e angel
ert, the
ould be

e sweet
r invite
been in

errors.
ne Ark,
d turns
mselves

varmth,
out the
g to be

now we
et with
ve and
Weldon

onfron-
tational attitude of a rap vocalist and the eloquent phrasing
of a poet.'   *Literary Review*

The Angel
in the House

KATE O'RIORDAN

Flamingo
An Imprint of HarperCollins*Publishers*

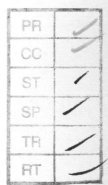

Flamingo
An Imprint of HarperCollins*Publishers*
77–85 Fulham Palace Road,
Hammersmith, London W6 8JB

www.**fireandwater**.com

Flamingo is a registered trade mark of
HarperCollins*Publishers* Limited

Published by Flamingo 2000

1 3 5 7 9 8 6 4 2

A catalogue record for this book
is available from the British Library

ISBN 0 00 225880 3

Set in Postscript Times Ten by Rowland Phototypesetting Ltd,
Bury St Edmunds, Suffolk

Printed and bound in Great Britain by
Clays Ltd, St Ives plc

For Jack and Jess, the angels in my house

Love's perfect blossom only blows
Where noble manners veil defect.
Angels may be familiar; those
Who err each other must respect.

Coventry Patmore, *The Angel in the House*

It was April and the swallows were back.

He could hear them chittering high up along the roof line. Hundreds of tiny blue wings fanning listless air. How did they know that the roof was their place? Or the young, still fleecy magpies know that decade after decade their ancestors had claimed the lower branches of the same wind-cut hazel? The sparrows set up shop, drill after drill, along strands of cable which once quivered beneath innumerable minute curled claws of their forefathers. Birds were endowed with an infallible sense of place. Humans floundered, in search of much the same thing.

But they had such a tendency to fall. Sometimes he experienced huge rolling tidal waves of pity for all the people out there, lurching from one pothole to another, desperately clutching at stray branches – tumbling. There were people he would have wished to be happy above any other wish. People he loved so fervently, he kept them in his head throughout every night dream. So that his wishes might protect and nurture them even as they floundered. Yet, ultimately they had to find their own way. Their own place. He knew that.

And he took comfort from the knowledge that somehow that was, after all, the way it appeared to work. The biological symmetry humans had evolved for themselves. Keep falling and eventually they just might get lucky. They might fall into money, success, happiness. All manner of good things. All manner of blessings.

They might even – fall in love.

1

Chapter One

There was his mother – dripping destruction. She waved to Robert from the deck of the houseboat, drawing her arms back then, to indicate her afternoon's work on the potted plants. A line of wet washing slapped at her plump face. Busy day. Bonnie's daffodil smile made Robert feel very unkind.

She mouthed 'Sunday?' and he nodded, a touch too eagerly. A few steps on, he stopped again, to study her pleasure some more, so that he could go on feeling guilty and thus kindlier toward her – but she'd gone inside.

Further along the towpath, the sky over Richmond was full of sharks. A bloated, low-slung Jumbo with white underbelly and exposed landing genitals almost grazed the top of his head, it seemed so close. A sleek, nifty little number devoured Richmond Bridge in one flashing mouthful. Eastward, higher up, the pale autumnal sky was scarred with evidence of a mid-morning feeding frenzy – the transatlantics had been late.

It was funny how the patterns of the sky became part of your life. How, in the garden, voices rose and fell in a constant sing-song to accommodate the noise overhead. A plane landed every forty-five seconds on the northern runway – and to get there they had to pass over his house. They had to pass over somebody's house, so there was little point in getting irritated about it. All the same, the occasional visitor sometimes did, making him feel he should apologize or something. At the very least, keep them indoors.

Mrs Leitch across the road in Isleworth, couldn't go to bed until the ten o'clock Concorde had passed. It closed the day for her, she said. Robert understood. Sometimes he felt lonely when the sky fell silent.

He was on his way to Peter and Anita's, for a late lunch or early supper, whichever Anita deemed appropriate. Peter had been Robert's best friend since their first day at school together. They'd been pretty much equals in those days, except for the fact that Peter always had a seemingly endless stash of boiled sweets, and he was slightly plump and uncompetitive, not to mention the copper tinge to his hair – all in all, exactly what you'd want from a best friend. Now that he was an orthodontist, he'd dropped the sweets, started to compete endlessly, but he was still plump and still Robert's best friend. Even if Peter had become a touch too hyphenated for his own good. As in double-fronted Mock-Tudor in tree-lined cul-de-sac. All of which lay at the next sharp turn right.

He fed the ducks as usual. Only the disenfranchised Marty sitting on his customary bench to whom he'd say:

'All right, Marty?'

'Just about. You, mate?'

'The same.'

Just once, Robert would like to say something different. Catch Marty's eye, man to man, so to speak. But there was nothing different to say to a man who sat on a bench all day. Even if Robert possessed the gift of the gab, which he did not. Right now, wouldn't mind one long swig of the Tennant's Extra though. Could rip that can open with his teeth.

It was that sort of day so far. Bills and a rickety kitchen table – greenfly all over his roses. Nothing epic, just enough to make the smallness of his malcontent a distasteful little nugget in itself. Two unreturned messages on Felicity's answering service. Why had he made that second call? It was so unlike him. Especially when she'd spelled it out so clearly on their last date: she was looking for an all or nothing sort of bloke – no

4

half measures, she wanted someone, the right someone, to be devastatingly in love with her. That was the actual word she'd used. Dev-astatingly. Tossing her auburn hair like that. But it was the bloke word that really did for them. It conveyed how she did *not* see him. Still, he'd phoned twice, even after he'd figured that much out. At a push, on a cavernous Saturday night, skulking shamefaced in front of the box, he could have made himself as devastatingly in love with her as the next bloke, say.

Anita flung the door open.

'Robert!'

'Anita!'

She called over her shoulder.

'Peter! Robert's here.'

Robert brushed his feet on the doormat which had been pointed out as usual by Anita's jiggling finger movement. As if it were an unconscious gesture on her part, nothing to do with her. Robert entered as Peter bounded down the staircase. They awkwardly clapped shoulders. Waiting for Anita to rescue them from the first what-to-say moments. As though they hadn't spent all of last Saturday together at the rugby match and later in the pub. Chat was always easier on neutral ground; homes invoked histories, comparisons, unsettled the feet. Homes were, well, home – to one party, making an alien of the other. In a few moments, that would all pass and Robert would allow himself to be absorbed. But first there was the other lacuna in Robert's life to get over.

'I'll call the girls,' Anita said. 'Tamara! Vanessa! Come downstairs a moment, darlings. Uncle Robert's here.'

The girls, nine and seven, hurled themselves at him in a way which was pleasing to their mother. They were dressed in layers of Oilily, little labels attached to socks and petticoats and the sides of their shoes. They made a big noise, just as children should. They flounced and petted, one dancing conspicuously while the other patted him down for goodies. Two Kit-Kats

5

and a pack of Chewits each slipped out of his trouser pockets not a moment too soon.

'Uncle Robert!'

'Nessie! Tammy!'

Robert wanted to get past the inevitable exclamatory greetings for all their sakes. He searched for something to say which might make it appear that he'd been there for hours already, so his own sense of discomfort wouldn't rub off on them because they deserved better than that.

'How's school, girls?'

'You always ask that,' Tammy pouted, 'and the answer's always the same.'

'Crappy?' Robert used her word, patting her golden head. She was his goddaughter. Bright as a star. No – twice as luminous. He wished she were older so he could marry her.

'Nessie, you look very pretty today,' he lied. Poor little Nessie took after her mother. Which was not to say that she wasn't pretty or anything – Robert would have argued that point with his last breath – but she did have that slightly ticcy eye and such sharp little teeth. The piranha, Bonnie sneeringly called Anita, hitting the nail on the head with her customary sledgehammer.

'Come through.' Anita led the way. 'We're nearly ready to eat. Lamb – is that all right?'

'Lovely.'

'Lovely if she doesn't burn it,' Peter joked. 'As usual.'

Anita laughed goodnaturedly and Robert nearly swooned with relief. Really, they were the most compatible couple he knew. Now he not only wanted to marry their daughter – he wanted them to adopt him.

Peter fixed gin and tonics. 'How's that for you?' he enquired.

'Perfect.' Robert took a sip.

'I'll just get cosy for a second before I go back in the kitchen.' Anita dropped into a squashy armchair, tucking her shoeless feet under her bottom. 'Cheers!'

6

'Cheers.' Robert raised his glass. He had his spiel prepared. 'Well, this is such a treat on a Wednesday afternoon – gin and tonic, food served up to you, good company . . .'

Stop *now*, a voice inside his head growled.

'Oh rubbish – it's your birthday tomorrow, it was either this or take you out for a meal but Peter said you can't stand restaurants . . . There's a little something for you over there, yes, by the window – just a token. Don't get all embarrassed now. Go on – open it.' Anita pointed to an exquisitely-wrapped package.

Robert flushed deeply. He didn't know what to say. So he said: 'I do like restaurants.'

With the very best of intentions they couldn't find a response to that so they just nodded politely as Robert unfurled ribbons in an access of misery. How could he claw that one back? Now they'd think him an ungrateful brute and the awful truth was that he did hate restaurants. So why had he felt compelled to disagree? Envy. That had to be the reason. The day was only halfway through and already he'd been unkind, envious, tongue-tied and –

'It's ideal,' he cried, sounding a bit hysterical to his own ears. The leatherbound personal organizer was indeed ideal of its kind. Peter had even thoughtfully bought pages beginning mid-year. 'I've always wanted one of these,' Robert added. 'How did you know?'

'Oh we just took a wild guess.' Anita smiled graciously. 'You will use it now, won't you?'

But Robert wasn't listening. He was desperately trying to find a route back to the subject of restaurants. None presented itself so he settled for another silent toast instead.

'Here's to thirty-six,' Peter touched his shoulder.

'Don't remind me,' Robert grimaced. That was better. He'd seen others do that.

'So – what's the plan?' Peter asked.

'Well, I'm thinking of a – a career change, or something . . .'

7

'No, no.' Peter smiled. 'I meant tomorrow night – your birth-day. Are you taking . . . what's her name again . . . ?'

'Felicity.' Of the answering service. 'Emm, yes. Don't know what we're doing yet.'

'Maybe she means to surprise you,' Anita offered.

'Sure.' They knew he was lying. They knew it. He was sweating.

'Is she the *one* then?' Peter had a nudge and a wink in his voice. A little look passed between himself and his wife.

'Give him a chance, Peter,' Anita protested, jokingly. A frown flittered across her brow.

'It's still early days, isn't, Robert?'

'Well, yes.'

Luckily for Robert, their attention was diverted from his unspectacular love life by the sound of feet pounding down the stairs.

'Tammy! Nessie! Come and say goodbye to Uncle Robert before your walk,' Anita called to the girls in the hallway.

They entered sullenly, pulling at the top buttons of their coats, which Anita promptly fastened again, making a little clucking sound with her tongue. The nanny hovered by the open door. Tamara flung an arm out toward Robert, catching her sister square on the nose.

Vanessa howled obligingly.

'She did that on purpose!'

'Did not. You stupid little . . .'

'Now, girls.' Peter made a feeble attempt at separating them, his eyes seeking out his wife's.

'She's voodoo,' Vanessa shrieked, knuckling her nose plain-tively.

'Trouble is – they're just too close if anything,' Anita was saying with a dreamy expression as Tamara slammed her head sideways in a well-practised headbutt, catching her sib-ling's crown with a sickening crunch. Two seconds shocked silence before Vanessa headed home to that familiar place, where, as second child, she felt most comfortable – Hysterialand.

'Girls! Stop it! Tammy! Say you're sorry. Nessie! Stop bellowing like that. You should see your face. Nanny! Best take them out – they need fresh air.' Anita fired a hail of exclamations.

Through the window, Robert could see them, still trying to get at one another, with Nanny airlifting them down the drive. Their stickish legs pedalling invisible bicycles. The outraged hollers receded. Sometimes he thought their honest anger more accessible. The girls said what they thought. There was something too polished in the language of their parents, almost quaint in its burnished veneer. As if they constantly hovered above themselves monitoring their own performance. Or maybe it was just his own sense of exclusion. At any rate, Robert only very rarely, and with great reluctance, had to concede that he sometimes found their polite, skirting interlocution a bit of a strain.

Anita pulled a mock despairing face.

'Don't have kids, Robert,' she said without conviction. 'No. I don't mean that. I'll be punished. They're adorable really.'

'Fuck – errr.' Nessie's howl echoed up from the river. And Robert had to conceal his smile behind a sip of gin and tonic.

Sometimes the little tic under Anita's left eye reminded him of a panting cursor on a computer screen. He felt that if he pressed his fingers against her face, he could access the internet.

As he helped Peter set the dining room table, he began to feel more at ease – a warm, spreading glow – at being part of their unit, if only temporarily. He wanted to say something pleasing to Peter, to thank him for the hospitality, for the birthday present. Sentences rolled over in his head, but as usual he left it too late and Peter punctuated the silence.

'A career change?'

'Well, yes. Maybe.'

'You never said anything about that before.'

'I haven't given it a great deal of thought, to be honest.'

9

None. Precisely.

'It's just something . . .' Robert broke off with a shrug.

'Ah-hah – you've been thinking about what we were saying about getting out more, haven't you?'

'I have.'

He was – now.

'You know, what you do is great, don't get me wrong. But it means so much time by yourself, doesn't it? Can't be good for a person. Maybe gallery work or something . . . Still, you're doing the evening lectures at the V & A, that's bound to widen your horizons.'

Peter lit candles on an elaborate silver centrepiece.

'Peter – I quite like being alone, you know.' Robert felt niggled. Every now and then, they took the nurturing a bit too far. Peter had acquired a stock of phrases, a certain elevated tone which made Robert want to remind him of the days they used to light matches to their farts after school. Restoring other people's pictures for them wasn't Peter's idea of a real career. He never said it outright, of course, just as he never openly *said* that Robert should have pursued his own art thing, even if he wasn't much good. A grander failure altogether, if success in orthodontics wasn't your first choice.

Robert had taken on the museum evenings at Anita's insistence. She worried about him, she said, spending so much time on his own. He should get out more, meet people. Stop thinking about everything so much. Just do. Standing up in front of an audience, one evening a week – it would do him the world of good. Get him out of himself a bit. Whenever people said that, they forgot that if you got out of yourself, it would help if you'd someplace else to go.

He didn't have the heart to tell her that the lecturing business was turning out to be even more torturous than he'd anticipated, and that was saying something. The very idea of addressing a whole bunch of strangers, the act of assuming their interest, then holding that assumed interest – most of the time he'd rather swallow a stranger's spit. But he perservered because he didn't want to disappoint his well-meaning friends.

'It's funny,' Peter was saying. 'After all these years, I still look around –' he waved an arm expansively '– and think – this could be you. Not me.'

Robert thought he meant the house, the hyphens. The teeth.

'Anita, I mean,' Peter explained.

'Anita what?' She entered with the garnished lamb. 'Quick, quick, someone – a placemat, this is roasting . . . Sorry, darling, you were saying?'

'Oh, I was just thinking out loud – if Robert hadn't introduced us . . .'

'You mean if he'd dated me first instead of my sister.' Anita checked the settings. She motioned for Peter to bring the decanted wine to the table, then playfully flicked the corner of a napkin at Robert's face. 'Isn't that rather assuming that Robert would've asked me out in the first place?'

They laughed lightly at that. But Robert felt that a response was expected of him. He stared hard at the steaming lamb.

'Fantastic. Better than any restaurant.' He breathed an inward sigh of relief. Managed to get round to that bloody restaurant faux pas after all.

'Rob-ert . . .' Anita rolled her eyes in mock exasperation. 'You're supposed to say you'd have fallen madly in love with me – if you'd met me first. Honestly. You're never going to get the hang of it, are you?'

'The hang of . . . ?'

'Smooth talk, I think she means.' Peter began to carve. 'Women like that.'

'Not always we don't.' Anita kept a chuckle in her voice, but the sound of dry twigs crackled there too. Robert had noticed that before, but for the life of him, he could never understand that strata of sounds between couples. They went up, they went down. They went in, they went out. There were things other

11

than what was being said. Perhaps it evolved with marriage – a silent language beaded between the words.

'Sometimes we prefer honesty,' Anita argued. 'Take Robert here, for instance.' She swivelled to face him, hand extended as though he were a specimen in a display case. 'You could say he's shy. Or too serious. Or he weighs everything up too much – that cute little stop he does, before he says anything – but I think it's 'cause he's fiercely honest. Yes, I do,' she added thoughtfully, her hand fleetingly closing over Robert's tightly bunched fist. 'He just can't be bothered with the small talk the rest of us . . . Well . . .'

Robert concentrated so hard on the gleaming mahogany table, his eyes watered. He hated when they entered their own airspace like that. It made him feel a bit freakish. Which was without question, the last thing on earth they ever intended. He assumed.

'Oh yes?' Peter was teasing. He winked at Robert. 'So small talk is out now. We're all going to talk big from now on, is that what you're . . .'

'Drop it, Peter, okay?' Anita interjected sharply. A fork screeched against a china plate.

Inexplicably, Robert thought of his mother.

The Irish said 'sorry', the English said 'pardon' or 'excuse me'. Angela reckoned she'd said 'sorry' at least twenty times just trying to get out of the carriage. The English said 'thanks' or 'thank you very much' or 'how kind, many thanks'; the Irish threw it all into the one pot – to be on the safe side, they said 'thanks a million'. Other than a few petty things like that, there wasn't all that much of a difference when you came right down to it – in spite of her aunts' many warnings to the contrary.

London was full of perverts and worse, they'd bleat. Worse? Yes – pagans. The perverts and pagans she'd come across so far at the hostel weren't all that bad really. She could handle them, she repeatedly told the Aunts on her visits home. Handling was too good for them was the usual baleful response. Wasn't that only what the devils wanted? Usually this stupid exchange would meander late at the end of a tiresome day. Angela would sigh with a welter of Social Science behind her. Was there a suggestion they'd care to make? She'd picked up enough of London by then, to attempt a sigh like that – exhausted, past caring. All-knowing. But the Aunts were indefatigable – and good Catholics to a woman. Shoot the feckers, they'd bay. Would that be before or after a trial? Angela would try an amused, condescending inflection. During! they'd shriek, thrilling at her dismay. That'd teach her to patronize them.

They were like a Greek chorus in her head some days, commentating, chiding, mocking her responses to situations. There were times she wanted to rip open her head, plunge a hand in and pull them out, kicking and screaming. But they were much too cosy in the cushion of her brain cells to try a forced eviction now.

She was late as usual. And uncertain if she was on the right tube platform to change for the Piccadilly Line. A voice over the tannoy advised them to expect delays to the District Line due to a body on the tracks. Avoid if possible. Could be one of her men stretched out there in a mangled heap for all Angela knew. They'd been known to target the District; maybe they just wanted somewhere familiar for the final stop. She made a sign of the cross and squinched up her eyes to read the tube map squiggle. Somewhere around the middle, the blues melted into reds, the reds into yellows. She'd never work it out.

A couple slobbered drunkenly over one another nearby. The girl pressed her groin against the considerably older man, who was spoiling the whole effect by looking so pleased with himself. She undulated her hips, holding her head back at an awkward angle to grin up at him. There was something about her anxiety to sustain that pleased rictus on his face that fascinated Angela. She almost wanted to mimic the young woman – just to see what the angle felt like. Her neck was craning back of its own accord when she stopped it in time. For a brief moment she envied their abandon, their total preoccupation, until she noticed the full-length ladder climbing up the girl's black opaque tights. Bet she'd feel mortified about that in the morning, telling herself it didn't matter who'd seen, as long as *he* hadn't. The skirt rode higher – the ladder led to a wide gash showing white naked flesh. The little gleaming oval looked so vulnerably revealing, Angela felt a hot spasm of embarrassment for the swaying creature.

What if she went to work tomorrow in those tights? With a terrible hangover maybe she wouldn't notice. And the entire office would be sniggering – because maybe that man was actually her boss, and everyone knew about the affair . . . Suddenly Angela felt lightheaded with worry. It was never worth it to her to be left loose in the city for any period of time. She had to live everyone's trauma for them, real or imagined. The Greek chorus yowled and cackled in her head.

She had to get away, but now it was possible that they might even stagger against her as she tried to pass by – a terrible thought. She froze, put money in the chocolate machine, pressed buttons and got nothing in return. It was broken. She blushed, thinking the entire platform was looking at her. Plunged her hands in her coat pockets and stepped quickly to the side.

The girl peeled away from her lover. She moved to the machine, asking with raised eyebrows if Angela was finished. Angela kept her head down, studying her shoes, nodding quickly in response. She made to move forward then backtracked on a hot, sympathetic impulse, pressing her mouth to the girl's ear.

'It's broken,' she whispered. 'And look it, I'm really sorry but you've a deadly ladder in your tights.'

'An adder? Where where? Oh Christ!' the girl shrieked, slapping down on her thighs.

Angela fled, heading for a platform she thought might be the right one. As usual, no idea where she was going. Her feet had

broken into a stilted, half embarrassed run. They were mara-
thon feet by now – in for the long haul. They couldn't stop
even if she wanted them to. And she did. Because she should
just ask somebody. Am I on the right path for . . . ? Plead
ignorance. But she hated pleading ignorance in an Irish accent.
Halfway down the long, tiled tunnel, it occurred to her that
this was pretty much the story of her life so far really –
heading feet first for a platform she thought might be the right
one.

She had to have a roll of ten-pence pieces in the pocket of the
navy raincoat. Had to, Robert thought, as he watched her stop
at every begging bowl on the long subway leading from South
Kensington station to the Cromwell Road. She was short and
slim, the hem of her coat almost brushing concrete. Spiky short
dark hair. He wanted to see her face. What sort of person came
out, prepared for beggars?
    She'd stopped to talk to a young man with a 'hungry and
homeless' card. Robert passed by, then turned for a quick look.
To his surprise, she was patting the man's head. She glanced
up and caught Robert's eye momentarily, or at least he thought
she had, but no, she was staring right past him into the yawning
tunnel ahead. Her face was very pale-skinned, triangular,
with large dark eyes of indeterminate colour. Mid- to late-
twenties – he couldn't focus any better in the fleeting moment
afforded. His feet slowed down, so that she might move ahead
again.
    All the way along, she stopped. By the time they were nearly
at the exit, Robert was walking like a man let out of his wheel-
chair for the day. He dropped his lecture notes at the steps to
slow him down some more. Out on the Cromwell Road, she
appeared to be heading in the same direction as him. He wondered if by chance she was also heading for the V & A. It
seemed like a pleasing enough coincidence, though for the life
of him he couldn't figure out why that should be. Maybe he

15

was just fixating on anything or anyone available, to offset his usual pre-lecture nerves.

She'd stopped on a traffic island mid-way across Exhibition Road. He thought she was waiting for the lights to change, but she was clearly debating something. Her little head turned this way and that as if no longer certain where she was heading. He wanted to get to the island to ask if he could be of help, but the stream of cars was constant. The thin shoulders inside the much too big raincoat went up. They stayed up by her ears for a few seconds, then just as the lights changed, she darted forward – much too quick for him – and veered left on the other side. Away from the museum.

Standing on the island, Robert watched her break into a peculiar sort of run. A few fast trips then slower, walked paces again. Fast then slow, fast then slow, all the way up the street until she faded out of sight. The lights had changed again and he was stuck on the island for another while. Feeling strangely disappointed. A tenpence piece shone brightly under a street-light by his shoe. He bent down to pick it up and slipped it into his pocket. Maybe it would bring him luck. It joined all the other coins and buttons and paper clips, which hadn't. He was glad they were making coins so much smaller these days, other-wise if his luck ever did change, he would be too weighed down to run after it. A final glance up to the left, just to see if she had doubled back for any reason. The far view was blocked by a laughing bunch of Spanish students, arms linked, spreading out across the pavement like a paper chain. He waited – but only air closed around the space behind them. She had evaporated.

Chapter Two

Bonnie said that shyness was a form of conceit. A person was just so full of their own self-importance, she said, it made them dither like geeks over every word, instead of talking any old crap same as everyone else. Standing there like puffed-up penguins, nervously hopping from one foot to the other – like anybody *cared* for chrissakes – oh they just twisted up her insides sometimes, twisted her right up. All that, as she darted him baleful glances from slitty, heavy-lidded eyes one afternoon as he took her rubbish out. Robert had to concede a saltgrain of truth in her words – it only took a grain to make an old wound sting – but he felt anything but self-important right now as the sea of faces focused all their attention on him. Self-conscious, certainly. To the point of suffering. He took a deep breath. Imagined himself through their eyes, exhaled again.

'Now where shall we begin?' He walked purposefully around the glass centrepiece in the Europe and America Gallery, hoping that they would think that he knew where he was going. They trudged dutifully along in his wake, a few snickering Italian girls, mid-west Americans, mini-bussed old ladies from anywhere, a couple from Norwich, an enormous Frenchman, more interested in the contents of his nose than a dissertation on Victorian furniture and china.

'Ah yes – if you look to the right, you'll see the magnificent oak sideboard designed by Ferdinand Rothbart in a style known as Gothic Revival . . .'

Several yawns. Unstifled. Robert felt his own responsive yawn clack at the back of his throat. He had to turn it into a cough. But the glazed eyes would stay with him to the bitter end, that much he knew: they'd paid their fiver entrance fee and if a guided tour or lecture – of any description – was going, they were up for it. Actually, it was worse if you had the occasional expert or aficionado, because then there were the endless questions to cope with, often designed to catch him out. His voice rose and fell, independent of him. Blabbety blabbety blab. God, he almost felt sorry for them.

'Now, the Victorians are often denigrated for being mere copycats. It's true that they pilfered from every age but the quality of their workmanship, their intense dedication to detail, must surely go some measure toward overriding these criticisms. The relatively new middle class wanted to display their new-found wealth. Take Mr and Mrs Turner over here for example. Look at the busts they commissioned for posterity. A little pompous you might say – done in the *ancien regime* like that – but Mr and Mrs Turner were . . .'

'Prats.'

'Sorry?'

'Prats,' Mrs Norwich repeated.

'Yes, yes. I suppose you could say that.' Robert checked the Frenchman's watch which was clearly on display beneath a forefinger still rooting around in his nostril. 'Emm – this way people please . . . ? Right, here we have an excellent example of . . .'

But the tone was set by that interruption and now they would all feel obliged to take a pop off him. It was him versus them. It happened. The American woman's eyes had narrowed – just waiting her opportunity. Robert obliged.

'The Victorian ideal of womanhood centred on marriage and home. Woman's mission in life was to be the guardian of moral, spiritual and domestic matters. She was the ah – "the angel in the house" to quote Coventry Patmore the poet . . .'

'The *what*?'

'The po . . .'

'Nah – that other shit – she was the what?'

'Oh the angel you mean?'

The old ladies had sighed collectively at Patmore's coinage, now they glared steely-eyed in agreement with the American. Robert tried a knowing smirk. To also distance himself from the Victorians. The American's eyes were dark slits now. She chewed gum furiously. Nothing personal but somebody was going to have to pay for the fourth lecture she was enduring this touristic day. Robert swallowed, moving them onto safer territory – a dinner service.

Mid-blah, he heard a little rustling sound at the back of the group. It was *her*. Short dark hair plastered to her scalp with rain. It runnelled down her cheeks onto the severe navy rain-coat. She was making little apologetic faces for being so late, to no one in particular. Robert caught her eye just as her tongue darted out quickly to lap at a straying raindrop. She flushed slightly and the contrast with her near-bleached white skin was deeply striking. The eyes were dark and shadowed in this uncannily pale, heartshaped face. Although by no means the best judge of these things, Robert could have sworn that there wasn't a trace of make-up on the delicate features. But it was the quality of her aloneness, her separateness, that made him stumble mid-blah.

'We done here or what?' A male American voice.

'Not quite yet.' Robert gestured toward the door. 'I think you'll find the William Morris room interesting. But first – a quick glance at the Library perhaps . . . Everyone all right with stairs?'

The old ladies said yes immediately. Robert had the strangest thought – with red lipstick she would be strikingly pretty. No – beautiful. No, maybe neither of those, attractive certainly, but there was no doubt in his mind that she would have photo-graphed or painted superbly. Triangular faces always did.

There was nothing to indicate that she'd seen him earlier.

19

He turned the ten pence over in his pocket, feeling curiously elated. Clearly, she had been heading for the museum and just at the last minute distrusted her instincts and went off in the wrong direction.

He was conscious of her brushing rain from her shoulders behind him. A few drops pinged against the grey mosaic-tiled floor in the Medieval Treasury Hall. Click clack of thirteen pairs of shoes trying to keep up with his quick strides. Halfway up the sweeping stairs, he had to backtrack for the old ladies who had veered wildly left at the base of the stairwell and were now clustered around a sixteenth-century figure of Christ on a donkey. Oohing and aahing, but, in reality, taking deep breaths for the inevitable ascent.

'All right, ladies?'

'He's lovely that donkey. Isn't he?'

'He certainly is. The stairs are right through here . . .'

She was ahead of him now. Razor-slim ankles flashing beneath the length of her coat. Ugly, childish shoes with a buckle on the sides. She kept her hands in her pockets even as she ran up the steps. As if she had to pin herself in. At the top, she surprised him by turning.

'Sorry I was late. I got lost in the tubes first – then on the streets.' Soft Irish accent. The eyes were slate grey, close up. Rain, not mascara, making spikes of the long lashes.

'Not to worry. You didn't miss much.'

'D'you do this every Wednesday night or is it just the once off? I mean – I could come again maybe . . .'

'Yes. Yes, you could. Next Wednesday if you like. I'm afraid I can't tell you what the subject will be though – you could check with Reception on your way out.'

The grey eyes clouded.

'Oh, you mean it's not always about the Victorians so?'

'Not necessarily – that's just my subject. The museum covers so much mo . . .' Robert glanced behind, white perms like a patch of cauliflowers stacked up along the stairs. 'To your left, ladies, please.' As they filed past, he continued: 'Actually, I think it is me next Wednesday. In fact I'm sure of it.'

He gave a little spiel about the Library and the group dutifully lined up to take turns looking through the glass on the closed door. As expected, they saw books. Mrs Norwich saw shelves not too dissimilar from an idea about shelving a neighbour of hers had back home. Only there were more of them here of course, and the room was about twice as high as her neighbour's entire house, and of course there was a dearth of paperbacks in the V & A's library but apart from all that – and the rows of scholarly pews – she could have been outside, looking in at her neighbour's front reception.

Robert nodded politely. Everyone else had gone downstairs again, following his instructions to the original Refreshment Rooms. Mr Norwich had stopped halfway down to wait for his wife, a bald, resigned stoop to his head, stubby fingers plucking fluff from his jacket. He winced a little at Robert's approach. Prepared, if required, to do a little male eye-rolling at his wife's naivety. Surprised, when Robert said that he thought it quite amazing that a Norwich neighbour had acquired such fantastic shelves. Mr Norwich agreed, he'd seen them himself and they were exceptional. Mrs Norwich glowed.

The group's interest perked up a bit in the Gamble Room. Robert brought their attention to the tiles on walls, ceiling and floor.

'The idea was that every part of the room should be immediately washable. Behind you, on the eastern wall, you can see the familiar blue and white Delft-like tiles, which were hand-painted by local women for a pound a piece, thus generating work for . . . Ah you're anxious to move through to the Morris Room I see . . .'

He was about to follow his wandering minstrels, when he spotted her over by the huge iron and brass range. Her hand trailed over the various oven doors.

'You can imagine the heat from it,' he said.

She almost jumped from her reverie and he felt sorry for disturbing her.

'My Aunt Bridie has one in her old house. Well, a much smaller version of course, but big and black. Like this one.'

'Has she? It's probably worth something these days.' He didn't mean to turn her memories into money. Felt that she would think less of him for that. Then wondered why it bothered him at all, what she might think.

'Ah, she'd never sell. Couldn't anyway. Not with Uncle Mikey above in the attic.' She smiled, as though he understood, and followed the group into the next ante-chamber.

Robert wanted to ask who Uncle Mikey was, and why he was above in the attic, but he could hear the increasingly impatient coughs and hrrmphs within. She was very thin, he thought, following after her, the bony shoulder blades sticking out, it seemed to him, in a vulnerable way through the oversized rainmac.

In the Morris Room, he thought her eyes took on an extra sheen when he delivered his brief homily on Victorian home life, avoiding words like virtue, morality, thriftiness because he felt that demeaned a whole era. As a generation, he felt that they were entirely misunderstood. He directed the end of his speech at her. And never once saw that familiar glazing over to the dark grey eyes. If he didn't know better he would have said that she was entranced.

There was a polite little clap when he ended his spiel. The Americans asked if the Natural History Museum did late evenings too and one of the old ladies tried to slip him fifty pence. He demurred politely, but she insisted telling him that she'd been a waitress for forty-five years. Up North. Silver Service. Robert had no option: clearly she was down to tip the whole of London.

His eyes quickly took in the few remaining stragglers. She was gone. He felt a spasm of disappointment. From the entrance to the Poynter Room, he saw a flash of navy coat tail round

22

the corner ahead. Robert mumbled his apologies as he brushed past the departing group. She was standing by the glass containing Christ on the donkey. She smiled as he approached, then her brow furrowed quickly.

'I never thanked you for the nice talk,' she said. 'I only go out hardly ever, so I forget my manners sometimes.'

Robert moved his head sideways, flapped a hand up and down to show her that there was no need for thanks and besides it wasn't much of a talk and her manners were perfectly adequate. He had to scratch his head to stop himself.

'I'm not much good at this sort of thing,' he managed finally.

'Oh I don't know about that,' she said. Her eyes were on the wooden figure of Christ again.

'You like that, do you?' Robert asked.

'He's got such a – smiley – sort of a friendly face,' she responded with her head to the side. 'At home, in almost all of the pictures of him, he looks so sad and – miserable really – for want of a better word. Starving too.'

'At home? You're visiting?'

'Oh no, I live here now. London, I mean. Five and a half years.'

'Have you been to the V & A before?'

'First time, would you credit it? Every week I say to myself, Angela, this is the week you'll make it to the V & A, but somehow, time sort of runs ahead of me, you know?'

Robert did know. Still, five and a half years could match any record of his.

Angela.

'You need to spend a good day here really – Angela,' he added, allowing the name to lap over his tongue for the first time. It suited her. 'We only managed to cover a tiny section this evening.'

'Evenings are best for me,' she said, with an air of regret.

'Weekends?'

'Not much good either. I sort of . . .'

'Work?'

'Sort of. At weekends.'

'Sounds like a very difficult job. That you do, Angela. Robert, by the way.'

A quick shake of her hand and a sigh of relief. That was his name out of the way. Things were progressing.

'It is. Well, it isn't.' She was trying to decide if her job was difficult or not. 'It takes up a lot of time though.'

'What do you do?'

He'd blown it. One question too many. Robert bit his lower lip and mentally sent his shoe up his rectum. She was flushing again, a uniform pinkness spreading across her cheeks. A pained little frown creasing her forehead. He had annoyed her.

'Sorry – I shouldn't be so nosy,' he said hastily. She flushed harder.

'Oh not at all, not at all,' she was searching for words. 'I'm a – a social worker actually.'

'That is hard work.' Robert went for a dry tone. It sort of worked.

'Yerra,' she said self-effacingly. The pink was receding from her cheeks, leaving a smooth white canvas again. Robert realized with a start that they were both staring speechlessly at one another. He had been mentally sketching her for a few moments. Now he should casually ask her to join him for a cup of coffee or something, wryly adding something to the effect of her making the most of her rare free time. He should. He swallowed.

She was shrugging. Taking little backward steps so that she could skirt around him. Her entire body curled into a scythe, making an embarrassed goodbye.

Robert rubbed an eyelid and let out a protracted 'emm,' as though they had just paused in mid-conversation and he had yet to finish his sentence. It worked, because she stopped moving away and now gazed expectantly at him.

'You're interested in the Victorian age then?'

'Well, to tell you the truth, I came here for my mother.'

'I se-ee.'

'What I mean is – she's the one with the interest. Not saying I didn't find it interesting. I did. I do. I'll come back. The thing is, her grandmother went up to Dublin to see Queen Victoria when she came over for a visit. The whole city was out. My great-grandmother was only a girl herself but she said it was the best thing she ever saw. Said Queen Victoria wasn't half as ugly as people made out. She went on about it so much, my own mother took to reading everything she could lay her hands on about the Queen and the times and what have you. So I promised her I'd come to the Queen's Museum and send her back a brochure or something.' She checked her watch anxiously, adding, 'I suppose the shop'll be shut now, will it?'

'No. It stays open, I believe . . . But tell me, why doesn't your mother . . .' Robert allowed his voice to trail off but his eyes finished the question.

'Come here, d'you mean? Ah God, she could never do that.'

'No?'

'Well, there's Aunties Bridie, Regina and Maisie for starters and then there's . . .'

'Uncle Mikey . . .' Robert's eyes signalled upstairs.

'Exactly. Above. Well below really. Above below in the other house.' She gazed up also. Robert seized the moment.

'Would you – I mean, have you got time for a cup of coffee, Angela?'

She seemed surprised and a little flustered by his request. The plain leather-strapped watch received another check.

'It's a bit late for coffee. I'd better hit the road. But sure . . .' She chewed her bottom lip, hesitating. 'Next week – maybe?'

'All right. Great. I mean fine then. Next Wednesday. Fine . . . Sorry, Angela – the exit and the shop are *that* way.'

Later, sitting by an empty fire grate at home, Robert thought about Angela. The phone rang several times around midnight, birthday wishes no doubt, but he let the answering machine take them in the hallway. He felt uneasy, preoccupied, slightly excited and couldn't quite put his finger on the restless feeling. Pacing up and down the living room did little to relieve the sensation. He switched on late night television, quickly turned it off again. Then it came to him – for the first time in so many years, he was experiencing an overwhelming desire to sketch something. It was in his fingertips. A physical craving.

At first, he thought it might just go away if he ignored it for a while. But the tension increased to the point when he had to run upstairs to the spare bedroom to rummage through half a dozen cardboard boxes of clutter until he found the old, yellowing sketch pad and a box of charcoals. His heart pumped so furiously he could hear the blood surfing through his head. He was breathing like a man surprised to find all the old familiar feelings come thundering back, at an unexpected sighting of an ex-lover. Not sure if those feelings were trustworthy or just a momentary nostalgia which would fade as soon as a word was spoken, or in this case, as soon as his arm brushed over the dense, inviting paper – back and forth in mental preparation.

Downstairs again, he quickly cleared a table, bundling stacks of newspapers, half-read books, unwashed mugs and crumbed plates into the recess by the chimney breast. It was taking too long so he impatiently gathered the remaining items into one big pile against his chest and just dumped everything at his feet. Broken china crunched under his shoes. He wiped the table with his sleeve, placed the pad on top, opened the box of charcoals, inhaling that delicious woody scent. It had been so long.

Just as he sat down, Professor Helmut Schneider's words came back to him. His teacher at art college before Robert had submerged any dreams he had and settled on a Fine Art degree.

'Crap, sveetheart. Hallmark Cards at a shove – or push is it? Ya, push. Vatever. You tink too much vit your head. Nice guy, don't get it wrong, you understand me? But more, there should be more ... it's too much *taught*, ya? Too much.'

26

It took Robert another year to figure out that the Professor meant *tight*. But by then he'd pretty much given up hope of being the new Hockney in any case. He was adequate. So were lots of people. And they weren't at college where adequate wasn't even the least you should be. Technically he was okay. He could draw. His watercolours even won a prize once. Enough to fool an impressionable young boy, looking for direction. Seeking approval from any quarter. And then there was Bonnie, eager to blow her only child's hobby out of all proportion, until the day he had to sadly tell her that he was fashionably minimalist all right – as in talent, sadly.

Still Professor Schneider was good enough to set Robert up in his years-long apprenticeship with a renowned picture restorer who taught him hard and well. It was painstaking, extraordinarily exacting work but also very satisfying. His own personal reputation was established by now. But on occasion the inescapable longing to do something original would slip into his dreams again. You simply couldn't guard yourself against dreams. They attacked late at night when a person was at their most vulnerable.

So what was it that made somebody who knew full well that they were just about adequate – and that on a good day – go on trying? Go on perservering? Yes, there was that element of hope, that if you tried long enough, hard enough ... but the voice of pragmatism could easily counter that. It passed the time? Sure, there was that, if your life wasn't dictated by acquiring hypens. No, there was something else entirely, there was hope – fragile, tenuous: at worst self-deluding; at best, sweet, tender, floral and perfumed. It lay in looking at the thing that was flawed, and knowing how it should be. And maybe if you flawed long enough, just maybe that one incredible, exquisite bouquet might take form, suddenly and inexplicably, perfect. It only had to happen once. Just once. If Robert could do that, he knew his life would change profoundly.

And there she was – on the page. Before he'd even started

27

to analyse, to deconstruct. It was a clumsy sketch, nothing to write home about, the product of another man's bored Sunday afternoon – yet there was more. If he lived to be a thousand, he couldn't put his finger on it. The heartshaped face, head down, eyes upcast but away from him – it was there. He could see her. Even if nobody else ever could, he had the clearest, most perfect picture of her lying there in front of him on the paper. He exhaled loudly and leaned back, arms cradling his head. He knew instantly that he was in love with her image. And he knew that now, he would not sleep through another night until he had painted her. Never mind that she would have to agree, that she would have to sit for him. Somehow, he was going to have to persuade her – next Wednesday night.

He did another quick sketch, more shadowy – Angela smiling. The upturn of her mouth, stretching the pointed little chin into a clearly delineated arc. She had a dimple on her left cheek. He hadn't even noticed, until the charcoal picked it out. The eyes were the most difficult. Big enough, lashed enough, they should have been relatively easy, the grey irises so large they swamped the eye, making the whites fight for space. But there was something else, he had the curious feeling that the dark pupils were crowded. Other beings were living there too.

Five quick preparatory sketches on, he felt tired enough to attempt sleep. A sidelong glance in the mirror over the mantlepiece showed a darkly smudged face, streaked where his fingers had drawn down his cheeks. He wished his reflection a happy birthday. Certainly it was the happiest for the longest time.

In the hall, he flicked on the answering machine. Peter singing for he's a jolly good fellow, echoed by Anita in the background. They hoped his evening went well at the V & A, that the next evening was pleasant with what's her name and if he was free next Friday night, Anita was having an old schoolfriend for the weekend and what about joining them for dinner, by no stretch of the imagination an attempt at a blind date or anything vulgar like that. But do come, all the same.

Felicity, to say she'd got both messages. It wasn't that he wasn't a nice bloke or anything, in fact she was certain he'd make a very good friend, but it was patently clear he wasn't anywhere nearly so much in love with her as she would need him to be at this point in time. The messages lacked passion. She absolutely had to have that, if nothing else. Her voice grew muffled and slurred until Robert realized that she was crying. At the end of the long garbled message, it was only when she snarled that he (Reggie?) could go screw himself anyway, that he realized that she was not just crying but was very drunk. Robert pressed the erase button, silently toasting the unknown Reggie godspeed and a long and healthy life.

Then, Bonnie.

'Rob? It's me. I know you're home so pick up the phone . . . Rob?'

'Rob-ert,' he muttered between gritted teeth.

'Happy birthday to you. Happy birthday to you. Happy birthday dear Ro-o-b, happybirthdaytoyou. D'you get my card today?'

Robert shook his head. He sat on the last stairtread with his hands tucked under his buttocks.

'Uh-oh, you won't have it – know why? 'Cause I'm looking at it right here by my sewing box, where I put it so's I'd remember to mail it when I went looking for the black cotton for the . . . Oh never mind. Cards don't mean a thing to you anyway. Or you'd send them. I'm reading it now Rob – are you listening? Get this – it says . . .'

Robert only caught her brittle shard of laughter at the end because he'd put his hands over his ears. Instinct told him that she'd read the soppy, over the top message – something to the effect of 'Son, you're the greatest' – in a voice dripping with sarcasm. She was angry because she knew he was there and hadn't answered the phone.

She ended saying she'd give him his present on Sunday when he came for lunch. She was going to make a carrot cake and put a candle on it, whether he wanted her to or not. Goodnight, and remember that she loved him more than anything in the whole world. Robert smiled. When she wasn't angry, Bonnie could be incandescent with charm. The trouble was, he could never be sure which face would present itself when she opened that door to the houseboat. It was like riding a gigantic roller-coaster – exhilarating and terrifying by turns, extremely wearing when you could never get off.

Perhaps everyone had someone in their lives who was both a conduit of pleasure and of torture. Maybe we even went looking for that person, actively sought them out, to complicate our lives. It was the most simple and inconsequential of things which could thrust a person off track. His chance meeting with Angela, perhaps. Then, just as his eyes were closing, he thought of Mrs Norwich and wondered if her neighbour knew, or ever had the slightest inkling as to how much those shelves had cost the marriage of the people who lived next door.

Chapter Three

Mary Margaret was in filthy form. Angela stood upwind of the gales of stale gin wafting in her direction. Total avoidance was next to impossible because Mary Margaret was shouting, soaking the air in Gordon's Dry. She was also thrusting her head forward, to punctuate her words, which made a big throbbing vein stand on her neck, and the black hairs on her chin stand out individually, as if to attention.

'I'm very sorry. Really.' Angela repeated for the third time. Meek as could be.

'Ah sure, what good is that to me? You're always fecking sorry.' She leaned back, rubbing her temples. 'My heart is half-broke trying to run this joint with the bunch of Lulus I've under me. What do I ask of you?'

'Not a lot.' Angela responded by rote.

'Not a helluva lot. That's for sure. Where is it that you say you took yourself off to again?'

'The Victoria and Albert Museum. They do nights now.' Just in time, Angela remembered to keep her eyes lowered. She twiddled her fingers for effect. 'I had it in my head that it was tonight – Thursday – that you wanted me for . . .'

'I can only make a stab at what that brute Dr Goldberg makes of us. Shovelling out pills left right and centre, and not a one at all here to put a name to a face for him or whatnot.' The ringing phone interrupted her. 'That's probably himself now,' she added darkly. She cleared her throat and grimaced before lifting the receiver. 'Hello yes? Who? Oh for feck sake don't be bothering me with that bollocks.' She slammed down the receiver. 'Some old fart back from the Missions – wanted to take a look around, if you don't mind,' Mary Margaret explained sourly to Angela. 'It must be the week that's in it. Staff hiking off to museums . . .'

'I'm very sorry. Really.'

'. . . Not to mention the two bozos they sent us down from Camden last week . . . Are you keeping your eye on them?'

'Both eyes.'

'Good. Because they're trouble with a capital T, I'm telling you. All right. Get out.'

Angela was just about to get out with a sigh of deep relief when Sister Carmel came rushing in. She was breathless and clearly very disturbed because she'd pushed her veil so far back in her agitation that her few last wisps of white hair were on show.

'He's at it again,' she cried.

'Who's at what?' Mary Margaret barked.

'The one from Camden – what's his name?' Sister Carmel stopped with a finger to her pursed lips. 'Oh dear, it's gone from me again. You know the one with the . . .'

'Don't mind his name – what's he at?'

Sister Carmel approached timidly, her voice lowered. She pointed to a part of her anatomy. 'He's after showing it again,' she whispered.

'What's he after showing, for Christ's sake?' Mary Margaret bawled.

'His tallywhacker,' Sister Carmel answered in a rush.

She was so flushed, she must have a temperature, Angela thought with sympathy. Poor old Carmel was heading for eighty or was it ninety? It was difficult to tell with the older ones.

'Right.' Mary Margaret slammed her fist down on the desk. Both women in front of her jumped. 'Follow me.'

She stalked out into the corridor. Carmel eyed Angela with

trepidation before she tripped after her like an ancient, bird-like Chinese woman with bound feet. They followed Mary Margaret's determined march down to where the corridor widened into a sort of ante-chamber which led into the refectory. A crowd of men had gathered around a huge giant of a man who was roaring some Scottish ballad and jiggling his hips so that his considerable penis, unleashed from the zip of his pants, bounced up and down and swung from side to side in time to his efforts. The men either sniggered or sang with him. They parted at Mary Margaret's approach. A few of them threw Angela a lascivious look. She stared back with dead, unimpressed eyes.

The giant stopped for a moment. Threw his head back and laughed before he aimed his penis like a firehose, soaking the nuns' legs in a spray of urine. Then he staggered to the side, knocked against a wall, shook himself, and resumed his ballad. The men were cackling now. Angela closed her eyes momentarily. Carmel twittered. Mary Margaret stood stockstill.

'Have-you-drink-taken?' she hissed.

'Whassat, hen?' He could barely stand.

'I said – have you drink taken?'

He was glowering at her menacingly then. Took a few faltering steps toward her unflinching frame. The penis waggled in his hand again.

'On yewr knees, woman. Pray to tha',' he said. The men erupted but stopped at one shrivelling glance from the Mother Superior.

'Put him away,' she enunciated quietly. Angela felt compelled to advise her about the better part of valour. This could turn nasty. They'd seen it before.

'Whassa'? You widnae liketa geez a wee lick noo? Justa wee suck. I widnae tell.' He stuck his tongue out and slurped. He tried to focus on Angela. 'Come oo-on yew beauiee yew . . .'

Mary Margaret moved like divine lightning. She darted forward, catching his penis in the clamp of her hand. She twisted, grunting with the effort. Beads of sweat on her brow. He roared. She twisted harder. The men winced. The giant teetered for a moment before he went down. Mary Margaret bent on her haunches with him. Still twisting. Angela could see that she was grinding it tighter and tighter in her closed fist. He couldn't breathe never mind try to protect himself. His guttural grunts matched Mary Margaret's as they knelt, eye to eye, for the briefest of moments before she abruptly released him, allowing him to keel over sideways with a long, deeply satisfying moan. The Mother Superior rose slowly, wiping droplets of pee from her navy skirt. Then she rubbed her palms along her navy v-neck, eyeing the onlooking, quailing men with her black gaze.

'Never let it be said that I didn't warn ye boys the day ye walked through that front door there,' she said quietly. 'No drink. No pricks. And no-oo fucking with me.'

She turned on her heels and strode back along the corridor toward her office, calling over her shoulder: 'Ship him out, Sisters. Back to fecking Camden for all the hoots I give. Only ship him out fairly lively now. Before I read him his last rites.'

The men were drifting off, one by one, when Angela called to them to give her a hand with the Glaswegian. He was still sprawled on the ground, panting, having tucked the offensive penis back inside the flap of his trousers. He stank of Scotch and cider, and looked decidedly sorry for himself now. Mumbling something about 'Nae need fur that, nae need fur that typa carry oo-oon,' in a deeply aggrieved voice.

Sister Carmel fell to her knees beside him and stroked his hair. 'Now, now, Jim. You know the rules, pet. You can't go round breaking them like . . . Mother Mary Margaret gets fierce angry if her boys do that.' She beamed and rooted around deep in her habit pocket, pulling out a miniature picture of Christ pointing to his heart – 'I am the Way, the Truth and the Life'. She shook her head, replaced it and pulled out another. 'We want something a bit more softer, don't we, lads?' she said, nodding with approval when the next picture showed two kittens with huge, glistening eyes. The inscription said something about love. Sr Carmel wrapped his unfurled palm around the picture. He held it tenderly, eyeing her with drunken bemusement. Angela often saw the men look at Sr Carmel like that. Even the diehard cynics and the psychos had a tender spot for the elderly nun. She treated them all equally. Dishing out holy pictures and lemon bonbons as she glided past them, usually lost in the labyrinthine corridors of the Shelter. Maybe they saw something, a singular, gentle spark from the dark recesses of their childhoods in her. Something at any rate, a moment they had long forgotten.

They were heading for the second floor, two of the men hauling the Glaswegian from the front with Angela and Sr Carmel pushing from behind. The men slept in cubicles called clusters, little cells no more than seven by eight with a bed, a chair and a tiny locker each. They were closed off by calico curtains. The clusters opened onto a corridor containing two toilets, one with a shower, to service up to thirty men at any given time. Further down the corridor, there was a small communal room with a few chairs, a fridge bolted to the floor and a kettle. This kettle was the subject of interminable disputes, being the only removable object in the entire area and therefore a prize, a possession, something which might be owned. At present, George, a schizophrenic former doctor from Weybridge, insisted on sleeping with the kettle and made the others sign a register in order to use it. He was six foot four and mad as a badger which meant that invariably Sr Carmel had to be prevailed upon to get the kettle back from him. What had cost others innumerable teeth usually took no more than three bonbons with her.

The first, second and third floors of the building, which was originally a Victorian workhouse, were devoted to clusters. A few of the older nuns still had rooms on the fourth floor. Angela preferred to stay with them. Mother Mary Margaret and others had their own self-contained flats in nearby areas throughout

East London. On the ground floor, there was the men's refectory, a small, dark TV/games room, tiny chapel, the nuns' offices and the soup kitchen, a huge rambling room which serviced the homeless with hot meals by day and when the weather was bitter, doubled up as an extra patch of floor for sleeping on.

The vast red brick building had been divided into two separate shelters with the homeless women housed next door, with their own entrance and appointed staff. The majority of the women were on the game, using the refuge if they were on the run from their pimps or other prostitutes. Angela had worked with the men since her arrival. The reason for this was quite simply that the nuns were safer with them than with the women. It was mostly non-clerical in the female section now. Due to the acute shortage of nuns.

In the main the men came from the streets. Or on referrals from other shelters with too few beds. Some drifted in and out, wanting only a bed, warmth and regular food for brief periods. Vacationers, Mary Margaret sneeringly called them. A few of the older men had been there for years. It represented home now. Then there were those who were waiting for that greatest prize of all – a flat. Usually they were younger than they looked. They had hoops to jump through still. Mary Margaret still advocated priesthood with an occasional one, but mostly she just insisted on sobriety and a measure of quietude within the four walls of the shelter. They could drink, fight, show their genitals, whatever got them through the day – outside. But come eventide, she decreed that they put their toys away and play the real game. Lots of sucking up and plenty of 'yes Mother' and 'no Mother' to keep her content. She ran a tight ship. And as much as every man who ran the gauntlet of the shelter vowed his miserable, hopeless, persistent life to Sr Carmel, while fantasizing nightly about Sr Angela, he abided in mortal terror of the hairy matriarch. She was the unchallenged High Priestess and for the life of her, Angela could never understand how the bearded, squat-legged, gin-breathed, foul-mouthed creature

36

had come to represent the apotheosis of all that Angela strove for daily, and with the greatest of difficulty, to become herself. Often, she thought she should take up gin. Or vodka. Maybe she should bypass all that and go straight for the heroin. Mainline her way to Mother Superior.

Or maybe it was all some sort of divine joke. If so, then the joke was on Angela, she thought, as she patted Glasgow's shoulder, about to leave him weeping quietly in his cluster for the night.

'Ahm no' al' bad,' he blubbered.

'Ah now, pet, no one, no one is *all* bad,' Sr Carmel assured him. 'Not a bit of it.'

Someone roared loudly down the corridor.

'That bleddy kettle.' Angela rolled her eyes to Carmel who stopped her with her little wren's pincers.

'I'll get it off of him, darling, you make pet here do his weewee for the night.'

'I think he's done that already, Sister.'

'Ah, he'll have another little strike, Sister.'

George the doctor came panting in to them. He was wild-eyed and sweating, the kettle clutched to his breast. He looked about frantically in his wake. A couple of men loped after him, not over-serious in their intentions.

'What's going on?' Angela tried to mimic Mary Margaret's tone.

'We only want to make a cuppa,' someone wheedled.

'Sign the register!' George boomed.

'Ah, now, pet,' Sr Carmel advanced.

Dr George's eyes looked glazed. A bad sign. Angela tried to stop Sr Carmel reaching for the stainless steel prize.

'Sister, I think we should . . .' she began.

'It's no' hiz ke'le,' Glasgow interjected, hoping to shrug off some guilt.

'Give that over to me, pet.' Sr Carmel reached out.

'What? What?' George hugged the kettle harder. It was the

love of his life. More important by far than three beauteous daughters, the youngest a model, and a wife of seven and a half stone precisely, who rode purebred geldings and entire villages.

'The kettle, darling. You'll give it over to me, won't you? There's a lovely man. Of course you will. Sure what business have you with that old thing? It only works – what does it work? – only half of the time. Sure what good is half the time? I'll get you a one tomorrow, your very own, that'll work most of the time. Now so. What have you to say to that?'

Angela held her breath. George looked so out of it, she couldn't believe that the frail, elderly nun could work her magic yet again. There had to be a place called stop. Angela lived in fear of it. And yet, there he stood – all six foot four of him – mulling. His face, which was always readable especially when murderous, could only be described as – mulling.

'I have to think about it,' he said.

'Course you do.' Carmel rooted for a bonbon. 'What have I here at all?' She held it up, looking surprised.

'I'd prefer – well the thing is – I've always rather fancied one of those, you know, cafetiere jobbies,' George offered reasonably.

'Oh?' Carmel was genuinely intrigued.

'Yes. You know with the . . .'

'Bassard,' Glasgow steamed. 'Taffy-nazed geek. Ge' oo' ah mah clus'er. Ge' afuck oo'. Fore ah looz mah heid.'

'Pardon me?' George appeared perplexed. Then a dangerous expression as the Glaswegian's words sank in. 'Stand up, you appalling animal,' he added quietly.

Angela didn't like the way the light in his pupils seemed to come from a distant galaxy. That meant serious trouble. She tried to quickly elbow Carmel from the cubicle, shaking her head and rolling her eyes in a manner she thought must convey something universal.

'Whew're yew callin' a nanimal?' The giant of the Gorbals sat up on his bed. He looked small next to George.

38

'Speak the Queen's English,' George roared. 'You Hebridean halfwit.'

'Hebrid-eeean? Hebri-fu'in-dean? Issa' wha' heez callin' mee?'

Angela was about to run downstairs for Mary Margaret, when Carmel pulled another bonbon from her other pocket. She popped it in her mouth and made a loud sucking, delighted noise. Then she plucked it out and crammed it into George's gaping maw.

'Now suck,' she said.

He looked at her. He looked at Glasgow. He looked at Angela. He sucked.

'Tasty,' he said.

Sr Carmel crammed the other bonbon into the Glaswegian's mouth. 'Think of your Mammy,' she said, as she always did, at times of intense stress.

It worked. As it always did. Carmel's magic. And Angela could only gasp on her way downstairs, at the illogical, irrational vagaries of life, nuns, men and lemon bonbons. And her own inability to fully, wholly, cohesively, come to grips with any of the above.

She felt exhausted but the evening's chores still stretched ahead. Check the clusters, lock up, paperwork, soup-making, a little light supper before Mass. Followed by tea, telly and two nightly cigarettes in her room, followed by merciful sleep. Sr Carmel was already wandering off, humming to herself, stopping only to slap one of her pre-gummed puppy pictures against a wall. As full of energy and commitment as she'd been at the crack of day. Probably even looking forward to Mass. Every corridor a shrine to her enduring optimism. God was love. Kittens were love. Puppies were love. Angela felt very unworthy.

A feeling which intensified when she saw that Mary Margaret was signalling her to the office again. A click of the fingers and a point at the door. Sr Oliver, who was at least a hundred and hardly visible behind the shield of holy medals she wore pinned

to her habit, shuffled past Angela, whispering out of the corner
of her mouth:

'You're wanted.'

Angela scowled after her. Young or old, no nun wanted to
be summoned to Mother's office twice in one evening. She
entered with her hands plunged deep within the pockets of her
jeans.

'Yes, Mother?'

'I had a phone call.'

'You did?'

'From Auntie Bridie.'

'Oh dear.'

'And well you might "oh dear." "Oh bollocks" I'd be more
inclined to say myself if I was you. But of course I'm not you.
Am I?'

'You're not, Mother.'

'Are you giving me lip? Because I won't put up with . . .'

'No. I swear. I was only agreeing . . .'

'The thing of it is, is this.' Mary Margaret rose to add the
appropriate measure of gravity to her painful words. 'Uncle
Mikey.' She enunciated slowly. No more needed to be said at
that particular juncture. Those two words, which had resonated
like no other two words throughout Angela's life, had been
uttered. Had been hurled out into the late evening air, to make
of them whatever an innocent bystander might. Simple enough.
On their own – 'Uncle Mikey' – hardly nuclear, heralding in
themselves no especially cataclysmic connotations. Except to
Angela.

'Oh,' she uttered. Forlornly.

'Doubtless they'll be wanting you home,' Mary Margaret
offered, somewhat redundantly.

'They will.' Angela took a deep breath. 'Throwing stuff and
the like?' she added tentatively.

'Worse. Much worse.' A pause for effect. 'He's been tipping
the po out the window.'

'He did that for a while a few years back,' Angela responded, trying to sound lighter than she felt. She felt like a small mountain range.

'I know he did.' Mary Margaret wouldn't be outdone. 'Auntie Bridie told me at the time. But then it was only fluids, wasn't it?'

'Ah he's not . . . is he?' Angela grimaced.

'Saving them up by all accounts. Waits until he has a half a dozen cacas or so, then out they go. Missed a nine-year-old girl by the ribbon on her hair according to Bridie. Her little shoes got splattered though. Gorgeous black patents, Auntie Bridie said. The poor child. Your aunts are in pure bits.' A note of censure to her last addition. As if everything was Angela's fault.

'I've a few days coming to me . . .' Angela began.

'It'll have to be after the weekend now.'

'Wouldn't it be better if I . . .'

'I need you here to show that fecking missioner around. He's insisting on staying. Doing some class of a study on poverty third world and real world or what have you. Give him the runaround before you see to Uncle Mikey. You could go from next Tuesday or Wednesday say. But only for the couple of nights. We're running short as it is. Remind me to book the aeroplane ticket in the morning. All right. Get out.'

Angela hopped from foot to foot. There was never a good or right time to broach certain subjects with her Superior, but she might just have the sympathy vote now after the inevitable censure.

'Mother, I was wondering if you'd given any consideration to . . .' She stopped, searching for the right words, remembering too late about she who hesitates.

'You're not going to bang on about the bleddy Missions again, are you?' Mary Margaret rummaged in a desk drawer and pulled out a packet of Afton Major. She lit one and drew with satisfaction. 'Here is where you're needed – for the moment.'

41

'Yes, but I thought the *idea* was for me to – to sort of move on after a while. I'm here over five years now.'

Mary Margaret chuckled darkly.

'Angela Angela Angela,' her head hung low, ghostly spectres from the cigarette tip dancing between them. 'You've notions, that's what's wrong with you.'

'Everyone has notions of some class or other.'

'Not everyone has a notion to be a nun.'

'I do my job well enough, don't I?'

'Am I on about the quality of your work here, am I?'

'I got my last exams.'

'I've no doubt you'll make a fine social worker or whatever it is that you're up to.' Mary Margaret inhaled deeply and hissed the smoke out between gritted teeth. She opened her mouth to add something, thought better of it. 'It'll come to you,' she added wearily, before signalling the door with her head.

'I'm sure it will if you'll just give me the chance,' Angela cut in eagerly.

'Not that, you fool.' Mary Margaret stubbed out her cigarette. 'Look it,' she began, choosing her words with rare caution. 'I don't mean to be down on you like a ton of hot bricks all the time.'

Angela looked sceptical.

'But I'm responsible in a way for your future, Sister.' Mary Margaret steepled her fingers. Her brow buckled under the great weight of her responsibilities. 'And what I'm trying to say is – you've no fecking business being a nun.' She added that last in a hot rush.

Angela gasped – this was the first time that her Superior had come right out and said it. After five years of diligent, hard work, it seemed more than a little unfair to say the least. Before she could begin to protest, Mary Margaret was off on a hack again, waggling her finger at the door.

'Look out there. What have we? A shower of decrepit bazoobas – the nuns I'm talking about. Half of them, what's left, don't even know where the feck they are most of the time. Then there's the precious few in their thirties or forties still, with their faculties, but all sorts of stories hanging to them.'

'Isn't that all the more reason . . .' Angela tried to interject.

'Shut up and listen,' Mary Margaret barked. 'Sr Aloysius is there because she might as well be somewhere. Carmel came out of the womb in a habit. Frances was ugly as the day is long and got chased by the Sisters of Clare for her troubles till she gave in. Marie-Therese is French. A couple of them got fiddled with by their uncles . . . You weren't fiddled with, Sister, were you?'

'Not that I know of,' Angela responded sullenly.

'But they all have one thing in common – they've a very healthy belief in God and all that stuff. It's sort of what you might call, necessary, if you're to make those final vows.'

'What are you saying? That I don't . . .' Angela was shocked.

'You believe in yourself as a nun first, is what I'm saying. It's not your fault. The Aunts filled your young head with notions. You've a pretty picture of yourself in the middle of Africa or someplace else hot, doling out food left right and centre to the poor starving black babies, with a big sunhat on your head. Getting your photo in the paper back home for them all to see. Maybe even going on to win the Nobel Prize or something. Telling Pat about it on *The Late Late Show* – making the entire country warm to you. Oh like I can't read you like a book.'

Angela shifted uncomfortably. No one liked to hear their fantasies sound like dull, concrete lumps falling from the mouth of another. She was doing her best. Her youth and good health allowed her to work harder than most of the other nuns put together. She knew that she was good with the men, probably because most of them reminded her of Uncle Mikey.

'And you've another serious thing wrong with you.' Mary Margaret hiked two hands under her large breasts, a habit she had when pontificating.

43

'Have I now?' Angela gritted her teeth.

'You're too pretty.'

'I'll keep my vows,' Angela said in a deliberately prim voice, knowing full well that her Superior wasn't above hauling some poor misfortunate dosser into her gin chamber in the early hours of the morning. She wanted to say: 'And what made *yourself* want to be a nun, hah? Oh don't tell me – your kind, caring nature, was it? Or maybe it was the beard that did it.' She pressed the tip of her tongue between her teeth.

'Only because you never put yourself in the way of breaking them,' Mary Margaret countered, curling her top lip knowingly. 'That's not a vocation, Sister – that's hiding.' The voice softened suddenly. Mary Margaret would often do that in the middle of a berating, which totally disconcerted Angela. She nearly preferred when the onslaught remained shrill, harsh and strident. At least she knew where she stood. 'Now so, I've ten million things to do before the night is out,' Mary Margaret was saying in that scary, softer tone. 'While you're at home, you might think on what I just said, Angela. Before your options run out on you and you'll have no choice left but to be standing there with your lip half chewed off and two big red cheeks on you, like you have. And ring Auntie Bridie before she rings me again.' She lit another cigarette, dismissing Angela with a wave of her hand. 'All right. Get out.'

Angela stood outside the door with her middle finger raised for a while. She kicked a leg into fresh air, imagining Mary Margaret's ample rear. Out in the vegetable gardens she saw Sr Carmel bustle purposefully to the end of a pathway, she turned right, stopped, put a finger to her lips, then swerved off left instead. A few shouts echoed down from the clusters upstairs. Bunking down for the night. The perennial smell of simmering soup drifted up the corridors from the great hall. The aunts cackled with outrageous glee in her head.

There was that uncomfortable ring of truth to much of Mary Margaret's words. Yet it was so unfair. It wasn't Angela's fault

44

entirely that she'd made a few bad choices along the way. Her first sojourn with the silent Sisters of Clare had been a total disaster. A year of biting her lip during the awful, silent meals and shivering with extreme cold throughout early morning matins in the pitch dark, her knees imprinted with the knobbled ridges of the small chapel's stone floor. Until the day she woke up talking and couldn't stop. She just could not stop. Gabbling like an eedjit. They thought she had a fever and sent her home. Auntie Regina had her first stroke about then and Angela had to nurse her for another year.

Then followed the two-year stint as a novice nun/nurse at the Bons Secours in Cork. Another disaster. She could never get to grips with the awful yowls of pain made by the women in late labour. Angela could mop their sweaty brows well enough. Even squeeze their hands reassuringly when called upon, but when they threw their heads back like that, all purple-faced and knotty-necked, Angela threw her head back and howled with them. She was put into the office for a spell but she still wanted to go to the Missions. So she returned home for another while, which was just as well because Uncle Mikey started acting up really badly for the first time, and she was the only one who could put any sort of hold on him.

The short stay, prior to an unrealized teacher training course, turned into two years, while she remained neither one thing nor the other. A sort of novice limbo. Until Auntie Bridie took the matter into her own hands by calling her old domestic science pupil, Sr Mary Margaret in London, who agreed to take on Angela at the shelter, as a carer then a postulant for three years, then a novice for two. Her every attempt at taking her first set of vows brutally staunched by her Superior. As near now to being a fully paid-up nun as she was to Africa. And Uncle Mikey was still above in the attic.

Angela had her hand on the receiver of the communal phone when she remembered the tall, slender guide with the tobacco-coloured eyes at the V & A yesterday evening. It must be all

45

of two hours since she'd cast him a thought. Now her cheeks burned hotly when she recalled again how she had fudged telling him her true vocation. What had possessed her? And more than that – she'd even agreed to have coffee with him next Wednesday even though she hated coffee. Thank God she'd be in Ireland instead. With her mother, the Aunts and the Uncle. She need never bump into him again. Need never see the way the lines cracked on his cheek when he smiled crookedly like that – almost shyly she'd have said, if he wasn't a man. He didn't even seem to notice the rapt attention of his audience. They hung on his every word – he'd made the museum seem so interesting – so alive. Angela'd overheard a gum-chewing American woman say that his lecture was the only thing worth listening to, since she'd come to London.

A man like that could seriously complicate things for Angela. She hadn't invested so many years of her life to blow it all over a cup of coffee. She'd had a couple of crushes from time to time over the years, visiting medics and the like, a particularly handsome, boyish chaplain at one time. Nothing to worry about, a few nuns a couple of decades closer to her own age, had assured her. Perfectly normal. Just biology. Years of chastity, soup-making, hard work, harder prayer, and all that biology stuff would just fade away. In truth, the way they put it – Angela wasn't sure if she felt comforted or horribly saddened by their advice. All in all, it was a very good thing that she'd never see him again. A tremendously good thing. In spite of the way he – no – none of that, nothing of him ever again. Thank God. Thank *God*.

'Excellent rib of beef, Bonnie.'

'Uh huh.'

'Mmm.' The meat was so rare a little runnel of bloody juice ran down Robert's chin. Bonnie silently handed him a wad of scrunched-up toilet paper from under her sleeve. Well, at least he didn't have to worry about mad cow disease – there was plenty of that in the room already and he'd managed to survive so far.

'Uh huh.'

She was rankling over something, sawing at her meat with fast, furious strokes. Chewing with her gaze fixed firmly in the distance.

'Lovely. Thank you,' he murmured again, wishing he could stop doing that, complimenting everything so lavishly, saying thanks over and over again. It was such an annoying habit, but he was just trying to fill the ominous silence. Staving, was the right word, he considered.

Finally, she looked at him. Eyes narrowed to a squint.

'The lemon,' she said, indicating the slice in his empty gin and tonic glass.

'I'm sorry?'

'The lemon. You never thanked me for the lemon.'

Robert set his fork and knife together on the plate. He leaned forward, resting his chin on the bridge of his hands. He did this though every tendon in his body screamed at him to run. She was angry: she would hurt him. That was the pattern. She would be sorry. She would be guilty. And he would say it was all right really, that she hadn't hurt his feelings even though she had because she always managed to find a way *in*. No matter how hard he tried to deflect or ward off or even retaliate, she found a route to get to him. And every time he mentally ejected her again, another little segment of his soul had to freeze within to protect what was left.

'Right,' he said. 'Are you going to tell me what's bugging you this time?'

'*This* time? How dare you.'

'Well you're in a gimp over something.'

She gave him a sour look and speared a pink, limp slice like a panting dog's tongue. A fourth roast potato next to that, squash and mashed swede, a big dollop of black gravy, then she cubed and diced making a wet peak to one side of her plate.

Enough salt to make Robert suppress a grimace, before she discarded the knife and plunged at the pile repeatedly with her fork. Her face a streaked palette of deeply unhappy colours, as she chewed in silence.

'Well . . . ?' Robert persisted.

'I'm hurt,' she said finally. Dropping her fork. 'There's no point in me trying to hide it any longer.' She fixed him with angry, accusing eyes. 'You told me – you sat there and you *told* me how you was gonna partner me for Barry Manilow. You know I feel a fool on my own.'

'What's the problem? If I said I'll go, I'll go.'

In truth, he had forgotten about her concert tickets. Amnesiac kindness on his mind's part, no doubt. The prospect of two hours listening to Bonnie's idol while surrounded by a drift of swooning elderly women – himself, the token heterosexual male, in the midst of them – *with his mother* – Well, it was at best, unedifying; at worst, self-mutilation came to mind. Still, if he'd agreed to accompany her . . .

'Friday night?' she rasped. '*Next* Friday night?'

'So?'

'I bumped into Peter this morning – that's so. Told me you had a hot date at their place, said it was all fixed up. You might have told me yourself.'

'A hot . . . ?' Robert racked his brain. 'I have no such thing. I seem to remember Peter leaving a message on my machine – but there's nothing firmed up. I'll just call him and say I can't come.'

'What is it with those two anyway? How come they're always trying to get you to do this, get you to do that. Why can't you tell them to get screwed – you'll get your own girl thank you very much. With all her full schaboodle too, I could say, but I won't.'

She was mindlessly sifting salt again. Robert gently extricated the cellar from her hand, giving her a quick squeeze at the same time, because he understood about loneliness.

'They weren't supposed to know she wore a wig.' Robert referred to their last attempt to fix him up with one of their acquaintances.

'The wig was the least of her problems.' Bonnie's eyebrows lifted meaningfully.

'Anyway, I cancelled now so's you can see what they got for you after all.'

'Why did you do that? You might at least have checked with me first. If push came to shove, you could have gone alone or got someone else. You know you wanted to go to that concert.'

He could have added – so why shoot yourself in the foot? But he didn't bother. Both Bonnie's feet were cratered in imaginary buckshot. She so often jumped right in, making an altogether workable situation utterly untenable for herself, just to enjoy the heightened frisson of self-pity. Once that exquisite moment passed, all too quickly, she was left to cope with the more enduringly miserable results of her own sabotage. But she'd never learn. Time and time again, she went for the moment, with the impulse. The 'flashes' Robert called them. If only she could learn to stop occasionally, to think things through. Follow a sequence to its logical conclusion. Naturally enough, she accused Robert of doing little else but that – to his own detriment.

'It's done now,' she said airily. Regret written all over her face.

'Ah, Bonnie.'

'Most likely you'd've looked a complete geek there anyway – *with your mother*,' she flashed.

Robert scraped his chair back.

'That's it. I'm going home. Ring me when you've stopped feeling so sorry for yourself.'

'Sit down.' She tugged at his sleeve. 'Rob? C'mon, sit. I'll act nice. I promise.' She looked so like a penitent puppy dog, with her long grey curls bobbing and the glistening blue eyes widened so appealingly, he couldn't resist. He sat again, shaking his head, giving her a look of mock exasperation. She giggled, in reality just as pleased as he was that the little spat was over.

'You know me and that Peter.' She munched happily. 'What is it about that guy? He just has this way of getting on my tits. She's even worse.'

'They've been good friends to me, Bonnie, you know that. I don't know why you always seem to go into one – every time you meet him.'

Her eyes narrowed at that for a moment. Evaluating. No – not worth another spat. She shrugged.

'Beats me.' She reached for the salt again but Robert got there first.

'Your heart,' he said.

As far as Robert could make out, Peter had never been anything but polite to Bonnie. Maybe that was what she distrusted. Even when they were kids, she used to tease him to his face, but Peter always chose to play on the boat rather than bring Robert around to his house. On occasion, he brought Bonnie sweets from his stash which made her laugh and deride him all the more, but nothing daunted him. He hopped along the gangway, all neatly creased shorts, wobbly thighs and parted copper hair, as if he were heading for Ali Baba's cave. Robert was an altogether more mishmash of a specimen in those days. Just throwing on whatever Bonnie left out for him, holed sweaters three sizes too big from the local Oxfam, and multicoloured socks, though rarely in pairs.

But Peter had been fascinated by the boat, by the fact that people actually lived on it. Robert in turn, longed for the mellow red brick, paved front garden and solidity of Peter's terraced house in Hounslow. No undulating in your bed at night, or creaking when your boat listed against the next one. Still, he had very fond memories of himself and Peter, punting up the river in Bonnie's little dinghy, taking it in turns to be Christopher Columbus or Vasco da Gama. Until Bonnie would blow it all by calling to them from her half-deck with her long hair waving madly behind, nothing but a stripey hand towel just about covering her front. Robert, painfully conscious of the fact her rear had to be exposed to neighbours and the towpath above. Luckily, the other boatdwellers were pretty eccentric themselves. And they certainly knew how to throw a good party.

Parties notwithstanding, as soon as he feasibly could, Robert took out a mortgage on a small, two-bedroomed brick cottage a few roads away, in Old Isleworth. Terraced Victorian, circa 1870, with two sash windows above and a rounded bay below. He spent his first night there, planting window boxes, scrubbing floors and just lying on the floor upstairs, feeling the solidity permeate his bones. Not a list. Not one undulating swell. No duck or heron calls in the midnight hour. No constant ring of the phone. Just peace and quiet and the wind gently tapping brick after brick. It took him the better part of two months before he could sleep properly.

When she was nineteen Bonnie had worked in an ice cream parlour in Upstate New York until she'd saved enough money to do Europe. She made it to London, got up the spout, and never went back. She was from a family of thirteen in any case, so it was unlikely that she was missed she told the young Robert. Irish mother, Italian father – meant that she used her hands and mouth a lot, frequently at the expense of her brain, Robert often thought. His own father, she'd explained, once he was old enough to ask, was okay in small doses. Whatever that meant. Sometimes he'd wondered just how big was the dose that had made him. Or how small. A dosage of no great significance either way it transpired when Bonnie was dumped at the first mention of her inconvenient condition. Her first and only love, she'd said, many times through the years. Robert believed everything Bonnie told him until she told him otherwise, which happened with regularity. Then, he believed whatever revised version of history she chose to give him. It was easier that way. Easier too, to grow quieter and quieter the more vocal she became, until there was a period in his teens when he wondered if he really could speak at all or if his own voice was just a figment of his imagination. By then, he was a short-back-and-sides merchant, with matching grey socks. While Peter grew long copper tresses over patchy sideburns and had taken to emulating Bonnie's sayings in an American-tinged accent.

Still, now when she was at her worst, goading him, he tended to remember the comforting smell of her when he got home from school. The milk and cookies. Standing over him every night as he did his homework. Pushing him forward for every scholarship going. Watching his face, though she pretended not to, when she took him to the bookshop in Richmond every month for his new supply, paying for them with the money she earned as a hospital auxiliary cum barmaid, cum whatever.

'That beef was organic, in case you're wondering,' Bonnie cut across his thoughts.

Robert was clearing the dishes. He turned, she was still seated at the table, picking at the leftovers – meagre pickings. He could see the round, soft contours of her Hitchcockian cheeks chomping still. A tiny bald spot on the top of her head – piglet pink – amidst all that hair, made his heart swell. He felt a strange compulsion to lean forward and touch his lips to it.

'Organic,' he smiled with fondness. 'Surprise me.'

'Robert?' She turned to meet his eyes, a worried little frown bisecting her forehead.

'You're not still, you know, well – ashamed – these days, are you?'

Robert swallowed a great rock in his throat.

'Oh, Bonnie. How can you say that? I was never ashamed of you. Never,' he lied.

'I meant the boat,' she said in a quiet voice.

Chapter Four

'There's rain in that moon,' Auntie Maisie said from her arm-chair by the window. Auntie Bridie sidled over and looked out.

'Not a drop of it,' she proclaimed.

Auntie Maisie's cheeks flushed with heat and ire, as she fumbled with the window latch and thrust it open, craning her head outside.

'Have one look out, let you – a good look. Now tell me there's no rain in that moon.'

Auntie Bridie stuck her head out, Angela could only see the cut off stumps of their bodies, asses wriggling in sisterly rhythm. Auntie Bridie pulled back first. She fixed her hair from the wind.

'There isn't a ounce of rain in it, mark my words,' she said dismissing her sister's claim.

'Close the window, Auntie Maisie, you're letting the cold in,' Angela said in her sternest voice. She rolled her eyes at Bina, her mother. The argument could go on all evening if someone didn't put a stop to it. But Bina was immune to them, she was busy as usual putting out the cups and plates for tea. Mother's Pan slices with triangles of Calvita cheese and processed smoked ham laid out in folded-over curls. Buttered brack for afters. Angela was about to scald the teapot but her mother got there first and circled the handle with her raw, chapped fingers.

'Don't I always do it?' She glared accusingly at her daughter.

'I'm only trying to be of help.' Angela stepped away. So far – only one day – she'd managed to avoid the little arguments which circled the square, open dining room cum kitchen, like a thousand tributaries in search of the big river. What started on one side of the room, between a pair of the Aunts, trickled out and forwards until the entire room became submerged. Sometimes, they diverged into a delta, but even then they managed to send out little probing rivulets to get to one another. Mostly, they were just passing time.

Maisie closed the window with a great show of reluctance. She hmpphed and sat on her chair again, pursing her mouth knowingly at the moon. She could wait.

Auntie Regina made a slobbering noise in her corner. Angela went to her.

'What is it, Reggie?' She cupped her hands to holler because the elderly woman was all but deaf. 'Your feet, is it? Are they bothering you?'

Regina's mouth turned up on one side. She was always grateful if someone could understand her. The last stroke had left her semi-paralysed. Angela patted her head.

'Her corns need a good scraping,' Auntie Bridie interjected. She lifted her own feet. 'My own could do with a doing, God knows.' She cast Angela an abject, wheedling look.

'You've no corns. Bunions is what you have,' Bina muttered under her breath, taking the teapot to the table. 'Well, are ye going to sit down or d'ye want me to eat it for ye too?'

From their respective corners the sisters closed in around the formica-topped table. A slow, vampiric procession. Each groaning louder than the other.

'I have so, corns.' Bridie was offended.

'I'll have a look tomorrow,' Angela offered, to keep the peace.

Silence reigned for a moment as they buttered their bread and peeled the silver foil from the cheese triangles, no easy feat with their swollen, arthritic fingers like oversized Twiglets.

Angela cut Regina's into bite-sized pieces and popped them into her mouth. She wiped a spool of dribble and inserted a dab of soft cheese, catching her finger between the toothless gums for a second. Regina half-smiled apologetically. Maisie continued to concentrate on the moon, willing it to vindicate her with rain. Bina, the youngest sister, at sixty-eight, sat down, last to the table, making a hurried sign of the cross before she poured tea for everyone. She stood up quickly again, and half-ran, half-hopped like a dog just brushed by an oncoming car, for the forgotten tea cosy.

'Now so, tell us all about your lovely school in London.' Bridie turned to Angela.

'It's not a school, Auntie Bridie,' Angela corrected her for the millionth time. 'It's a shelter for the homeless. We don't teach them anything.'

'Don't ye teach them to cop themselves on, come in out of the cold and have a roof over their heads like normal people? Isn't that something?'

'It's not like that.'

'Well what business have you there if it's not like that?' Bridie was only talking, not interested in the slightest in any response Angela might attempt. In truth, she was really just showing off to the other sisters that poor enough as her own understanding of the situation in London was, as they called it, it was still far greater than theirs. There was the situation in the attic, and the situation in London. 'And the first set of the old vows, Angela?' she wheedled again.

'Soon now. Fairly soon anyway.'

'You got sick, pet? The last time, was it? You did sure. And why wouldn't you?'

'I did not get sick,' Angela protested hotly. 'Mary Margaret made me wait. She said I wasn't – wasn't, you know, *completely* ready in myself to . . . Soon enough now.'

'In your own time, dotey. Bina, would you be a darling and boil me up a nice brown egg? I've a taste in my mouth for a egg for some reason. Isn't that the most extra-ordinary thing? I had a one only yesterday.' Bridie pawed at her youngest sister's sleeve.

Bina rose with a deep sigh. Angela hopped up quickly. 'I'll do it.' She urged her mother to remain seated and was rewarded with a baleful glare. Angela sat down again.

'Don't I always do it?' Bina said over her shoulder.

Auntie Bridie's broad grin took them all in.

'Isn't it nice that we have the pet back with us of an evening, sisters?'

Regina drooled. Maisie grunted, but her gimlet gaze was still in thrall to the golden satellite throwing slats of broken light on the bog outside.

'Will I bring Uncle Mikey down his tea?' Angela called to her mother. She noticed the little involuntary shiver the Aunts made in unison. Bina nodded sourly.

'He's being very bold.' Maisie interrupted her moon-gazing to whisper.

'Very very bold,' Bridie added, her eyes widening.

Angela waited for them to continue, a morsel of cheese poised on her forefinger, unaware that Regina was stooping forward in a vain attempt to get at it. Her head hit the table.

'God, sorry, Reggie.' Angela hoisted her back again. This time, she allowed her aunt to suck the cheese from her finger, feeling the noduled tongue lick around the rim of her nail. It tickled.

'He'll listen to you, Angela,' Bridie urged.

Angela nodded, unconvinced. It had been getting more and more difficult to get Uncle Mikey to listen to her over the past few years. She'd been putting off the moment since she arrived earlier in the day. If she could have her way, she would wait until breakfast time, when she might feel a little fresher, but they were relying on her intervention – and besides, he needed his tea.

'I seen those in black on a young one in the Post Office,' Bridie said, fingers scrabbling at Angela's blue denims.

'They come in most colours now.'

'Is that so?' A pause. 'No one on the bus would know you're going for a nun.'

'What bus would that be, Auntie Bridie?'

'The bus what took you home this morning.'

Angela gave another dab of Calvita to Regina.

'I did tell you,' she said in an over-patient voice. 'Only the older ones wear the habit now.'

'That's hard on you.' Bridie chewed impassively.

Angela looked at her mother who was applying herself to buttering bread with the same fastidious, yet distracted, air she remembered from childhood. Bina had refused to meet her eye since morning.

'I got you some brochures from the Victoria and Albert Museum, Mammy.'

Bina's eyebrows rose, then collapsed again. She continued buttering.

'You'd've loved it,' Angela perservered. 'I only got to see a tiny bit, but there was a talk for free. Well, included in the price anyway. You could've heard a pin drop when this tall, thin fella went on about the Victorians and what they got up to. There was this lovely – statue, I suppose you'd call it, wood like, of Our Lord on a donkey. He looked so happy.'

'The donkey?' Bridie asked.

'Our Lord of course.'

'That'll be English museems, for you,' Bridie murmured. She was deeply affronted at the thought of a happy-looking Christ because she was sighing heavily, unable to chew the clump of dough under a prominent cheekbone. Milky grey eyes fixed on the window now, like her sister beside her. If she pulled out the false teeth, she was seriously aggrieved. Here we go, Angela thought, at the distinctive-sounding thud on the tabletop.

'Put your teeth back in, Auntie,' she said, looking up at the ceiling.

'My gums are at me,' Bridie responded, sulking.

57

'I thought it was your corns that were at you.'

'Wait till you're old. You won't be so saucy then.'

Half her face was gone without the teeth. She coughed piti-fully. Her rheumy gaze searched for Bina who rolled her eyes and brought the unasked for glass of water into which Bridie plunged her beaky nose as though it had suddenly caught fire. For a moment, it looked as if she had collapsed into herself. All brittle bones, hair-netted hair and acrylic pearl-buttoned cardigan, a masque of human misery. Maisie, several years younger, wide of hip and hair curled into severe sausages, looked like a fecund Nero beside her elder sister. Always the sneak, blowing with the most prevailing wind, mostly Hurricane Bridie, she shot her niece a heartbroken look, which would have won her accolades in any old-time silent movie. 'What'll become of us now, after what you've done?'

Angela sent her back a quick frown to warn her off. The unspoken accusations bounced back and forth across the walls. Bina took the opportunity to savour her only daughter's dis-comfort.

'You've the life,' she said, reaching across to fill Regina's open, plaintive mouth before Angela could get to it. 'Sook sook,' Bina soothed, as though feeding calves or newborn lambs.

Angela jumped to her feet.

'Right. I'll just go and ... Uncle Mikey,' she said, rubbing herself mentally from their censure.

'Take the torch, let you,' Maisie shrieked.

'Of course I'll take the torch,' Angela snapped.

She stepped into the back kitchen, where all the cooking was done, to prepare Uncle Mikey's tray. Bridie was extracting mileage from the denim jeans and the smiling Christ in the main room.

'They're sore out, my poor old gums,' Angela overheard.

'You've gums on you like Gibraltar,' Bina was responding sourly. 'Put your teeth back in like she said and stop your going on.'

'There's no sympathy in this house.'

For a moment, Angela felt that time had stood still in her life. Nothing had happened, not the Sisters of Clare, not the Bon Secours, not London, nothing. She was back in her childhood, a human repository for all their misery. Guilt rubbing against her shoulderblades in an endless chafing massage. She wanted to go out there, clap their stupid, mindless heads together, stomp on their withered, brittle bones. Make them sing with pain. Rip their gums open with her fingernails. That would give them something to –

'Okay so, Aunties? I'll head away down.' She carried the tray through.

'Mind yourself, dotey,' Bridie mumbled, popping her teeth in again. 'We'll sit up for you.'

A cold blast of air outside momentarily cleared the Aunts from her head. She balanced the tray on her outstretched arms, holding the torch in one hand. White moonlight was sufficient to pick out the more treacherous ruts on the track in any case. The house behind her stood on a slight gradient. Halfway down, she turned to look back at it. Even in the semi-darkness she could make out the peeling walls. It needed a good lick of whitewash. The three front windows upstairs remained unlit. Downstairs, lights on only in the porch and the kitchen. The good parlour to the left of the porch was only used for the Stations, or when somebody died such as Auntie Imelda a few years back, or when the priest visited. In truth, the house and the surrounding sheds were practically falling down around them. But the Aunts cared less, not least because it wasn't their childhood home. Only Uncle Mikey still resided there, all alone, in the Ruin at the bottom of the track.

Angela continued to pick her way down, pausing to steady the tray as she brushed wild brambles away from her face. The narrow road, such as it was, was nearly closed over with hedgerow. To her left and right, bog, spreading out as far as the eye could see from the moment the track levelled. A couple

59

of stunted, leafless bog oaks here and there, grimly outlined by the moon, and way out in the distance two undulating hillocks like the contours of a woman lying on her side. Heaven lay behind those hills according to Bridie when Angela was a girl. But you had to be holy enough to see it, she sometimes added, hedging her bets. Angela sniffed the air, rich with peat and the high, sedimenty smell from the nearby pig farm. Almost suffocating in the summer.

She bore left and there was Uncle Mikey's house. It had a naked granite facade with a mesh of creeping cracklines. The lower windows were boarded up, the porch almost concealed behind a screen of ivy. She had to use the torchbeam to pick out the door handle. Inside – darkness, the moon excluded. No electricity for the past twenty years once Bridie had deemed that it might as well be cut off. It made no difference to her brother.

The porch opened onto a wooden stairwell. Angela heard a slithering above her head, when the first few steps creaked under her weight.

'Uncle Mikey,' she called up. 'It's me. Angela. I'm home. I've got your tea.'

She ascended slowly because the stairs had gaps where the wood had rotted. The slithering increased as she started on a second, narrower set of steps which led up from a small landing.

'Uncle Mik-ey. Open up.' She had to balance the tray in the curve of her waist, while her other hand pointed the light at a recessed door in the low ceiling. A rattle as the door lifted up and fell back with a clang of metal latch. Angela waited. He always hesitated for a while when she first came home.

'It's me,' she said softly, to reassure him.

She could just make out the glint of two black eyes, blinking rapidly in the torchlight. Evidently, he was satisfied that it was her because he moved back and grunted for her to come up. She had to swing herself in from the side of the trapdoor, having pushed the tray ahead.

He was hunkered down, studying the contents of his tea. Angela allowed the torchlight to trickle over him. She shook her head. Hair so long now, it would take a pair of shears to cut through the matting. And they still had done nothing about those nails. Crooked and twisting like unicorn horns.

'What're you doing in the pitch dark?' she said more to herself, gazing around for the paraffin lamp. He jumped a little when she lit it, washing the low, angled room in shadowy half-light. She touched his bent head, the foul stench of him nearly making her gag. His slightest movement sailed wafts in every direction. She would scrub him from his toes to the top of his skull first thing in the morning.

'How are you, Uncle Mikey?'

He looked up and grinned, showing a line of blackened and holed top teeth.

'I hear you've been up to your old tricks, hmm?'

The grin broadened. He pointed to the ceramic potty in the corner and chuckled throatily. Although he rarely spoke, and then only in grunts or the occasional barely decipherable word, he understood perfectly well. Bina said that he hadn't spoken much as a boy either. Just the odd curse and then he pretty much gave up on that as well.

'I'll empty that out for you in the morning,' Angela said. 'The proper way,' she added sternly. 'Understand?'

He chewed on one side, probably where the teeth were the least rotten. He remained on the floor, sitting cross-legged before the tray. The black eyes followed the line of her gaze to the potty again and his shoulders began to heave up and down.

'It's no laughing matter.' Angela had to hide her own smile. 'There'll be no more of that craic. The poor kids have to pass by your door on their way to the top of the road for the school bus. It's not fair on them. How would you like it – if – if . . .' She had to break off, pinching her nose at the thought of the sky raining turds on the unfortunate youngsters.

Long enough they'd called up to him, generation after generation, mocking, jeering, sending him shrieking to the skylight window to howl down at them in impotent rage. The window had become his solitary outlet on the world, until he'd blackened it with a mixture of saliva and dust.

He was still cackling softly.

'Eat your tea, I'll come early.' Angela spoke in a low voice. Normal conversational level sometimes startled him.

She crept downstairs backwards, keeping a palm flat against the side wall for balance. Just as she reached the intermediate landing, the trapdoor clanged shut above her head again.

'Night night,' she called. But if he grunted, she couldn't hear him.

The aunts would be circling, fizzing with questions, wanting to know if she'd managed to get through to him. She never knew how to respond to that. Yes, he was very co-operative? He apologized unequivocally and will never, ever, toss his turds out the skylight window *agayyn*. He's copped himself on and will be seeking employment in a bank forthwith? She'd have to spin them some line or other just to make them go to bed. It would all start again in the morning in any case. In the meantime, her feet took small, slow steps up the track.

There was a time when she could be sure that she'd get through to him. His hands would clap with delight when she tripped into his garret in her green school uniform with the red tie. She brought him comics and read them aloud, motioning any action bits, slitting throats with her forefinger, feet lashing out in karate kicks. She fed him undissolved cubes of jelly sometimes, smuggled down from the sisters' kitchen in the gusset of her knickers. He turned somersaults for her, over and over again, careering around the tiny attic, his long feet scraping against the beamed ceiling. Making her laugh. And on quieter days, when his vision fixed on a point beyond her shoulder and his forehead creased into an endless, confused frown, she would rest his head on her lap and stroke his hair until he fell into a deep sleep.

No one knew for sure why Uncle Mikey went up into the attic. Everyone had their own piece of conjecture. Mostly it centred around the death of his father. According to her mother, Bina, whose memories weren't always entirely reliable as she had been so young herself at the time, he'd taken to spending long spells up there as a boy, prior to and after the death of their mother. Bina herself was only a child of six then. It fell to Bridie, the eldest at sixteen, to step into the breach and help her father bring them up. Which she continued to do after his death, eight years later. Five girls, one boy. Maybe Uncle Mikey simply made up his mind that he didn't want to be the only male left in the house of females. Maybe he just liked the attic. All anybody knew for certain was that he went up the morning after his father's funeral, and he never came back down.

According to Bina, in response to her young daughter's questions at the time, efforts were made, valiant efforts, to get him down. They tried starving him. Got the priest and the canon to shout up to him. Masses were said and holy souls invoked for favours. Finally, St Jude, the patron saint of hopeless causes, was prevailed upon after the nightly rosary, but evidently he was busy elsewhere. After a while, the sisters gave up the cause and brought up his food three times daily, a change of clothing and wet face flannels once a week, fresh blankets every fortnight, and emptied his bedpan every morning. He grew boils which they learned to lance because he would not permit the doctor upstairs. They scoured him for lice and fleas every now and then, but apart from parasites and the occasional cold, he remained in remarkably good health. In over fifty years his eyes had not blinked in the full light of day nor had he held grunting converse with any, other than the sisters and then Angela, who, for much of her early youth, thought that everyone had an uncle in the attic.

When Angela was old enough to worry about the subject, Auntie Bridie dismissed her concerns with great airiness. He was as well off where he was. No doubt he'd only be causing manly wreck, like so many others, if he was out and about in the local village. Besides, by that time, Auntie Bridie had come to see herself and the sisters as her very own private sect, realizing, in a fashion, her own thwarted ambition to be a nun. Her mother's death had put paid to that and for years Bridie had pined most grievously for convent life. She was made for it, she knew. Anything else would be a poor second. But when Uncle Mikey obliged by going up, the all-female house came to fulfil her albeit second-rate desire. She was militantly virginal. Consecrating the souls and vaginas of her sisters to the glory of God in likewise fashion. Whether they wanted to or not. In those days, Bina had further explained, no one crossed Bridie, who took over as the sole teacher in the nearby National School in order to spread her evangelical word all the better. She taught one subject, apart from Catechism, and that was Domestic Science. Generations of men in the area had the greatest of difficulty with fractions and algebra evermore, but they could raise a madeira cake to perfection.

Years had winged by with the sisters running the farm, or what was left of it after their father's death. The bank man had visited and left with sheaves of paper which turned out to be acres. Auntie Bridie ran her school, Maisie and Regina did a bit of sewing, Imelda, who tended towards weak and watery, was always having to concentrate on getting better, though she'd never really got any worse. And Bina eloped at the age of thirty-nine.

Angela couldn't remember her own father, Ambrose Dooley, but by all accounts, primarily her mother's, he was a nice man, with big hands, two three-piece suits and a liking for a pipe on Sundays. He was also on the middle side of fifty, which was probably the reason why Bridie never saw him coming. He lived with his bedridden mother less than half a mile above the sisters who only ever saw him at Mass, or so Bridie thought. No threat at all, especially as he was renowned the district over for being particularly slow and sleepy in his ways. He liked a doze.

However it happened, Bina caught him in a wakeful moment, and she left her childhood home at the crack of dawn one morning, having scribbled a hasty note for Bridie. 'I'm gone. Sorry.'

They were married later that day and Bina moved into her new marital abode. It was difficult for Angela to imagine her mother as blissful, but certainly her account of the few years that followed conjured up a degree of sedate contentment. This, in spite of the fact that her sisters shunned and denounced her and crossed over the road if she met them in the village. Bridie had decreed that her very name, Bina, be stricken from their lips. The youngest was a traitor. Unnecessary lust of the loins, clouding a perfect five – Bridie would perform a quick sketch of the Virgin Mary with arms outstretched. Feet together, divine points one and two, tips of her extended hands, points three and four – top of her head, point one – Bridie herself, of course. Now sadly, Our Lady was missing a limb thanks to the unmentionable sister and her incontinence.

Angela was born on Bina's forty-second birthday. The same day, they lost Grandma Dooley. Maybe the excitement was too much for her. At any rate, it was presumed that she was happy to go because she'd kept a packed bag under her bed for a fortnight beforehand, and her teeth were in for the first time in years. When Angela was three, her father took a little doze at the nearby pig farm, and keeled over quietly into a tank of pig slurry. Death by drowning, the certificate maintained, discreetly.

Bina put on her widow's weeds and set about getting some work to provide for herself and her daughter. She kept hens and sold the eggs in the village. Little jobs came her way, like cleaning the priest's house and then the church on a weekly basis. She did a bit of mending for a tailor until she got her first big break – a wedding dress. Other commissions followed – wedding, bridesmaid and confirmation dresses – until her book was so full of advance orders, she had to turn people away.

A year passed with not a word from the sisters. Bina was busy and self-sufficient, passing contented hours with her four-year-old daughter, as they hand-sewed thousands of mother-of-pearl beads onto bodices. When asked, Bina made it perfectly clear that she was far too occupied to be heartbroken for the loss of her husband. Nevertheless, she added that she did miss him 'a good bit'.

Angela's hazy recollections of her early life began from around that time. She remembered her mother humming as the needle darted in and out like quicksilver. She remembered going down to the bog to fill her basket with loose turf for the fire, the curtains twitching in the funny old women's house as she passed. Asking her mother about them and the muttered response – something about witches. She always put her head down and ran past the house after that, in case they put her in a pot.

There were pleasant evening memories of the sky black and howling outside, while her mother and herself sat by the glowing fire with cups of cocoa before bedtime. And not so pleasant memories of vivid witch dreams, as hunched down they crept into her room in the dead of night to carry her away for their soup.

Not long after the dreams started, she became aware of the bushes rustling around her when she was out in the yard alone. Her mother, conscious of her daughter's vivid imagination, told her to cop herself on. But Angela's worst fears were realized the day she looked into the wild rhododendrons and saw four sets of eyes gleaming right back at her. In her terrified state, she ran in circles, screaming for her mother, until she was forced to stop when her shoes lined up with two tiny, laced boots. Rendered speechless and shooting little hot darts of urine into her knickers, Angela's eye travelled slowly up, past a navy pinafore with yellow, faded flowers, a gold dangling crucifix (which she thought might be a good sign) to a lined, pointy face with thin, compressed lips and squinched-up, small, black eyes. Auntie Bridie – studying the peculiar specimen of her niece. Angela quailed further, when three other bodies stepped silently from the bushes.

'Ye're the ones in my dream,' she screamed.

'Ah-hah,' Auntie Bridie said knowingly to the others. 'What did I tell ye? Visions.'

She tweaked Angela's cheek with bony fingers, sending the child into paroxysms of horrified tears. Sure as eggs were eggs, she was going to be boiled and eaten alive.

'Right then,' the thin, mean-looking one was saying, just as Angela rediscovered her feet and ran for dear life. 'Get the bags, sisters, and shout up to Mikey that we're away off.'

And all Angela's memories took on very different hues from then on, because that was the day the sisters moved in.

She was nearly at the house now, her feet dragging all the slower, when she saw that more of the lights were on, an aunt flickering like a candle, at every window. It occurred to her that she should be at the V & A round about now. She wondered what subjects he was covering. For her own part, she could have listened to him until hell froze over. Robert suited him. Usually Roberts were intelligent. At least, the few she'd met at the shelter tended to be less braindead than your average Seamus, say. But of course that was forming an opinion, and Mary Margaret hated opinions. Especially from nuns other than herself. They were there to feed the men, clothe the men, house the men and if, on occasion, a sad old dosser dropped dead in his tracks from renal failure, or his body gave up in the comfort, which happened more than once, they were there to empty his pockets (the easy bit), contact any relatives (the hard bit) and sing 'Lord Make Me An Instrument of Your Peace' over his wracked, unwholesome cadaver. Little wonder Angela longed for Africa or someplace like it. South America would have done just as well. Anywhere with small, needy children. She had a soft spot for them. Which was a bit of a worry sometimes.

What business had he asking her for coffee when he probably

had small, needy children of his own, waiting at home for him? Angela felt the hairs on the back of her neck rise. Most likely asked lone females for coffee every Wednesday night. The unbelievable cheek. And to think, she might even be there – sipping cappuccino in some small steamy cafe with hardly any of the lights on. Maybe there'd be a band playing soft music in the background. Jazz or what have you. Maybe she'd be saying 'Ordinarily, I hate coffee but this is quite extra-ordinary', as he reached across to put a spoonful of froth to her lips. Maybe then he'd be –

'There's no story, go to bed, let ye,' she said to the waiting, fizzing Aunts.

'You told him as our hearts are pure bleeding from the worry, Angela?' Bridie whispered plaintively.

'I told him to stop his carrying on,' Angela said in a firm tone.

'Now so, up to bed the lot of you.' Bina clapped her hands.

The Aunts looked very disappointed. This wasn't amounting to much of a performance. Angela felt that she owed them more. 'He said – well sort of – he said, well he *looked* fierce ashamed of himself,' Angela lied. 'I think I got through to him.'

That was much better. Any sentence carrying any permutation of the shame noun was always good. Auntie Bridie was toodling off toward the kettle, hoping now to extract another half-hour from the night. But Bina gripped her forearm and swerved her toward the door instead.

'Shoo – go on,' Bina urged, pointing upstairs.

When they were gone, two ascending creakily amidst a low thrum of grumbles and Regina to her cot in the corner of the kitchen, Bina set out her new interlocking machine by the fire. She was making curtains for someone.

'He's ashamed now, is it?' she muttered in her usual droll fashion.

'You know what they're like.' Angela tried to defend herself. 'I had to say something.'

'How long have you got this time?' Bina checked the tautness of her threads, gave the machine a little test run.

'I've got to be back for Friday afternoon.'

'Not long.'

'No.'

Angela twiddled her thumbs as she watched her mother turn the heavy brocade this way and that. The noise was deafening.

'Would you like a cup of cocoa, Mammy?' Angela shouted.

'No, thank you.'

There wasn't much point in sticking around, trying to shout over the machine. Angela shrugged, clapped her thighs and headed for the door with her overnight bag. She stopped, remembering the soaps. Pink cherubs wrapped in floral V & A paper. She held the package out.

'I got you these.'

'What's that?' Bina roared.

'Soaps – nice ones,' Angela roared back.

Bina nodded, she took her foot off the pedal for a moment. 'Put them on the table there.' Her voice softened fractionally. 'And you might as well leave those brochures you were talking about too – I could maybe take a look when I'm finished with this old thing.'

Angela did as bidden and tripped up to her room with a lighter heart. On the landing, she listened to the familiar rhythm of Bridie and Maisie snoring side by side in their bed together. Throughout her childhood her tiny adjacent bedroom used to pulsate, she could have sworn, with the sound of them.

Her mother's face, the day they all moved up without so much as a by-your-leave, registered stoical acceptance. It had only been a matter of time, she explained to the young Angela, who was far from stoical at the prospect of the witches taking up residence in her house. Hadn't they their own home at the bottom of the road? And why did her mother have to say no to piles of lovely wedding dresses, so that she could make their dinners and teas and wait on them hand and foot? Overnight, it seemed to Angela as though her mother had turned into Cinderella. She hated their intrusion and let them know at every opportunity. But her rants fell on deaf ears. Every now and then one of the Aunts, for that was apparently what they'd become, would tell her to 'whisht' or cop herself on. And then there was the strange man in the attic in the other house, who she fed and watered with her mother every day. At least he made funny faces and could jerk his thumb in and out and wiggle his ears in a way that made her giggle, which was more than the torn faces above in her own house ever did.

She couldn't even get away from them when she started school because Auntie Bridie was giving her the eye there as well. That funny way she had of looking at Angela, like she was waiting for something to happen, her head to explode off her shoulders or something. There were no more cosily-together evenings with her mother either, only prayers and lessons and more prayers. Bina was permanently exhausted and hardly ever smiled.

Angela's was an imagination waiting to happen. When she wasn't inventing new games for herself and Uncle Mikey in the attic, she took to gliding past the aunts, talking to herself in an effort to expunge their presence. At the table, she stared dreamily ahead, lips silently moving, ignoring their pleas for her to pass the salt or butter. Naturally, she pretended not to hear when they discussed this turn of events, Auntie Bridie strangely enough the one advocating forbearance. She'd seen the like of Angela before, she said. They had to wait and see where this was taking them. Suitably encouraged, Angela acted up even more. She took to elaborate faints, drifting to the ground in a series of sways, like a skein of ribbon. When she started babbling in her own made-up language, Auntie Bridie got seriously interested.

The woman had plenty of time on her hands now, since her school was shut down the previous year. In truth, due to a shortage of pupils, so parents sent their children elsewhere – but lack of funds was the posited excuse.

70

The lead up to Angela's Holy Communion was a heady time for the seven-year-old. Bridie encouraged her every vaporous display, nodding fervently, as Angela recounted her dreams with her eyes tightly shut, a hand to her forehead. When she got to a really juicy bit, anything with Satan or Archangel Michael, she couldn't resist opening one eye, just a slit, for a look at the aunts' faces. Bina sent scoffing missiles from the back kitchen from time to time but she was always too busy cooking or cleaning to interfere in earnest.

The Holy Communion dress was the subject of intense fizzing. That was Bina's domain and she managed to exclude them right up to the final moment, when Angela stood in the middle of the room, palms pressed demurely together, head down as her mother, on her knees, put in the final pins for the floor-length hem. Bridie barged in and nearly fell into a swoon. She hollered to the sisters, a look of triumphant vindication on her narrow face. They trooped in, ignoring Bina's censures, and all agreed that Angela's appearance was indeed a premonitor of the all-white habit she would wear in her early noviciate. It all sounded like music to Angela's ears.

If she had managed to make herself the occasional focus of the house before, she was now the undeniable pivot. The dreams (now visions) and faints increased, the Aunts barely suppressing screams of delight. They began to enact the wedding ceremony as it would unfold, the day Angela would finally become a true Bride of Christ. Singing as she slowly walked up the makeshift aisle in the kitchen, through a phalanx of candles on either side, to the altar, where Bridie performed the ceremony, invoking Angela to her final vows – and the most exquisite bit – placing the ring on her finger.

It was only a matter of time before Angela felt a pressing need for a miracle incumbent on her. All manner of suggestions were put forth, but Bridie finally decreed that there was no real rush – the event would happen the day she took those vows in reality. That was a touch too nebulous for her niece. She wanted to know something concrete – peace on earth and all that stuff wasn't exactly what she had in mind. A crock of treasure under the floorboards, or something like it, was a much more edifying prospect. Auntie Bridie who was by now as adept at secondguessing her niece as the other way around, happened on the perfect miracle. Uncle Mikey would come down from the attic. That was very appealing. At the age of seven, Angela was growing increasingly aware that he shouldn't really be up there in the first place. To be the instrument of his descent – now – *that* was sucking diesel.

There was never a question as to her vocation. If you didn't have to question it, Bridie put forward, then you had one. Occasionally in her teens, which Angela found to be a particularly trying time, she sought advice from her mother. But Bina only shrugged. Time was when she'd have given advice, but Bridie's little pet was too above herself to listen. She'd made her bed now, and she could lie in it.

Lying in it, listening to the creak of her mother's heavy footsteps up the stairs, the rumbling snores next door, the permanently wind-rattled window, Angela sighed deeply and turned over to her sleep side. She was just drifting into a pleasant unconsciousness when she remembered what she'd forgotten again. Her nightly prayers. She made a mental sign of the cross, and fell asleep.

Christ on the donkey turned slowly, to taunt Auntie Bridie with his wide, infectious grin. Only it was that fellow Robert, at the V & A. Now he was getting annoyingly invasive. Entering her sleep like that. There was only one thing to do. In her dream, she got out of bed, knelt down by the side with her hands pressed together. She would pray him – *out*.

Chapter Five

There were two things in life you could be sure of, Robert thought, as he stared at the smiling phalanx of Japanese faces – death and disappointment. For the melancholic nature, brief moments of happiness were always tempered by the prospect of the moment thereafter, and Robert was, for the longest time, so reconciled to enduring disappointment, he could hardly believe that just this once he hadn't prepared himself appropriately. Hadn't forewarned himself that it was, in fact, more likely that she would not turn up, than probable that she would. He had abandoned a lifetime's code of pessimism only to discover that it was well-warranted in the first place. Stupid really. Just a glitch, now he could go back to his normal state of mind, before that little, preposterous bead of hope had glittered on the periphery of his vision.

And yet, it had to be said, it absolutely had to be said, that, standing there by the entrance to the Poynter Room, he had the overwhelming feeling that he didn't want to be disappointed anymore. If she turned up now, he might have to suppress an urge to shake her a little. It didn't make the slightest bit of sense, but somehow she'd managed to change everything. The pattern of his life was no longer fixed in solid, dependable, almost geometrical shapes, stretching ahead until they merged into a fixed, dun line. Comfortingly so. No, the future was blurred now. Mutating colours and out of control.

All day he had been hopeful. Thinking about how he would

broach the subject of his painting her. Wondering what they might talk about before he came right out with it. A direct approach was the course he'd settled on. Followed by profuse apologies if she balked. Seeing, in his mind's eye, the grey mosaic floor widen to accommodate their separation should her refusal put distance between them. He was, in every respect, prepared, he thought. Except for the little fact that she hadn't actually turned up. There was no way he could think out all the angles on that one. A bald truth just slapped you in the face and made nonsense of any premeditation.

'You can see that every surface of the room is covered with tiles . . .' His hand waved expansively. Shiny, black heads swivelled back and forth in perfect rhythm. Not five words of English between them. And yet, they were easily the most attentive group he'd addressed since he started this lecturing thing. They nodded, bowed, smiled, oohed appreciatively and aahed sympathetically, taking their cues entirely from the timbre of Robert's voice or the expression on his face. When he stopped momentarily, trying to remember what to blather on about next, they stood with their heads cocked to the side, all patient, dappered studiousness. Robert shot a finger up toward the ceiling. He saw a line of upturned chins, a row of eggs waiting to be tapped.

'My life's a mess,' he said, then stopped. Appalled. The chins came down. Robert blinked rapidly. He opened his mouth to tell them about the delft-like tiles painted for a pound a piece by local women.

'I mean – God knows why I'm telling you this,' the strange voice continued. 'You probably have your own problems. Only you wouldn't dream of talking about them right out loud. To a complete stranger. Not the Japanese way at all, I imagine. Quite right too. Absolutely.'

They seemed pleased by his vehemence.

'It's just that – well – I don't know really – I was expecting someone this evening. I didn't realize how much I was expecting this person until right this minute, to tell the truth. It's crazy. Angela's her name. You'd like her.' He must have smiled because a uniform line of smiles beamed back at him. Robert anxiously looked over his shoulder, in case anybody might have joined them. No, they were still the only group in sight. He moved into the Gamble Room, making frantic sweeping movements with his arms now to keep the Japanese heads swaying back and forth.

'You have to believe me – this isn't like me in the least. You'll have to take my word for that, of course. If you could understand, you'd be calling me a madman, or worse – no doubt. At the very least you'd be looking for your money back, and you'd be perfectly entitled. Perfectly . . .' He pointed toward a corner, to test them, and they turned obligingly. 'If you could understand what I'm saying, you'd probably figure – oh, he's just at it again. But I swear to you – I'm not. At it again. This is really the first it – I've been at . . . if you see what I mean – which of course you don't.' Robert paused to sigh heavily. A woman followed suit, until the room heaved in a wave of regret. Robert folded his arms and eyed them piercingly.

'What I'm trying to say is – does true love exist? What do you think? Or do you just settle for less and less as time goes on? You start out with a set of ideals, you know – requisites – then fear of old age, loneliness – for God's sake – childlessness, sets in, and next thing you know, you're compromising. Or do you mould the next eligible person you meet into the perfect image? Is that what I intended to do with Angela?' Robert sighed again. 'You tell me . . .' he added, as they returned in kind his perplexed stare.

One of the more mature women had a peculiar glint in her eye. Robert's heart raced for an instant. He quickly shot his hand up at the ceiling, her gaze duly followed. Just to be sure he did a quickfire crisscross which sent them into a spin. Satisfied that they didn't understand one word he was saying, he led them into the Morris Room.

'Oh there have been ... No – I was just about to lie to you. Telling you that there have been others, times when I thought I was nearly in love. But I'm not going to lie to you. It wouldn't be fair now, would it?' Half of them nodded, the other half shook their heads. 'Rachel was a nice girl. For that matter, so was Denise. Why, I could be sitting on a sofa with either of them right this very minute, drinking a gin and tonic with our son on my knee listening to his bedtime story. So why aren't I? you'd doubtless ask, if you could. Why indeed? This is the question I keep asking myself. Why do I always insist on messing it up? What made me think it would be different with Angela? Is this what they call a nervous breakdown? It's not so bad really. Don't be afraid if it comes to you. Thank you for your attention. You may exit through here. Good luck with your lives and very much *Sayonara*. Okay?'

They clapped politely, bowed in unison and filtered through the doorway. Robert felt for the wall. He laid his cheek against the cooling olive frieze. Rivulets of sweat streamed from his forehead, making his eyes sting. He laughed helplessly for a moment, then straightened abruptly as a colleague cast him a curious glance from the distant outer chamber. Well at least he wouldn't have to suffer this next Wednesday night. It was his night off. He could take every night off if he handed in his notice. Maybe some people were just not cut out for this type of thing. Maybe it did their heads in, a little. Or a lot.

Soon he would be safely tucked away in his little cottage, surrounded by the accoutrements of his life. Where he could be happy, lonely, sad or just indifferent, entirely at the behest of his own free will. He was cross with himself for his uncustomary optimism earlier in the day. Better to be alone with possibilities than to be alone with none. This whole ridiculous Angela thing was an invention – just his mind fixating on something unattainable so he wouldn't have to put any effort into meeting anyone else. Peter was right. Bonnie was right. It was a shabby little cold comfort truth, but a truth nonetheless – he was terrified of commitment. His mouth curled, he could hear Bonnie's drawl – 'Like *you're* such a prize, huh?'

But prize was not the way he saw himself at all. He would be happy to commit – if he could understand who it was that he was committing. His sense of self had grown so foggy and blurred around the edges, especially over the past few years, that he sometimes wondered if he wasn't just another figment of his own imagination.

The urge to get tucked away indoors propelled him most of the way home, until he alighted at St Margaret's station and found his feet heading in the direction of Peter and Anita's. He had no idea why that should be. Maybe he just needed the company right now.

At any rate, he was there. Feeling like a Dickensian character with his nose practically pressed up against their living room window, staring at the mellow lamplight within, flickering blue of the television screen in the far corner. Peter and Anita were stretched out together on one of the long, deep sofas. Shoeless feet entwined. Robert could just make out the contours of their bodies, both heads fixed on the TV, Anita's lolling slightly back to rest against Peter's shoulder. That. Was what he wanted. Nothing less would do. Robert crept away, feeling like a petty thief who, in trying to steal a sliver of their marital bliss, had ended up with a snapshot which would only serve to haunt him all the more.

Home didn't provide the usual settling, levelling quality he craved either. The rooms looked smaller than usual, dull and cramped and crammed and well, bachelory. This Angela person, if he ever did meet her again, would have a lot to answer for. Then again, if he was this unsettled after just one meeting, he would probably have to be hospitalized after another. Resuscitated certainly. All in all, it was a very good thing that he would never set eyes on that cordate face again.

Robert kicked off his shoes. He stood in the little lobby which separated the downstairs rooms, drawing his hands down his face.

'Why am I such a complete and utter and total . . .'

'Schmuck?' Bonnie surprised him by stepping out from the shadowy kitchen. 'Because you just are.' She waved his charcoal sketches of Angela. 'Hey – these are *good*.'

'Eeeny meeny miney mo, catch a nigger by the toe . . .' Sr Carmel tapped her last bonbon between the newest arrival, a stocky, silent young man, and a bemused Rastafarian.

Angela came to a skeeting halt in the corridor, beside them.

'We don't use the N word anymore, Sister. It's bad.' Angela cast the Rastafarian a watery grin. He had his fingers out for the bonbon.

'Oh dear.' Sr Carmel pressed a hand to her lips. She thought for a minute. 'Right. Eeeny meeny miney mo – catch your Commonwealth brother by the toe . . . is that allowed?' She was truly disturbed at the prospect of having caused offence.

'Don't like sweets anyway,' the young man mumbled, about to wander into the soup kitchen. 'Let him have it.'

Angela took a couple of quick strides to keep abreast. He scowled sideways at her. It was hard to tell his age: the square, jowly face with deeply serrated forehead lines, old shiny scars and mesh of thread-veins, could have been set on middle-aged shoulders quite easily. But the diluted blue eyes were still strangely young. Two sapphires rimmed in red and egg yolk where the white should be. Eighteen at most, Angela figured. Burnt out, used up – ready for his own room or flat where he could drink cheap cider all day, maybe watch the daytime soaps. In return for the room, he would just about tolerate the nuns' twitterings, the enforced rules of the clusters, even if it took a few months. The waiting list was so long now, he had no idea that he would be their reluctant guest for at least a year – if he chose to stick it out that long. Most of the younger ones couldn't hack it. After a few months, their bodies longed for benches and doorsteps again.

He was longing already. Angela could detect all the telltale signs. The way his clubby frame seemed to recoil from her nearness. The bunched fists. The way his breath came in a series of high-pitched hums, as though he could not bear to share her air. She tiptoed beside him, mindful of his acute unease. There was the business of the day to perform, however. Mary Margaret had charged Angela with this new recruit.

'Where d'you come from, Steve?' she asked. 'Originally, like.' Meaning before the streets. Before the shiny scars. As if she couldn't butter toast with his saturated Sarf London accent. The questions were just part of the routine – psyching him out. Her eyes quickly travelled the length and breadth of him, pausing for a pitstop at the severely scored wrists – most probably the work of the penknife bulging in his back pocket. She made a mental note to deal with that later. Homemade tattoos across his knuckles. No needle tracks.

He didn't answer – just jerked his head to indicate somewhere.

'Been on the streets long?'

'Long enough.'

'Mother Mary Margaret went through the rules with you, yeah?'

'Yeah.'

'And you're okay with those?'

'Yeah.'

'Grand.' Angela held the door to the soup kitchen open for him. She could sense his body flinch as he passed her by. 'You have a bite to eat now and I'll meet you up in your cluster after. You'll have to take a good shower before we go see Doctor Goldberg, all right?'

He stopped inches from her. The scowl was a mean glower now. 'I'm not seeing no fucking doctor.'

'It's house policy, Steve. Doctor Goldberg has to check you over for – well, for different sorts of stuff like. All the men see him. He's okay really. He can give you something to help a bit, if you need to deetee . . .'

79

Usually, the men couldn't get enough of doctors. Seeing them as elevated creatures of immense power, with unlimited access to little brown glass bottles which contained pills to fog them up. Or they could tell a man his liver was shot to pieces and he was one drink from death, when that was the diagnosis required to assist a man's abstinence. Conversely, when that abstinence was beginning to wear very thin, the slightest verbal hint of a physical improvement could be timed nicely, with relapse. 'The doctor said . . .' How they loved to begin sentences with that. It had an important ring to it. Somebody was yet responsible for their wellbeing. But from the dour expression on Steve's face, he wasn't about to agree to an examination so easily. Angela sighed wearily. 'Look, we'll talk about it later.'

He slouched toward the kitchen counter. Outside in the court-yard, a long, shuffling queue was already starting the midday seep into the big hall. This was the best time to feed them, any earlier and most of them would be groggy still from their few hours kip. Any later, and they wouldn't want nourishment. The soup served as ballast for the long day ahead. They came from everywhere, of every age, and every one of them had a different story and the same story. Some didn't even drink. A few pre-sented themselves quite spiffily each day, having washed and combed in the public toilet beforehand. They had their own hierarchical code which in the main they adhered to quite strictly. Feeding time generally meant truce between old enemies with raw, punctured faces and scabby hands. Others looked like scrunched-up paper bags, and spoke to no one. Apart from the odd ranter, the nuns were treated with defer-ence and a degree of helpless gratitude.

The tables were full of ragged men elbowing soup. They scrabbled at tufts of bread. Almost silence except for slurps and hacking coughs. A smell of human decay and piss hanging in the air – the bodies uniform in their brownness. So little colour. It was as though they'd shrugged off all that was primary and subsumed themselves in dank neutrals. Varying shades of shit really, Angela thought, as she watched Steve draw his bowl close against his chest, one hand clutching a wad of crusts. The posture spoke of an institutionalized life. She wondered about him. Which was not necessarily a good thing. It had taken her the best part of her time here to learn how to stop wondering. There was little point in conjuring past lives or imbuing them with futures, for that matter. The men were to be dealt with in the here and now. There was a conveyor belt which occasionally stopped for soup and the odd kind word, then moved on. Getting involved meant accepting responsibility and the inevitable disappointment which would surely follow.

Nevertheless, sometimes a man slipped through a tiny gash in their self-protective nets. There was something in Steve's flickering gaze, the sullen yet frightened set of his lips that reminded Angela of Uncle Mikey. She knew instinctively that she was treading on dangerous ground here and decided to ask Mary Margaret to put him in someone else's charge from tomorrow. What with her constant and most irritating thoughts all week of that Robert fellow and her near date for coffee, the last thing she needed was a new obsession. Or anything that kept Uncle Mikey in mind.

She'd spent practically all of her last couple of days at home tucked up in the attic with him. He'd seemed even more distant than usual, warily watching her from the corner for the longest time, until she finally managed to crack a laugh out of him. His eyes had fixed on that spot over her shoulder as though he were deeply preoccupied by something nobody else could see. When she moved to touch him, he had trembled, before allowing her fingers to move in strokes through the matted hair. The fingers couldn't get very far with the knots but she persuaded him to allow her to use a long-tined comb eventually.

'Uncle Mikey – what's the matter,' she'd whispered, cuddling him. 'Tell me.'

He just turned his face into her shoulder.

'C'mon now. Why've you been acting up? Are you a bit sick, is that it?'

He shunted closer still, so that his nose was flattened against her clavicle. She leaned her head back and crooked a finger under his chin. Trying to see his eyes.

'Should we call a doctor, pet?'

A low whine and he was scrabbling for another corner.

'Shh. All right. Whisht – we won't do anything you don't want,' she murmured. 'But you'll have to stop the potty carry on – d'you understand me?'

He nodded eagerly and she thought he was crying quietly then. Snuffling into his sleeve. But he was laughing again. She had to laugh herself. He put his arms out straight for more cuddles. She went to him.

'Ah, Uncle Mikey. What are we to do with you at all? Sure you'll never come down from this attic, will you?'

More tears and clinging to her when she crept up to say goodbye. Staring up into his black eyes before the trapdoor clanged shut, she felt that each departure was another betrayal. He was all emotion, a crouched suppurating wound. Sometimes she felt that she was all he had, and he had precious little.

Steve was making snorting, angry sounds through his nostrils, trying to jostle for table space. Angela watched from the side-lines, ready to move quickly if necessary. But his build and quiet menace ensured he got what he needed before his anger spilled over into violence. Whoever got him would have to keep a very close eye.

Sr Carmel and Sr Oliver were in charge of the soup today. The enormous blackened cauldron simmered on top of a gas stove, the rim of the pot so high, the smaller nuns had to reach up to tip contents in, dunking like basketballers. Some of them, like Sr Carmel, tended to get a bit carried away with their soup-making. They couldn't bear to see anything go to waste and would shove bits of crust or half-eaten apples under their sleeves, surreptitiously chucking their spoils up in a well practised arc, eyes darting left and right all the while to check if they'd been spotted. Angela had found a gob of chewing gum clung to the base once when she administered the weekly scour. Another time, she found a holy medal and the flimsy remains of a sacred picture, for all the world as if the nuns would force the men to ingest God by whatever means came to hand.

Right now, Sr Carmel was doing her skulking routine, moving toward the pot in stops and starts, hands tucked away under the loose sleeves of her habit. A quick glance around, while blinking innocently like an owl, until she caught the purse of Angela's lips.

'What have you there, Sister?' Angela approached. She indicated for Carmel to reveal her stash. The guilty start confirmed her worst suspicions. Carmel slowly unfurled her palms.

'Ah, Sister Carmel,' Angela shook her head. 'How many times . . . You can't put dairy products in – you just can't. You'll give them botulitis or something.' She held her hand out for the half-eaten Dairylea triangle still in its wrapper and the cube of Turkish delight.

Sr Carmel looked shamefaced but when Angela's back was turned, she heard the familiar little plink which told her that she'd missed the nun's morning egg.

There was a furore starting up in the queue outside. Angela rushed to the door. Mary Margaret had her dark glasses on, marching up and down the line of men until she'd pulled a skulking, emaciated elderly man from the ranks. With a bellow of outrage, Mary Margaret turned him around, drew her leg back as far as it would go and shoed his bony ass so hard he nearly stumbled to the ground.

'Thought you'd pull one over on me, hah?' she howled, drawing back for another kick but he was skiddling off as fast as he could. 'One year you were here, you fucker you. One whole year you got fed and found and soup. How many times do I have to tell ye? How many times? There's no soup – when you've got your flat. Make yer own soup.'

The culprit was gone but his misdemeanour had to be impressed upon the others. Mary Margaret strode up and down, slapping a rigid palm against the length of her thigh. She pulled her face up close to a chewed-looking misfortunate. 'I know every fecking thing that goes on here. Everything. Whatever you might be thinking of trying – don't try it. I've eyes in the back of my skull. Which means I can see you *twice*. Twice, d'you hear me?'

The men nodded soberly. Mary Margaret drew back, giving them permission to shunt on in the line with a curt nod of her head. She enjoyed a good bollocking. It gave her a thirst.

She must have caught Angela's disapproving glare because she beckoned to her.

'Why've you that face on you, Sister?'

Angela shrugged. She knew better than to express her reservations in front of the men. From the corner of her eye she could see Steve's scarlet face and his fists tight as molluscs. Clearly he wasn't too keen on Mary Margaret's brand of discipline either.

The Mother Superior peered into Angela's face, willing her to dissent aloud. When she was satisfied that the bait was not going to be taken, she humphed, hiked up her bosoms and marched inside. There was an audible sigh from the queue, a general subsidence as hackled shoulders went down again. Auntie Bridie whooped triumphantly in Angela's head – 'She's the one that'll soften your cough for you girl *heh heh heh*.'

A woman from the Salvation Army side-slipped a Bangladeshi into the line and approached Angela with a determined glint in her eye. Here to argue for a cluster no doubt. But there wasn't a bed to be had, not for another month at the very least. Angela sighed and prepared to listen to the lengthy, pleading monologue, knowing that she would have to refuse at the end in any case. All the candidates were suitable, even if some were more deserving than others insofar as the criteria for allocating spaces were concerned. But you couldn't make beds appear from nowhere. And even when some sorry tale, of which there were too many, tore at her heartstrings and she still had to say no, she had to move on and never give up, because that was what nuns did primarily – they never gave up. Angela had to concede as the Sally woman stepped closer, that right this minute, she felt far from constant.

There was something about the way he perched right on the edge of the bed, hands drooping listlessly over one another, that scalded her with thoughts of Uncle Mikey again.

Steve's head jolted upright when she entered the cluster. As though he'd been switched off and she had just pressed the on button. She was pleased to see that he'd showered as instructed.

'Are you ready, Steve?' Angela asked softly.

He nodded, grabbing at his jacket. Maybe he was on her side a bit after seeing Mary Margaret in action earlier in the day, or maybe he needed pills for the withdrawal – whatever motivated his capitulation about the doctor visit, Angela was just relieved to avoid the argument.

She forced herself to be chatty as they headed for Dr Goldberg's clinic in Whitechapel. Angela and Steve to the fore, Sr Carmel and Sr Aloysius nearby and nine lame ducks following at their own desultory pace behind.

'Mostly the doctor comes to us,' Angela explained, 'but when we've a good few to see him, like today, he prefers if we go to him. You're all right about it now, are you?'

'Yeah.' Whatever Steve's story was, he wasn't much of a talker.

Pshhht. From the rear. Angela strode on. People were turning their heads to stare after the motley caravan. *Pshhht.* Sr Aloysius, who didn't get out often, nearly jumped out of her skin.

'What was that?' she cried to no one in particular. Angela could tell her history from the nun's peculiar walk – head sloping forward, both hands hanging down rigidly in deference to the two buckets she probably carried around the farm all her young life.

'Never mind,' Angela said.

Pshhht. Pshhht. That familiar sound of half a dozen ringpulls of Tennants Extra – they'd probably lose a third of the men on the way as they slithered sideways into yawning doorways. Angela knew the score. She'd told the doctor to expect around six or so. Looking back, she saw that she'd estimated just about right.

'D'you think he'd take a wee look at that knobbledy bit on my ankle if I asked him?' Sr Carmel enquired.

'Oh I'm sure he would.'

'He won't think I'm taking liberties with his time?'

'Sr Carmel – Doctor Goldberg thinks everyone takes liberties with his time.' Next to Mary Margaret, Angela's least favourite person, on a worryingly increasing list, was the good doctor himself. He was half mad from arrogance. And filthy rich from this cushy little sideline earner away from his more genteel clients in Mayfair. He always had a special little lopsided smile for Angela, a supercilious crook to his left eyebrow, as if to say: 'Anytime you're ready, my dear, just bend over that and I'll give you what you're so afraid of.' Angela knew that look so well. Every man that gave it thought he was the only one.

She was only a little afraid the time she nearly went all the way with Dinny McGrath in the shed behind the Youth Club after the Hallowe'en hop. That was in her mid-teens when she felt like she was being split into two for a while, torn between the aunts' pageants at home and loving every minute of her destiny, and the deep, unsettling longings which had sprung up out of nowhere not long after her first period. Auntie Bridie had foreseen all this of course and when she found a lipstick in Angela's room she bought her a bicycle.

After her sixteenth birthday, Dinny told her in no uncertain terms that he was going to have to look elsewhere for comfort if she didn't give him something more than a handjob. 'Take one look at me,' he'd cried plaintively. 'I'm the remains of pure lust.' Angela was indeed moved to pity. Which led to the nearly-all-the-way scene in the shed if Auntie Bridie hadn't come looking for her, shrieking, 'Angela! Come quick! Uncle Mikey's got diarrhoea again.' A second before penetration. Angela ran from the shed and Dinny got himself another girl-friend.

The longings were never so intense now as in her teenage years. She still felt a bit feverish from time to time, especially a couple of days after a period, but it was containable. The main thing, a couple of nuns had told her, was never to give in to it, in case you acquired a taste and ended up like one of those rampant terriers always wrapped around someone's leg. Sr Catherine, who had since left the convent, advocated soap, a good sniff of a bar of Lux and you'd be right as rain in a matter of minutes. Evidently her own bar had finally dissolved or something, but Angela held onto the advice and found that it worked most of the time, strangely enough.

Dr Goldberg slid back the halfdoor to his surgery, peering through to the waiting room to see what they'd brought to him today. Like a priest in the confessional. He was a tall, angular man with bushy eyebrows and full lips, which he liked to curl into scrolls of barely concealed disgust. He sighed and flapped a hand toward Angela and Steve, signalling them in.

'This is Steve, Dr Goldberg,' Angela began. 'He's new so we need you to give him the full exam . . .' Her voice trailed off as Dr Goldberg closed his eyes, looking as though he were in great pain. When he opened them again, he ignored her.

'You look fine to me,' he addressed Steve. 'What do you want?'

Steve shrugged and looked to Angela. What was he meant to say?

Dr Goldberg checked his watch, he drew back the sliding door again to check how many were left. With another pained sigh he riffled through his prescription pad. 'What do you want?'

he repeated. 'Lithium? Prozac? Valium? Come on, come on. I haven't got all day here.'

'I don't want anything.' Steve was confused.

Angela stepped in hesitantly.

'Emm – he's just here for the check, Dr Goldberg, you know?'

For some reason the doctor seemed to find that highly amusing. He threw his head back and brayed.

'I like that.' He wiped his eyes. 'Oh dearie me – just here for the check ... Aren't we all?' He grew serious again. Wrote something quickly on the pad. 'Right – valium it is.' He ripped a sheet off and handed it to Steve. 'Don't kill yourself – today. Okey dokey. Next!' he bawled.

Angela saw that Sr Carmel wouldn't get any joy out of him today for the knobbledy bit on her ankle. He was in one of *those* moods. Sometimes he was kindness itself to the men, attentive and courteous to the point he nearly had them crying. Mostly, he amused himself at their expense. Now, he was sucking at his teeth and glaring in a mean way as his next patient shuffled in. No, he was not in the mood for the whining voice, the unctuous cap-doffing of this one-legged moron from – Wales, was it? Or someplace equally awful. He cut across the whingeing diatribe about the sort of sharpish – but it could be dullish too – type of pain the man had in his stump when he –

'Librium?' Dr Goldberg snapped.

'Yeah, great, thanks, Doc.' Cardiff limped out again.

'You still here?' The doctor barked to Angela.

She felt her cheeks glow hot as griddle cakes.

'Dr Goldberg – you know our rules of admission. I have to insist that you give Steve here, the proper examination. Please.' She added, hating that last submissive note. But he required it.

'Jesus H. Christ,' he muttered impatiently. 'Right, get your kit off,' he continued to Steve. Left eyebrow up for Angela's benefit. 'Are you intending to watch or what, Sister?'

Angela gave Steve an encouraging smile and slipped outside. She rolled her eyes at Sr Carmel. They could hear the doctor's familiar God routine within.

'An atheist do you hear me?' he was booming at Steve. 'If God exists – then I'm *it*. Bend over.'

'Oh he's in one of his moods,' Sr Carmel whispered to Angela. 'I don't think I'll bother with the . . .' She pointed to her ankle. 'Not today.'

'I think that might be wise, Sister,' Angela sighed.

The rest of the men rocked back and forth on their chairs, studying the smoke-grimed ceiling. Suddenly there was a resounding smacking noise from behind the wall, followed by a roar from the doctor. Steve burst through, cinching tight his jeans belt. His face was the colour of cranberry juice. He made an inarticulate snort, knuckled his shaven head and stormed out into the street. Dr Goldberg staggered into the waiting room, pinching the bridge of his bleeding nose. He glared at Angela.

'Will you please, once and for all, ask dat – dat Shaman – if we can eliminate de haemorrhoidal check from de examination? What business is it of hers if de bloody men have piles or not?'

'I don't know, Doctor,' Angela said, all sweetness and light. 'Mother Mary Margaret always says we should start with the inside and work our way out. Sort of the same as yourself only backwards. I'd put a lump of ice against that, if I were you,' she added, throwing a sly wink to Sr Carmel who was sucking one of her own bonbons with extreme relish. Her dainty little feet tapped out a jig on the floor.

Steve had calmed down by the time they left the surgery. Pacing up and down the pavement, he paused only to spit and knuckle his head, but he nodded when he saw Angela and stepped into walking rhythm by her side. When she stopped to cough, she noticed that he stopped too. He was her new shadow. The thought was not displeasing. She gave him a little smile and was rewarded by something approaching a reciprocal smile sketching his lips.

When he was through the door ahead of them, Angela lightly pressed Sr Carmel's bony hand. She didn't mean to sound so urgent but there was a quavering, almost disturbing underlayer to her voice.

'Don't you ever have doubts, Sister? Never?'

Sr Carmel sucked hard. She hid her eyes which could be surprisingly astute.

'D'you mean about being a nun or God himself, pet?'

'Oh everything.' Angela scuffed the doorstep. 'No, not God. I don't mean that. Oh I don't know what I mean. It's just that sometimes I wonder what makes us the way we are – Doctor Goldberg say, or Steve there, or my own Uncle Mikey for that matter.'

Sr Carmel scratched her veil.

'Wisha – I can't answer all that, pet. Look it, I've a pack of iced caramels upstairs if you like?'

'Thanks.' Angela grinned. 'Yeah, I haven't had one of them for ages.'

They stepped through the long, dark corridor.

'I suppose God has a hand in it, same as ourselves,' Sr Carmel offered.

'He must have a hell of a sense of humour then,' Angela said.

'Oh laughing morning, noon and night, I'd say.' Sr Carmel licked the gum on one of her holy pictures. She slapped it onto a door. It told of how her day would come – when the meek would inherit the earth.

The quietness of the chapel late at night. That was what Angela liked the best. When the whole building seemed to swoon into a deep sleep and she could almost hear the walls softly breathing. Sleep, like death, levelled everything and everyone. You could see the child they used to be, in the men's faces when they

90

were asleep – even the roughest of them. Sometimes she wished she could inject them in their peaceful slumber, put them down. Most of them would have thanked her. Most of them would have done the job themselves if they could sustain a moment long enough to feel worth the trouble.

She could hear her own heartbeat. Thu-thunk thu-thunk thu-thunk. She wanted to believe that she was the only person awake in the house. Prayers or the memory of them from childhood flitted through her head but didn't pause to make themselves heard. The truth was, she didn't want to think about anything at all. Just listen to the silence and maybe know a moment's peace. If she sat there for long enough, maybe one of her old trances would come, and she would have a feeling of God.

Tossing and turning in her bed earlier, she'd given up trying to sleep and slipped on her warm candlewick dressing gown to creep down the backstairs. In here, by flickering candlelight, she usually felt cocooned and safe. She could remember why she was here in the first place. The scents of must and wax and lemon polish from the gleaming mahogany pews had a comforting, maternal odour. Like she was being taken gently to someone's bosom. The doubts of earlier in the day faded away, her jangled nerves were soothed. She wanted to be a good nun, give herself to God the way Sr Carmel did. She wanted to see the path of her life moving off into the distance, her feet taking solid, definite steps in that direction. Surely that was the wonderful thing about a vocation – it gave you one huge thing to fix upon, making incidentals of everything else.

But that nagging voice was insisting – even here, where she'd always managed to find some measure of certainty. It told her that she'd been on this path for so long, she was too afraid to choose another. When all was said and done, she was no different from the lines of men snoring upstairs in their clusters. Wavering, staggering through every day, sheltering from the world outside – nothing certain about her at all.

91

She told herself to cop herself on, blew out the candles, genuflected in the dark and tiptoed out into the corridor. There was a light on in Mary Margaret's office. Angela checked her watch. It was past two in the morning. The Mother Superior was still there, a dark carbuncle hunched over her desk, sets of budget figures spread out across the top. Bottle of half-empty Gordon's Dry and an overflowing ashtray vying for space. The sound of muffled, distant shouting from the street outside made the nun glance up quickly. Angela heard it too and flattened herself against the corridor wall, expecting Mary Margaret's approach. But she'd gone back to her figures, one hand uncapping the bottle of gin with well-practised dexterity.

The woman should have been an accountant, Angela thought, as she slipped upstairs again. For a moment she felt infinitely superior: at least she was in a chapel if she felt the need to burn some midnight oil. Yes, she felt good. She might even sleep now. That was something.

The glow didn't last long. Back in her room, she felt restless again. She pulled the cord of the candlewick and moulded the long white nightdress to her body by bunching it at the back. She had to stand on the bed to get a long view of herself in the mirror. Not bad. She opened the top buttons to show a little cleavage, pouting at her reflection. 'Cappuccino? Don't mind if I do,' she drawled, raising her left eyebrow in Dr Goldberg fashion. 'No. No buns. I have to watch my figure. Oh go on then. You've twisted my arm. Just that weensy little eclair there.'

She hopped down and drew a cupid's bow on her top lip with a red pen. Black for eyeliner. Shame to stop there so she fixed a little beauty spot to her cheek. 'They make the most maw-vellous coffee here, don't they?' Ah *stop* it. Stop it. If there was a bar of Lux around, she'd have eaten it. They had such lovely soaps in the V & A, she should have got a couple for herself. She would. There. That was that decided. She'd go back next Wednesday night and buy some soaps. And if that Robert fellow was giving another lecture, it wouldn't do anyone the slightest bit of harm if she hung around for a while to listen. No coffee though.

Curled up in bed, burrowed deep under the covers she might have slept if her breasts weren't at her. Lolloping around like that inside her nightie, just begging to be squeezed.

Suddenly, her door was crashing open. Sr Carmel and Sr Oliver were fizzing there with their wispy hair awry, looking like twin geriatric nightmares in their flannel nightwear. Ten thousand volts apiece, and still standing.

'Come quick, Sister!' Sr Carmel beckoned. Angela ran after them.

'What is it?' she gasped.

Sr Carmel had to stop for breath on the stairwell. She was wheezing.

'I saw him from my window – he was down on the street. Shouting his head off, bless us and do good for us – *roaring*, up at the women's next door. He must have slipped out a window or something.'

'Who? What? Take a deep breath, Sister – now, who was roaring up at next door?'

'Young Steve. He was fierce upset in himself. Then he must've got back in and he's below now, making a parade. We can't put a hold on him, at all at all. He's the men in a desperate state.'

'Did you call Mother?'

'I thought she was home in her flat. We'll get her so.'

'No, no. Don't bother her. I'll handle this,' Angela said with a great deal more confidence than she was feeling.

The floor of Steve's cluster was in uproar. Men keening, huddled into foetal positions or stalking wild-eyed through the narrow communal spaces. George, the doctor, clutched the kettle to his chest and had somehow managed to squeeze himself into the confines of a small cupboard. He kept demanding that they sign the register.

Angela clapped her hands as she'd seen Mary Margaret do

93

on countless occasions. Jimmy Scallopjaws, who was a lifer, and who usually assisted the nuns whenever there was an outbreak, was nowhere to be seen.

The loudest din came from Steve's cluster. Angela drew the curtain back. He was howling, alternately knuckling his head and smashing it against the wall. A nasty gash over his left eye sprayed the cell with blood, every time he drew back for another headbang. The louder he roared, the more disturbed and frenzied the men grew around him.

'Don't go near him.' Sr Carmel clutched at Angela. 'The eyes are back in his head. What'll we do?'

It had to be serious if Sr Carmel wasn't administering her usual palliative. Not a bonbon in sight. Angela frowned, to make them think she was contemplating something. She was. Running.

'I'm going for the Mother.' Sr Oliver was about to totter off. 'She can't hear what's going on from her office.'

'Hold on one sec,' Angela said tentatively, she took a step toward Steve. Auntie Bridie shrieked hysterically in her head, the warnings trailing off into *heh heh heh*. Sr Carmel could only peep through one eye. Rosary beads racketed through her fingers.

'Steve?' Angela almost touched his shoulder. He froze. Then bawled something incomprehensible before launching his head at the wall again.

'Ah, Steve, pet, come on now. You'll have to stop this carry on.' She was trying her Uncle Mikey voice, half-chiding, half-joking, anything to bring him down from the height in his head. 'Keep this up – and they'll all be wanting a wall.'

A dollop of free-flying blood caught her neck and trickled down the length of her torso. She had only seconds to make decisions. To take his measure, which was what she was trying to do as she cautiously lowered her buttocks onto the edge of the bed. She murmured all the time, nothing sounds, animal sounds – chook chook chook, nyya nyyah. He was rigid, the scrubby block of his head faced away from her. Fists clenching and unclenching, fingers splaying like a starfish when he released them.

'Sook sook.' Angela inched back on the bed. Feet pointed at the door, poised for flight, just in case.

He hadn't roared for a while which was a good sign. The turmoil beyond seemed to have abated somewhat as well.

'What's the matter at all?' Angela spoke to her toes. 'Calm down a bit, will you? You'll see – everything'll be just grand. Just grand.' She knew if she touched him now, he would kill her. 'I'm thinking maybe you've got yourself worked up something cat, and you don't know what way to get out of it. You'd love a sleep now, wouldn't you? If you gave yourself half a chance. Maybe that old doctor business got to you. But, d'you know – you could put your head down, right here on this pillow, and be gone in seconds. You're saying that to yourself, aren't you? If I could just put my head down, I'd be asleep and everything would go away.'

'*You* go away,' he choked. And she knew she had him.

From the corner of her eye, Angela saw Sr Carmel draw aside and Mary Margaret was standing there with Jimmy Scallopjaws. Angela put a finger to her lips and frantically indicated for them to withdraw. Steve slumped onto the bed, inches from her, head still turned to the wall until he swivelled it quickly into the waiting cup of his hands and rocked back and forth, moaning softly. Angela patted his back for minutes, the finger of her free hand still to her lips, warning the others off. When she was certain that he was calmed for the night, she creaked herself up and stepped out, swishing his curtain closed behind.

'What's going on?' Mary Margaret hissed. The smell of sour gin nearly knocked Angela over. 'He got himself worked up.' She shrugged. A quick warning glance to Carmel and Oliver so that they wouldn't tell about his being outside, shouting up at the women's shelter. That would mean certain expulsion.

Mary Margaret looked deeply suspicious. The peering head

of the Gorbals giant showed around a curtain, making her eyes narrow – wasn't he supposed to be gone? He grimaced when he saw her and quickly slipped inside again.

'Hmm,' she said. 'I have me doubts about that one.' She indicated Steve who was sobbing quietly now behind the curtain. 'Grave doubts. He's trouble. I think we'll have to let him go.'

'Ah he's all right,' Angela said lightly. Another quick frown to Carmel. 'He's new is all. Just getting used to being off the streets. You know how it affects them in different ways. Only just this minute he was saying "Thank God for Mother Mary Margaret."' She crossed her fingers. Sr Carmel had turned green as a pickled gherkin.

'Hmm. We'll see. If he pulls another stunt like this – out he goes.'

'Yes, Mother.'

'And I'll thank ye not to be running around in nighties, if you don't mind. At this hour. Ye're supposed to call for me, or lock the door to the clusters. Let them at it. If they've a mind to kill themselves, they will.'

'Yes, Mother.'

Angela was doing her best to conceal the little triumphant smile playing on her lips. She'd managed Steve all by herself. Maybe he was sent to her, a key that would finally unlock Uncle Mikey. Yes, she felt sure of it.

As if reading her mind, Mary Margaret humphed suspiciously again. She eyed Angela with a mixture of disdain and sly canniness.

'Sister – don't dabble, that's all I'll say to you. Even good-intentioned dabbling can cause ruination. There are people, just like things, that get broken and they can't be fixed. We're not here to fix them. All we do is keep a hold of the pieces in our pockets for a spell. You follow me?'

Angela hesitated, then nodded. But she wanted to skip with her fists punching the air. Praise be to God, His Holy Mother, all the saints and martyrs and all belonged to them – she just might make a nun yet.

'And another thing.' Mother Margaret slitted her eyes. 'What, in the name of Christ, have you on your face?'

Chapter Six

Peter knew tears when he saw them – his wife had them. She was humming quite happily in the kitchen now, preparing dinner for their guests. But only the other evening, as they stretched out on the sofa, watching TV, he'd thought she was laughing at something, her body was shaking so uncontrollably, and when he rubbed her cheek, he discovered tears. That was not the first time. Lately, it seemed as though she was permanently on the point of eruption. Sobbing and sighing in the bed beside him, when she thought he was asleep. Snarling viciously, if he so much as traced a finger across her breasts.

Then, days when she was up again, humming and shopping with renewed vigour. He wished that she would hum more and shop less, but shopping and sex went hand in hand with her, so he couldn't complain. Really, he should ask her what was the matter. Not just cluck sympathetically when the floodgates opened. He should come right out with it and ask – what is the matter with you, you crazy bitch? But he didn't care to just yet. In case she told him.

Robert would be on his way by now. Probably stopping to feed the ducks en route. Peter smiled and polished the silver canteen of cutlery. His own distorted reflection – dozens of Peters – smiled back at him. He liked silver, it gave such a satisfying response to the slightest rub.

Anita's friend, Louise, sat by the fire with her back to him. She was riffling through a magazine. They were both banned from the kitchen as Anita was preparing a surprise. Something she hadn't prepared for a long time, she said. Try a moist vagina, he thought, hawing on a knife. No, that wasn't fair. They were just having a funny patch. Lots of couples did. The trick was to ignore it. Don't read too much into things. That was the rock on which people perished. Keep smiling, polish the silver, remember birthdays and anniversaries, surprise with flowers occasionally and never, ever, ask what's *really* the matter?

Robert would be staring across at Bonnie's houseboat by now. Hands plunged deep within his pockets. Probably whistling in that low, soft way he had. Doubtless wouldn't even want to disturb the ducks. It was funny how things had turned out. How the balance had altered so completely in Peter's favour. Back when they were kids together, if you'd asked anyone which of them would be the trailblazer, the response would be Robert, undoubtedly. He always seemed so sure of himself in those days. Always got the girls. Peter didn't mind. Much.

Now, Robert didn't know what he wanted. He was drifting, to all intents and purposes. Peter very much knew what he wanted. And he had it. Tearful wife notwithstanding.

Louise stretched her legs and turned, raising her eyebrows to check if there was anything she could do. Anita hadn't seen her for over five years. It seemed to Peter that they didn't have a lot to say to one another. She was pretty enough, though a long way off being a threat to his complacency. Long dark hair. Too many split ends for his liking. Lazy too, in a single woman sort of way. She'd pretty much lounged around since her arrival. And she hadn't brought so much as a bottle of wine – nothing for the kids. But he'd liked the way her eyes blinked rapidly as she complimented the house, when he took her from room to room. Giving her the guided tour. Lots of blinking in the half-acre garden, something she'd always wanted, she'd said, most gratifyingly.

He made a pooh-poohing sound. Waved a hand expansively. It was all under control. Nothing at all for her to do. If there was one thing he and Anita excelled at – they gave good dinner. No, he decided, inspecting some tongs to the light, he didn't much care for this Louise person.

Perfect for Robert, though.

The dessert wine popped with a satisfying little glutchy noise, a wet, sugary cork that had waited twenty years for oxygen. They could sit back and enjoy the rest of the evening now that the cringing was over. Louise had told them about her new American boss. A vulgar animal. No manners whatsoever – they should see him eat. Still, she had to say, he wasn't that exceptional by American standards. At least not by the standards she'd encountered. Could anyone around the table, hands on their hearts now, say that they'd ever met an American they actually liked? Robert had said, yes, he had. In a very quiet voice. Perhaps she mistook his whisper for lack of vehemence or maybe she just enjoyed a challenge, but no one could get to her in time before she insisted that he share the information with them. He was pretending, she was sure of it. Go on, give them a name. Bonnie, Robert said. As in 'my Bonnie lies over the ocean'? Louise sang. What was she anyway? A childhood sweetheart? Holiday romance? My mother, Robert said.

That was all past now. More wine and cheese and thawing to come. The usual humpbacked bridges of dinner parties, crossed and behind them. Peter beamed at Robert. Who was surreptitiously staring at the twin livid spots, high on Anita's cheeks. She'd barely uttered a word for the last half hour or so.

'You'll try a sip of this, Louise, won't you?' Peter did a mid-air flourish with the bottle, before positioning it on the rim of her glass. 'I mean, a little sweet German isn't against your principles, I trust?'

'No. Please . . .' Louise gestured him on. She turned to Anita. 'Really – I'm so sorry, Anita – about the Beef Wellington. I should have said something. Entirely my fault – oops!' A dribble of German escaped her lips. 'Lovely. Quite lovely.'

'Isn't it?' Peter swilled his glass.

'I suppose I should have asked,' Anita said, tersely. 'I mean, so many people've turned vegetarian these days. I'm out of touch.'

'Nonsense.' Peter sipped and did a mock swoon at the taste.

'If I'm out of touch, I'm out of touch,' Anita barked, softening her tone toward the end. She managed a self-deprecating giggle.

'Well, all I can say,' Robert felt compelled, 'is I'm so glad I'm not a vegetarian – no slight to you of course, Louise ... But that was – well, it was special. Yes.'

'Thank you, Robert.'

'I should've said,' Louise repeated. She toasted Anita. 'A superb meal, sweetheart. You always knew how to cook. Me – I can't even boil an egg.'

'Now now,' Peter chided. 'Any fool can boil an egg.'

'Well, this particular fool – can't.' Louise smiled, but Robert felt the chill in the air take on an Arctic quality. Around the table, they'd been plunging toward extreme temperatures for what seemed the longest time. He had no idea why that should be, apart from Louise's vegetarianism, but he was close to frostbite.

'You used to like meat once?' Robert asked, to close the silence.

'Oh yes. But I always felt it was, you know, wrong somehow.'

'Did you?' Anita placed her chin on the bridge of her hands. 'I don't remember that.'

'Well, I never said anything of course. But then I saw an ad in some paper or other, something to the effect of – if you're thinking of turning vegetarian, call this number. So I did. And I haven't touched meat since.'

'Isn't that interesting?' Peter held the small dessert glass to a candle flame. The wine swirled like a thick syrup. 'What a colour. Marvellous. So tell us, Anita – no cravings at all? For a bacon buttie or somesuch?'

Louise scrunched her face into a purse of horror.

'Listen – the group I joined were so militant, we weren't supposed to even *dine* with people who eat flesh. For ages, I couldn't have Sunday lunch with my own family. But now I think that's taking things a tad too far. Live and let live, I say. Let people see the light in their own good time.'

'That's very big of you.' Anita was toying with the cheese board. She sliced and chopped until every wedge was dissected into bite-sized morsels. Then she cleaved them again.

'I think we can manage the rest ourselves, dear,' Peter chuckled.

'What?' Anita stared at her handiwork. 'Oh yes. I'll get the coffee.'

Robert followed her into the kitchen. She stood with her back to him, arms folded, staring out the side window.

'Can I help?' Robert asked softly.

'It depends on what you mean by help.'

'With the coffee, I . . .'

'Yes, yes, I know you meant the coffee. Sorry, Robert. I'm in a bit of a mood, I'm afraid.' The gust of her sigh fogged up a windowpane. She turned quickly and set about putting tiny rosebud coffee cups onto saucers.

Robert didn't know which way to look. He'd never seen Anita like this before. Or maybe he had, and just never noticed properly. At any rate, he felt that he should say something. He chewed the soft flesh of his inner lip.

'You don't know what to say, do you?' Anita caught him offguard with a piercing glance. She had little diamond tears in her eyes. 'Of course you don't. There's nothing to say.'

'I suppose it must be upsetting – after all that effort,' Robert mumbled.

'What? Oh, the bloody meat you mean. I couldn't care less. Not really. To tell the truth, I wish I'd never asked her. I'd forgotten how much I disliked her at college. We don't have a thing to say to one another. Not like you and Peter.'

102

'We don't really say a lot to one another either, Anita.' As he said it, Robert knew it to be true.

'Maybe it's different for men. Peter's always on about what good friends you are. How you signed a blood brother pact, when you were kids.'

'Did we?'

'Well, he says you did. He's always on about you, you know.'

'I'm amazed.'

Anita studied him with her head cocked to the side. The tears had frozen. She gave him a lopsided smile.

'Yes. I suppose you are. You have no idea the effect you have on people, Robert. That's your problem. Peter won't be happy until he's fixed you up with someone.'

'Why should that be?' Robert was genuinely perplexed. But Anita was only reiterating what Bonnie had been saying for years.

The coffee went putta putta putta.

'Maybe – maybe he wants you to be like him.' Her voice was dry as sunbaked concrete. 'You know – happy. Happy happy happy . . .' Before Robert could say a word, Anita indicated the tray. Robert passed it to her. She ran a finger along both eyelids. '*She's* been giving you the eye – bet you never noticed.'

'Louise, you mean? I don't think so.'

The tray fell, clanging against the tiled floor. Anita's hand extended, but she was not reaching for the tray, as Robert supposed, her fingers fluttered through air, near his left cheek.

'Oh, Robert – are you really so blind? Can't you see that I . . .'

She froze. Her hand fell limply by her side. She was glaring at her daughters over Robert's shoulder.

'Girls! How many times do I have to tell you? When you go to bed, you stay there.'

'We're thirsty,' Tamara whined.

'Both of you?' Anita widened her eyes.

'Yeah, we get thirsty together,' Vanessa said.

103

'Any chance of that coffee?' Peter put his head around the kitchen door.

'It's coming,' Anita snapped. 'Girls! Bed!'

'Just a glass of water.' Tamara sidled toward the fridge.

'Or there's Coke there.' Vanessa pushed her luck.

'No water. No Coke. Bed!' Anita swivelled them to face the door.

'You're being totally unreasonable,' Tamara said, reasonably.

'Robert – will you please tell these girls to go to bed? They don't listen to a word I say.'

'All you do is shout at us.' Vanessa looked up at her mother, ticcing eye, match for match.

'That is not all I do!'

'You're shouting now, aren't you?'

'Milk, not cream, for Louise please, Anita.' Peter's head popped around the door again.

'Girls – what's going on? You should be in bed.'

'Look – you bring the coffee through,' Robert softly urged Anita. 'I'll bring the girls up to bed.'

'Thank you, Robert.'

'May I just – a glass of water to share, maybe?'

'Fine. Fine. Whatever.' Anita conceded defeat. She would not meet his eye, Robert noticed.

Tamara and Vanessa swooshed triumphantly upstairs, ahead of him. Robert could hear Peter chortling to Louise about how he, Robert, had those two girls wrapped around his little finger. Shame he wasn't a father, himself. Still – all in good time, eh, Anita? Robert didn't hear Anita's response.

The girls gambolled through the wide landing toward their room. A montage of limbs, bits of arms and legs sticking out like a Degas painting. Pure, unadulterated energy. Belonging – to someone else. Robert felt breathless with envy for a moment. Such a disgusting feeling. It gobbled up a person's soul and constantly reduced them. So that he was often left wondering how much of a person's self was really formed by comparison with

104

another. As though he were defined by what he did not have, and what was left was his paltry measure. He didn't care about the hyphens, the house he could take or leave, but this, *this* – the flailing limbs, the enclosure by strong, protective walls, the circumference of it all, the upstairs-downstairs day-to-dayness of it all, the alluvial odour of established marriage – this, he envied.

He sagged against the bannister rail for a moment wondering what Anita had been about to say, earlier in the kitchen. It was all very strange. Everyone seemed to have such sharp edges tonight. He couldn't for the life of him figure out what agendas were circulating around and around, though he was certain they existed. He longed for the solitude of his front room. Maybe Peter and Anita were right – he spent so much time on his own, he was no longer capable of interacting in the layered fashion of his species. He felt incredibly inadequate. Just one single layer – a topsoil, to others' rich and peaty humus. He thought of the dinner, the conversation with Anita and the diamonds in her eyes, the fact she'd intimated that Louise appeared interested in him – if it was true, why couldn't he see that? What was the matter with him? How could any of it be important to anyone? It all seemed so mindlessly trivial. Yet it was the stuff of life – and he had no part to play in it.

Lately, he'd grown more and more uncomfortably aware of his isolation. Withdrawing from the simplest of conversations, because he would feel unaccountably stung. Days when the caustic impatience of shopgirls as he fumbled for loose change could play on his mind for hours. Nights when he felt loneliness bear down on him with a crushing, palpable force. Sometimes he felt that he was walking around without his skin on. He'd even found himself wandering into a Disney store, for no other reason than to enjoy the broad, uncomplicated smiles of the staff. That was pathetic. They were paid to smile – yet it was nice, while it lasted. The next time, he'd felt obliged to buy something. Two presents, stashed away for Tamara and Vanessa's birthdays.

'You're in a dream.' Tammy pulled at his jacket, drawing him into the bedroom. The girls sat up expectantly on their bunks. No notion of sleep. He passed them the glass of water. They made glug glugging sounds, as though they were gasping. Tammy patted a space beside her. Robert sat.

'I can't see you now,' Nessie whined from above. She quickly shunted down and snuggled in beside her sister. 'That's better.'

'Why aren't you married, Robert?' Tammy asked. They'd had this conversation a hundred times before.

'I told you, Tammy – I haven't met the right person, I guess.'

'You'll have to hurry up,' Nessie sniffed. 'You're old now.'

'Any chance either of you would have me – in a few years say?'

'Gro-ooss!' They shuddered.

'You'll be all wrinkly and stuff.' Tammy looked genuinely disgusted.

'Maybe I could have a facelift.'

'Look, Robert.' Tammy touched his arm sympathetically. 'It just isn't on. Come on now – let's think. There has to be somebody you could marry.'

'What about Louise?' Nessie asked her sister.

'Nah.'

'Why do you say that?' Robert was curious. He loved the way they endlessly trawled their parents' acquaintances in search of his future wife.

'She's no fun.'

'And you think that's a priority?'

'Oh God yeah.'

'I think you're right. So let's go through the checklist again – what are we looking for?'

The girls wriggled accommodatingly, ticking off their fingers. They smelt of soap and strawberries. He could have licked their cheeks. Then, he had an idea.

'One sec,' he said, 'I'm not being totally honest with you girls. I did meet somebody recently.'

'Ooo-ooh,' they said.

'I wonder what you might think – you know how important your opinion is to me – let me run her by you . . .'

'Will you tell her to get stuffed, if we say?'

'Of course.'

'Go on then.'

'Well.' He stopped to think, conjuring Angela's face as he had so many times when sketching her over and over again. If only she knew, that right this minute, she lay draped over his dining table, naked. He felt a bit ashamed about that. It was a touch ignoble, but it had started with her neck and shoulders, his conjuring of them, until he had had to continue – to see the rest of her. She was quite lovely in fact. A perfect image. From his imagination.

'You're dreaming again,' Tammy interrupted, tapping her fingers impatiently. 'Is she short, tall, thin, fat or what?'

'She's shortish. Thin. Black, shiny hair – cut like so . . .'

'Spiky.' Nessie said. 'Yeah, go on.'

'She's a social worker.'

'What's that?'

'They help people.'

'That's good. Go on.'

'Guess what her name is?'

'No. Tell us.'

'Angela.'

'Angela. Angggella.' They tried it out.

'Like it?'

'Is she like an angel?' Nessie asked.

'I think so.'

'Does she have wings?'

'She could have. I haven't seen any yet. But you never know.'

'Wow. That'd be well cool. What else about her?'

'She's Irish – her voice goes up and down, you see? A bit like that . . . Her eyes are grey and big with masses of lashes. And she kind of half-runs, half-walks everywhere . . . Like this . . .'

'That's funny,' Nessie giggled.

'She's from this big, really close family in Ireland. Aunts and everything – they all live together.'

'Happy?'

'Oh, very happy. Quite blissful in fact. And . . .' He stopped, they looked so serious, ticking off fingers one by one. They waited. '*And* – there's an uncle in the attic.'

'How d'you mean?' Their fingers hesitated.

'Well, I'm not entirely sure what I mean, to be honest. But apparently he's up there. Maybe he's disabled or something and everyone wants to put him in some awful, mean institution, except Angela and her family – so they keep him up there, so they can mind him for ever and ever.'

'Excellent!' Fingers ticked. The girls did a silent tally, whooping excitedly at the total.

'She's the one,' Tammy shrieked. She gave Robert a congratulatory hug. Nessie wrapped herself around his neck. Robert made exaggerated choking noises.

'*Who's* the one?' Peter's silhouette asked from the doorway. Robert couldn't see his face.

'Angela!' The girls shouted together.

Peter stepped into the room. His mouth had curved into a fixed smile.

'You never told me about any Angela,' he said with a hint of accusation.

'Any Angela! Any Angela!' the girls chanted.

Peter held his hands up for silence. 'Oh she's just someone I met not long ago. Nothing serious.'

'You'll have to bring her for dinner. Won't he, girls?'

'It's not *that* serious. Really.'

Peter's eyes grew round as pennies.

'Is dinner serious, Robert?'

Robert sighed. You wouldn't have thought so.

*   *   *

'Just a couple of hours or so,' Angela responded to Steve's query. 'I'll be back before you know it.'

He nodded, sucking hard on his cigarette. He'd followed her outside when he saw the navy raincoat.

'Go on,' she prodded, 'have a game of ludo or something.'

He didn't seem inclined to move. She saw that he was watching the movements to and fro next door in the women's shelter. A couple of young girls tottered out in dagger heels. Short leather jackets, skirts practically grazing their crotches, their painted faces parodying their sex. Big eyes, big mouths, big hair. Steve studied them from under a furrowed brow, swollen where the gash still glistened viscerally.

'Steve,' Angela remonstrated, 'if you're seen so much as talking to any of the girls, you'll be thrown out. Understand?'

'Yeah.'

'And stop knuckling your head. You'll wear what's left of your hair away.'

'Yeah.'

'Go on now. Go back inside. You're safer there than out here.'

He stubbed out the cigarette, expelled the last drag in a hissing stream, hitched up his shoulders – and obeyed.

She felt good about that, all the way in the tube. Didn't once get mentally embroiled in her fellow passengers' sagas. Happily googled at a small baby in its mother's arms. It was in that place where babies go when neither fully awake nor fully asleep. Angela was an avid baby watcher. This one had lizard eyes, half-moons for lids, drooping down, almost closed but she could make out the constant flicker from side to side of the eyeball within. Faint track of a brow curving up for an instant, then down again. Breath coming in foal-like snorts from dilating nostrils. Lower lip, extruding, wet and full, kidney-red. A slut. Angela thought that girl babies looked like delicious sluts; boy babies all looked like Frank Sinatra.

She made her googling noise again and was rewarded with

a slow, lazy smile. The mother's lips curved too, quickly, while she checked Angela's ring finger.

All along the tunnel to the Cromwell Road, the pound coins for her soaps jangled heavily in Angela's right pocket. She kept her roll of ten pees in the left, dispensing as she moved. She was determined that she would go and make her purchases first and foremost. Then maybe a little saunter to take in some of the stuff she'd missed last time. She might have a cup of tea in the cafe. Might pick up some more brochures.

But her feet headed straight for the Europe and America Gallery, taking the rest of her with them. Her heart gave a little leap when she saw a small crowd gathered around a speaker. It had to be the same lecture. She murmured her apologies, working a path through the assembly. Same lecture, different lecturer. A woman with a black bowl of hair, pointed them in the direction of someone or other's dinner service, circa 1850. Angela's shoulders slumped. She thought she might slip away when they moved to another room but the woman with the bowl had caught her eye on arrival and smiled slightly. So that was that. It would be unbelievable rudeness not to stay for the whole thing now. Even if the talk didn't sound half so good as the previous time.

In the Poynter Room, Angela swallowed yawns like caves in her mouth. In the Gamble Room, she lifted her forehead to keep her eyes staring fixedly at the ceiling. But there was a snore, on her feet, in the William Morris Room. Not a snore you could turn into a cough either. The full nostril-quivering, throat-glugging thing. Accompanied by a start and a dazed glance around, just in case anyone was left in any doubt. The woman with the bowl haircut gave her a cutting smile. Angela put the back of her hands to her cheeks to cool them down.

When the lecture was over, she stood by the glass case of the Christ figure, studying the donkey this time round. The prospect of buying the soaps didn't seem in the least exciting. Not anymore. She'd just drop at a Boots on the way home and get some regular own brand Boots soaps. As good as anything and twice as cheap. Brochures? She'd plenty really, to keep her going. If she wanted to be kept going. The hot cup of tea might cheer her up, though. Better than a poker in the eye. She sighed, plunged her hands into the pockets of her coat. That was that. So long cappuccino. Adieu, adios, goodbye, good luck, good riddance.

Probably.

She turned on her heel and careered headlong into Robert. He had to grasp her shoulders to prevent her stagger turning into a fall.

'Angela,' he was saying so softly, she had to strain to hear him. 'So you came back after all.'

'Robert!'

'I missed you last week.'

'I had to go to Ireland. Uncle Mikey was acting up.'

'He's all right now then?'

'Oh grand.'

'I'm glad to hear it.'

Angela hopped from foot to foot. She could feel the slow burn creep up her cheeks again. There was something about the way he was looking at her. Not discomfiting exactly, but intimate, like he could x-ray through her clothes. She almost had to check that she was still wearing any.

'Have you a talk coming up?' she asked.

'No. It's my night off actually. I came – well – I came on the off-chance you might be here . . . Sorry – was that the wrong thing to say? I didn't mean to . . .'

'No, no. That's grand.' Angela pulled at her nose, stared at her feet so hard she thought they really would kill her. She didn't know how to talk. What to say. How to say it. That simple dialogue could be so entirely excruciating, that words could be so painful and come so bloody far apart – of this, she knew nothing. And to tell the truth, he didn't appear to be such great shakes at it either.

'Angela – I have a great favour to ask of you,' he was saying with difficulty. 'It's not something I ask lightly. Not at all. And of course I've no right to ask a perfect stranger in the first place . . .'

'What is it?' Angela interjected.

'Well, I – d'you think we could go somewhere? I mean, it's a bit awkward here. Have you got the time?'

Angela checked her watch. She'd be back much later than she'd anticipated. She said yes.

'Great! Look, there's a little coffee bar around the corner – not far.'

Angela took a swigful of air.

'Before we take another step – I think I'd better – well, I've a confession to make.'

'You have?'

'Yes.' She swallowed. 'Robert – look it – I *hate* coffee.'

'What about tea?'

'I love tea.'

'So do I. I don't know why I suggested coffee – maybe it just sounds altogether grander or something.'

'Oh,' Angela giggled with a hand to her mouth, 'I'm afraid you'll be finding nothing grand about me.'

Robert looked at her intently. For the scariest moment she thought that he was going to contradict her. Then she'd have to throw herself under the tube. But he just gave her a crooked smile. And placed a tentative hand to the small of her back. As if to guide her.

'Tea,' he said. And didn't – praise be to the Lord God on high – add 'for two'. The tracks of the tube lines receded from Angela's vision. Instead, she saw cups, saucers, teaspoons and a ginormous bar of Lux with a cake knife sticking out of it, between them on the table.

Chapter Seven

Their uncomfortable silence was covered by the heated argument going on between the couple at the next table. Angela sipped her tea and tapped her feet. Robert could see that she was doing her best not to blatantly stare at the fighting couple but her eyes kept sliding in their direction. A worried frown creased her forehead.

'She's going to cry, I think,' she hissed under her breath. 'Oh no.'

The young woman had indeed erupted into a series of loud, anguished sobs. The man gazed around furtively, his body wafting waves of embarrassment. Then he began to shovel food into his mouth, ignoring the weeping creature on the other chair. The louder she sobbed the faster he shovelled, as if he could eat her into silence. Robert tried to quench his own twinkle of amusement when he saw the throb of sympathy in Angela's grey eyes. The whole cafe was staring now, mouths agape in mortified wonder at the baying woman who had begun to rock from side to side in her chair. It was not a comfortable sight certainly but Robert had to compress his lips tightly every time he looked at the shovelling man. He turned an escaped gurgle into a cough. Angela stared openly, her pupils dilating and contracting in tune with the sobs. Her face blanching and flushing alternately. She squinched up her eyes and spoke out of the side of her mouth to Robert.

'What'll we do?'

'Do? What? What do?'

'I don't know. She's hysterical. Somebody should do something.'

'I don't see what we could do really.'

He was trying to sound more sympathetic than he felt. What he felt was embarrassment and irritation with this couple for making total strangers party to their own particular misery. He wished the woman would stop making those ridiculous heaving sounds. Wasn't she aware that she was making a spectacle of herself? Or perhaps that was the point of the exercise. He wondered why her partner didn't do something to try and stop the scene. Tell her to shut up at the very least. But no, there he sat, a human slot machine, just piling it in. Angela, on the other hand, looked taut as a fiddle string. Her entire body seemed to be listing toward their table. As if drawn toward some strangely irresistible perfume. The heart of her face mirroring the woman's tragedy. Three fingers tapped against her mouth, unconsciously peeling down her wet lower lip. The tip of her tongue protruded between two rows of small, even, white teeth. Robert was reminded of a cat and made a note to himself to remember that for another sketch. Suddenly she caught his eye sharply and he focused on the couple again.

'Look. There's nothing we can do. Really. They wouldn't thank us for getting involved,' he was saying, but Angela was already on her feet, grabbing a wad of paper napkins which she thrust under the nose of the crying woman.

Robert closed his eyes, anticipating a real scene now. One in which he might very well have to become a participant. He wanted the ground to open. The ceiling to fall. At the very least, a power cut would do. He concentrated on the pot of tea, topping Angela's cup to the brim. A clearing of his throat before he dared sneak a sideways glance to find Angela seated beside the woman who was loudly blowing her nose into a scrunched-up white posy. The weeping had subsided. A tinkle of chatter from other tables permeated the room. Cups met saucers and forks danced with knives. The man was saying something quietly about post-natal depression or something. He seemed relieved not to have to devour the contents of the table any longer and conveyed his sense of impotence by means of compulsive shrugging instead. Angela was murmuring something soothingly. Robert couldn't believe how much energy seemed to radiate from her body. Her pale face gleamed like a waxy moon. He noticed how her skinny nimble fingers darted around the woman, never really touching but casting spells all the same. The man squeezed his wife's hand briefly before tucking his own hands under the table once more. A pang of remorse and self-disgust welled up in Robert for his compulsion to laugh earlier. Naked emotion like that always made him want to laugh or run away. What Angela did, jumping right in without an invitation, was inconceivable to most people, he considered, looking around at the other diners who all appeared reassuringly on his side of the boat. Still, it was admirable. The woman was nodding with the posy pressed against her nose. She gave Angela a crooked smile to reassure that she was all right now. The man called for the bill. Angela returned to her seat.

'That was very brave of you,' Robert said, for something to say.

'Brave?' She seemed genuinely surprised. And he thought – she has to be faking it. Has to. The couple were leaving, both extending a sheepish wave in her direction. Angela took a sip from her cup, sloshing the full contents over the rim. She leaned across the table like a fellow conspirator, eyes gleaming with the interest she assumed he would naturally reciprocate. Robert was fixated on the satisfying little puddle in her saucer.

'They've just had a baby. Been trying for-oh-years. She can't understand why she's not up there with the stars. Poor thing. No, don't get me wrong. She loves the baby. Adores him. But apart from him everything's gone black she says. Well, not black exactly. Grey. Greyish. Your man's at his wits' end what to do for her. Feels like she hates him. Isn't that the saddest thing you've heard in a long time?'

She sipped and sploshed again. Robert thought – no. It is not the saddest thing I've heard in a long time. In point of fact the saddest thing he'd heard in a long time was – was – well, it was something far sadder than that. Far. A sobbing woman in a restaurant with a loved baby just didn't cut it as far as he was concerned. True enough she was genuinely and quite visibly upset but hormones and all that stuff. Sad – no. Mildly dis-comfiting – yes. Worthy of a conversation when his precious time with Angela was ticking away – definitely no. On the other hand, what was so precious about this time after all? Clearly she was a bleeding heart. Oh, worthy enough in its way. Maybe it was an Irish thing. Or a female thing. Not a thing a red-blooded heterosexual man should understand. Unless he was absolutely determined to fall in love. And he was not that. Neither absolute nor determined. In fact, he wasn't entirely certain that he wished to paint her if it came right down to brass tacks. Uh-uh. Wasn't entirely sure that he could paint for that matter. Why was he sitting here when he could just as easily and certainly more comfortably be sitting at home? Not painting. Not having some strange woman's personal pain being forced down his gullet. Not looking at the swell and contraction of Angela's absurdly large pupils.

The trouble with going out and interacting with other humans was the less than human way you felt afterwards. This is what he thought. Sitting there, sipping tea, watching the way the spikes of her hair cut shapes into the white forehead. The way you felt stung and slightly soiled and tainted by self-loathing and repulsion afterwards. The stupid things you said, the little secrets you revealed with that particular comment, the bits of you that were mummified in the rarest internal tomb that sud-denly insisted themselves on an unsuspecting public when you loosened the hold on them for just one split second. The way you needed a bellylaugh at this comment, a sympathetic head-

116

nod at that. The smoky scent of boredom wreathing another's hair after a while. Being with other people demanded far too much. And the payback was far too little. Alone, you could please yourself. Quite literally. Alone, you could even at times labour under the very pleasant illusion that you liked yourself.

'What's the favour anyway?' Angela cut through his thoughts.

'Favour?' He wanted to buy some time. Checked his watch to do that. 'Look, I think on second thoughts – it mightn't be such a good idea. I've no right to ask anything at all of you.'

'No. I'm fierce curious now. Please ask.'

'I don't think so. Really.'

'Fair enough so.'

The way she was trying to blink back her disappointment and sip the overflowing tea at the same time made him want to rip open his chest with his own nails. Tear it open, plunge in his hand and slap his beating heart on the table. She would see for herself the scabby smallness of it. No larger than a butter bean. And she would run and be protected from him. She had seemed so at ease and confident moments ago, now all that nervous agitation and those jittery limb movements were back. Robert checked his watch again.

'The museum is open for a while yet. Would you like me to give you a quick show around?'

'Oh yeah, please.' Angela's pupils dilated again.

'What in particular would you like to see?'

'I don't know. Whatever you like.'

'Give me a clue.'

'No. I meant whatever *you* like. The things you like best.'

'Okay.' Robert grinned. It was a place to start. He signalled to the waiter for the bill and flipped open his wallet. She was watching him, flushed again, pulling coins from her pocket.

'Let me. It was only tea,' he said.

'How much d'you think it'll come to?' She worriedly made a stack of ten pence coins. Another separate stack contained three pound coins. She explained that she had been keeping

117

them for soaps but it didn't matter if she didn't have enough in the ten pence coins for the tea. Three things became apparent to Robert. First, she had to pay her own way, couldn't even conceive any alternative. Second, the stacks on the table represented every penny she possessed at this precise moment. Third, she had absolutely no idea whatsoever of the cost of a cup of tea in a cafe. He wondered what planet she'd been living on. In his anxiety to pull a note from his wallet he didn't notice something flutter onto the floor. Angela scooped the small square up and handed it back to him. A photograph of Tammie and Nessie.

'They're lovely,' she said.

'Yes. They are. Lovely girls.' He was about to explain who they were when the waiter interrupted. In her rush to pay her share Angela sent her tower of coins rolling in every direction. Robert quickly paid up and helped her scrabble about on the floor catching as many as they could. Her cheeks were incandescent. She kept muttering sorry over and over again and he felt another little stab at his heart. He helped her up and they ran for the door.

Outside they both inhaled a rush of polluted London May air and Angela broke into her peculiar half-run, half-walk toward the V & A. Robert took long strides to keep up. All along the subway she dispensed her ten pence coins to beggars in a dizzy, distracted fashion. Clearly thrown into confusion by the fact the money was loose and not in a tightly-contained roll. Again he was plagued by that sense she could not be for real. But she didn't appear to be looking for a reaction from him one way or the other and furthermore he'd seen her do this very thing when completely unaware of his presence. Maybe she was that rare beast, a genuinely goodhearted person.

As they stepped into the Medieval Treasury Hall, Robert couldn't suppress his curiosity any longer.

'Do you always do that? Give money to every beggar?'

She considered for a second, pulling her mouth down at the corners.

'I suppose. Yeah.'

'I just wondered.' Robert wiped an imaginary fleck from an eyelid. She was moving rapidly on then stopped abruptly, awaiting directions from him. 'Why?' Robert asked.

'Why what?'

'Why the money? The beggars?'

The grey eyes swivelled from the mosaic floor to the ceiling, down again. She shrugged. He thought the inside of her ears looked like mother-of-pearl.

'I don't know.' Another shrug. 'I mean, why not? Don't you?'

'Only at Christmas, I'm afraid,' Robert answered, straining to catch the scent of disdain or false piety from the top of her head. But he couldn't catch a whiff. They might just as well have been discussing apples. The like or dislike thereof. He waited to see if she wanted to add anything. There had to be a comment coming to let him know how morally superior she was. But she in turn was waiting for him to tell her which way to go.

'This way,' Robert said, delighted by the little trip-trop beat of her shoes behind his.

He took her through the Dress Gallery, thinking this would be of most interest to her. She was so absorbed by the intricate needlework on the first eighteenth-century garment they came across, it was difficult to move her on. The changing trends and fashions of the ages didn't concern her in the least. But the fretwork on a particular mantua held her enchanted gaze. She told him that she used to make wedding dresses with her mother when she was a child. As they moved upstairs to see the Great Bed of Ware, Robert tentatively asked about the Aunts and Uncle Mikey in the attic.

'God that is a big bed all right. Huge,' she marvelled. He explained that it was commissioned in the fifteenth century for an inn in Ware, Hertfordshire. How it was designed to attract the custom of those travelling to and from London.

'It's even mentioned in Shakespeare's *Twelfth Night*,' he added. 'You were saying – Uncle Mikey . . . ?'

119

'I've never seen the like of those carvings,' she said. 'The hours of work that must have gone into them. Look at that. And I thought wedding dresses were hard.'

He pressed again on the way to the Twentieth Century Gallery. A ring of desperation on the way up to the Glass Gallery. But for someone who'd so casually mentioned her eccentric uncle practically from their first moment's meeting, she was now being reticent in the extreme. He felt that he was boring her and wanted something back. His voice grew weary and disinterested as he pointed out this and pointed out that. He thought she wasn't even listening after a while. He felt the purse of his heart tighten against her. They rushed through the Glass Gallery and he decided he wouldn't show her the Luck of Edenhall after all. Her head was swivelling, trying to take everything in. Robert had taken all the colour from his voice.

'Is there something you really like here?' she asked. And it suddenly struck him that she was so engaged, so completely intent on absorbing as much as possible in the limited time frame, she hadn't even heard his questions about the Aunts and the Uncle. Moreover she hadn't the slightest idea of how he'd cheated her thus far – showing her stuff that meant so little to him. Tourist stuff. Obvious stuff. They were about to leave but he touched her elbow and guided her back.

'This is the Luck of Edenhall,' he said, pointing to an elaborately scrolled vessel.

'It's special?'

'Very. You see, glass hardly ever survives. So fragile. But this passed through generations of the Musgrave family of Edenhall in Cumberland. And the story goes that a party of fairies were drinking around a well near the Hall but they were interrupted by humans. They were frightened and ran away and the last fairy screamed out, "If this cup should break or fall – farewell the Luck of Edenhall." That's the myth behind it anyway. Now we know that it's actually a perfect example of thirteenth-century Syrian glassmaking. Probably found its way to England in the baggage of a returning Crusader. So it must be lucky to have survived this long don't you think?'

She nodded her head fervently.

'And I'm so lucky to see it now. Thanks a million.' Her eyes were shining wetly, the curve of her smile took up most of her face. Robert's fingers itched with an overwhelming desire to trace the hollowed dimple on her left cheek. On impulse he grabbed her shoulder and quickly propelled her from the room.

'If we're quick we might get one more thing in,' he said, catching her hand to fly them downstairs, across the main concourse and over to the Henry Cole Wing. It was only when they were in the lift, both breathless and light-headed, that he realized he was still holding her hand. Angela was realizing too because her eyes were glued to the knotty bunch of their fingers. Robert let go abruptly and she nervously sifted her hair into spiky pleats. The ascent to the top floor seemed to take for ever. There was something absurdly intimate about this enforced claustrophobia. At last the doors opened and he led her directly to the portrait.

'Look, I don't know why I'm showing you this really,' he felt obliged to apologize. There were so many things he could have shown her instead. So many bigger things. This was just an ordinary pastel when he could be showing her a Constable or the Raphaels, for God's sake.

'Oh.' Angela peered up close at the portrait of the unknown woman. And Robert knew that he hadn't made a mistake. He also understood the connection – why hadn't he thought of it before? It was so blindingly obvious at this particular moment. His eyes swept over the heart-shaped face inside the frame. The pale ivory skin, gentle dreamy-eyed expression, slight tilt of the head, the exquisitely-executed black fronds of eyelashes below the firm line of eyebrow. How many times had he stood in this spot admiring and envying the quality of the workmanship? And envied the artist his knowledge of this woman who seemed so fleshily of this world but of another world too in her

121

slightly distant smile. A smile that spoke of secrets. His eyes darted back and forth between Angela and the unknown woman. And he allowed himself the thought – perhaps she was not so anonymous after all. Perhaps he knew her.

'She's so – so . . .' Angela broke off with a shrug.

'Perfect?' Robert offered.

'Yeah.' Angela nodded. 'Look at those eyelashes. How did he do that?'

'Beats me. Especially when you consider the medium. Tiny details can be buggers with pastels.'

'That's what this is, is it? A pastel. Imagine.'

Robert prayed that she would continue scrutinising every detail for a while longer. He was so busy himself, scrutinising her.

'She's like your wife, is she?' Angela kept her eyes trained on the portrait.

'My –? No. I'm not married.'

'You're divorced, is it?'

'No. I've never been married.'

'I see.'

'What? What do you see?'

'Ah, sure nothing.' She let out a heavy sigh and turned with a hugely bright smile.

'Thanks a million again.'

Robert felt dazzled. Blinded by the sheer breadth of that smile. He felt as though the fog of his life was lifting. All the confusions and hesitancies of the past were solidifying into one concrete, tangible shape. She was there, right there, standing in front of him. An angel. A real-life angel. He would make himself deserving of her. The fact that he even thought he could make himself deserving of her was a gigantic step in the right direction. He held her smile and felt the tight little butter bean in his chest swell and expand until he thought it would surely burst. His hand snaked out instinctively and touched the dimple on her cheek. Her eyes were glittering, radiating with flux and

122

movement, unlike the fixed curve of her lips. The rest of her face had frozen also.

'Angela,' Robert said. 'I'd really like to paint you. If you'd allow me. Please.'

'Paint me?' She looked shocked. Utterly. He had the feeling he couldn't have shocked her more if he'd asked for a quickie on the museum floor. It occurred to him how sudden and immediate and intimate his plea must have sounded to her. A huge jump from showing her a picture to becoming his picture. It further occurred to him that she might very well have a guardian angel of her own. Waiting for her right this very minute. It was just that she hadn't given any indication before.

'Oh God, I'm sorry,' he blustered. 'I just landed that on you, didn't I? I don't know what I was thinking of. I don't really paint anyway. Well, not any more. You wouldn't have the time in any case. Even if you were available. Available to paint, I mean. And you've lots of commitments haven't you?'

Her mouth was still open. The smile was definitely gone. The sun had crept behind a cloud and there was nothing he could do to bring it back. But his tongue was wagging now of its own accord and there was nothing he could do to stop that either.

'You yourself are committed, I suppose.' He nodded her response.

'Committed?'

'To someone. Are you? To someone?' Robert held his breath.

'Well. Yeah. I suppose that's one way of putting it.'

That should have been it. The pattern of his life had not altered after all. She was unavailable. Otherwise committed. She was somebody else's angel. Could never be his. He should walk away from her this very minute, back to his small miserable mink of a life. This was the credit roll and there would be no lights camera action. He was alone with possibilities once more. The amount of hurt she could have opened him up to in any case. The staggering width and breadth of it. If anything he

123

should feel relieved. No harm done. And the possibility of all that harm could now be avoided. Hurray! He opened his mouth to say goodbye.

'Angela – would you let me paint you anyway?'

No sign of Steve in the refectory or the television room. A couple of the men were playing ludo in one corner; the others were glued to the television. Angela was always struck by the way they appeared to believe that everything on the screen was real life. They constantly bickered and argued through the soaps, defending their own special character if another said something derogatory. Even the ads held them spellbound. A suave, urbane man was trying to sell them a sofa, as a blonde woman flitted around in the background. Why they could take it home today. And not have to pay a penny. Not for four years. No deposit. Interest-free credit. Not for one year. Or even two. Not three. For four years. Not a penny for four years. The man kept repeating it as he danced around a sofa with the blonde. The giant of Gorbals hitched up his sleeves. Peering ever closer at the screen.

'Good deal tha',' he nodded.

'Yeah,' somebody answered.

'Anyone seen Steve?' Angela asked.

'Bloody good deal tha'.' Gorbals fisted the arm of his chair.

'Am I talking to myself?' Angela asked, looking around at a sea of furrowed faces concentrating deeply on the ad.

'No' a penny. Fur four year. Good deal tha'.'

His legs were jiggling. Debating. He stopped still and turned to the others with a deeply perplexed expression.

'Where would yewse put it?'

Angela lifted her eyes to the ceiling and left them to it. She had a sneaky feeling she really did know where Steve was and just didn't want it confirmed.

Mary Margaret was laying into George the doctor along the corridor.

'Gimme that kettle. Give – me – that – kettle.' She was trying to prise it from his grip.

'Woman! You are unspeakable,' George boomed, close to tears. But he relinquished his prize. No one could stand up to the Mother Superior for long. The door to the office slammed shut after her. Angela gulped a deep breath and knocked tentatively.

'What?' rasped the voice from within.

Angela entered, feeling like shark bait. She waited until Mary Margaret finished scribbling something, a fag dangling from the corner of her mouth. She sucked and eyed Angela through dancing phantasms of blue smoke.

'What d'you want?'

'I was at the Victoria & Albert Museum again yesterday evening –'

'Here isn't museum enough for you, I suppose. Oh, go on, yeah . . . ?'

'And. Well. What it is is . . .'

'Oh for feck's sake, get on with it.'

Angela studied her shoes. She took another breath and crossed her fingers behind her back. She knew her cheeks were two strawberries.

'I was wondering if I could have Sundays off for a while –' Angela plunged ahead. A raised hand stopped her going on. She could see the silence that followed. It had a colour.

'Sundays?' Mary Margaret finally mused. 'That would make sense, yeah. Oh dearie me. You want to be a nun and you want Sundays off. Okay. Got that. And what do we want Sundays off for?'

'Well. It's this, emm, painting course they're doing at the Museum. On Sundays. What I mean is – history of painting. I'd like to do it. If it's all right with you. I'd still be here to do all my stuff in the mornings.'

Mary Margaret leaned back. She took two rapid puffs together, expelling a long stream from the other corner of her mouth. Angela didn't dare to meet her eyes. Her feet scuffed at a tear in the floor.

'Uh-huh.' Mary Margaret closed one eye. 'A history. Of painting. That's what's got your juices going now, huh? Came at you like a runaway train I suppose. One minute you're standing there in a museum. You see something on the notice-board, is it? Something along the lines of: "If you've nothing better to do with yourself of a Sunday afternoon, come and do the history of painting." Like that was it? Oh-hoh. Ah sure now.'

'It's a thing I've always wanted to do. Since I was a little girl!' Angela cried in her most plaintive voice.

'And what's the other thing? Ah, yeah. Being a nun. Sure maybe you'll give up that notion altogether and turn into Leonardo da Vinci. How would it go? Angela – da – Vinci. Ah, yeah.'

'I don't want to paint,' Angela said through gritted teeth. 'I want to learn about it. That's all.'

'Indeed, then I could say you've the same approach to nunning. But I won't.' Mary Margaret stubbed out her cigarette and returned her attention to the layers of paperwork spilling over the desk.

'Well? Can I?' Angela hated the wheedling sound in her own voice. Auntie Bridie.

'Off with you. Who am I to stand in the way of your childhood dreams?' She dismissed Angela with a stab of a finger toward the door. 'Oh, one thing, while I have you here – I'm not one bit happy with that Steve boy. I caught him outside this morning sniffing round next door. What's he up to at all? Where's he now?'

'Watching telly. Quiet as a mouse, Mother.'

'Uh-huh. Well watch him. All right. Get out.'

Angela got out. Hot angry tears scalded her eyes. Sr Carmel was about to scuttle past but stopped in her tracks when she saw the expression on Angela's face.

'Pet?' Sr Carmel said.

'She hates me. She really does.' A tear escaped and plopped on the ground.

'She does not. How could she?' Carmel looked genuinely concerned.

'Why's she always picking on me then? Making me feel bad. I do my best here don't I? I work all hours. But all I get is sarcasm sarcasm sarcasm. It's not fair.'

'Ah, that's just her way, pet. She grew up in Kilrush don't forget. Before the family moved county. That'll be it. What thing is she picking on now?'

'I want to do the history of painting. Art, like.'

'Well, sure.'

'She makes a mockery of everything I do. What's wrong with wanting to learn about painting?'

'Not a bit.'

'Yeah.' Angela wiped another falling tear. 'That's how I look at it. For God's sake it's not like I'm doing anything *wrong* is it?'

'Oh Lord, no.'

'I mean you could say it'll inform my sociology studies in a way.'

'Indeed you could.'

'It's a perfectly innocent desire, isn't it?'

'If you say so, pet.'

'The way I look at it – it's only right to educate yourself. No. More than that. It's your duty. How can you really help people unless you've the proper education?'

Sr Carmel's bony forefinger pressed against her lips as she thought about that. Her other hand scrabbled deep within the black habit for a pack of bonbons which she offered in a distracted fashion. A tiny little sausage of frown stood out on her forehead. She was debating something. Finally she offered:

'D'you know – I never went on to the Secondary myself. Yerra there was always so much stuff to be done on the farm and what have you. I said to my mother – "D'you know, Mammy, I don't think I'll be bothered going to that old Secondary. I'll stop home with you instead." And she was grand with that, may she rest. The day after she passed away was the day I packed up a bag, blue it was I remember, and off I went to the convent, a two-mile walk. Then I got sent over here. And d'you know you're right, Sister. Maybe I should have got that old education when I'd the chance. But sure anyway. I'm past it now. I'm thinking it's a different world these days and you have to have it.'

She patted Angela's arm encouragingly and trotted off, sucking hard on the bonbon which meant that she was deeply preoccupied. And Angela felt a spear of remorse cleave into her soul. Sr Carmel was the simplest, most goodhearted of creatures. Every day she helped the helpless without a thought for education or her own motivations which were as pure as a daisy and entirely unsullied by the complications an educated, inquiring sort of mind must necessarily evince. She stood at the very summit of altruism. And now Angela felt that she had made less of her, all so she could continue to unfurl the elaborate screen she was constructing in her own head. The history of art how do. She'd never been inside an art gallery in her life. Never wanted to. The Aunts were shrieking in her brain cells at her duplicity. Auntie Bridie loudest of all. 'Now so. Off you go to your fancy man. With his two children and the mother of them he hasn't even married or divorced. That he only pays the odd call to when the urge overtakes him. And he says he wants to paint you. *Paint* you no less. No doubt he painted her too and that'll be the two children for you. Without a stitch on, what can you expect? Oh that'll be the next thing. And you only thrilled with yourself. Thinking about those brown eyes looking at you, eating you up. If it's the painting that's interesting you how come you didn't tell him what you really are?'

'So what am I?' Angela shrugged to fresh air. She put Bridie's *heh heh heh* cackles aside. The Aunt was just trying to wrongfoot her as usual. Yes. There was a certain degree of flattery going on here. And yes there was something about him. God, the way he could make anything sound interesting. That story about the fairies and that glass thing. Not to mention the way he could listen as well with his head cocked to the side like that and those tiny crinkly bits at the corners of his eyes. All the way along the subway as he walked her back to the tube, he'd asked her about the Aunts and Uncle Mikey, never once making her feel a bit of an eedjit or that she was from a strange crew the way other people did. He wanted to paint her and what was wrong with that? Nothing. Only if you'd a bad mind. And Sunday afternoons were so boring anyway in this place. Sure she didn't like the way the contents of her stomach seemed to churn over every time his face filled her mind like a close-up in a movie. Or the racing of her pulse. On the other hand, she did like it. Of course, another way to look at this whole painting and seeing Robert on a regular basis business was it could simply be looked at as a test. Her own final test to herself. And once she'd passed, she'd be a nun. There. Simple. That was the tack to follow. Angela plunged her hands deep within the pockets of her jeans and whistled softly to herself as she went to look for Steve. Her heart felt a lot lighter now.

It plunged heavily once more when she saw him skulking by the women's front door again. He caught her angry glare and knuckled his head anxiously.

'Steve, what're you doing here?' she hissed.

'Nothing,' he responded sourly, not meeting her gaze.

The door opened and a few women spilled out. Steve's head shot up as his eyes scanned the faces. Suddenly he let out a yell and dived into the middle of them, hauling at a twenty-year-old with fiery red hair and Cleopatra made-up eyes. She tottered on stilettoes and furiously hit back with her shoulder bag. Before Angela could make a move, the other women screamed and hurled obscenities, raining blows on his shaved head. Steve just roared like an enraged bullock, trying to prise the redhead from the group. Angela could see the slow cruise of a police car approach from the distance. It stopped at traffic lights. She leapt forward, pushed past the screaming women, managed to armlock Steve's head and pulled him back sufficiently for the red-head to jump clear. 'Fucker!' the young woman screamed over and over, the tendons in her neck bulging with rage. The face still seemed strangely white behind a canopy of loose powder.

'Steve! Stop this at once!' Angela remonstrated. It was all she could do to hold onto him. The police car was drifting closer.

'Lemme go!' He tried to shrug her off but Angela could sense that a lot of the fight had gone out of him. He seemed strangely affected by the appearance of the redhead. She could sense the hot, bitter tears coursing around inside his head. The object of his desire or whatever it was he felt toward her, cast him a look of curdling contempt. She adjusted her pvc mini and spat a gob on the pavement. Angela realized that her own feet were dangling high up off the ground as both arms were still locked around Steve's neck. She didn't know whether or not to let go as the panda approached.

'Everybody shut up!' she cried. 'Not a word, Steve – okay? I don't want the police getting involved.'

Evidently the women didn't either because they clustered around again, not too close but close enough to nearly block Steve and Angela from view. They lit cigarettes and muttered among themselves. The redhead laughed then shot Steve a most peculiar glance. Angela couldn't quite sift through the mixed contents of scorn, anger, pity too and something else. Something quite unexpectedly soft. The panda glided past, a cop just throwing the girls a cursory glance, perfectly aware that this wasn't their turf so there was no need to move them on. Steve was working up to a series of howls, the prelude humming already at the back of his throat. Angela's arms were stretched to breaking point and she had to let go. She grabbed the back of his sweater instead.

'Nicola.' His voice was a hoarse whisper. 'Nicki!'

The redhead batted an eyelid. She was about to move on with the others when she thought better of it and approached him.

'Steve – how many times do I got to fucking tell ya? Keep away from me! I'm sick of your fucking following, okay? It's doing me head in. Piss off!'

'Who are you?' Angela asked.

'Mind your own, okay? Just keep him away from me.'

Steve reached out to touch her cheek and Nicola flinched as though scalded. Her eyes which Angela now saw were like two icy emeralds, shifted past his great head and locked onto hers instead. She delivered her warning in a voice that matched her irises.

'I mean it, you know. Or something really bad's going to happen.'

With that she turned on her spiky heel and sauntered away with the women who amassed in a protective shield around her skinny frame. One of them turned and gave Steve the finger. But he was concentrating only on the retreating Nicola, little gurgles erupting from his throat. Angela was at a loss. She still held onto his sweater just in case he loped after them but his body was visibly sagging. The fight punched out of him until the next encounter. That there would be a next was the one thing Angela could be sure of. She stepped around to block his view and pushed her face as close to his as she could reach.

'What?' she cried. 'What was all that about?'

No response. The head was taking a furious fisting. His lips twisted to prevent tears which lapped behind the eyelids.

'Steve?' Angela adopted her Mary Margaret voice. 'Who is she? Who's Nicola anyway?'

'My sister,' he replied hopelessly.

'Your *sister*.'

From the corner of her eye, Angela spotted Mary Margaret coming through the men's door. She fixed a smile on her lips

131

and nodded her head as though she was engaged in a deeply interesting conversation with Steve. Which was not the easiest thing to pull off, seeing as he insisted on gazing into the distance, snorting and knuckling to beat the band. Angela could sense the gimlet gaze before Mary Margaret sauntered up to them.

'That's great, Steve,' Angela said loudly. Her eyes silently begged him to play along but he couldn't see.

'What's great?' Mary Margaret asked with her tongue poking around her back teeth, looking from the women's door to Steve and back again.

'Steve here's been telling me how he took communion this morning, Mother. Isn't that right, Steve. *Steve?*'

'What? Oh yeah.' He ran a length of palm up under nostrils.

'Catholic, are we?' Mary Margaret sucked the other side of her back teeth.

Angela couldn't remember for the life of her what, if any, denomination was registered on Steve's chart details. He gave her a quick shifty look to let her know she was on shaky ground.

'Turning.' Angela smiled sweetly to the Superior.

'Uh-huh. It might be in your interest and the Church's interest God knows, Sister, to let this young man know that we take holy communion after we've "turned".'

'Oh yeah. He knows that now. I just told him.' Angela grabbed his elbow. 'Right then. We'll have that game of ludo so, Steve.'

She marched him off with the heat of Mary Margaret's eyes burning holes in her back. Steve loped beside her like a chimpanzee doing his daily performance. He broke away from her when they got inside and she assumed he was running off to his cluster. There was a group therapy session going on in the television room so Angela quickly took her place within the circle. Snores, farts and belches all around. A young counsellor was trying to prise his story from one of the new men. Some of them loved to talk. Most of them didn't. This particular Paddy fell into the latter category. A tight little walnut with

132

sleek black hair, no teeth and a crooked zip of flesh where his left eye should be. Angela noticed the fresh, ragged edges to one of his earlobes. No doubt recently chewed while he was stretched out in a drunken stupor by an old bench mate with a grudge. That was how the revenge system operated. An extra share of liquor, whatever was handy, an extra cigarette, watch, wait for your buddy to keel over. Then a broken bottle rammed in the eye or a chomp of an ear. No hard feelings after that. Just try not to be the one to keel over first, next time. Doubtless, Paddy was avoiding someone. The someone he'd glassed in return. He'd only last a couple of weeks at the shelter. Just a little recuperative sojourn before his head hit the concrete streets outside again.

But the group were bored. Anyone new who didn't want to give it up and essentially admit to how worthless and unenviable a human being he truly was, usually got hectored and bullied until he broke down and gave them what they wanted. A sort of initiation and acceptance rite, but mostly it passed the time. Once the goods were delivered little else was required. It was just a levelling thing really. Reassurance that they were in the gutter together.

Angela felt in need of the chapel so she excused herself quietly and left.

She entered, feeling as though she were going for a shower. The lies of the day were taking their toll. She felt impure and tainted and longed for the soothing simplicity of the little room. For flickering candles representing the wishes and desires of others. For light sifting through in coloured blocks from the stained glass window. The cool touch of polished wood where she would rest her cheek against the back of the pew ahead. For the Stations of the Cross carved along the walls depicting Christ's journey to Calvary. She would pray all the way with Him. Genuflecting at each Station and clasping her hands together tightly to help her concentrate on His suffering. If she could feel His pain, she would be purified. Made whole again

133

with a clear path set out in front of her. By the time she stood before the first Station – Jesus is condemned to death – she was already beginning to feel a little better.

A strange, harsh snuffling attracted her attention. It was coming from the wooden confessional at the back. With her head cocked to the side she approached cautiously. The peculiar choking sound increased. It couldn't be one of the men at Confession. There wouldn't be a priest around at that time of day. To be on the safe side, she checked through an open gap at the top of the middle door. Empty, as she'd figured. So it had to be emanating from the other side. Her hand snaked out for the knob and she pulled the door open quickly. Steve was huddled up inside. Knees pressed against his chest, hands wrapped around the hedgehog of his head. He glanced up quickly. Tears runnelled down his cheeks. His eyes pleaded with her to let him be and she nodded her assent, but first she trailed her fingers across his scalp. A quiet close of the door and she tiptoed down to the altar. She lit a candle for his intentions. And another for his sister, on impulse. She prayed for them. For Uncle Mikey. And for the men outside. Not knowing what she should pray for. The rank odour of unremitting hopelessness stung her nostrils. Steve's agonized weeping accompanied her Stations of the Cross and by the time she reached the final fourteenth wall panel – Jesus is placed in the Sepulchre – Angela was crying helplessly too.

Chapter Eight

Tiny golden thermometers streaked the sky where evening sun caught small jetstreams. Through the open french windows, Robert's garden sang with joyous colour. Orange and cream calendulas lifted their hopeful faces to the last shafts of full rich sunshine. Scarlet geraniums blazed in terracotta pots, the heads of the tallest blooms skimmed by full drooping heads of palest pink clematis. His cottage garden reflected how Robert would like to be – full, busy, bursting with life and colour. In love with itself.

A few doors along, someone was lighting a barbecue and the woody aroma drifted in and out through net curtains and yawning sash windows. Robert hummed happily as he squeezed the last lemon, and grated rind for lemon mascarpone tart. Louis Armstrong in the background assured him that it was indeed a wonderful world. The oil painting he should be surface-cleaning of various accretions stood on an easel covered by a thick white cloth in the front room. He hadn't done a thing to it for the last couple of days. He would be late in returning the Victorian flower piece to this particular collector who also happened to be a good and regular client and not someone you'd want to let down too often, but Robert didn't overmuch care at this precise moment. In fact, on a scale of one to ten, he cared about one and a half. Because lemon mascarpone tart cut out a good chunk of the best part of two days if you took into account the buying of the ingredients, the making of sweet pastry a day in advance and then the slow, slow whisking of the mixture to get it to just the right consistency without curdling the eggs.

He wanted it for Angela on Sunday. It was his best gift. She wouldn't know that of course but that wasn't the point. He would watch her bite into a zingy, creamy slice and he would know that he had made this for her. Bonnie received a whole tart for her birthday every year. When the mixture was ready, poured into the waiting pastry case, he let it set in the oven for five minutes before immediately transferring it to the fridge. The kitchen was alive with the bright astringent scent of lemons. The remote possibility presented itself that whoever she was committed to, could also and perhaps had also, offered this particular tart, but that was too remote to interfere with his overall feeling of wellbeing. He could resume work on cleaning the painting now. So he decided to go for a walk instead.

In fact he was feeling so good about himself and the world in general, he thought it just about the right time for a fellow to pay a visit to his mother. If not the only time. On his way out, he spotted Mrs Leitch from across the road scooting along full throttle on her motorized buggy. Robert didn't run errands for her any more since she'd acquired wheels but he wasn't entirely sure if this was a good thing or not. She drove like the escaped prisoner she was. Turning the buggy in through the gate and up to her front door had become a performance act. She kept missing the narrow entrance, reversing in a fury, zooming down once more, far too quickly, only to miss again. Never happy until neighbours were on the street, shouting offers of help which were met by her acrid scorn. She was a gnarled little thing with pink eyelids and cataracts like onions. Robert crossed over. Steeling himself for the ten-minute battle before she would allow him to gently steer her into the passageway.

'Go away!' she was screaming at him now. 'I can do it.'

'Fine.' He folded his arms and tapped a foot. Sometimes she gave in after five minutes. Reversing then shunting past the gate every time. Over and over. Refusing to listen to his reasoned argument that if she would only slow down long before the sharp turn right, she would get the hang of it. Maybe she enjoyed the sheer cussedness of the everyday drama. Fair enough, Robert thought, examining his fingernails. The roar of a cylindrical 767, low above their heads, drowned out her expletives. Robert followed its trajectory.

Wondering briefly about all the lives, all the hopes and dreams, that passed over his head. It still seemed strange to him that so many strangers could quite literally cross his path. They seemed so vulnerable up there in their tin can.

'All right. Guide me in.' Mrs Leitch obliged by an early yield. Her bony, brittle shoulders slumped in defeat.

Robert steered her to the front door: she gave him the key.

'You never get used to it. Growing old,' she said. He nodded, placing her shopping bag inside.

'You'll get the hang of it.'

'I'll be dead then. Not old.'

'The buggy I meant – anything you want me to do while I'm here?'

'What happened to that nice Sarah lady I used to see in and out of your place?' She screwed up withered petal eyelids to peer at him. Robert shrugged. *Sarah?* She was aeons ago.

'We broke up. Just one of those things. It was mutual.'

'So you always say,' she said balefully. 'I saw her leaving your house. She was crying. You shouldn't do that your ladies, Robert. It doesn't become you.'

Sarah crying? He wasn't sure if that was a good thing or a bad thing. He'd thought they'd just sort of slipped into an agreement. Not to go on. 'Why Sarah? Why now?' he asked, drawing her curtains for the evening and switching on the television. She could barely see but it did for company. She kept a copy of the *TV Times* on top with the programmes she was going to watch for the week, marked with red crosses. Double crosses for favourites.

137

'I don't know,' Mrs Leitch sighed. 'I wouldn't want you to be old and alone, I s'pose. It's no fun at all, like I say.'

'D'you want me to fix supper and sit with you for a while?' Robert was touched by the tremble of her lower lip. Not a relative in the world. It was a sad way to end your days.

'I met Mr Perfect once,' Mrs Leitch continued dreamily. 'I did. And you know what happened?'

'Tell me.'

'He was waiting for Miss Perfect too. And she wasn't me.' She flapped a hand at the door. 'I'll make my own supper, thank you very much. But I'll tell you the one good thing about being old – I can say what I like. So there.' Her jaw jutted out and she nearly ran over his toes as the buggy shunted further into the room.

Robert closed the door and sighed heavily. He walked on toward the river. Bonnie's boat listed gently from the constant wash of cruisers up and down the stretch of water. The penny-unblinking eyes of a grey heron fixed on him momentarily then looked away again. Chevron tracks glinted on the water's surface where the dying sun caught a duck family's trail. He could hear a loud peal of his mother's laughter through the narrow windows which lined the top of the houseboat. He wasn't so sure about a visit now after all. But she came to the door to throw scraps to the ducks and he was spotted. She waved and called him in.

Mr Gibson sat inside beside his overflowing ashtray. Robert had met him a few times over a long period of years. All of Bonnie's gentlemen friends were called Mr something or other. It was better than 'Uncle' Robert supposed. The boat was so confined it was difficult to avoid them when he was growing up. Though he did his best. But the sound of their laughter in the room next door to his, late at night, and the corresponding earthy chuckle from his mother, often made him fall asleep with his hands cupped over his ears. Even then, he knew that she was perfectly entitled. She was lonely. She was an attractive woman with plenty to offer – still it was a touch discomfiting every now and then.

'Hon, you remember Mr Gibson?' Bonnie poured him a shot of whiskey.

'Of course.' Robert sipped, sitting as far away from the man as was physically possible.

'Haven't seen your good self for the longest time,' Mr Gibson offered affably. As though they were old friends. He was a short, bald man with yellow teeth and two tan fingers from chainsmoking. The lines on his face were heavy, pendulous, so heavily scored that, from a distance, he appeared to be streaked with dirt. Even his eyeballs were sallow. The crumpled grey suit had concentric circles of old piss stains around the crotch. A travelling salesman. Chocolate bars, Robert gathered. Still, he wasn't unpleasant, except for the bray of a laugh which usually ended in spluttering coughs and sounded utterly insincere. Robert didn't know what to call him. 'Mr Gibson' sounded ridiculous and using a first name, whatever that might be, would lend the man a status, a familiarity, none of the other Misters had acquired.

'You're well?' Robert asked.

'As well as I deserve,' Mr Gibson thought that was very funny for some reason. He cackled, coughed, took a sip of whiskey to settle himself and lit another cigarette. Robert rolled his eyes, wondered how to get out of there as fast as might be deemed decent. The rolling eyes stopped at a sketch of Angela, framed and hung above the cast-iron brazier. Robert did a double-take. Her naked torso stretched up with her hands cradling the back of her head, the protuberant nipples elongated by the stretch. Just a whisper of dark pubic hairline where the woodframe met it. She was smiling, a touch dreamily like the pastel of the unknown woman in the V & A. But there the resemblance ended. He choked back a stinging mouthful of Jameson's.

'I took that one,' Bonnie was saying. 'You don't mind, do

you, hon? It's good. The best thing you've done in a long time.'

'You had no right –' Robert's protest was cut off by Mr Gibson's wander over to the portrait.

'She a friend?' He crooked a thumb and Robert felt sick with disgust at the knowing moue the man's mouth made.

'Sort of.'

'How come I never met her?' Bonnie shot in.

'You don't meet everyone I know,' Robert said testily. He moved to the brazier wall.

'Damn right I don't,' Bonnie sniffed. 'I'd remember her. Hey! Whatd'ya think you're doing there?'

Robert had almost elbowed Mr Gibson out of the way. He was reaching up for the frame. Practically wrenching it from the wall.

'This is my property, Bonnie. You can't just come and take whatever you like that belongs to me.'

'Oooh!' she mocked. 'So you *really* like her, huh? When do I get to meet her in the flesh?'

'So to speak,' Mr Gibson insinuated in that darkly toasted voice, buttered in catarrh.

Robert wanted to bop him one. But he fixed a tight smile instead, firmly placing the portrait under his arm.

'Ask. Before you take, Bonnie. Okay?'

She had the good grace to flush a little.

'She isn't anyone you're going to meet,' Robert continued in a softer tone. 'Just an acquaintance. I hardly know her to tell the truth.'

'Looks like you know –' Mr Gibson's cheesy grin collapsed at the searing glance Robert sent him. The man stubbed out the cigarette, hitched his shoulders up, looking around for his car keys.

'I'd better make tracks. Thanks for the drink, Bonnie. I'll swing by in a coupla weeks maybe?'

Bonnie walked him to the door. Which wasn't far. They chuckled something to one another and Robert felt his insides

140

tighten. That deep throaty sound brought back a flood of uncomfortable memories. The kind that knotted his large intestine. When Mr Gibson was gone, he downed the last swallow of his drink and made to leave also. Bonnie placed a hand on the picture frame. She was doing her let's be pals smile.

'C'mon, you can get this on the way back. Walk me for a while. It's still hot as hell. I get stir crazy in here. Aw c'mon, hon.'

Robert hesitated. On the one hand he really did feel quite cross with her. She would never learn the boundaries of his house. That was his place. Seperate from her. He had spent so much of his life trying to stop her looking inside his head, whatever was left inside there was pretty much concealed from himself now too. The little bits he did know, he had to protect. On the other hand, she was alone, just like Mrs Leitch. Abandoned or unwanted by Mr Perfect. His own father.

And it was a lovely evening and she did look pretty, smiling like that. He told her so. She flushed with pleasure, reaching up to kiss his cheek.

'C'mon,' she said. He left the picture and followed.

They walked in companionable silence for a while. Bonnie linked her arm through his. A white butterfly rested on her hair and she stood still until it moved on again. She giggled with her hand cupped over her mouth. When she laughed like that, her whole face opened like a flower. And Robert could instantly remember all the reasons why he loved her. By turn, instantly forgetting all the reasons he did not. Suddenly her face clouded over dramatically.

'I wouldn't want one of those,' she said.

'A butterfly?'

'No. Those.' She was pointing to a sleek silver cruiser gliding toward Twickenham Bridge. 'I'm happy with the boat I got. A big showy thing like that?' She jabbed an accusing finger. 'It's all bullshit.'

'Maybe the man who owns it just really likes boats.'

'Yeah, maybe. Tell you what's funny peculiar though – the older I get the more I'm coming round to thinking folks don't really want things for things at all. You know?'

'No. I don't know.' He instinctively felt this was somehow going to end up as a slight to him and screwed up his eyes to follow the boat's wake. Deeply interested in its progress.

'It's a syndrome. That's what it is.' Her brow was furrowed as she considered her words with care. Which was a rare enough occurrence.

'Ye-es?' Robert said cautiously.

'Well. The real buzz is other people wanting what you have. So it's not so much the thing. It's the wanting the thing. Other folks' wanting. Yeah?'

'There's some truth in that, I suppose,' Robert conceded, relieved that the subject wasn't directed at him after all.

'Starts in the goddam play-yard. Remember you and Peter? Always comparing. "I can piss higher than you. No you can't. Well my piss is liquid gold so nahh." If nobody looks at what you got – nobody wants what you got – where are you then? Nowhere is where,' she added, nibbing him in the end.

Robert opened his mouth to argue and saw where her sudden dark mood had sprung from. Peter and Anita were strolling toward them further along the towpath. They appeared to be arguing, Anita's hands making angry sweeping gestures. Then they spotted Robert and Bonnie and cleaved together with almost comical haste. Peter threw back his head as though laughing at something hilarious Anita had just said.

'See what I'm saying?' Bonnie's voice had taken on the low snarl she reserved for Peter. 'All front. That guy's chasing happiness so hard he wouldn't know if it bit him on the ass. He checks in the mirror. Compares what he's got to – you, say. Tells himself: 'Hey, I'm a lucky guy! Even if I am a greedy little porker got up like a dentist.' She let out a series of honks from the back of her throat.

'That's not – Bonnie, has it ever occurred to you, that you're the one who gets upset by Peter's success?'

'Do not!' she protested furiously. 'Don't matter a flying racoon's fart to me what the guy's got. It's the smug way he sidles up to you that gets on my tits. You should stand up to him more. Or sit on him a spell – like when you was kids.'

'Bonnie –'

'Listen up. Some day you'll get something he hasn't. Something maybe he'd kinda like to get. That'll put you in charge again, the boss again. You'll see what a pal he is then. You'll see.'

'Bonnie, if I live to be a hundred I'll never figure out how your mind works.'

'You got that right,' she winked. Fixed her lips into a sarcastically friendly smile at Peter and Anita's approach, adding out of the corner of her mouth, 'I'm always looking out for you, son. That's all you need to figure . . . Well lookee here – don't you two make a pretty picture?' She called across to the couple who were now inextricably wrapped around one another, Peter's face a study in uxorious fondness.

'Robert! Bonnie!'

'Peter! Anita!'

Bonnie clicked her tongue and turned away from the air kisses.

'What a lovely evening.' Peter stared around expansively. 'You do look well, Bonnie.'

'Yeah? Well, I am well.'

Peter hawhawed. Said – good good. In that peculiar accent he exaggerated around Bonnie. Over the years Robert had come to notice how his friend who spoke perfect Hounslow when they were boys, now appeared to deliberately keep his top lip pulled down low and tight over his teeth. The effect was to make his words sound slightly clipped and affected. Sentences ran together with little raised or lowered intonation. Which was of course a mark of lower-class speech. Emotional inflections were something to be derided, except for an occasional hearty snort or hawhaw which signalled still waters running very deep indeed. The other habit he'd adopted was to say 'oh right' over and over when listening to someone. It came out 'O-raht'. 'We had a damn good shoot last weekend.' 'O-raht.' Conversely, Bonnie became more American. And since she'd left at nineteen, never to return, her concept of the lingo was somewhat dated. Lots of gottas and wannas and heys. At times she sounded like an American putting on an American accent. Robert had even heard her say 'swell' one day. 'Groovy' couldn't be far behind.

Anita was studying the ground. Her eyes looked puffy, swollen, as though she'd been crying for a long time. Robert was surprised when she suddenly shot him a darting glance. The ticcy eye spasmed uncontrollably. She concentrated on concrete again. Peter and Bonnie were sparring around one another in their usual fashion. Usually it started simply enough, a couple of put-downs, a few sarcastic remarks until one of them grew impatient to draw blood. Bonnie patted Peter's growing paunch. She said nothing but her eyebrows lifted knowingly. He flushed. Laughed heartily. Patted it himself.

'Cost rather a lot of money this.' The old cliche. 'Good food. Too much of it maybe. Still, better than pizza every night eh, Bonnie?'

'Every other night, Petey,' she corrected, using the diminutive he loathed. 'Pizza or a fat, juicy burger. Don't take a lot to make me happy.'

'Aren't you the lucky one?' Peter gritted his teeth.

'Aren't I just?' Bonnie gave him a blistering smile, nudged Robert to move on again.

He was still staring at Anita, the sad expression on her face, while simultaneously trying to decipher the strange, recondite code that passed for exchange between his mother and his friend. One thing was clear, had always been clear from their childhood days, Peter both wanted to impress Bonnie, sought

144

her approval, yet also wanted to punish her for withholding that selfsame approval. Acting for all the world, Robert often thought, like a surrogate son. They were about to move on when Anita tugged his sleeve.

'Your girls keep on about this new friend of yours, Robert.' She always said 'your girls' like that, implying a degree of ownership which Robert was not averse to. 'What's her name again? Oh, Angela. That's it. She sounds – well – lovely. Talks funny, walks funny. Your girls say.'

'I don't know her all that well. Really.' Robert spotted the clamped jaw of his mother from the corner of his eye. She was staring beadily across the river. Peter picked up on her exclusion and homed in merrily.

'When did you say you'll bring Angela over for dinner?' He put an intimate spin on the name. Angela. Oh already he was so familiar with this stranger to Bonnie.

'We'll have to see, Peter. She has a very busy schedule. When I see her again, I'll ask, all right?'

'You see her often then?' Anita smiled with her head to the side.

Bonnie sucked her teeth noisily. Her foot tapped.

'Very rarely as it happens. Her long hours and so on . . .' Robert let his voice trail away.

'Remind me. What does she do again?' Peter cast a gleaming eye in Bonnie's direction. Her sucking and tapping had taken on an almost maniacal rhythm.

'Social Work. Something like that.' Robert patted his hands against his thighs. 'Right, then. Might as well get the last of the light. Let's go, Bonnie . . .'

'Lunch? Next Sunday, Robert?' Anita touched his arm again.

'I – I can't, Anita. 'Fraid I'm busy next Sunday.' Robert quickly moved on before anyone could ask what or who he was busy with. When he looked back to check on Bonnie, she was trailing after him, head down, muttering sourly to herself. He tried to quickly pull all the pieces together inside his head. All

145

the pieces of him. Sometimes he could gather them, erect a protective shield of fog and impenetrable mist, so that she couldn't get through – if she flashed. He felt a flash coming on. Coming, coming. Her face was twisting. She ran a couple of steps. He smiled seraphically at her. Although his eyes had taken on a stunned, opaque quality. The eyes of a dog waiting for a kick. He hummed a tuneless tune under his breath.

'This Angela person. She's what you're busy with on Sunday, right?'

'Oh, maybe. Nothing fixed yet.' He hummed harder.

'And she's the one in the drawing?'

'What? Oh, yeah. That's her.'

'Petey and Neety can meet her, huh? Not your own mother, though. I'm not good enough to meet her, I guess? Huh?'

'Look. What is wrong with you people –'

'You people? You *people?*' She shrieked across him. 'I'm not people. I'm your mother.'

'I'm not getting into this.' Robert hastened ahead. He didn't want to get angry because it cleared the protective mist inside his head. Carved a pathway for her. Best to stay blank, fuddled, impenetrable.

'You know your problem, Rob.' She was tripping after him, slightly breathless. 'Your problem is . . .'

He hummed so loud his throat ached. She caught his arm. He swung around unleashing the anger. Which was what she wanted. Licence to kill.

'Whatever is bugging you – don't say it. I don't want to hear. You'll only have to say sorry afterwards and that's not good enough any more. I'm tired of sorry. I'm tired of being your punch bag whenever it suits you. And I'm sick to the back teeth of everyone's ridiculous interest in my private affairs. Who I see and who I don't see is entirely my own business. Got that?' He shrugged his arm free. On impulse, decided against the walk, turned back on the towpath, toward home.

'Oh I got it all right!' She called after him. 'Loud and clear,

Buster. You're gonna drop this Angela so fast we don't even get to meet her. Just like all the others. Great, just great.'

'You don't know anything about her. And that's the way I want to keep it,' he called over his shoulder.

'Oh yeah . . . ?' She trotted faster. He felt it coming, coming. The final flash. It was on its way. Winging toward him. An Exocet. He hummed. Tried to go blank again. But the sound of its whistle carried through air and space. Her mouth was open behind him. He knew. He just knew.

'Keep pushing them away, Rob. Yeah sure. Go on. This Angela's another angel, huh? Poor girl don't know how quick her wings'll be clipped. Second she starts being a real human being.'

Robert stepped up his pace. Infuriated, her mocking voice hollered at full pitch.

'Poor baby don't wanna fall in love with a real person. Oh no. All that messy schmessy goo they leave behind. When they go . . . *Just like Mr Fielding*. Huh?'

Bullseye.

Too late to close her passageway to his head now. She always got there in the end. Bingo. The eagle had landed. Uncle Sam had won the day. And the township of Robert was well and truly gadzooked, Nagasakied and nuked. He tucked his hands crossways under each armpit. His head listed forward, while he carried on home with his chin resting on the blade of his chestbone.

Poverty, chastity and obedience. The three vows Angela would undertake when her novitiate was finally through. The first was easily taken care of, in that she lived on the meagre allowance given to her monthly from the communal funds. She dealt in cash, no question of a cheque book. Or credit card. It was pocket money really, but if she needed something for work or for personal reasons, she could make the request in her quarterly budget which all the younger nuns had to forecast. The elders took whatever was given to them and usually gave most of it away to charity anyway. Mary Margaret monitored the budgets. And the money came from the Church, the State and fees they could accrue from any outside activities such as fund-raising and teaching or counselling services. All in all, the State got a very cheap deal. The shelter building was owned by the nuns. But they ran it on a pittance.

Aside from the more than considerable day-to-day involve-ment in the shelter, the younger nuns like Angela held literacy classes, ran youth clubs, bereavement groups. Then they were seconded to schools in the Boroughs, single-mother associ-ations, any group that ended with the suffix 'anonymous', and care in the community hostels. Any given week was full to overload.

Which helped considerably with the second vow. Chastity was all right if not a downright requisite when your schedule barely allowed for sleep, never mind sex. Or so it had always seemed to Angela. Until these irritating dreams about Robert had entered her subconscious. At least she figured they had to be something to do with him. Since they met last at the Museum, she kept dreaming that she was some kind of animal. It was the strangest feeling. She would wake all hot and sweaty to find herself still groaning inchoately, her head buried in the pillow with her ass stuck somewhere up near the ceiling. And on Wednesday she found herself so tightly wound up in the bed-sheets from the height of writhing, she could barely extricate her own legs. Chastity was a difficult one. And would remain so until the blood congealed in her veins and she took to wearing a sheath of holy medals as Sr Oliver did, like badges of honour. Her fantasies were really quite disturbing. On Thursday night during Benediction she found herself pressing the tops of her thighs together and thinking about . . . Oh God . . . No. She just couldn't think about *that*.

As for obedience. Well. She was just about to blow that one. Again.

Sr Carmel was getting a bollocking. In front of several of the men. It was not a pretty sight watching the elderly nun's spindly legs tremble and her little wren's jaw wobble uncontrollably. Mary Margaret was only getting started.

'You changed the bleddy sheets? And they on not even this last two weeks? Where is your head, Sister – where is it?'

Behind Sr Carmel's quaking figure stood the object of the Superior's ire. A full laundry skip of soiled sheets. It took all her energy just to pull it. The men's sheets were due for change once a month. She had whipped off this particular batch within two weeks and left a clean, pressed pair on every bed in every cluster. Angela knew that sometimes Sr Carmel got sidetracked in her measure of weeks. Not to mention years. It was no big crime. But Mary Margaret couldn't see it that way. As she ranted, nostrils flared around her. Men who could say nothing because they knew their worth, which was precisely nil nada zilcho, could only steam silently in favour of Sr Carmel, their adored cherub, or distil noisy, impotent harumphs from their collective nostrils. George the doctor pawed the ground with one foot like a frustrated stallion.

'Is it some clip of a hotel you think we're running here, Sister, or what?' Mary Margaret fumed. 'I mean, in the name of good God and his blessed mother and all the holy saints belonged to him – where is your fecking head sometimes? Hah? I'm going to take a good long look at your duty roster and so I am. And I'll be taking you off certain things and that's for sure.'

Sr Carmel's eyes misted over. A lump of bonbon stuck out under her cheek. She couldn't summon up the interest to suck it now. There were so few things left that she could actually handle physically any more, depriving her of further duties was like a kick in the teeth.

'My fault, Mother.' Angela heard her own voice before she knew she was going to speak.

The gimlet gaze fixed upon her.

'I got mixed up in the rota. Didn't I, Sister Carmel?'

'Ah no, love, you didn't, sure it was my own mistake –' Sr Carmel began, noisily slurping the accrued bonbon juices in her mouth. But Angela talked across her before she could continue.

'D'you remember, Sister? We were talking about this and that what needed doing – only yesterday it was – and I seem to recall saying something about the sheets. I'm sure I did.'

Sr Carmel's brow knitted. There could be truth in that. Conversations of yesterday were not always the clearest things in her mind.

'So I've you to thank for the extra laundry bill.' Mary Margaret's chest swelled with righteous indignation. Lord but it was so much sweeter giving a bollocking to a younger woman. Huuugely satisfying. Her mouth twisted with the vast choice of invective that presented itself. She didn't have time to make her selection before Angela shot in, hiding a quick wink to Sr Carmel.

'So it'll have to be my roster you take a look at, Mother, instead.'

Mary Margaret's eyes narrowed. She knew a snookering when she saw one. Angela's commitments were already stretched to back-breaking point. To relieve her of any duties would mean that the Mother Superior would have to take them on board her good self. The older nuns were too unreliable, not to mention knackered.

The watching men nearby didn't have a clue what was going on but they could sense a slight hesitancy on the Superior's part. A turning of the tables in Angela's favour somehow, and ultimately this meant in Sr Carmel's favour. Mary Margaret tapped fingernails against her teeth. She eyed the laundry skip, gave Angela one flinty glance which promised retribution sometime in the future but for now she was conceding defeat.

'I'll let it go. This once. But them men'll lie on the new sheets an extra two weeks now. Have you got that?'

Angela nodded meekly. As she passed Sr Carmel, she noticed with satisfaction that the elderly nun was once more sucking happily on her sweet. Angela stepped out from the shelter and swallowed mouthfuls of air. She was up against Mary Margaret on a daily basis or so it seemed these days. There was little doubt in her mind that these mini contretemps were merely preludes to the inevitable showdown which couldn't be far off. There would be only one survivor. One nun left standing. And Angela wasn't even a nun. Yet. The missions receded further with every passing minute.

She plunged her hands into her jeans' pocket and headed for the women's shelter, still brooding on her nebulous future. A gaggle of women passed her on the stairwell, clearly dressed for business. One of them giggled and blew a stream of smoke in Angela's face. It wasn't ordinary tobacco but she ignored them and made her way to Nicola's door. The women's rooms differed from the clusters in that there were paper-thin walls and doors instead of curtains. The walls ended before the ceiling so that the effect was like rows of toilet cubicles, and the actual rooms themselves weren't much bigger either. She knocked. Timidly at first, harder when there was no response. But she could sense a presence behind the door. It was yanked open suddenly, Nicola's face twisting with annoyance. She'd been anticipating one of the other women and her irritation turned to surprise. The emerald eyes looked so young without the black Cleopatra rim. Angela reckoned she was much younger than she'd previously figured. Definitely not in her twenties yet. The naked vulnerability of her face without make-up was quite disconcerting. A little like seeing a plucked chicken for the first time.

'What do you want?' she rasped, quickly glancing over Angela's shoulder to see if Steve accompanied her.

'Can I come in, Nicola?' Angela said. 'I'm on my own if that's what's bothering you.'

'Fuck sake,' Nicola muttered with a sneer, as if there were very few things in life that could bother her. She stepped back with ill grace to allow Angela through.

'You were worried that I might've brought Steve with me,' Angela said softly. Trying to find her angle into this conversation. If that's what it could be called, because the hostile stance and slitted eyes of her reluctant interlocutor didn't exactly promise much in the way of idle banter. Nicola was sizing her up, from head to toe, which didn't help. She plucked a wad of gum from her mouth, pressed it under the narrow metal bed, lit a cigarette and sat sullenly waiting for Angela to say something so that she could throw her out. Angela smiled nervously, indicated a chair, might she sit? Sullen nod. Might she hand the ashtray to Nicola? Sullen nod. Silence.

Nothing on the walls. Usually they gave some clue to the occupant's history. Posters or photographs, something that Angela could point to and ask about. A way in. No books or magazines to act as prompts. None of the usual clothes draped across every surface. She was scanning the tiny room with a growing sense of desperation. It was an impersonal cell and no more. Nicola smoked and continued to eye her in contemptuous silence.

'I have a couple of fags at night. In my room.' Angela winced at her own clumsy let's be buddies attempt.

'Don't tell us – your one vice?'

Nicola's eyebrows were lifted in utmost disdain. She folded her arms. The power was all hers. Angela's uncomfortable gaze settled on an elaborate array of bottles and tubes containing every type of make-up, face cream and lipstick imaginable. Expensive brands, top of the range, doubtless nicked. This was the one solitary clue to Nicola. She liked make-up. It wasn't a lot to go on but Angela took a deep breath and plunged ahead. She was here to find out about Steve, and the only way forward was to find out about Nicola.

'Great collection you have,' she said, idly fingering the various bottles. 'I'd love to wear make-up.'

There was a flicker of something like interest at that. Nicola could barely absorb the concept of a woman who didn't paint her face. She inhaled deeply, blowing out a stream that made Angela's eyes sting.

'Can't cos you're a nun?'

'Not really. I mean we could wear make-up if we wanted, I suppose.'

'What'd be the point though?' Nicola examined a strand of red hair, flicked it back over her shoulder again. She was looking at Angela as if she were a strange, pathetic breed of insect.

'Well, I don't know,' Angela faltered. 'A woman might just do it for herself, mightn't she?'

Nicola made a scoffing sound. Long painted talons clittered over bottles of varnish and upright sticks of lip gloss.

'I could do you. If you wanted.' A smile almost escaped. 'Yeah. That'd be a first. My first fucking nun.'

'Nicola. Be fair. Don't deliberately use that sort of language when I'm sitting here. Please.'

'Did I ask you to sit there? Did I?' Nicola rasped, quick as a flash. The green gaze was full of silent challenge once more. Angela sighed inwardly. Nicola was one of those nuts you'd never crack. The layers of shell were adamantine at such a young age. By thirty, if she survived the streets intact, she would look like ploughed concrete. For now her face was pretty enough in a pointy, angled sort of way. She had one top incisor missing which lent her a piratical quality. A vixen of the high seas.

'It'd be grand if you'd do my face one day though,' Angela tried, feeling her way again.

'Here – gimme.' Nicola stubbed out the cigarette, summoned Angela's hand with an impatient flutter of her own red claws. Placing the offered hand palm down on the little rickety table, Nicola unscrewed a bottle of pink glittery lacquer and began to apply it fastidiously to each nail. Her tongue poked out of the corner of her mouth. Concentrating hard. When she had finished, allowing Angela a chance to admire the neat work, she summoned the other hand.

153

'That looks really nice, Nicola. Not one blotchy bit on any nail.'

Nicola kept her head down, applying herself to the other hand.

'S'wat I do, innit?' She almost smiled again. 'One day I'll get me own parlour – well clinic, like. I do most of the women here. That's who I thought you was. At the door there. One of 'em. Wanting their faces doing. I'll be fuc – I'll be damned if I do 'em for nothing for always,' she added on a bitter note. Thought sounded like fought and nothing was nuffink.

'But they're good for practice.' Angela smiled.

'That's it, yeah. Got to practise on someone, don'tcha?' There was a pause as she pressed down on Angela's cuticles with a look of scorn. 'You need your cuticles looking at too. If I do your face I'll go over 'em as well. Soak first though. Soften 'em up.'

'I'll do that.' Angela wondered if Nicola herself had softened up enough for her to shoot in a question or two. But she was surprised when the girl got to her first.

'It don't do to let yourself go, you know. Even for a nun. How come is that anyways?'

'I didn't realize I was letting myself go,' Angela responded, slightly miffed. 'How come is what?'

'The nun malarky. What's your problem? Raped, was you?'

'I was not.' Angela retorted with indignation.

Nicola shrugged. Fine, okay, whatever. No odds to her. She was just making conversation. And it occurred to Angela that she herself was making some assumptions here. She was assuming the right to ask the questions, to lead the enquiry. She hadn't really been interested in anything Nicola had to offer other than as a means to get to the subject Angela wanted to get to. Namely Steve. The high moral ground subsided a little under her feet. She decided to start again. So she bunched up her knees, wrapping her arms around them and began to tell Nicola the history of the Aunts and Uncle Mikey and her dream of the missions. Nicola nodded from time to time while applying foundation, powder and blusher to her own face, the trademark Cleopatra kohl around the emeralds, lip liner followed by the shiniest gloss Angela had ever seen.

She noticed a black enamel box with a padlock on a shelf under the table. For jewellery she assumed, seeing a key on a chain around Nicola's neck. Her gaze was distracted again by Nicola's almost violent throwing of her head forward to brush the red locks with fast, frenetic strokes, tossing it back with an upward sweep again until it billowed out like a burnished cloud. They finished almost simultaneously. Angela her story and Nicola her transformation. A little silence ensued. Angela cleared her throat.

'Thing is – you see, Nicola – your brother, Steve, well, he reminds me of Uncle Mikey in a funny kind of way. Don't ask me why. It's the way his head goes to the side like this – or the hurt look he has, like he'd say things if only he could but he can't. Something puts me in mind at any rate. And – and, I'd like to – if I could at all, you know, help him. If I could. At all.'

Her voice trailed off. Nicola was smacking her lips in the mirror. She shot Angela a green glance.

'How "help" him?'

Angela shrugged. It was a very good question. Nicola efficiently screwed the tops back on all the bottles. Shunted the lipliner back into its sheath. Shut the powder compact with a resounding smack. A quick lightning nudge to the black box, out of sight, indicating that she'd caught Angela's curious glance. She swivelled around.

'Could be said I help people, too.' The incisor gap was revealed by a wide cheesy grin. 'Punters like. Give 'em a bit of relief. Same as you.'

'You don't have to work the streets, Nicola,' Angela protested, sounding ridiculously prim to her own ears but she wasn't about to buy into this stale old logic she'd heard a

155

thousand times before from the women on the game. It was just too crass and simplistic this nun versus prostitute thing.

'No?' Nicola's eyes were flashing. 'Says who? You? Blessed Mary ever Virgin?'

'Oh.' Angela interjected, taken aback. 'You and Steve *are* Catholics then?'

'Am I fuck,' Nicola spat. But the green eyes were glittering with amusement. 'Look, sister, or whatever you call yourself, I don't come on your turf tellin' you not to be a nun, now do I?' Her eyebrows raised inquiringly. Angela could only nod and look at the door in misery. Expecting to be shown it any second now. 'What it is is,' Nicola continued, in the reasoned voice of a tutor instructing a pupil. 'How'm I supposed to get my own beauty clinic otherwise?' Ovverwise.

'I don't know. How do other people do it?'

'Cos they got someone looking out for 'em, don't they? I know who looks out for me. Oh yeah. I work my own patch, got my own set room to take the Johns to. I pay nothing to no one, no greasy Tom taking chunks outta what I make. Kip down here where I'm safe from the likes of them vultures. And I don't do drugs like most of 'em here. Don't nearly drink. Vodka every now and then maybe. Mostly with a punter, like. Got it all sussed. Two, three years tops, I'll be wearing a white coat with me own business. So don't gimme shit, okay?'

'Okay,' Angela said meekly. 'So where does Steve figure in this plan?'

'He don't.'

'He seems to care about you a good deal,' Angela persevered. Nicola curled her lips in disgust. There was something about her putative rags to riches story that didn't ring quite true for Angela. Something she couldn't put her finger on exactly. Or maybe it was just the way Nicola related it. As if by rote. It was just too pat, yet another cliche, the tart on the make, pulling herself up in the world by the elastic of her knickers. Angela knew full well that one of the ironies of this place and places like it was that, in order to get the bed, the cluster, the room, the flat, you had to spin a good story. Not that whoever was listening didn't see right through it and know by turn that the drinking wouldn't really cease, the girls wouldn't stop plying their trade, the lies wouldn't stop. Bollocks and lies. It was just that there had to be some criteria – and a decently-executed yarn was as good a place to start as any. Anything which contained a permutation of 'I'm going to do' as opposed to 'What I've done' was always welcome in every hard luck story. Nicola was on the make all right, but Angela figured she hadn't heard what the young woman was really making for. That was between Nicola and Nicola. There were several of them in that one skinny frame, Angela didn't labour under any illusions there. You didn't get to be that tough with just one persona.

'Look, Nicola.' Angela leaned forward, trying to catch her eye. 'He's forever hanging around this place. A while back I had the devil of a job trying to get him to calm down and stop hurting himself. He was smashing his head something fierce against a wall. And it all comes down to him just wanting to be near you or talk to you or whatever. Couldn't you give him a few minutes, hmm? A little chat. Keep the peace.' Angela's eyes were nearly popping out of their sockets with the effort of her appeal. But Nicola brushed her eyebrows into feathery peaks, clearly unmoved.

'He's a psycho, innit? Pure and simple. Always been at that. Hurting hisself.'

'Don't you care any bit at all?' Angela couldn't help herself. 'He's your own brother, for pity's sake.'

'Oh for – don't gimme that crap. Does me fucking head in. Listen to me, wouldya – he's nothing to me. Not any more. I been trying to get away from the freak for years.' She turned, seriously angry now. Angela's head yanked back, the malevolent glare in Nicola's eyes was quite disturbing. The hairbrush went flying across the room. 'Prick follows me everywhere. Every dosshouse, every skip – I wake up one morning and there

157

he is. Knucklin' that stupid fucking head of his. Duh.' She did a fairly creditable mimickry of him, adding an open, drooping mouth and two limpid, lifeless eyes. It made Angela very uncomfortable. The look on Nicola's face was exactly the mindless lovelorn expression she'd seen him casting the women's shelter as he mooched around waiting for a glimpse of his sister.

'Does he have anyone else?' Angela asked softly, hoping to defuse the situation but Nicola appeared to be working herself into a frenzy. The twisting contortions of her narrow little face were not a pretty sight.

'Like who?' Nicola snapped incredulously. 'Only ever been the two of us. Me and the spaz. So help me God if he blows it for me this time I'll . . .' She checked herself. Fixed her face into a bland, cold mask once more.

'Blows what for you, Nicola?' Angela asked in a quiet voice.

Nicola dissembled, as she lit another cigarette her fingers quivered slightly.

'Nothing.' Nuffink. She inhaled with piston force and a nasty smile peeled back lip gloss. 'See? He gets to me. Gets right to me. I can't be doing with that, can I? Else I might turn out like yerself – a bloody nun or something.' Sumfink.

'Howd'you figure that one?' Angela asked.

'Well –' Another suck down to her toes. Angela was beginning to feel Mary Margaret was with her in every room. 'Well – wanting to help people and the like. Thinking Steve is another Uncle whashisname? What a load of – you're just scared intcha?'

'Am I?' Angela froze. She was the one supposed to be doing the analysis here. Already she'd conjured up their case histories. Abandoned by their mother, no father probably, a series of less than adequate children's homes, probably a few brutal foster homes along the way as well. The usual sad hotchpotch of misery. Doubtless a fairly unhealthy dose of sexual abuse thrown in as well. And the piteous vision of a brother wanting to hold onto the one thing that he could call his own. His sister. She rose to leave.

'I'm sorry I bothered you, Nicola. I'll leave you alone from now on. I was just worried that my Superior would catch Steve hanging around here and – oh well – if she slings him out she slings him out. There's not a lot I can do to stop her.' She had her hand on the doorknob, feeling utterly deflated.

'She's thinking of doing that?' Nicola's eyes had slitted again. 'No, wait! She throws him out he's going to be here, on my doorstep night and day. I'll never get rid of him. That'd well screw me over.'

'How d'you mean?' Angela's fingers were curling around metal, she was already out of there mentally but Nicola's eyes were flitting; she was reckoning something up. The talons summoned Angela again, indicated the chair.

'Sit, wouldya?' The green eyes looked tortured. Nicola was clearly wrestling with something that caused her great pain. Angela sat, knees pressed together, hands folded neatly on her lap.

'What is it, Nicola?' she encouraged, gently.

Nicola took several deep breaths. She pressed her hand against a bony indent in her chest and began to tell her story. Essentially, she was giving it up.

An hour later, Angela shifted position. Tears glistened in her eyes. Her entire body ached with cramp. She had been afraid to make the slightest movement while Nicola spoke. It was the usual sink of human misery and degradation all right. But it transpired that Nicola had a gift for articulacy which painted a strikingly clear picture of two young siblings in a morass of childhood quite beyond their control. The young woman's voice cast plangent echoes of loss around the room. Loss of parents, home, continuity, a place to start from, a place to head toward. Their lives were in constant flux, moved from one children's home to another once Steve had started acting up. Eventually no one could do anything with him but Nicola. By the age of

159

ten, she had become, in effect, his sole mentor. Keeping Steve in check became her full-time occupation. She wasn't allowed to go anywhere without him tagging along. His very presence in a room began to exhaust her. The weight of him. The responsibility. Angela thought of Uncle Mikey at that point and began to see why Steve had put her in mind of him. That was it exactly. The weight of Uncle Mikey had always pressed down upon her shoulders. Even from afar. He was always there, like the Aunts' chorus in her head.

Nicola's dull monotone eschewed self-pity. She kept her eyes trained on her bottles of make-up, occasionally flittering the shiny talons across the tops, as if they were touchstones representing some strange security that only she could understand. Perhaps they were the only constants in her life so far, apart from her brother. Perhaps, Angela surmised, they were the face Nicola could put on, the face she could rely on when everything behind the painted veneer was in such a sorry state of confusion and turmoil.

Gradually, as she continued, Angela increasingly began to warm to her. It wasn't right that children should have it so hard. They weren't equipped to deal with such deprivation. Christmastime was always the hardest. When they would compare their lot with other children. And know that what they had long suspected, occasionally resisted, but finally absorbed – was in fact the bald naked truth. They were utterly expendable. Surplus to requirements. Detritus. Nothing – nuffink – was the word Nicola used.

A chance came along for Nicola. She was fostered out to a couple who doted on her. They had lost their own little girl some years before and were too old to be considered for adoption. They lived in a big red-brick house on a sunny street off Clapham Common. They were kind and gentle and took over her education. After a year, Nicola was blossoming under their increasingly fond attention. Steve remained at the children's home. No one would foster him, too much trouble – Nicola

160

visited him at weekends. It broke her heart leaving him behind every time but there was little she could do for him. And the truth was that no matter how guilty she felt, the sense of relief, of having him off her shoulders, outweighed her sadness. All was sunshine in Clapham. She had become what she had always wanted to be – somebody's little girl. To all intents and purposes they had adopted her and she had adopted a new personality. Her first Christmas at that house was something Nicola would remember for the rest of her life.

Likewise, her second. Steve was rushed to hospital with wrists slashed so deeply he'd even nicked bone. He could not get through another Christmas holiday without his sister. And the pressure on her shoulders returned with a vengeance. The foster couple were sympathetic. They visited Steve with her, tried to incorporate him somehow in their tight triangle but Steve couldn't find a corner to fit. Finally, Nicola begged them to take him into the sunny house. They were reluctant but their fondness for their new daughter made them decide to have a try. It ended in disaster with Steve banging his head one night against their livingroom wall, spraying blood all over their cream fixtures. He was too institutionalized by then to settle in red brick without bars on the windows. His behaviour grew so erratic and violent, they had to send him back. And after the next suicide attempt, Nicola sadly joined him. Life with the couple was never the same after Steve's sojourn. She felt they'd grown colder toward her, distanced themselves as a means of self-protection. The trouble was, a taste of her brother had reminded them, in very vivid fashion, that Nicola had her own history. And it wasn't theirs.

The siblings were moved to another children's home, ostensibly to make a fresh start, but in reality because it was time to move Steve on again. It was as if the homes took turns with him. And this was the hardest place they'd been sent. Nicola didn't even have her own shadow any longer, Steve always stood across it. She had just reached puberty when the first rape occurred. One of the male outworkers. She didn't tell anyone then. Didn't tell anyone when the second rape took place. When Steve was dragged in the middle of the night from the boys' compound to watch, she told. And nobody listened.

By then, Steve was just a ball of inarticulate rage. No one bothered to investigate Nicola's story. She was considered a capricious piece of work with her face made up like a Barbie doll and skirts up to her panty line. Everyone knew that some of the older girls were charging for it anyway. Resigned to the fact that they might as well. Nicola learned a lot of lessons around that time. Not least that she had something which could earn money. But not enough. So she ran away at fifteen. And Steve followed, tracking her to a squat in East London. After a while, she wasn't running from the home any longer, she was running from Steve. Because she could not, no matter how hard she tried, expunge the memory from her mind – of his eyes watching. Bound to a chair, Steve was being taught his lesson as one man held Nicola down and the other entered without permission. Steve was being taught that if he didn't behave, harm would come to his sister. He was duly warned. In so many words. And never spoke of the incident again.

But his eyes haunted Nicola. They still haunted her. And he'd found her again.

'Oh, Nicola,' Angela could only say. She reached across to press Nicola's flat little fish hands into her own, but the young woman drew back with a sharp intake of breath. As if gentle touch would singe her. Her mouth twisted to the side. Under some irresistible compulsion, she reached for the gloss and lavished both lips in a mechanical back and forth fashion. With her mouth open wide, lips curling over her teeth, her voice was muffled.

'I can't be with him, see?' Wiv 'im. 'Does me head in.'

'I'll see what I can do – I'm not sure if there's anything.' Angela faltered. 'But I'll try to keep him away if that's what you want.'

162

'That's what I want.' Nicola looked up from the mirror. Her glittering eyes bored through Angela.

Angela nodded. She turned to leave and on a hot rush of impulse, swung around and squeezed Nicola's torso in a tight embrace. She knew the young woman couldn't bear to be touched at this moment but she couldn't resist the urge. She wanted Nicola to know that her terrible story could still touch someone's heart in a world where Nicola only ever saw the same story or similar, on every face of every woman she made up at the shelter. The gaunt little frame beneath Angela's fingers tightened, fistlike, at first, then gradually subsided into the embrace.

'I'll go now.' Angela straightened once more. Pressing the bridge of her nose to stem the tears that threatened. 'I'm so sorry, Nicola. For bothering you. Oh for all of it. I'm so sorry.'

Angela spun around and shot through the door before Nicola could see the flood coursing down her cheeks. She in turn, did not see the tight little smirk which curled up the corners of Nicola's super-glossed mouth.

Chapter Nine

Mary Margaret was all dressed up for an evening out when Angela returned. That constituted the wearing of her navy jacket over the perennial navy skirt. A starched white blouse with oversize collar wings from the seventies, white pvc clutch bag and God help us, Angela rolled her eyes, white slingbacks bought that morning, worn with black 20-denier tights. Only Mary Margaret could find white slingbacks these days. She was hopping nervously from foot to foot, waiting for someone to come out of the toilet. The other young man who was to accompany her this evening stared up at the ceiling wearing an expression not dissimilar to every holy picture of Saint Sebastian Angela had ever seen. Where the saint was being arrowed to death. Mary Margaret suddenly shot back into her office, practically braining herself in the process with a sweegee from the unaccustomed heels. Resounding slam of the door after her. Several quick snifters no doubt. To get her through the needful.

Angela had recognized the young fellow from his time at the shelter nearly a year ago now. The man emerging reluctantly from the toilet was also an old occupant of a cluster. They both had community housing flats now. Or bedsits of some order. They had been summoned to accompany the Mother Superior to some borough do or other where she was to receive a commendation from the Bishop and Lady Mayoress for her doughty efforts in getting the housing project completed. They could hardly say no. Angela offered them a sympathetic smile which was met by an involuntary groan from one of them. They were both staring at the ceiling now.

Mary Margaret emerged once more. The back of her hand swiped across her mouth. She was beside herself with nerves. Here she was head honcho, the queen of all she surveyed, the top of the heap – out there, she was just another fat woman in a navy suit with a neat line in bristling moustache. Her chunky calves stood about two feet apart the better to keep her balance on the silly heels.

'Right.' She took a deep breath. 'Tell me again what ye say if His Grace throws ye a word?'

'We owe it all to Mother Mary Margaret.' They chimed in unison.

'Right.' The knuckles desperately clutching the unfamiliar bag were white with strain. Angela almost felt pity for the woman. Almost.

The sorry little expedition party made their way out into the ether and Angela still had one thousand and twenty three tasks to perform before the evening was through. Then there would be the paperwork with her three cigarettes the thought of which recalled Nicola forcefully once more and she felt such a spear of intense pity she needed to check on Steve. He was watching or not watching, mindlessly adhering a glazed gaze to the television. He looked up when she entered. She couldn't think of anything to say so she patted his head like a dog and left to get on with her work.

Hours later, practically bent with exhaustion, she made her way to the chapel. Sometimes she had the feeling that God wasn't a person or a being at all, God was a place. It was a construct she had never dared voice to the Aunts or any Superior when they all knew perfectly well that God was a man, ancient as time, with a golden crook and a fierce long beard. But when she felt particularly tired or emotional or the Aunts were fizzing in a frenzy inside her head, she saw God as a safe place. Safe, soothing and neutral. Like the chapel.

Sr Oliver was praying in a back pew. Beating her breast which made the medals tinkle, which was of course the intention. Sr Oliver liked to be noticed when she was being devout. There wasn't much point in being the most pious person in God's universe unless somebody observed. The hunched little figure of Sr Carmel sat up front with her veiled head pressing down on a pew back. Probably taking a tiny kip, Angela figured. In contrast to Sr Oliver, Sr Carmel did her praying so quietly she might well be asleep. Often, she was.

The Aunts were restless tonight. Angela couldn't make out their incoherent mutterings and mumblings. The only thing she could discern with any clarity was the customary censorious strain that coursed through every bleat. She wasn't doing anything right. Would never do anything right. Look at the way they'd brought her up and look at the way she was turning out – rudderless, indecisive, at odds with her Superior. Auntie Bridie could have told her that was the sure way to wreck and ruin. There were those who should obey and those who gave the orders. Simple enough. Why couldn't she learn? If only she could shut them up, just once, she might be able to think straight. Perhaps a psychiatrist or some such might be able to help.

But what to say? I've Aunts in me head and they're driving me nuts?

Only thing was – if they ever could be driven out – what would she replace them with? They had formed her every opinion, her every ambition. They had moulded her into the quintessence of their every thwarted desire. Auntie Bridie bestrode any Mary Margaret like Boadicea herself. No contest. She might be a doddery old poodle with bunions now but in her heyday she was as formidable as a Rottweiler with a growl that was twenty times more persuasive. And now what with all that going on in one part of Angela's brain cells, the abject creature that was Steve reminding her of her duty to get Uncle Mikey out of that bloody attic and the adventitious rise of Robert in the whole scheme of things – she was fit to bust. The prospect of seeing

166

him again so soon, on Sunday, made her stomach join in the tempestuous cacophony of her head. Still, if all she had to do was just sit there, it might turn out to be a very restful process. *Hah!* shrieked Aunt Bridie.

Sr Oliver ostentatiously creaked her calcified bones upright, gasping at every turn just in case the young novice was in any doubt as to the level of pain she had to endure in order to kneel in the first place. Several groans of exquisite torture as the shaky limbs went down to genuflect, not once begod but twice. Angela held the door open as Oliver gave her a smile of deepest torment.

''night, Sister,' Angela said cheerfully.

'Goodnight, dear one,' Oliver offered with an airy wave of her hand. 'Be so good as to pray that I might sleep, Sister. I am sorely in need of a good night's rest.'

Sorely in need of a boot up the arse more like, Angela had the uncharitable thought, but she smiled sympathetically with her head to the side. Knowing full well where Oliver was headed – off to the kitchen to make her usual nightly raid – two Penguin bars, a packet of Quavers and a cup of chocolate Horlicks. As for the lack of sleep, she'd be snoring like a bull within thirty minutes flat. The rumblings from her bedroom often cut into Angela's meagre allowance of sleep.

Sr Carmel pitched sideways in her pew at the front. She awoke with a start and looked around as if checking where she was. Angela padded down and sat beside her. They remained in companionable silence for a while. Angela put her clasped hands to her forehead meaning to offer up a decade of the rosary for Nicola. But within moments she was immersed in one of her hot, feverish dreams about Robert. Her forehead was covered in a film of sweat when Sr Carmel gently shook her awake.

'Will we have the cup of cocoa?' Sr Carmel asked in a voice full of childish glee. As though she had suggested putting stink bombs in the Superior's office.

'Yeah.' Angela smiled and quickly made the sign of the cross. They linked arms on the way to the kitchen.

'I've been having the weirdest dreams,' Angela said.

'Is that so?'

Angela stopped in midstride. She knelt down on all fours, swivelling her head to look back up at Sr Carmel.

'It's like I'm some kind of animal or something. I wake up and this is the way I am. My backside stuck in the air and all these, I don't know, grunty noises coming out of my mouth. Are they a sign I'm coming down with something d'you think maybe, Sister?'

Sr Carmel pressed a forefinger to her tightly compressed lips. She closed one eye, deep in thought. When she'd given the matter due consideration for some time, she opened the eye and said:

'You've tried the old soap, Sister, you have?'

She was late. Or she wasn't going to come at all. You can't trust anyone, Robert thought as he stood outside Richmond Station, anxiously eyeing every emerging cluster of passengers. He'd arranged to meet Angela here and intended walking her along the riverbank to his house in Isleworth. Give them a chance to break the ice as it were before he commenced the first set of sketches. People were dispersing towards waiting black cabs and bus stops. It would be a while before another tube spewed out the next batch. This present lot were glued to mobile phones almost to a man. One woman told her husband or whomever to put the potatoes on now, she was catching a cab and would be home within minutes. And had he put the chicken in the oven precisely one hour previously? Robert could imagine her issuing forth an instruction at every tube stop. It was the way things were done these days, or so it appeared. Everyone wanted to walk into a readymade life. Readymade business meetings, readymade suppers. Soon enough the entire transactions of any given day could be dictated in advance over a line and a person wouldn't need to go anywhere at all. Or do anything at all for that matter. Physical presence would no longer be a requirement. Tennis matches and sex could be conducted over the phone. Well, perhaps that was going a bit too far. No one could really play tennis over a cable.

He wondered if the talk was of any greater significance now that there was so much more of it. Judging by the contents of these passengers' inane ramblings the answer was negative. The entire world had become addicted to communication. Internet, car phones, one-to-ones, CB radios, voicemail, e-mail, some new mail every other day. People frantically accessing the void. Using their phones to stem the epidemic tide of loneliness which the mobiles were only reinforcing in the first place. Because a phone that wasn't used meant that someone wasn't calling.

Robert had been lonely for such a long time, perhaps ever, that he didn't need a mobile phone to tell him that he had nothing to say. And no one to listen to him say it.

He decided to buy a strawberry tart at the French patisserie a few doors along. Sadly, his own lemon mascarpone had come to a bathetic end. All over his kitchen floor in fact when he wrenched the fridge door open too violently in his haste to get a bottle of beer after his fracas with Bonnie. As he chose his purchase her words rang in his ears. Mr Fielding.

How long ago was he? A long time. It must have been all of a week since he'd so much as crossed Robert's mind.

He was about to turn twelve when Mr Fielding popped into their lives. Pop being the operative word because one minute he wasn't there and the next he was, like a jack-in-the-box. He was different from all the other Misters. An Oxford graduate with baggy corduroy trousers, a line in knitted waistcoats and a variety of multicoloured bow ties. He wore his abundant hair swept back in two steel grey wings over his ears. He spoke posh too. And laughed like a drain, throwing his head back so that Robert could see that he had upmarket white fillings and none

169

of the dingy mercury stuff he and Bonnie settled for. He also had a huge rambunctious golden retriever called Sir.

Mr Fielding came out of nowhere and suddenly he was everywhere. With his gap-toothed smile and easy relaxed manner. Robert took to calling him Fielding which suited him because he was for all the world like some overgrown prefect. But naughtier. He set off fireworks one night on the boat causing half the other boatdwellers to nearly expire in their beds from shock. It was three o'clock in the morning after all. He introduced Robert to novels he would never have discovered on his own. Obscure Boy's Own writers with tremendous adventure stories to tell. He actually swam in the filthy Thames each and every morning, singing a different aria as his arms swung through the fetid waters, Sir's glinting head bobbing not far behind.

Every Thursday he met Robert at the school gates, much to Peter's intense envy, and took him to all the galleries in London. He appeared to know everything there was to know about art or so it seemed to Robert. More than that, he insisted that Robert had talent, serious talent, in contrast to what Professor Schneider was to evince many years later. He even asked Robert if he might keep a number of hasty sketches and Robert said sure, yes, expecting to see their scraps in the rubbish bin, immeasurably touched when Fielding had them all framed one afternoon and hung around every wall. He could speak on any subject and often did. At not inconsiderable length, so that a bleary-eyed Robert would have to haul his aching body to school from the sofa where he'd fallen asleep in the middle of some monologue or other the night before.

Not that Fielding didn't ever listen. He excelled at that too. And when he asked Robert a question he would sit, knees spread, fingers making pyramids, grey eyes dancing in anticipation of the response. The one thing Fielding never spoke about was where he had come from. Or where he was going. He didn't work but appeared to have money, not huge amounts but he paid his way which was a hell of a lot more than many of his predecessors. And he made Bonnie laugh. Her face was a constant daffodil. Fielding took her out, to the movies, for picnics in Richmond Park, boat trips down the river. Robert had never seen her even begin to approach such happiness. And almost more than all of that, when they were out, he got to mind Sir who was truly the most incredibly wonderful beast with a coat like silken gold and a floppy tongue which had a life all of its own. He didn't see a lot of Peter in those days, felt a bit regretful about that but not regretful enough to ever change the day's plan to incorporate Peter. Mr Fielding was just too damn enjoyable to share. Peter's father, a plumber whose only topics of conversation were boilers and grids, who Peter would have happily shared, was a very sorry specimen next to Fielding. And more often than not, Peter was turned away from the door of the houseboat he had come in no small measure to consider his real home.

Bonnie, Robert, Fielding and Sir were inseparable. Finally everything fitted for Robert. There were no more strange Misters interrupting his sleep, no more torrential monsoons of tears out of nowhere from Bonnie. No more idle musings on his parentage. He fished, walked, laughed and talked Fielding and Sir. He needed nothing else to complement the beginnings of his voyage into manhood. All the awkward, icky questions he could never ask his mother, Fielding provided the answers and embellished from his own personal repository of anecdotal tales. He saw Robert through wet dreams, inappropriate and humiliating erections, the pending drop of his balls. A man at last to talk to. Moreover, a man with a slobbery, endlessly affectionate dog who slept each night in the warm circle of Robert's arms and wakened him to soft wet licks and nose nuzzles each morning. A man whose presence permitted the young boy to succumb to the deepest slumbers, safe in the knowledge that he wouldn't suddenly have to jump up in the middle of the night to brandish the bread knife he kept under his pillow at some intruder who was heading for his mother's room. A man he came to think of as his long-lost father, but returned in a new light. Willing to accept and wear his responsibilities like a welcome coat on a frost-ridden day, instead of begrudgingly and with a sense of being hard done by, lumbered with an eccentric daffodil and her Oxfamclothed son.

Bonnie never said in so many words but she insinuated from time to time that it would not be inappropriate for Robert to consider Fielding in that light. Her hints confirmed his deepest suspicions that Fielding was in fact his real father. It made perfect sense. Robert was too content and far too besotted with his new life to harbour the slightest grudge toward the lacuna in his old life. The man was here now and that was all that mattered. Nothing embarrassed Robert any longer. The boat, his colourful mother, the patches on his sweaters. These things he could wear now with pride and a sense of adventure. Robert et al were the Nouveau Happy. And, boy, did it feel good. He was the truly appointed leader of the gang at school. Not one of them had a dad to even halfway measure up to Fielding who played rounders and rugby with them and never asked for time-out after only five minutes.

And then one morning Robert woke and felt an absence in the bed beside him. No Sir. A pad to the kitchen revealed no Fielding. He was a man – who was gone. Not a note or even a phone call. Nothing to explain the absence just as there had been nothing to explain the presence. All that remained were a few golden hairs and the lingering odour of dog on his bedsheets. He would never permit Bonnie to wash that cotton. Though after a while he told her he wasn't one bit upset by their departure. Not really. It was just a big adventure, wasn't it? It was time for a change again. This change manifested itself in his clothes, his hair, his socks. Ultra-conservative, just as Peter was entering a bohemian phase, Robert looked like a nascent stockbroker. The breadknife resumed residence under his pillow at night.

As did the last sheet Sir slept upon.

There were things Robert felt he should be explaining to schoolmates. To Peter. But there was nothing he could say. Other than he'd lost his father. Again.

The absence throbbed around the houseboat for years, if the truth be told. Bonnie was understandably devastated. She took to her room for what seemed months on end. Nothing would cheer her. Had Robert been able to think of anything at any rate. An air of doom and gloom and utter despondency followed the first few months after Mr Fielding's abrupt departure. But still there was a shred of hope that he might return.

That shred dissipated with the passage of time. Bonnie would not permit his name to be mentioned in her presence, not that Robert wanted to, just the vocalization of the name was enough to bring back a flood of haunting memories that brought lumps the size of boulders to his throat. No. He decided the best policy, the only way forward, was to forget Mr Fielding, insist upon proper shop-bought clothes now that his star was no longer in ascendency among his mates, and never ever to trust anyone again. With the moderate exception of Peter who in spite of his constant rebuffal had remained inversely a constant plump, occasionally irritating but always enduring fixture.

There was a lot to be said for someone who stayed.

'Seven pounds fifty, Monsieur,' the young French girl said behind the array of delicious cakes. 'Can I get anything else for you?' She was clearly flirting, even Robert could tell that. Probably flirted with all the customers.

'No. Thank you. I've got everything I need right now. Everything.' He smiled back at her, backing away with the tart tucked under one arm. It was in a white box with a pink curly ribbon. Much more appealing than anything he could have offered in the way of lemon mascarpone in any case. Shop goods were better presented. Better packaged. Why he had even considered offering something of himself, he couldn't begin to imagine. A

173

girl like Angela deserved only the best. That is, if you could trust her to turn up at all.

He headed back to the station. She was helping an elderly woman lift a suitcase into the back of a cab. She looked preoccupied, a nervous little frown flickering on the milky forehead. Robert just wanted to gaze at her for a while. The way she checked her watch, riffling the black hair into shiny exclamation marks. The agitated tap of sensible shoe against the pavement. She turned, saw him and her whole face split into a huge beam. For one fleeting moment he wanted to rush over, lift her slender frame into his arms, swing her into the air, carry her away for ever and ever. But the feeling quickly passed. She belonged to someone else after all. So he approached with an indolent gait, bending his head down to peck her cheek by way of greeting, caught the startled expression in the grey eyes, decided to shake her hand instead.

The Aunts had yowled the whole journey through on the tube. Angela had begun to think that other passengers would hear them in a minute. Her stomach churned something awful too, making loud pinging and squealing noises. She was so nervous she could hardly breathe. She alighted, fifteen minutes late and found he wasn't there after all. For a moment she didn't know whether to laugh or cry. Her fingers went to her hair automatically, splicing it into stiff peaks when what she really wanted to do was tear it out by the bushel. She had no business being here, on a warm Sunday afternoon, looking for a strange man who said he wanted to paint her. Probably rape her more like. She turned, and there he stood, leaning against a shop window, a cake box dangling by a pink ribbon from one finger. Such a warm, gentle smile on his face she could hardly smile wide enough in response. He came over, bent his head down, Aunt Bridie shrieked *sodomy!* and Angela instinctively flinched. But it was all right because he shook her hand instead, firm but polite and she figured Aunt Bridie had just been her usual previous self.

174

They walked along the riverbank, stopping to feed ducks with little clumps of bread Robert extracted from a pocket. He inquired about her week, how work was going, he hoped she wasn't too tired and apologized again for making these demands on her precious time. Angela assured him that she was fine really but she hoped he wouldn't be too disappointed by his choice of sitter. She remembered that her hair was sticking up like a punk's and flattened it quickly with a lick of spit to her palm when he wasn't looking. They crossed a scrolled cast-iron footbridge gaily painted in a delicate duck egg green or was it blue? Sort of an aqua shade at any rate, he offered. She agreed.

Along the towpath on the other side, Robert nodded and said hello to a vagrant on a bench, called Marty. They appeared to know one another, if not well. Up ahead, where the path ended, there was a cluster of brightly painted houseboats in varying states of repair. A glimmer of amusement and something like bafflement in the tobacco eyes when she said she really liked those. How amazing it would be to live on a boat like that, always on the river, so much – life all around. She was gazing at two elegant swans performing a graceful glissade across nutbrown water. A heron stood motionless on one leg on the other bank. Ducks congregated in little clusters of colour everywhere. So well fed, they were choosy about which scraps they darted toward. A passerby stopped to lean on the railing above them.

They reached Robert's small cottage after about fifteen minutes of unhurried walk and meandering chat. It was the strangest thing, even when they were silent, Angela felt that they were in some way still communicating. She felt such ease in his company. He didn't make one sarcastic remark the entire way, or make her feel that whatever she was doing it was the wrong thing, or that she should be doing something else. In fact, if anything, she felt decidedly sleepy by the time she stepped into the small front living room. Sitting on his battered

175

sofa, staring around at the contents of his life, she felt entirely at peace.

This was a safe place.

Robert apologized for the mess, which she said you'd hardly notice but you really couldn't help but notice. He went to get himself a bottle of beer and a cup of tea with strawberry tart for her. Light slanted into the room at an angle which threw the fireplace wall into a blaze of red relief but the rest of the room stayed a muted dark berry shade. There were old junkshop paintings everywhere, framed prints from museums. Properly bound books in stacks across bare floorboards, two pillars of them holding up a plank of wood for an ersatz coffee table. Her eyes quickly skimmed the marble mantelpiece and across various overladen bookshelves for photos of his daughters and perhaps a glimpse of their mother. She found what she was looking for in a gilded frame, two laughing scamps, heads pressed together for the lens. No shot of the mother though. A plump woman with wild bushy hair and a disconcertingly intense blue gaze in another frame. His own mother perhaps. So she figured he was still insisting on living the bachelor life, as the room confirmed, in spite of the pretty minxes. Right at the back, tucked away behind a dusty line of boys' adventure books, was a faded unframed photo of a genial looking man, dressed somewhat eccentrically with a spotted bow tie. A golden retriever stood at his side, looking up adoringly.

In the small bay window stood a trestle table with an electronic microscope. Beside it an easel which was covered in a splodged, once-white cloth. An old-fashioned oak set of freestanding shelves, redolent of an apothecary's display, stood behind the easel. Each shelf contained a huge number of small, labelled bottles, some containing various clear liquids, others had thick viscous substances. On tiny trays like miniature ashtrays there were powdery chunks of stuff that looked like copper turned green. Beneath the trays, in tubed stacks like chunky biscuits, were round jars containing vibrant tinctures in chalky

176

deposits. The last shelf held long rectangular wooden boxes with, it seemed to Angela, a thousand paintbrushes each. Some of the tips as fine as an eyelash.

She couldn't resist a quick peek under the easel cloth. It was a painting of flowers, just strewn about with no vase. The background was deepest brown with a mesh of cracks which caught the light. The flowers had faded in colour, the contours blurred with age and possibly damage. She jumped guiltily when Robert entered carrying a tray.

'Sorry. I was being nosy.'

'Here, let me.' Robert put the tray on the makeshift coffee table and swung the oilcloth clear. He eyed the painting solemnly. Shook his head. 'I don't know. I just don't know about this one at all.'

'Looks grand to me,' Angela lied. 'You did it ages ago, did you?'

'Me?' Robert laughed. 'Good God, no. This is early Victorian. Cost the buyer a pretty penny I can tell you. No, I'm restoring it. That's what I do,' he added to her confused expression. 'Aside from the odd lecture at the V & A.'

'Oh.'

'It's a big job this one. Best part of a month I'd say. I should've made a start already, but you know how it is.' He shrugged, about to drape the cover again.

'How d'you do that?' Angela stopped him. 'Restore, like?'

'Believe me you really don't want to know. It's a very boring process to anyone outside the –'

'No, really. I'd like to hear,' Angela persisted. 'If I'm not stuck in shelter life I'm stuck in –' She stopped herself from saying convent life in time. 'Oh you know. Work. Go on – tell me.'

She sat on the sofa again with her arms bunched around her knees. She pointed at the Victorian flowers.

'That, for example. Where will you start? I have to say it looks pretty shook to me.'

Robert hesitated for a moment then he smiled and turned the painting so that she could see the back.

'Well. First decision is whether it needs re-lining or not. That's the canvas lining here at the back, see? I'd have to take it to a specialist re-liner who would cut to measure and coat with a mixture of flour and animal glue called a paste. Luckily the lining isn't too bad on this so I can start from here.'

'Where d'you get them from? The pictures?'

'Referrals mostly. From private galleries or individual collectors.'

'They must trust your work a lot.'

'Well. Yes I suppose they do. These are their investments but I never look at them that way.'

'How do you look at them?'

He paused to consider that for a moment, cracked open a bottle of beer and poured tea for her. He was still considering as he handed her a plate with half the tart on it. Angela figured she'd be lucky to manage half the half but said nothing. Suddenly he replaced the beer and tapped the canvas with a knuckle.

'It's hard to explain. It's about getting to the truth, in a way. The truth of the painting. What's real, what remains of a botched restoration job already, what's retouched.' He was eager now to expand as he indicated the dark background area. 'Look at this, see – darkened varnish, oxidized with age, then there are the cracks, nicotine stains, soot stains, it probably hung over a fireplace for years. The first thing I'll do is fix the existing paint with glue. I use sturgeon's myself but you can use synthetic.' He picked up a fine paintbrush. 'Sabre,' he explained. 'Now I feed the glue under every fleck of paint. That'll take a day or so. I could use a syringe but I prefer the brush. Next I'll clean all the surface accretions with a very dilute solution of this.' He held up a bottle of clear liquid. Angela read the label – Synperonic N. Her mouth full of strawberry tart, she hoped he wouldn't ask a question. But he was off on a hack again.

'Sometimes I use saliva would you believe?'

'Shhaliva?' Angela mumbled. A crumb of pastry flew to the ground.

'It's an old trick. Anyway, next thing is to remove the old varnish with acetone or industrial methylated spirits maybe. This is the dodgy period because we're stripped right back to the basics now. We're in a very vulnerable state indeed. Totally naked.'

'Umm.'

'Now we need a new layer of protective varnish, don't we? – paraloid, say, but we also need all our gaps and holes to be filled in –' he stopped when Angela choked, continuing when she frantically waved him on '– with a mixture of chalk and glue. This will be applied to us with a spatula.'

His hands were moving back and forth across the painting, forming mental images for her of his hands rubbing, tipping, brushing, applying a spatula with delicate minute strokes. She swallowed hard. Rammed another mouthful of tart into her mouth.

'Now comes the really painstaking work,' he said. 'Powdered pigments to match each and every colour will be mixed with egg yolk and every inch of us will be worked over, section by section, in tiny minute detail. This will take two weeks of undivided attention at the very least. Look at that red there, appears quite dark and dingy, wouldn't you say? Well it's not. When it's stripped down, laid bare, brought up again, it'll be the reddest red you ever saw. Visceral red. And that mustard? It's not. It will be the richest yellow, not too far from a buttercup in fact.' He turned to her adding, 'After a while you just get an instinctive feel for these things. What colours you're going to find. It takes years. The reality behind the pollution, see?'

Angela nodded. Absently loaded another forkful. Totally engrossed.

'Finally,' he said, 'we need a new layer of varnish. Applied with a brush or a spray gun if you like but I've always preferred

179

to brush anything if possible. It's got a more precise and intimate feel. The protective coating will have to be something easy enough to take off in years to come. In case we need to be restored again in, oh, say ninety years or so. No point in putting something on you can't take off again is there?'

Her tongue was out ready to lick the plate. But she just managed to stop herself in time. Her head nodded him on.

'Now comes the moment where I stand back, I look at a polaroid of the original, the various stages of stripping and restoring. And –' he beamed at her ' – that's the best moment.'

'Because you've finished, is that it?'

'Well, yes. And also I've brought something beautiful, or at least beautiful to me, back to life. To a new life in a new home. And more than any of that, I've found the reality, the truth of the thing itself, detected every flaw, every crack, every pathetic fissure – and made it whole again.'

'Like a doctor really.'

'More like a make-up artist to tell you the truth.' He smiled.

Angela immediately thought of Nicola.

'But.' She cocked her head to the side. 'I'm not sure about this – but are you saying the reality is when you've it all stripped back to the bare essentials, what's really left, or is the reality the new restored work just because it looks exactly as it did once before?'

'Ah-hah,' he exclaimed. 'That's the big question.'

'And?'

'Like I say. That's the question.'

Deep in thought, Angela wet a finger and blotted up the last few crumbs of tart.

'The reason I ask is, well, I work with people who tell lies all the time. I'm not saying that's their fault, you understand, it's just their way of life. They keep telling me that nobody's interested in the truth. And for all I know, they might be right.' She paused, not sure what she was trying to say.

'Go on.'

'Well, it's like, like – is there ever a moment when you know absolutely, without a shred of a doubt, what's really true and what isn't?'

'You wonder about that, do you?' Robert said with his eyes flashing. 'So do I! All the time in fact.'

'You do? So I'm not such an eedjit after all.'

'You know –' Robert considered his words carefully ' – sometimes I think, or at least I'm beginning to think, that the truth can be how it is, on any given day. It's the way we see it that changes.'

'I like that.'

They smiled. Robert indicated her empty plate. Offered more.

'Oh no! I can't believe I ate that much as it is. I was so busy listening to you I did the pig on it altogether.'

'Right.' Robert pressed his fingertips together. 'Shall we make a start then?'

'Ye-es,' Angela responded doubtfully, wondering what was coming next. She was waiting for Auntie Bridie's outraged shriek but nothing came. She shifted nervously on the sofa, pressing her knees together with her hands folded tightly on her lap. 'What way d'you want me?'

'Well, if you could just . . .' He gestured for her to sit back a ways, let his hands flop loosely for her to follow suit. 'May I . . . ?' He checked before cupping her chin to turn her face this way and that. Angela could feel a blush start at her ankles working its way up. His eyes were slitted as he concentrated on the angle of her head. Finally he settled on a pose which instantly reminded Angela of the unknown woman at the V & A. She wondered if he was aware of this but he said nothing so she decided to let it pass.

He removed the Victorian flowers from the easel and replaced them with a large sketch pad. Angela was beginning to feel amoebic under the intense scrutiny of his gaze. As if she was no longer there in the flesh and he was seeing right through to her spirit. His hand brushed back and forth across a sheet of paper, fingers clutching a stick of charcoal.

'Angela,' he said with an apologetic smile, 'd'you think you could possibly take your hand down?'

'God, sorry.' She let the hand flop loose again from its python grip around her blouse collar.

He was measuring perspective with his thumb. Closing one eye. A quick stroke to the paper and he stopped once more, checking the light through the window. Something was troubling him. Angela's head began to wobble slightly from the strain of holding the pose which was awkward on her neck and she could feel a fit of the giggles burbling at the back of her throat. She spluttered, quickly turning it into a cough.

'Are you all right?' He sounded genuinely concerned.

'Grand, grand,' she splurged, trying desperately to resist. But this time there was no holding back, the laugh came right out, rebounding around the red room like a jackdaw.

'Sorry,' she said again, wiping her streaming eyes. 'God, sorry. It's just – It's just –'

'What?' He dropped the charcoal, afraid he'd offended her in some way.

'The thought of me sitting here like this with my neck – you know.' She mocked her own pose and cupped a hand to her mouth to stifle the giggles again. 'It's so not me. Oh I didn't mean . . .'

'No. You're absolutely right.' He waved her next apology away and laughed himself.

'Absolutely. As a matter of fact, the way you are right now, yes just like – *That's* you, isn't it?'

Angela felt his eyes skim over the hair she'd just unconsciously teased into spikes, down to where a dimple cleft her left cheek, finally resting on the curve of her laughing mouth. She immediately relaxed and had no trouble holding the pose. His fingers swept across paper with frenetic speed.

'Perfect, perfect,' he murmured, casting the window a cursory glance. 'Just this damn light – I forgot how faint it can be late in the afternoon. In this room.'

Angela was about to offer a move to the garden or wherever when the sound of the front door slamming shut after someone distracted her. The woman in the photo with the wild bushy hair and hot blue eyes bounded in. Robert didn't look too pleased.

'Bonnie,' he muttered.

'Only me,' she said. Effectively ignoring his displeasure by turning her back to him so that she could fix Angela in a penetrating scrutiny. A chubby pad of hand shot out.

'You're the famous Angela, I guess.' She shook vigorously. 'I'm the mother.'

'Angela – Bonnie. Bonnie – Angela,' Robert intoned in a wafer-dry voice.

'Pleased to meet you,' Angela said, a bit bemused and more so when she couldn't extract her hand from the pumping grip. Bonnie's eyes were half closed turning what light that could escape into twin searing lasers.

'Yeah. Okay. Yeah,' she kept repeating as if she could see things about Angela that no one else could possibly see. It was discomfiting to say the least.

'Bonnie. Would you mind returning Angela's hand to her now please?' Robert said.

'What? Oh sure.' Bonnie released her and offered a blistering smile before turning her attentions to her son.

'The light is shit.' Waved an airy hand at the window.

'We'll get by,' Robert mumbled.

'Tell you what.' Bonnie ignored him. 'I just been sitting there on the boat thinking this is where he should be doing his drawing.' She flicked sideways at Angela. 'You're a whole lot prettier than the sketches so far by the way.' Before Angela could ask what she meant she rattled on to Robert again. 'So. Tell you what I'm gonna do – I'll sit here nice and quiet, read my paper maybe, keep outta the way, and you and Angela here take the boat. A neat idea, huh? Now don't gimme that look. I'm not butting in. Honest. I'm only trying to . . .'

'Bonnie.' Robert replaced the charcoal firmly in its box. 'Bonnie – I know you're trying to help. I do know that.' Angela thought he sounded like a weary parent trying to reason with a recalcitrant child for the umpteenth time that day. A weary parent who was in danger of snapping any second now. Pushed to the absolute brink. His taut expression didn't knock a blink out of Bonnie who stood there smiling excitedly at him as though he were offering praise for her great idea. 'But this is my house. And I'll conduct my affairs my way, understand?'

Angela wasn't so sure about that word 'affairs'.

'Um. You were saying something about the light here,' she mumbled, thinking it mightn't be such a bad idea after all to move the whole situation onto more neutral turf.

'See?' Bonnie clapped her hands. 'Let's go!'

Robert looked at Angela.

'You did say you liked the houseboats on the way here. Would you mind terribly? I mean – I hate to move you around like this.'

'No problem. Really,' Angela almost shrieked. So many vessels in such close proximity. The light airiness of a boat compared to the almost palpable closeness of this red room. She jumped to her feet, following Bonnie's quick exit. Robert hastily gathered his things behind them.

'So. You work in welfare, huh?' Bonnie asked, checking over her shoulder as if measuring the amount of questions she could get into the time before Robert caught them up. He was already sprinting.

'Welfare?'

'Social whatever, you know.'

'Oh yeah. Yeah. That's what I do. Yeah.'

'Whatd'ya think of Robert so far?'

'He's umm nice. Actually I think you might have the wrong

idea here a bit,' Angela tried to continue but Bonnie just gave her a mischievous smile and bounded ahead.

The interior of the boat was everything Angela hoped it would be. Light streamed through a series of small rectangular windows all along the split level front deck. The lower half was the living area with a black wood-burning stove, a rocking chair with crocheted cushion, one high-winged damask easy chair and a pine chest for a table. All around the bow shape the walls were wood panelled and covered in pictures, similar to Robert's house. A pine dining table and several chairs just squeezed into the top half of the room. Dust motes swirled in the air where the piercing light came through a window at a shafted angle. A door led to a tiny galley kitchen and beyond that, Angela assumed, were the bedrooms. Robert had jumped down the gangway ahead of them and was hastily moving a framed picture out of view when she followed through with Bonnie. Who, Angela decided, was trying to make up to her son for something or other. She caught the slight tremble of the woman's hand on the doorframe, the little gaspy breath before everything she said to Robert and the telltale palpitations coming through the very ample cushion of chest.

'Okay!' she was exclaiming now. 'I'll get outta here.'

Robert stood with his head to the side, gazing at his mother with dry amusement.

'We wouldn't want to keep you,' he said almost with a chuckle when Bonnie appeared to hesitate. She nodded, cast Angela a last sunny smile and stepped up to the door. As though struck by an uncontrollable impulse she backed down again, caught Angela's hand and hauled her through to a dark bedroom at the end of a passage. She put a finger to her lips excitedly and reached up to the top of a large built-in wardrobe, pulling down a pink hatbox. Without a word, she unwrapped layers of tissue paper and extracted a silk shawl which shimmered exquisitely in the dim light. The colours appeared to change, to merge, coalesce then separate again, like petrol, Angela

185

thought, instinctively smoothing her fingers along the superfine weft.

'It's beautiful,' she said softly.

'Sure is.' Bonnie held it out fully for them to drink in the colour scheme to better effect. She chuckled and cast it about her shoulders. 'Never worn needless to say. A present from someone special. No. Not Robert. Just someone. Go on. Try it.'

'What's going on in there?' Robert called from the passage just as Angela threw the shawl on with a flourish so that one end wrapped right across her torso and dangled down at the back. Bonnie led her to a full-length mirror. Her blue eyes appeared misty.

'What d'ya think?' she asked in a hoarse voice. Noticed that Robert was standing by the door now and turned to him. 'What do you think, Rob? I thought it might be kinda nice for a painting?'

Robert was staring at Angela with his mouth slightly open. Then he turned his head this way and that. His brown eyes gleamed.

'God, yes.' he said. 'Where did you get that?'

'Oh just someone. A long time ago, hon,' Bonnie said airily.

Angela admired her own reflection. You couldn't help but admire yourself in a garment like that. She murmured 'beautiful' under her breath. Bonnie was playing with draping it, finally settling on high and bunched on one shoulder, slipping slightly deshabille off the other. She pulled her mouth down to see if Robert agreed with her. He did. Bonnie shooed him from the room to allow Angela to change in peace.

'Change?' Angela said in dismay.

'Well, sure, hon.' Bonnie seemed surprised that Angela didn't understand from the outset. 'If you take off the shirt you can just pull the brassiere straps to the side like this. No sweat.' She motioned how Angela could do it. Encouraging her to hurry up with a smile – the light would be fading soon. Her

186

enthusiasm was infectious certainly but Angela could only manage a glum lip-twitch in response.

Alone in the bedroom she considered her options. A:They were a mother/son duo specializing in a very select strain of perversion. In which case she should run. But it was probably too late already. B:They were perfectly all right, all was as it seemed and Bonnie was only making friendly overtures by offering the prized shawl. In which case, she should agree and remove her blouse. C:This was the main problem. Trouble was she never wore a bra. It was a cap-sleeved vest which could never be pulled down at the shoulders and after several washes at the shelter laundry had seen its whitest day long since. D:Remove the vest. Drape the shawl. Hold on for dear life.

She waited for the Aunts' strident opinions on all this. Nothing. So she opted for option D and quickly scuttled back to the living area with her fingers clenched around bunches of silky fabric. Bonnie fussed around her, fixing the off shoulder position while Angela's eyes burned holes in the floor. Robert had set up a makeshift easel on the dining table. He'd positioned a chair beneath a window for her. Bonnie continued to fuss, pulling here, tucking there, lifting her eyebrows for his approval when she moved a swathe. So concentrated on winning his approbations that Angela could sense the waves of anxiety emanating from the portly frame. Mingled with a pungent musky perfume, something like patchouli. She felt herself grow attuned to the scent just as she simultaneously tuned into Bonnie.

'Oh, c'mon,' Robert rasped, checking his watch.

'Ah, Robert, she's only trying to help.' It fell out of Angela's mouth.

Clunked onto the floor, each word like leaden weights. Bonnie's back was rigid with shock. Her face issuing tiny radial sparks of delight. Robert was drolly glancing from one woman to the other. Dear oh dear. What have we here?

Ah, Robert, she's only trying to help.

187

Sooo wifey-wifey. A spouse of a hundred years wouldn't have phrased it better. Bonnie's feet were making scuffling sounds preparing for imminent departure. But she gave Angela's shoulder a tiny pinch. As if to say, well, as if to say.

A yammering on the door cut into the stunned silence. Robert rolled his eyes.

'Jesus Christ, what's going on today?' He took the steps in a few jumps and angrily wrenched at the handle.

'Robert!' Tammy and Nessie leaped at him so that he bundled them together in his arms.

'How're my girls!' he cried, immediately forgetting his impatience of a moment ago.

Angela watched the way they coiled around him. Hugging, licking, kissing. She watched the way he nuzzled his nose to their shiny heads, breathing them in. Clearly he was a very fond father if a somewhat absent one. A thin woman with a handsome, horsey face and an eye that seemed to tic uncontrollably, stood watching the performance with an indulgent smile on her face. Angela observed that the smile was reserved for Robert and not the daughters. The mother, she assumed. And felt ridiculous standing there with no bra on and a silken shawl wrapped around her shoulders. The thin woman looked past Robert and the girls and the look she sent Angela was by no means pleasant. Downright hostile in point of fact. Bonnie had caught it too because Angela could hear a tiny haruumph from behind.

'We tried your house,' the woman was saying to Robert, 'and decided to have a look here. Your girls were absolutely desperate to meet Angela.' She came down the steps with her hand extended. 'Who must be you – I take it?'

Angela felt more bemused than ever. How many people had been talking about her then? What was this – some sort of freak show? Uncle Mikey's the freak in my family, she wanted to say but tried a tight smile and returned the handshake which turned out to be a very limp and quickly executed affair.

188

'Angela, meet Anita,' Robert was saying, 'and this pair of witches here are Tammy and Nessie. Say hello to Angela, girls.'

'Hello, Angela,' they chanted together, bounding down to check her out more fully.

'Robert says you talk funny.'

'And walk funny,' her sister reminded her, the one with the ticcy eye like her mother.

'Can you give us a go?'

'Oh God,' Robert groaned.

'How do I talk and walk funny?' Angela's jaw thrust out. She indignantly tightened her hold on the shawl.

'Where're your wings?' Nessie asked soberly.

'Wings?'

'Yeah. Like a proper angel's got. Where are they?' She was trying to peek around Angela's back.

'Girls, I'm sure Robert didn't mean Angela's a proper angel. Only a pretend one,' Anita said sleekly. She was busy eyeing the pretender from head to toe. Bonnie haruumphed again. Suddenly igniting into a burst of activity. She more or less prodded the girls ahead, signalling with her head for Anita to join them.

'Okay everybody. Show's over! Time to vamoose.'

They barely had time to resist.

'Why's she got that thingy around her?' Tammy asked on her enforced exit past Robert.

'Cos he's gonna paint her is why.' Bonnie turned and bathed Angela in one of her blistering smiles and Angela felt a warm glow after the icepick demeanour of Anita.

The girls would only leave after Robert promised that yes he would paint them too. And yes they might get to meet Angela again. Yes, properly next time. They waved her goodbye so enchantingly Angela thought that might be quite a pleasant prospect. Without the icepick though. To be fair to her, she had to concede, it couldn't be easy watching him entertain other women when he'd left her so casually with the two children.

189

To be further fair, the woman didn't appear to be harbouring a grudge. On the other hand, it was fairly clear from that first brief encounter that she was, however, harbouring a torch. Which was still very much aflame.

The door slammed shut with a flourish from Robert. He turned.

'Finally,' he said.

'Finally.' Angela smiled. She looked across to the chair. 'How d'you want me again?'

'Just as you are.'

He continued sketching preliminary drafts for a long time. Just casting her little smiles to check that she was all right and not feeling cramped or uncomfortable yet. She nodded that she was fine each time. Then found herself shifting ever so slightly so that he would send another quizzical glance. She felt so comfortable sitting there with warm sunlight sifting through the peaks of her hair, she nearly dozed off several times. Such a luxury, doing absolutely nothing. Even in the chapel there was praying to be done. And the nicest thing of all was that the Aunts had remained asleep or silent or utterly gobsmacked since she'd left the tube earlier in the day. She had to suppress a long lazy yawn. Sundays were looking better than they had for a long time. A thought struck her.

'How many more people did you tell about me anyways?'

Robert finished that particular sketch, ripped the sheet off and commenced another. He was grinning from ear to ear.

'Oh just about everyone I know. And the odd unsuspecting Japanese tourist,' he said.

Chapter Ten

Of course every man wants to see his best friend live happily ever after. Just not happily ever after before himself. And of course there were few things more pleasant to contemplate on a sun-drenched afternoon than new-found happiness visited upon a dear friend. Unless that contemplation was slightly sullied by a corresponding new-lost happiness visited upon oneself. Such was roughly the timbre of Peter's thoughts as he strolled along the towpath toward Bonnie's boat. He was plagued by many thoughts that Sunday, not all of them as pleasant as he might have wished. And if Peter wished for nothing else, he wished for pleasant thoughts. When he wasn't staring down at the wobbling proboscis of a patient's gleaming tonsils, he liked to eat well, drink above average wines, if not, on occasion, the odd stunning bottle, and he liked to walk by the river, thinking pleasant thoughts. Was that so very much to ask?

The problem, if he absolutely had to concede there was a problem, was his wife's emotions. She had too many of them.

Men should be warned before they I do'd. I do what? I do take thee to be my lawful wedded wife in the full and explicit knowledge that thou hast an extra rib, a spare chromosome and verily, ten thousand two hundred and twenty three extra emotions? I do take thee in the full and comprehensive knowingness that thou shalt be compelled to express these hitherto veiled and most deeply concealed tremors into one supreme distillation, refining all ten thousand hereforesaids etc, into the simplest of words? A single solitary word. Peter said it aloud: 'Anger.'

What women, or wives, to put a finer point on it, meant by feeling emotional, stressed out, pre-menstrual, taken for granted, usurped, menopausal, water retentive – any or all of the above and many, many more besides, essentially meant expression in the one guise. So many feelings. Indeed with so many provenances. One manifestation. Anger.

Perhaps they weren't such complicated beasts after all. Then again, why in the name of Christ were they so bloody angry all the time? She knew the deal. Signed the contract just the same as he did. Promised to love, honour and be angry for the rest of their lives till death did them part. And what for? Peter did his best. He provided a good home, no, make that great. Two wonderful daughters. She could be a childless C&A shopper with a husband on the dole, a council flat in Whitton with an Alsatian and a line of fertility clinics and clairvoyants behind her. Instead, she was in the lap of luxury with a gold card, no, make that several, and a line of vitriol reserved for him. She was spewing it out these days. Like vomit. He was even considering having a garden shed erected. Never one for pottering about much among the shrubs, Peter was beginning to feel that he could potter in the Himalayas. Echoes there of Hounslow and his father's stoop, fag butt in the corner of his mouth as he worked or, more to the point, hid, amongst his plumbing para-phernalia in the outhouse at the bottom of the crazy-paved garden. His mother crying Reg! Reggie! Re-eeeg! from the back door with a bottle of ketchup to be opened in her hand. The plebianfulness of it. Exit stage right notions of pottering forthwith. Enter instead, on a wisp of magician smoke, notions of a blonde mistress, about five foot two, blue saucers for eyes, mid-thirties – the right side of grateful – and oh, maybe a little lisp when she got excited. Now wouldn't that be so much more pleasant than a torn face each morning and an accusatory back each night?

192

Apropos torn faces, Anita's anger had started out innocuously enough. A little pointed barb at the odd dinner party. A dour sullenness the morning after. Evolving into silent weeks. He couldn't remember exactly when it had all begun. Some years back. He glanced surreptitiously from time to time at male companions and their wives, wondering if they were experiencing similar, well, difficulties. Ah-hah! A roll of the eye, just a touch too much white showing for all to be perfectly well at the Camerons'. A nervous laugh that went on that smidgeon too long at Gareth's place. A pointed offering of cigars from a wooden box in the expressly non-smoking Steed household. He was not alone. He felt certain.

He was entirely alone. He felt certain.

Nonsense! Pleasant thoughts pleasant thoughts pleasant thoughts. He willed them back and *voila* – there they were. It was just a matter of concentration. Yet there was only one thing he could state with any degree of certainty. The emotions/anger/tongue lashings/directed at him had swelled exponentially with the dawn of Angela in their lives. No fathomable reason why. So he intended to meet her for himself to do some fathoming.

And there were other disconcerting phenomena. The change in Robert for instance. Six weeks of painting Angela and he appeared to be a chemically altered being. Hardly showed at the house these days except to see the girls. And the way he was smiling. Well, it might be deemed smug – if Peter didn't know better. What had Robert to be smug about anyway? In comparison to, Peter, say. Not a lot was the truthful answer to that one. Moreover, the very reason why Peter had always felt such a deep compunction, if not downright obligation, to try and sprinkle some glitter on the drab, darkly grey silhouette of his friend's life was the lack of reasons to be smugful therein.

The girls were being painted too. Dancing with delight every Saturday before Anita tripped them along to the houseboat where she swore they remained perfectly still while Robert painted. He was going to do her next, she asserted in a rare moment of cheer. Yes, his family was a growing absence in Peter's weekend life. Not to mention the biggest tragedy of all, the absence of a fellow's very best friend to show off to. Now that was up there with root canals.

Yes. This Angela person had to be checked out. He was going to suggest travelling home with her on the tube. Seeing as he'd concocted a very pressing, notwithstanding tiresome, requisition of his presence at the clinic. On a Sunday. Not an ounce of scepticism from Anita either. Just glad to see the back of him for a few hours. By God he'd get the cut of this Angela's jib all right and sort out what all this nonsense was about once and for all. She could only be human, not the angel that Robert had been holding out for. She had to have feet of clay. And a lifetime's repository of anger the same as every woman. It might even transpire in the course of things that Peter could access that self-same vasculum and offer his friend a hint of what might lie ahead. Oh yes! There was nothing he wouldn't do for Robert. Nothing.

Except live through the Mr Fielding experience again. There was only so much rejection a person could take in one lifetime.

Unaware that paintus interruptus was ambling in their direction at the leisurely pace of a true gentleman, Robert was having a lovely time with Angela. The painting was good. Probably good enough to submit to the Royal Academy for next summer's show, if he could get the skin tone right. Now that he had the opportunity to scrutinize for as long as he liked and no longer had to engineer quick cursory glances, he was discovering layers of whiteness behind the whiteness. For example, Angela's neck was a delicate creamy hue, the tip of her pointy chin had a touch of strawberry-suffused milk. Under the grey of her eyes there were two shadows which sometimes showed through the sheen of skin like violet bruises. Tired bruises. She was clearly exhausted from work and he felt guilty asking her to travel such a long way, then sit as still as she could for hours on end. But she kept repeating that the entire procedure was in fact quite therapeutic for her. He insisted on reimbursing her fares however, but she wouldn't take another penny.

Every Sunday she arrived. A little late sometimes, but she always turned up. She wrapped the silk shawl about her shoulders in the manner Bonnie had suggested and he painted for most of the afternoon. Mostly they were quiet, him concentrating so hard he barely blinked, her drifting into a trance-like daydream before she invariably allowed her head to fall limply sideways as deep sleep overcame her. She was unaware that he would stop painting then. Instead, he would pull up a chair and sit with his chin resting on the bridge of his hands, elbows placed on his spread knees, while he would just simply and quietly contemplate her to his heart's content. It was a different kind of contemplation to that required for his painting. Incredibly more intimate somehow. He would have loved to tell her that occasionally she made tiny little guttural snores which ended in a whistle through softly pursed lips. Or that she squinched her eyes into minute black spiders when in the throes of a dream. Or that the lightest patina of sweat glinted on her forehead and small moans issued from her mouth when something was clearly disturbing her dreams. Or that a number of times, her tight hold on silk had relaxed sufficiently to expose a peach of breast with a hollowed dimple before a gentle curving swell to where the flat opaque nipple contrasted so darkly with translucent white. A nipple with a matt, velvety texture, similar to a rose petal.

He felt like a sordid thief at times like that. But a hungry thief also. He could not get enough of her. Hoping each time that the silk would slip further and further so that he might investigate the tiny pear-shaped mole in the middle of her rib-cage. Or the nub of protruding bellybutton that brushed the top of her jeans. A delicate geisha frame with sharply delineated contours of bone, especially by the clavicle and the ball-and-socket joints of her shoulders. It was uncanny how accurately

195

he had imagined her in the previous sketches of which she had no knowledge. When the shawl slipped he always ensured that it was carefully draped again before she awoke which was never an instant process with her, more a gentle series of fits and starts, nervous little cat jumps before the grey eyes peeled open, glazed and unfocused for seconds. By then he would be back behind the easel of course.

One Sunday he was trying to drape the fallen silk with excruciating care when his eyes were drawn to the nape of her neck. Little hummocks of bones stood out and the skin was coated in the finest down hairs. He bent down to inhale the scent of such a tender place and a little bead of sweat dripped from her scalp. He followed the runnel until it met material and remained there poised, a shimmering gem. Hardly daring to breathe he gingerly tipped the bead onto his small finger and tasted. She was made of milk the illicit taste confirmed, and salt, and something reminiscent of gardenia soap. After that lick, he was inexorably drawn to that recondite haven at the back of her neck. He blew softly on the feathery hairs, watching the way they swirled and separated as though invaded by a cyclone. And once, he could not help himself, he put his lips to the spot and kissed with such longing he felt certain she would wake. But she slept on. And he kissed again, unable to stop once he'd begun.

He wanted to ask her about the man to whom she was committed. But could not bring himself to face the unendurable torture of seeing her eyes light up at the mention of another's name. Or listen to her extolling his virtues with her lips curved into a dancing smile. No. Time enough for that torment when the day would come when he could no longer, in all conscience, protract the painting of this picture a Sunday longer.

When they did talk, it was just idle, meandering conversations. She told him about some of the strange-sounding characters at the place where she worked. She never said where or what the place was exactly but he was put in mind of some type of institution or other. That she worked ceaselessly he was in no doubt. But much of her life remained a mystery and she seemed to want to keep things that way. She was far less reticent about life growing up with the equally strange-sounding Aunts. And once shyly confessed that she often thought they were still in her head though she had left there years ago. It wasn't such an entirely incredible concept to Robert. He remembered that from the outset he had thought that there were other beings residing behind the huge grey irises. Now it made sense. He saw how they had shaped her life's history, considerably more so than she even thought, he suspected. And that Uncle Mikey – what was he doing in that attic? She always grew agitated and a touch upset whenever she mentioned his name, so they avoided the subject. But Robert felt certain that Angela had, for whatever reason, persuaded herself that her *raison d'etre* was to get the creature out of the garret.

In turn, he responded to all her questions about whatever he was restoring at the time. He kept waiting for the glaze of boredom but she apparently couldn't get enough. The simplest of things lit up sparkles in her eyes. She must have lived a very sheltered life, God alone knew, to be so interested in anything Robert had to say, he kept reiterating to himself, until one day he stopped. And talked quite freely, without stopping to establish if she was bored or not, and without constantly checking the last thing he'd said while simultaneously scrabbling about his brain to censor the next thing in advance.

Occasionally, if he finished early or felt the imposition of sitting for so long might cause Angela to get cramps, he suggested a walk. They strolled along the river bank, stopping to feed the ducks or sat side by side on a bench just quietly contemplating the rising swirl of river which was still tidal along this section. Seagulls were returning to their railing posts like beady-eyed sentries, signalling the incipient end of true summer. Strutting ponderously across the footbridge parapet, chests thrust out and wings like the white-suited arms of old men tucked and clasped behind their backs. Evening light would begin to fade from August and Robert didn't want Angela returning to wherever her flat was in anything other than full light. So he would have to hurry up. The prospect made him miserable.

They called on Bonnie a couple of times as well. She made them all a light supper and they ate in Robert's garden with citronella candles staked into the grass to keep the midges off. Angela had a sweet tooth and for some reason the sight of her flitchy fingers tentatively reaching out for another ginger stem biscuit caused a lump to rise in his throat. It was among a number of things about her that made him have to swallow hard. Another was the way she seemed to become embroiled in the least likely dramas even when the distance they had to cover between the boat and his house was hardly the span of eventful possibilities. But something always happened around Angela, a child's tipped-over tricycle, a woman's twisted ankle due to a loose paving slab – of which there were many. A collapse of a top shelf at the local corner shop spinning her dervish-like in an effort to pick up as many cereal boxes as she could manage in one swoop. Perhaps these little things were always happening. Perhaps he'd never noticed before. Or perhaps he was falling in love. And now everything she did took on a new complexion.

She'd even managed to pass the Mrs Leitch test with flying colours. The elderly woman was doing her reverse and thrust routine with the buggy one afternoon as they passed. Robert put his hand out to stay Angela's instinctive rush across the road. He gave her a droll look as if to say, he wouldn't if he were her. Too late. The repeated barks of 'keep bloody back' didn't discourage her either and Robert watched in bemusement as the women ended up chatting for a brief while and while she was still talking, oh so casually, so not noticeably, except to Robert, Angela's hands were guiding the buggy through the gate and up to Mrs Leitch's door.

She was fully asleep now. With her head listing plant-like toward a pane of sunny window, a slight breeze teasing spikes of dark hair into swaying anemone fronds. Was he falling in love with her? he asked himself for the thousandth time. Or was he falling in love with an idea of her? An image he was trying to capture on canvas. An image which would be all that remained once she'd returned to her normal Sunday routine, spent with this other man of whom she said nothing, it had to be said.

A sharp rat-a-tat-tat on the door made her jump. Instinctively Angela's hands clutched tight around the rim of the shawl. Robert stuck his brushes in a jar of linseed oil just as Peter came in.

'Peter!'

'Robert!' Peter wasn't even looking in Robert's direction. His gaze was entirely directed at Angela who was still coming to after a lengthy snooze. 'I've heard a lot about you, Angela,' Peter said with a wide enough smile. Though Robert thought his friend's voice sounded curiously like it was coming through screens of egg white whipped into stiff peaks. Almost but not quite meringue.

'My friend Peter,' Robert explained. 'Anita's husband. The girls' father.'

'*Your* girls,' Peter responded with an indulgent smile. 'As Anita keeps putting it.'

Robert thought he detected a strange dilation to Angela's pupils, a shivery intake of breath, but her face remained bland. Peter didn't wait for her to speak. He went through to the kitchen to uncork the bottle of wine he was carrying tucked under an armpit. Calling over his shoulder.

'I'm not interrupting, am I? Figured you'd welcome a break on this hot afternoon. I had a friend who was Irish, Angela. A huge laugh. Life and soul of the party. Remember Conor, was it, Robert? Where was he from again, now let me see –' The sound of a cork popped, glugging as three glasses were filled.

'County Roscommon, I think it was. Or Donegal maybe. One of those up there at any rate.' He came through with the glasses huddled against his chest. Robert denied him a quick peek at the painting by whipping the cloth over rapidly. Peter gave him a mock look of admonition then handed the wine around, raising his own in salute.

'To whichever county you're from, Angela.' A sip, exhalation of satisfaction. 'Which is?'

'Emm, Cork.' Angela took a swallow and looked utterly bemused. Robert felt sorry for her. Peter's brand of bonhomie bordered on strident if you weren't used to it.

'Must be lovely. I've never been. On the coast, I suppose?'

'Well no. We're more on bog, like. Where my place is.'

'How charming,' Peter said. 'A friend of mine goes to the coast, sails at, let me think – Kinsale – would that be the place?'

'Could be. Probably.'

'Excellent restaurants there. So he tells me.'

'Is that so?'

Robert figured Angela must be wondering by now how many friends Peter might allude to with tangential connections to Ireland. He couldn't tell her just then that Peter had friends with tangential connections to everything. He'd yet to meet any of them though, as they were always off sailing or deep sea fishing or something else incredibly daring or wonderful. He'd even had the sneaky suspicion a couple of times that all these friends, close friends and very very good friends of Peter's, were actually clients who happened to mention this and that. While he was peering into their mouths.

'Cheers,' Robert glumly said. Wondering how he could stave off the inevitable dinner invitation which was doubtless the reason for Peter's incursion. Up to this, he'd managed to steer clear of the subject, making sure he called to see Tammy and Nessie whenever Peter might be out. He would feel so foolish when Angela told them that she really was only sitting for the portrait. Oh dear, Robert wasn't her man, is that what they thought? No, no. Her lover was someone entirely different. Entirely. Taller. Younger. A much more athletic build. Rollerbladed with a bandana around his forehead and a Walkman plugged in his ears. Hip hop music. Very stylish. Something big in the city. Not something small by an easel.

'Well now.' Peter splatted into the rocking chair, lifting one ankle and crossing it over the other knee. Settling in. 'Isn't this nice? I've been meaning to pop up here every Sunday. To meet you, Angela. But you know how it is. Hectic.' He rolled his eyes at the impossible hecticfulness of his schedule.

'Mmm.' All Angela offered.

'Have you had to take people's children from them then, Angela?'

'Sorry?'

'One of the downsides of social work I imagine. Though I have to say, there can't be too many upsides either. Terribly hard work. Is it? Yes?'

'Well, sometimes. But I never have to take child –'

'Where?' Peter cut across. He scratched his nose with the stem of the glass. 'Where is it you're based again? Did you tell me, Robert? I can't remember.'

Robert's eyes narrowed.

'What is this?' He shot across to Peter.

'What? What is what?' Peter feigned confusion, a steady beam again to Angela, his eyebrows up, waiting on her response.

'Near the City.' Angela appeared flushed. She was squirming visibly on the chair. Robert sensed that reluctance again on her part to divulge such simple details as her place of work.

'You live thereabouts too?'

'Sort of.' She looked very uncomfortable now. 'It's, emm, complicated.'

Peter eyed Robert. Pulled his mouth down at the edges. What could be complicated about living near work for heaven's sake? Robert decided it was time to step in before Peter started asking

201

far more awkward questions. He drained his glass in one gulp.

'Right. Back to work, I think. The light is still good. Okay with you, Angela?'

She checked her watch, spilling most of the wine in the process.

'Oh give the girl a break, Robert.' Peter stood up. 'Enough for one day. I have to go into the clinic now in any case. Sort of an emergency you could say. Why don't I walk you to the tube, Angela? We might even be going in the same direction as it happens. Where exactly are you – ?'

'I'm grand for time actually,' Angela interjected. 'Thanks a million anyway.'

Robert jumped through the window of opportunity.

'Don't let us keep you, Peter,' he said, pointedly stepping up to open the door. 'It wouldn't be fair to make some poor patient wait too long at the clinic now would it? Especially an *emergency* case. No no. I wouldn't hear of it. I'll walk Angela to the tube myself. As usual.' He didn't wait to give Peter a chance to buy more questioning time but practically poked his friend up the steps and through the door. 'I'll catch up with you during the week,' he added to the clearly disgruntled features.

'But – but – dinner . . .' Peter managed to splutter. 'I wanted to arrange –'

'Yeah yeah. We'll do that on the phone or whatever. Thanks for the wine. Bye, Peter – See you!' Robert swung the door shut as fast as he could, realizing only as he turned to Angela, that he'd actually shut it in Peter's gobsmacked face.

Angela appeared deep in thought. Mulling something over.

'Peter's married to Anita then,' she said with a little puzzled frown flitting across her brow.

'Yes. Didn't I say? Is there something bothering you, Angela?'

'Oh no. Nothing at all. I'm just thinking how different things are these days. To the way they used to be is what I mean. The arrangements people come to.'

'You're right. They'd probably just live together nowadays. Wouldn't bother getting married. It's just a piece of paper, isn't it?' he added airily.

'I suppose. Still, it's probably a good thing for the girls that he married their mother. Security and so on. Good for them to have something – someone – well, stable in their lives.'

Robert rubbed an eyelid. He couldn't figure for the life of him where this was leading.

'Stable? As opposed to?'

'Well. Not there. Someone who runs away from their responsibilities. Ducks them for whatever reason. It's hard for children to come to terms with that. At least that's what I imagine.'

Her face had grown steadily more thunderous. Now she appeared to be glaring accusingly at him, increasing his growing bafflement. 'That someone who runs away can leave a trail of trouble behind them,' she blurted suddenly, adding, 'troubled kids who grow into ginormously troubled adults. Listen – I deal with the end results every day. It's my job. It's what I do!'

Robert poured a glass of wine. Didn't so much drink it as inhale it.

'Okay okay, Angela. No one's arguing the point here.' She looked so upset he thought he might offer some consolation. Thought of Mr Fielding – said: 'You know, some kids get over things better than others. They learn to cope. It's life.' He shrugged.

His words did not produce the desired effect. She was steaming now. Wrapping the shawl ever tighter, standing to leave.

'Well I think that's a very cavalier attitude if I may say so.'

'*Cavalier?*'

But she'd already brushed past him on her way to the bedroom to change. He shook his head. Inhaled another glass of wine.

'Angela?'

'Actually I do have to go now,' she called to him. 'I made a mistake. Actually I've been making a fierce mistake.'

'What have I said to upset you?'

'Nothing. Nothing at all.' She flitted back through the room, stepping in that half run, half walk which was so familiar now. He caught her arm, swung her around to face him.

'Angela?'

She pulled her arm free.

'I'll walk myself to the tube thank you very much.'

'What've I done – said – what?'

'I have principles,' she said primly.

'Well I'm sure you do. I didn't doubt that for one moment.'

'Fine then. Just so's you know.'

'Okay. That's settled. I would never doubt that you're a principled person. Never. Now let me walk you to the station. Please.'

She pointed down, tapping a foot, quite imperiously he thought.

'What are they?'

'Pardon? Oh – feet.'

'Precisely. One and two. Perfectly capable of walking me to the station by my own self. Goodbye, Robert and good luck to you. And if I just might say, if I just might say, it would behove you to put yourself out a little bit every now and then. Consider the feelings of others. Children come to mind is what I'm thinking of. Involving yourself a fright more than you do with their wants and what like. A whole fright more than you do, it seems to me.' She turned for the door. 'That's all I've to say on the subject.'

'*Behove?*'

'Yes. Behove.' She swivelled again, her eyes flashing.

He caught her by the shoulders and kissed her. It seemed the only thing to do at the time. Really there was precious little else a person could do when someone said behove to you. Her lips parted in indignation, well, it was hardly passion. And in

204

case she said behove again, he kept on kissing. If she has the slightest feeling for me she'll go limp *now*, he thought. Now or now, maybe now – no, she was rigid as a beanpole. It wasn't like the movies after all. How to get out of it was his current problem. Did he love her because he'd kissed her so impulsively, was his next concern. Most immediate of all, what to say when his fastened lips finally let go? Damn it all, they seemed to have a life of their own. She was lovely. Oh so lovely wrapped up there in the curve of his arms. The lips made a smacking sound like a plunger as they decided it was time to release. Truly, it had nothing to do with him. They were such careless beasts.

She stood without a movement. Her own lips twitching, twin, waylaid rabbits.

'Next Sunday okay, Angela?' he said.

'Okay,' she whispered. And fled.

Peter sat in a state of morbid disconsolation on a bench by a vagrant named Marty. At least that's what the man with the Tennant's Extra kept telling him. Saying his own name over and over – Me, I'm Marty – giving the clear impression that it wasn't the done thing to sit there and not say, And me, I'm Peter. But Peter did not wish to engage in such glittering repartee. In fact, he did not wish to sit there at all. But her Royal Supremeness of the House of Angry had been told of an emergency and there were hours to kill yet. Kill was a good word. Certainly more patrician than, potter, say.

The look on Robert's face as he closed the door of the boat. Impatient. Irritated. Anxious to be shut of Peter. Intent on someone else. It brought back all those days after school when Peter would trot down the gangway, his head filled with the adventures they would have, only to be told that Robert and Mr Fielding were going fishing. Or boating. Or just about anything that didn't include Peter. It brought back all his pathetic attempts to win Robert back, the pen that took the woman's clothes off when you dipped it – Uncle Harry had brought him that from Canada no less. The world's largest gobstopper – a week's pocket money that was. Not to mention the playing cards with the vestal virgins – divested. Nothing would do. He'd even offered his entire collection of Dinky cars one afternoon in an access of despair. But Robert had said thanks but he wasn't collecting any more. It wasn't that Robert was ever especially cruel or heartless in the way he more or less told Peter to bog off, that might have been something, a ray of hope even. No, it was the way his eyes didn't appear to register his erstwhile friend's presence, never mind existence.

Good grief, it got so bad he'd resorted to hanging about with his father down at the outhouse for a while. Handing him that monkey wrench there. No, that one. Jesus H., didn't he know a monkey wrench when he saw one? What were they teaching him in that school? Get up to London and be an orthodontist fast was what they were teaching him, Peter could say now. But then, he'd said: Aw this is boring. Why don't you *do* anything? His father, the plumber, had told him to sod off now, there's a lad, go and annoy his mother.

There was no one sadder than Robert when Mr Fielding left. And no one happier than Peter. It was around that time the thought ignited in his head, he, Peter, might have a purpose after all. Might be a candle that was simply unlit – thus far. His effulgence was, oh, breathtaking. Dazzling. He had to shield his own eyes from his starry new self. While Robert's flame diminished to a stubby, equivocal flicker. The new regime. Peter's purpose to colonize the abandoned pedestal from whence he could look down evermore. Robert, at the base, head craning with the effort of looking up.

Wholly addictive.

His forlorn trance was distracted by the curious gait of a woman passing by. She would take quick decisive steps, no, trots, one second, as though she knew where she was going and was in the most terrible hurry to get there; the next minute, she was walking at a snail's pace, thoughtfully, ruminatively, as though she didn't want to get where she was going at all. She stopped once with her hand pressed to her chest. A person in turmoil. Or pain. A toss of her head and he knew that one all right, could smell it. Anger.

He squinched his eyes up. Heavens. Yes. It was Angela. She broke into a trot again just as she passed. He opened his mouth to call out. Marty said – Me, I'm Marty. Thought about conducting his interrogation in front of *that*. Thought better. What would be the harm in following her for a while? It looked like a lovers' tiff. Maybe he could discover something about her which might be of assistance to Robert who was of course a novice when it came to dealing with angry women, in so far as they never seemed to last long enough to expend a sufficient amount before he gave them the boot. If she was angry then Angela had possibilities. It was entirely possible that she might even harbour within that petite frame the wherewithal to fuck up his friend's life to a greater degree than Anita was fucking up his own. Oh rapture!

He sidled, trying to appear nonchalant, until he ran. He had to. Because she did. From time to time. It was awkward to say the least, trying to mirror that peculiar gait of hers. At the station, he hung back, melting behind a pillar in true 007 style. Slipped into the next carriage when she boarded the tube. Stuck his head out at every stop to make sure she hadn't alighted unbeknownst to him. Got out at Whitechapel, followed her up the escalator, remembering to constantly scratch his forehead so that his hand was hiding his face in case she turned suddenly. At the summit, he waited a few moments before sliding his ticket through the barrier. Nearly lost her at the top of the exit steps. The winding grubby streets she trotted along grew dingier by the minute. Sunday-deserted. He relaxed his pace. There was little chance he'd lose her now, he had such a clear view ahead.

She turned a corner sharply just as he'd slowed to an elegant strolling rhythm once more, one hand plunged deep in a pocket.

He really didn't want to run in case his footsteps echoed sharply, but he had to. He was panting and redfaced by the time he'd rounded the corner himself. And she was gone. Disappeared. He listened for a distant echo of her peculiar trot but a car passed and then there was silence. Damn!

Nothing but rows of mainly dilapidated Victorian buildings, their façades blackened from years of pollution. The sour odour of stale piss from a few boarded-up doorways along his path. It was a far from salubrious area wherein the mysterious Angela resided. For some reason, his curiosity only intensified and as he walked back to the station, he promised himself that he would follow again and next time he would see exactly where she ended up. A series of lewd catcalls and hisses made him turn around. A couple of hookers eyeing him up and down. He raised an eyebrow at them in what he considered a suitable gesture of both irony and reproval. One of them, a thin, pointy-faced thing, with black fishnets and a pvc miniskirt and eyes done up like an Egyptian, cast him a wink as she passed. Her green gaze mocked him to his face. He stopped to cough to give them a good headstart. The Egyptian turned, said something to her mate and they both cackled in a deeply offensive manner. Peter felt very put out. Remembered a rather nifty Chablis waiting on chill for him in leafy East Twickenham. Cheered up a bit and headed home.

His cheer was short-lived unfortunately. Anita had had a bitch of an afternoon with the girls. And while she'd been more than happy to see him go, she was less than happy that she'd paid the price. It was one of the usual no-win situations he found himself embroiled in these days. She slapped their dinner plates on the table in a surly silence, having sent the daughters to bed at little past six o'clock. Peter stretched and yawned expansively. To remind her that he had, in fact, been working.

'Tired?' she snapped.

Hesitant pause as he considered the various minefields looming ahead.

'Oh just a little.' Surely that was middle of the road enough. Even she couldn't find a bone in that.

'You've never had to go in on a Sunday before.'

He fetched the crystal wine glasses. Hawed and polished. The Chablis was chilled to perfection in a silver ice bucket. Thought he could push the envelope. Just a tad.

'It's been so busy. I hate to turn anyone away.' He gave her a pointed look. 'Where did you say we're going in September again?'

'Seychelles.' Gritted teeth. She was onto him all right.

'Great!' Time for a little retreat. Then he just couldn't help himself. A plaintive yawn. 'Looking forward to the rest.'

'At least you get a rest.'

'Pardon?'

'You heard me.'

No, this really was unacceptable. He had to make a stand. 'Your life is so incredibly difficult, I'm to take it? Why is that exactly? Please do tell. I'm sure if you'd explain in simple mono-syllabic fashion without the accompanying histrionics – I might understand.'

She was standing perfectly still, the cruet set gripped in one hand. Petrified like a figure from a Pompeii catacomb. In his mind, Peter woefully commended his spirit to God the father. For he had stretched himself with some malice and no afore-thought upon his very own Calvary.

'You are such a pompous arrogant little git.'

He swallowed. Starters. Entree was on its way.

'You have absolutely no appreciation of all I do around this place. Not to mention that I'm bringing up those girls practically singlehandedly.'

He decided to let that one go. The Presbyterian nanny wasn't worth another laceration. His mind was churning furiously, try-ing to stem this onslaught before certain annihilation.

'Look, Anita. Darling.' He was about to reach out but her eyes widened and swivelled, fixing him with a glare worthy of

Medusa herself. 'Why don't we go away for a weekend? Just you and me. Like we used to. We're both under stress. It's just what we need.'

'What you mean is – why don't we go and shag ourselves silly – and that'll make everything all right, will it?'

Well yes. He thought. Of course that's not what he meant. He said.

'Besides.' She put the cruet set down with a bang. 'I can't go away until Robert has done me, remember?'

'Pardon?'

'My portrait. After the girls. He's promised that he'll start any day now. I wouldn't want to mess up his schedule, would I?'

Robert's schedule. Robert's everything. Once again, all the action was taking place on that damn boat. And Peter was excluded. It simply was not fair. Not fair at all. The cork from the Chablis slid out with a resounding pop. Peter poured two glasses, perfectly aligned teeth chewing his lower lip, thrashing even. He extended her goblet.

'Glass of whine, dear?'

Chapter Eleven

Aunts were dropping like flies. First the call came on Tuesday that Regina had suffered her final stroke and before Angela could fly out on the Wednesday, it transpired that Bridie, never one to be outdone, had suffered a stroke of her own and was gamely clinging on until Angela would arrive. At least that was Maisie's interpretation over a crackling line. Maisie herself was in rude health and doubtless would bury them all just as Bina had always predicted.

Mary Margaret was surprisingly magnanimous about the amount of time Angela would have to take off. Even suggesting in her practical way that the best scenario all round would be if there could be a double funeral. Save a lot of hassle and money that way. Angela just nodded and ummed. Inside, she felt stunned and full of sadness. Auntie Bridie hadn't cackled in her head since the first Sunday with Robert, and now she was dying. It wasn't as though she'd actually miss the chorus, just that it had been there for so long, the emptiness felt hollow and lonely too. Truly it was the end of an era.

There was so much to do before she left, she didn't have much time to think about last Sunday and that kiss. God Almighty! Where was her head at all? And to think she'd said that she would return – for more – there weren't enough saints in Heaven to pray to. Him with those lovely sparky little girls who so clearly loved him even if he'd cast them aside like half-eaten toffee apples. It wasn't as if he were a bad man, she could tell that from his eyes, just feckless and yes, cavalier, about his obligations. Wasn't it Auntie Bridie herself who told Angela as a young girl, that the class of people who chase after personal happiness in the extreme, are the very ones who end up more wretched by far than those who bow down to their duties and responsibilities? The woman had a lot to say in those days. And she said it. And a whole slew of it made perfect sense. Indeed it did.

Then there was Steve to sort out before she left. Over the past few weeks since her exchange with Nicola, Angela had managed, with the greatest of efforts on her part, to keep him calm, keep him at a distance from his sister. She didn't dare to broach the subject of the rapes, fearing that he would go off the rails entirely, but by means of subtle and persistent little remarks to the effect that Nicola was fine or Nicola was perfectly safe, she saw that she was assuaging his fears and he didn't hang around the women's shelter quite so much. He did keep a distant eye on Nicola's comings and goings however, but Angela figured that was acceptable. Once, she'd managed to intercept him as he was just about to run after his sister and she explained calmly and rationally that if he caused trouble, Nicola might be thrown out and then he would have to start looking for her all over again. Who knew where she might end up? Effectively, the same tack that had worked on Nicola, in reverse. To keep him in check however, she did dangle a further persuasive carrot, by promising that she would in time engineer a meeting between the siblings when he could verify to his own satisfaction that all was, in fact, quite well with Nicola.

She decided another dangle of that carrot might be in order before she caught the plane. Just to keep things running smoothly while she was away. Her bag was packed as well as a small rucksack full of prayers and holy pictures from Sr Carmel for the intentions of the family, when she sought him out in the television room.

Some of the men were leafing through a pornographic magazine when she entered. Paddy with his one good eye squinched up to match the other gash. A few snorts of approval here and there. They didn't bother to hide it from Angela. Steve was in his corner, alone as usual.

'How's it going, Steve?'

'Okay.'

She pressed his hands in a clasp and leaned forward so they wouldn't be overheard. His fists instinctively bunched but he didn't withdraw.

'Look it, I have to go away for a little while, Steve –'

'Away?' He looked startled.

'Few days. A week maybe. I can't say for sure, my Aunt Regina's died and another Aunt – Bridie – well she's not doing so good. So I just wanted to tell you before I left. And make sure you're all right with everything. You know what I'm saying?'

'You said you'd get me a talk with her.'

'I know. And I will. But you have to be patient. You don't want to panic Nicola now, do you?'

'You don't have a clue. That's what it is.' His top lip curled in disgust and his fists pulled back from her grip.

'I do. Honest I do, Steve,' Angela cried, then remembered to lower her voice again.

'Just give her –'

'Yeah time,' he hissed across her. A fist began to roughly knuckle his crown. 'You don't know. That's what she ain't got. Doing what she's doing. They'll get her.'

'Who'll get her?'

'Them.' The fist began to violently pummel the top of his head. Angela sensed a full-blown explosion on the way, her mind whizzled rapidly trying to get the right words. The soothing mantra that had so far managed to calm him down.

'Look, Steve. Look at me now. Into my eyes. Nicola is safe, okay? She's getting on with her life and she's fine. I promise you. I know you're worried about her – what she does – but there's nothing I can do to stop her, any of them, you know,

213

on the streets and such like. But she's a –' she stopped herself calling Nicola a clever piece of work '– a bright girl. She's a fair idea how to look after herself, you know – out there.'

He cast her a look of savage disgust.

'Yeah.'

'Promise me you'll behave while I'm away. Please, Steve. Or you'll only make trouble for yourself and Nicola too. She's comfortable next door. Give her a break.'

'Yeah.' A snarl.

Wearily, Angela rose to leave. He was shutting down, shutting her out again and she knew he was best left alone for a while. There was nothing more she could say or do to protect him while she was gone. It was in his own hands. And Mary Margaret's. She headed to the chapel with a deeply heavy heart and a sense of foreboding. Lit a candle for him and prayed as hard as she could with her fingers scrunched together so tightly her knuckles remained white for a long time afterwards.

She continued to pray all the way on the flight and the subsequent bus journey to the village near the farm. Several cars stopped to see if she wanted a lift during the two-mile walk from the bus stop but she waved them on. She needed to find some peace of mind before she faced the absence of one aunt, the looming absence of another. And how would all this affect Uncle Mikey?

The small suitcase grew heavier and heavier as she kept up a steady pace through bog country. White and yellow wispy flowers dotted the long, coarse swathes of ropey grasses. Streaked mats of deep pink heather cut across the layered effect of muted colours. The flat landscape curved at two points: a medium gradient leading to Angela's house, the Aunts' old dwelling place containing Uncle Mikey at the bottom; and a steeper gradient far out on the western horizon. All the way to that point, slick black apertures yawned wet and glistening where the earth had been peeled back and carved into heaps of rectangular peat blocks. A few outlying families still cut for their own winter fuel, methodically spreading, turning, footing, stacking and drying the sods in the old way. The piles looked like triangular stacks of sun-dried cow dung.

A few sheep here and there, clusters of small, grey granite boulders and a number of twisted bog oaks and that was pretty much it really as far as the eye could see. Behind and to the right of that one distant hill, the outline of a chimney stack could be made out behind a screen of Scots pine, the pig farm where her father took his fatal doze. Auntie Bridie used to tell her that heaven lay behind that hill. When there was only one rising point in the distance to fixate upon as a child, and low-lying bog land dark beneath swatches of ever-present rain was the more immediate daily vision, it didn't take very long for the young Angela to swallow a tiny nugget of scepticism and believe, with no little degree of optimism, what her aunt told her. That undulation in the otherwise flat terrain vied with Uncle Mikey as a focal point for her thoughts. She had to see for herself, in spite of Bridie's repeated warnings that if you went up there, you might never come back.

So she had packed a prodigious amount of sandwiches, in case she did happen to encounter any difficulties on the return leg, a large screwtop bottle of milk and a set of pyjamas, for the selfsame reason, and headed off one morning just as the cockerel set up his ululation in the yard. It was a long trek for a young girl. Her legs ached and were covered in nicks and scratches from sharp, wiry grass. Her shoes and socks looked like they'd been plunged in a sedimenty gravy which wasn't too far from the truth. Sometimes a leg got sucked down to the knee by soft, squelching potholes of bog. All the sandwiches and milk were long gone by the time she reached the base of what looked like an increasingly sinister hummock of sheer rock. Crows circled the pointed apex, their glossy black coats reminding her of the village undertaker's suit. A little peaty stream gurgled somewhere at the back.

It occurred to her that she might walk around the hill. But

that seemed a cheat for some reason. Part of the deal had to be that you actually climbed up. Hours had passed by then. Her mother would be worried, the Aunts would be fizzing back at the farm. Her eyes sought out the comforting contours of both farmhouses way way back in the distance. A light drizzle wreathed everywhere in a mantle of grey. She wasn't so sure she wanted to see heaven after all. Maybe she should wait. Just like everyone else. Then again, there was always the possibility, if not probability, that this was yet another of Auntie Bridie's tests. Maybe she wanted Angela to prove once and for all that she did in fact possess a singular destiny, albeit somewhat murky as yet. If she did see heaven, managed to survive and come back down again, what better way to prove to all of them, herself included, that indeed she had been touched by intimations of grandeur? Perhaps one day, she might even lead Uncle Mikey by the hand – out into the light, out onto the bog, and over the hill – to a place which would surely prove infinitely more comfortable than an old dingy attic.

Such thoughts sustained her over the next few hours when her legs kept slipping on rainswept rock and her fingernails cracked in nasty little sharp-edged fissures which were all that were on offer as a means of gaining purchase. Her knees were gashed and bleeding. She felt unspeakably cold. The light drizzle had worked itself into drifting sheets of hard rain that stung her cheeks and made every step up an exercise in slippery endurance. She was so thirsty her tongue lolled out permanently to lap what drops she could.

Just as she was about to heave her aching body the last few footholds, the cloud of rain cleared and a shaft of sunlight streamed hot and warming on her back. There was a patch of watery blue in the sky almost directly above the summit. She thought it had to be a sign. A whisper of sunbeams on her upturned face and she felt a last hot surge of energy course through her blood. One final haul on a protruding clump of jagged rock and she was at the top. She was panting. On her knees, faced in the wrong direction. Her home in the distance called a familiar song to her. She imagined Uncle Mikey staring from the roof skylight. Bloodied fingers curled in a limp wave, just in case. Well, she hadn't been struck by a bolt of lightning yet. She took several gulps of air, closed her eyes as tight as she could, and turned.

Bog. More bog. Stretching out all the way to a small cluster of farmhouses in the east. Triangles of turf heaped here and there, just as on her side of the hill. Just rough bands of colour, straw, hemp, pink heather, spring green patches of fresh, newer grass, lichen-covered hunks of bleached granite. Bog.

She put her face in her hands and wept tears of outrage and frustration. There was no heaven here. No radiant smiles from circlets of winged angels around a benign, glowing-faced man on a golden throne. No offering of a deliciously thirst-quenching drink, Fanta maybe, from a silver, gem-encrusted goblet. No vision of a man she would instantly know as Father, waking from his afternoon nap to cast her a welcoming beam, his arms stretched out in fond embrace.

Grown-ups lied. Far more to the point, Auntie Bridie had lied. And if you couldn't believe her, who could you believe? Angela wept and wept. She crumpled up the list of favours she had been about to ask and threw it down to the bog below. It melted into marsh as she watched. Clearly, there was to be no short cut to getting Uncle Mikey out into sunlight.

The descent took just as long as the ascent. She nearly slid down several times. Now her buttocks were sorely scratched as well. Every now and then she would have to stop for another feast of hot indignant tears. By the time she reached the base, the sky overhead had settled into one long stretch of indigo gauze. It was nearly full dark as her tired legs finally staggered past her uncle's house and up the track toward her own. She looked back only once at the hill of disappointment silhouetted against the grainy sky.

Above it, winking with a quiet desperation – one brazen star.

Bina slapped her face and told her that the whole place was out looking for her and would a couple of boiled eggs and toast do now or what? Angela could hardly stand from the tiredness as the Aunts fizzed en masse around her listing frame. Slowly, she told her story. Casting Auntie Bridie a glance of furious accusation at the end. You told her what? Bina pinched her elder sister's bony shoulder. Maisie's chubby fingers danced in and out through the sausages of her hair with crazy glee that their undisputed leader was being taken to task. Get out of this one, let you. Only Bridie remained impassive. Eyes of black jet, narrowed and dismissive, remained glued to the window, as if there were certain things only she could see. Her lower lip stuck out defiantly. Finally she fastened the top pearl button of her cardigan. And who could say that heaven wasn't bog? There wasn't a person could say that for sure. Not for absolute. Yerra, get away with you, Bina scoffed, boiling eggs.

Angela fainted from exhaustion and was put to bed without the eggs in any case. She awoke from dark, peaty dreams in the middle of the night to find the scooped shadow of Bridie resting on her bed. Twin dancing gleams of light from her eyes burned through the blackness. Reminding Angela of the winking star. Bridie spoke low and hushed. She repeated over and over that Angela was indeed among the chosen, no matter what anyone else said. The thrust of the whole thing was not that Angela had found more bog on the other side of the hill, that was as maybe, and there would be a point explained about that in due and full course, the main point for them to focus on right at that moment however, was that Angela had come back down at all. That was the thing of it. There was a lot of thinking and scrutinization to be given to the matter yet. Oh no, it wasn't a disappointment by a long shot. In fact, when you came right down to it, you had to come at this one by way of the back door. The twin gleams swivelled and fixed Angela to stone. God, Auntie Bridie was fierce persuasive when she got going.

In fact, in point of fact, it had all been a test that she, Auntie

218

Bridie, had set her niece, the hushed voice was saying. And if she, Angela, couldn't overcome her disillusionment with heaven, or what God himself had chosen to show her – at that particular time and so forth – well. Well? Angela couldn't help herself. But Bridie would only repeat just – well. They welled back and forth for some considerable time before Angela felt her eyelids drooping heavily again and the last things she saw before darkness were the two Old Testament eyes glittering with renewed fervour.

Now, she had to shield her own eyes from a garish sun as she stared across the bog to that hill. Uncle Mikey's house was not far up on the left. Nothing ever seemed to change around here. Just the shifting colours of marshy grasses. She felt that spear of loneliness that always hit her on coming home. Here was everything she knew. Everything she'd come from. Her understanding of life was somehow inextricably linked to that bog. So many walks as a solitary child on the sponge of soil. So many effervescent dreams sending her back to the house and her daily chores, breathless with anticipation for the future. But if you left home – then it became the place you went back to. It would never again be entirely Angela's. And it made her lonely. Because she had moved away while her memory place had remained fixed. Stretching out before her to where the dun land appeared to seep into sky in a faint colourwash stroke.

She hesitated outside his porch. Wondered what her uncle had been told about his sister's demise, decided it might be best to check in advance. On the way up the track, she met Bina carrying a tray for him. They said hullo. Angela put down her case to give her mother some sort of a hug or touch but Bina had already passed by. She called over her shoulder that Regina was in the morgue already, she, Bina, wasn't up for a wake or what not and Bridie was slipping in and out of her senses and Angela'd better hurry up if she wanted to say goodbye. From the set of her ramrod back, Angela could tell that her mother was worn out already from seeing to the Aunts and the endless retinue of visitors who would have called to offer sympathy and required endless pots of tea. Sometimes she thought her mother was a little cold to her. But then she would look at the stoical, resigned face, gaze forever distracted by whatever had to be done next and Angela would quickly remind herself that Bina had her own way of coping with the heavy mantle of responsibility which had been thrust upon her shoulders. All the extra mouths to be fed, clothes to be stitched, a farm to be run and a brother stuck up in the attic of another house. Little wonder Bina had no time for smalltalk or energy-sapping hugs.

Still, a simple handshake would not be unwelcome from time to time.

Maisie rushed out to greet Angela, her mouth pulled open in silent movie scream. She beat her chest most piteously. Had to lean a hand on Angela's shoulder to get her breath back. Angela waited, rolling her eyes. No doubt Maisie was griefstruck in truth but the performance was over the top as usual.

'Thank God and his blessed mother you're here, child.' Maisie sniffed.

'I'd better go to Auntie Bridie.' Angela patted Maisie's hand, edging away slowly. The pincers tightened.

'She's gone from us!' An anguished shriek.

'What? Bridie?'

'Regina! We'll never do without her.'

Do what exactly? But Angela thought it best to just murmur soothingly. Of course it was sad. The sisters only had each other and their brother. They had spent their entire lives together notwithstanding a brief lapse on Bina's part. But poor old Reggie had been gone from them a long while since. It was only her shadow that had hung around the past few years. Angela was gently trying to prise Maisie's pinching fingers from her shoulder when she heard a croaky, feeble call of her name from upstairs.

'I'm coming, Auntie Bridie!' she called up.

Maisie released her and burst into a fit of genuine sobbing. Angela felt a spear of real pity. Whatever about Regina, Maisie really would be lost without Bridie. Had even slept with her all her life. In the blink of an eye, or more like the flash of the grim reaper's scythe, everything was falling apart and in this tiny corner of the universe, life amidst the bog would never be the same again. She climbed the stairs with her heart sagging somewhere around her knees.

If she'd secretly harboured any doubts about Bridie's mortality, they were quickly dispelled when she saw the wizened sultana face. Bridie's mouth turned down dramatically at one corner, a spool of saliva flowing constantly into the crepey crevices of neck. She was the colour of burnt ochre as well with the cataract-ridden eyes hollowed and sunken into folds of flesh.

'Hullo, Auntie Bridie.' Angela sat on the bed and pressed the old woman's limp hand. She could feel every bone contract a little. A skeleton.

'I'm dying, Angela!' Bridie tried a screech but the voice once so strident and commanding was now reduced to a slurred and guttural whisper. Angela had to conceal a tiny smile: it was so typical that the person most surprised by the prospect of death was Bridie herself.

'Shh now. Don't be talking like that. Sure you're grand, aren't you?'

'I'm not! I'm dying!'

'Ah whisht. Look – will I boil you up an egg? A nice brown egg. And I'll make little strips of toast how you like them. You'll be right as rain after that.'

'I'll try a egg,' Bridie said, slightly mollified. 'Ye've the priest on lookout though, haven't ye?'

'He's always on lookout. But I don't think he'll be needed here today.'

Bridie considered that for a while. She sniffed.

'He's Regina to do first anyway. It's true.'

221

'You see? So you can't go off inconveniencing the poor man even if you'd a mind to.'

'Fair enough.' Bridie was relaxing by the second. One eye closed. 'I could nearly try a sleep.'

'Course you could.' Angela had to purse her lips. That other eye was awful reluctant to close as well. She dabbed the trail of saliva from the folds of her aunt's neck. Brushed and combed her hair using the mother-of-pearl set on the dresser. Plumped up the pillows, patted the sheets straight, then casually, with a deft flick of her thumb, shut the still open eye. Bridie snored.

She didn't inconvenience the priest in the days that followed as it turned out. Regina's funeral was a sad little affair with a cluster of people standing around in a gale force wind that had struck up suddenly and violently out of nowhere. Driving rain battened chins down onto chests. The priest said a few nice words about Regina and sisterly love and so forth, reminding them all to pray for Bridie also, who everybody in the village knew to be a rock of the church in those parts and furthermore was a fine teacher in her day and ran that school singlehandedly until it was so rudely taken off her. The odd guilty glance amongst the bowed heads at that one. The odd wink as well.

As they stood before the gap of scooped-out earth, waiting for the coffin to be lowered to its resting place beside her parents and sister Imelda, Bina's shoulders began to heave. Angela was startled. She'd never seen her mother cry before. And somehow it was all the more shocking for the way she did it. The face impassive as ever, just full fat tears rolling down her cheeks, not a sound, the shoulders heaving up and down mechanically. She reached out to squeeze her mother's hand and was further shocked by the intensity of the rebuff when Bina shot her clasped hands to one side, out of Angela's reach.

'Mam? Mammy?'

'Shut up. I'm fine.' But Bina shot her a look which made Angela intake a sharp breath.

222

She couldn't tell for sure what was in that glance. Accusation certainly, a touch of contempt and a hint of the deep well of sadness that had always resided somewhere at the core of Bina which she had tamped down behind an impenetrable shroud of busyness and resignation.

The final prayers were read for Regina, the earth was being sealed just as Bina resealed her inner self once more. The shoulders ceased heaving, the tears stopped. And as they slowly walked away, Angela took a furtive sideways glance and Bina's eyes were staring straight ahead, blank and lustreless as ever. Her own head hung limply, oppressed by the crushing weight of her mother's unspoken anger. For the first time in her life, Angela realized that it had been ever thus.

Maisie took to the bed beside Bridie who was slipping a little further every day. Maisie could not be prised from her sister's side. She was beset by unholy terror that Bridie would slink away without saying goodbye. So there were three sets of trays to be prepared for every meal. Uncle Mikey appeared to understand that Regina was gone and Bridie was going, when Angela explained to him what Bina, for whatever reason, had not. He was sombre and pensive each time Angela climbed up to the loft. She was grateful to see that his hair had been cut recently and his nails had been pared.

When she wasn't attending to the Aunts or helping her mother prepare the endless trays of food, she sat with him for hours, quietly telling him about life at the shelter. He listened with his head cocked to the side, sometimes flashing a rotten-toothed smile, but his eyes were immeasurably sad. It seemed to Angela that there were things going on within both houses of which she had no understanding. Perhaps it was just the scent of death everywhere. She seemed to carry it in her nostrils as she moved around. The sickly, cloying odour of a dying generation. The old country as it used to be, supplanted by smart shiny jeeps and ersatz country farmhouse kitchen cupboards replacing the real thing. There wouldn't be an attic nowadays, to accommodate an eccentric uncle – it would be a smart loft conversion with Velux windows and an en-suite shower room.

She tried to cheer him up, performing cartwheels all around the attic one day, as she used when a young girl. He laughed and made one feeble attempt himself which she took as a positive sign. He was amazingly agile for his age. The only exercise he ever got was circling the perimeter of the room, which he would do for hours at a time. But just as he managed to swing both legs into the air he went limp again and sat in his usual cross-legged manner. Glazed eyes staring over her shoulder, barely registering her presence. When she clicked her fingers in front of his face, he started and offered her a watery smile again. She patted her shoulder and he nestled his head with a quiet sigh. Sometimes they would both drift off into deep sleep. Once when she thought he couldn't hear her, Angela gave in to the tide of tears she'd been restraining since her arrival. Just everything seemed so sad and hopeless. In spite of her best efforts, nothing had changed while everything had changed. It was all out of her control. Soon there wouldn't be an aunt left and her uncle too would just quietly slip away one evening having never left his self-imposed prison cell.

Auntie Bridie was very quiet one morning, so quiet that Angela feared the worst when she tiptoed in for the first check of the day. Maisie put a finger to her lips. They listened to the rattling sound of Bridie's breaths. Maisie whispered: 'She's awake the whole night long, dripping with pure fright. Says she's going to purgatory till you get himself below out of that place.'

'Oh, rubbish.'

'It's what she says, I tell you.' Maisie's eyes widened. 'She can feel the flames lick at her ankles is what she's after telling me. When're you going to take them vows, Angela? When?'

Bridie's eyes opened suddenly. It was true that her desiccated face, what was left of it, was indeed a mask of taut fear.

'When?' She repeated Maisie's question in a whisper dry as sticks of kindling.

'Soon enough.' Angela felt a spurt of anger. All her life she was subject to their demands. Even at death's door an aunt was still exercising control.

'I'll be burnt to a crisp.' Bridie's doleful response.

'D'you hear that, Angela?' Maisie remonstrated. 'Go back and do your duty.'

'Oh, for God's sake. Is there no let up with the pair of ye at all,' Angela shouted. 'My duty. I'll make my own decisions, thank you very much. If it's right at the time to take the vows, I'll take them. It's pure nonsense this business of purgatory and what have you. You're just making up stories like you always did, to force me into something. Remember that hill over there?' Angela leaned against the windowframe, looking out. 'Heaven how do,' she added with her lips curled.

'I'm not making up stories!' Bridie tried to lift her head from the pillow but it wouldn't budge. She was sweating, dribbling and clearly in great distress. 'You don't understand. You don't know.'

'Know what?' Angela snapped.

'What I done!'

There was a long silence.

'What have you done?'

Maisie too was all ears but Bridie's mouth had clamped firmly shut again except for the issue of drool from a small gap at one corner. Angela walked across to them and planked her behind firmly on the bed.

'What're you on about, Auntie Bridie? What is it you've done? Tell me.'

'I can't!' A muffled shriek. One scrabbling hand pulled the sheet up over her face. 'I can't!'

Maisie and Angela exchanged puzzled glances. Whatever Bridie had done, she was going to the grave with it. Moreover, by her own estimation, she was going to purgatory with it. And

Angela's vocation was fixed in her mind as her sole means of salvation.

'I'd have a egg,' she wailed from beneath the coverlet.

'I'd lay an egg,' Angela sighed, standing up, 'as soon as figure you out, Auntie Bridie. You're one of the divine mysteries.'

'Ah, sure you're still making something big of her,' Bina said in a voice laden with contempt. She was standing at the open door with the morning tray already prepared, a brown egg gleaming in its cup. She stepped across and whipped the sheet from her sister's face. 'When all she is is what she ever was. A foolish old woman that was given far too high credence and not half enough shoes up the hole. In this house.' Bina neatly tapped the top of the egg off and shovelled a spoonful into the shocked open jaw on the pillow.

For the longest while there wasn't another sound in the room to be heard other than the slurpy mastications of said jaw. At one point, Angela caught her mother's eye and thought she saw a glint of amusement there. Angela ventured a shy smile and was rewarded by something similar. Just a quick fleeting curve of Bina's lips, but a smile nonetheless.

A little while later, Angela's feet didn't touch the ground as she took Uncle Mikey's breakfast down the track. She was walking on air. A feeling not too dissimilar in fact to how one tiny honest part of her felt after Robert's impulsive kiss. She had managed to shove that hot memory into a recess in her brain ever since that Sunday. Whenever it tried to peek through into her thoughts, she had quickly sent it scurrying back to its bolthole. There was just no dealing with it. Here it was again even as she placed her uncle's tray on the attic floor. He was gazing up at her with his head cocked to the side in his usual fashion. She knelt down and clasped his hands as a sigh issued up from her underbelly.

'Uncle Mikey,' she began in a frank, matter of fact voice, until Robert's face floated before her eyes again. She stopped and bit her lip. 'I'm a lie,' she said simply. He nibbled a toast

226

soldier and kept the dark eyes trained on her face. Angela wanted to turn away, to hide from the penetrating orbs, but she couldn't.

'If I am a lie,' she continued, 'then I don't know what's the truth. All I've ever known to be – is a nun. And what's wrong with that? What's wrong with being sure about one thing? Lots of people aren't sure about anything. But if you take the nun thing away –' her voice faltered, she shrugged '– then I don't have the first clue who I am. Not a clue. First man that gives me the nod, well a kiss actually – oh God, this is so mortifying – well that's it, isn't it? I'm away off on another hack. But I really like him. I mean really like him, Uncle Mikey. And now who I thought I was, I'm not at all. And what I thought I wanted – I'm not so sure. And who is it anyway that's doing the thinking or the wanting? Who is me? I'm damned if I know.'

Angela stopped for a breath and watched him from the corner of her eye. This me, I, want, business was truly disturbing. And yet she felt certain that it was all in some way connected to her mother's mutiny with the Aunts earlier. Bina might have muttered or complained in the past but she had never actually done anything contrary to Bridie's wishes. The fogginess in Angela's head that had plagued her childhood and young adulthood had lifted for one brief instant but the shaft of light had been shortlived and now the dark fumes subsumed everything once more. How could anybody know themselves so little, she wanted to ask him, but what could he understand about that? His needs were so basic, so uncomplicated. It wasn't fair to burden him with such thoughts, so she made to rise from her haunches. His hands clutched hers with surprising speed. He cocked his head to the other side and pressed lightly with his thumbs against her palms. She realized that he wanted her to go on. Tell him more.

So she told him about Bridie's fear of purgatory and what Bina had said to her. He was very still for a minute then bolted down the remaining toast and honey before attempting another cartwheel. This time he nearly executed a perfect turn but it got away from him right at the very end. Nevertheless, he appeared quite pleased with his effort and slurped back his milky tea with gusto. Every now and then his nose would wrinkle up as he grinned happily to himself. It was the longest time since Angela had seen those grins and she sat back contentedly to watch him. Before she knew what she was doing she was telling him all about Robert. How they met, the Sunday painting sessions, the tour around the museum. He listened avidly, looking up when he wanted her to go over something again like the Edenhall vase or her description of the mosaic floor in the V & A Treasury Hall. He flapped a hand, signalling more again when she got onto the pastel miniature of the unknown woman. A thought struck her forcefully.

'That's me, isn't it, Uncle Mikey? I'm the unknown woman. I might as well be looking at a picture of myself plastered up there on the wall beside her. Ah sure, this kind of codology will get me nowhere. I've to set my mind on things again. See straight ahead. There's no point in looking in here, is there?' She tapped the side of her head. Hard enough to hurt. The smile on Uncle Mikey's face faded. Suddenly she felt a spasm of irritation with him. What was that dreamy smile implying anyway, every time she mentioned Robert? Was he another one saying she'd never make a nun?

'Look it,' she cried, drawing her hands away from his grasp. 'I might've made him sound cock of the walk or something but he's a man with two children of his own, lovely little girls, and he hasn't the time of day for them. How could he be a good man with that sort of attitude, I ask you. Anyway, I've no notion of seeing him again – ever. So you can wipe that smile off your face once and for all.' Angela stood up abruptly. Turned her back to him so that he mightn't see the hot, prickly tears which stung her eyes. She dabbed the back of her hand against her nose. A solitary, sympathetic grunt from Uncle Mikey and the verbal torrent took her over once more. She began to tell him about Robert's line of work. It was as if by conjuring every minute detail of her meetings with him, she could somehow reach in and exorcize him from her memory bank.

A feeble sun was doing its best to peer through the dust-grimed skylight. It struck Angela that she might just get away with something at this juncture. She kept right on talking, waving her hands about to describe things, dabbing an imaginary paintbrush when she described the painstaking process of picture restoring. She was standing by the window then. To illustrate the procedure, she licked a finger and wiped one tiny corner of glass clean. Another and another, talking at a staccato rate all the while, until all ten fingers were black as night and the window retained only a faint veneer of smudged-in dust. His eyes followed the newly revealed dust motes streaming in one shaft of light. She decided to let it at that for now. One step at a time. Soon it would be entirely transparent again and he might at least look out. If nothing else, he would have his own personal picture of the world restored to him.

Before she left, it occurred to her that it was Robert and not herself who had in fact finally succeeded in restoring some light to her uncle's life. The thought was not unpleasant. She let the notion meander a little, grow legs as it were, until very soon it took on a life and meaning of its own. Surely this was how she could justify the whole Robert business altogether. The covert meetings, the intrusive dreams, damn it – even that kiss. If she stepped out of her own head for a moment, a place where she singularly did not wish to remain, if she maintained a forward course again, toward the nun thing, the getting Uncle Mikey out of the loft thing – then, really, in a curious fashion, it might well be adduced that Robert was just part of the overall design.

The whole world looked lighter and brighter as she climbed down from the loft. By the time her feet hit solid ground – she was back on course. A huddle of small children with glistening eyes and broad, toothy beams sang to her from the Missions so far away. She understood what her life was about, her vocation, her destiny. It had got a little murky in London for a while there. But now the Aunts were out of her head and she was in control of her own future. And as that had always been to be a nun, why should she change in midstream now?

Change? Where had that come from?

On the way up to her own house she remembered that it was Sunday. She'd missed early Mass and would catch the twelve o'clock with Bina. She suddenly stopped by a wild rhododendron bush with a cupped hand against her mouth. All that idle talk about Robert and she'd forgotten to send so much as a note to say she wouldn't make her sitting this Sunday. She didn't have a phone number. He would think she hadn't turned up because of that kiss. Well, she told herself, there was every chance she wouldn't have turned up. Every chance that her proper senses would have returned to her during the course of her week's duties at the shelter.

A snowball's chance – in purgatory, say.

Chapter Twelve

Silly bints wearing their hearts on their sleeves were the curse of Nicola's life. Them and that spaz brother of hers. But by the end of a week of constant surveillance and the absence of the silly bint to stop him, Nicola was beginning to sorely miss the screening presence of Angela. Every time she left the shelter, there he was, mooning by some corner, kneading that thick, stupid head of his. Oh he knew what she was up to all right. And it was only a matter of time before he messed things up for her. She had to do something about him and quick.

Later in the afternoon she was supposed to pick up some decent gear from a source near King's Cross. Keep her in sales for a good month or so. And it would be high-quality shit too, which was vital in the early days of laying claim to a piece of turf. A good section of the streets around belonged to her now. Her reputation growing every day. Wouldn't want to have to start all over again, like so many times before, because that moron had tracked her down and made taking care of business next to impossible.

You had to have serious guts to take over the streets at Nicola's age, being a woman and on the game which put her out there for every rival turk to take a pop off. But Nicola knew her head didn't work like the rest of the crapped-out dopeheads in here. She had a brain that went clickety-clack. That was the sound. She could have sworn she heard it sometimes. Turning over. Sizing up. Turning some other sap over.

Clickety-clack. She bought stilettoes to make that noise. Made her laugh sometimes when she'd see a John looking her up and down. Judging what she'd on offer down below by the shoes. It was what she had up top that went clickety-clack. Still, how could they know. Until she'd roll one over so fast he thought he was still in a daydream.

As a kid she'd been lightning fast too. Got fostered out more times than any one else in all the institutions put together. Except for Steve. Got sent back when it suited her, mostly when she got bored of listening to some silly bint telling her she was pretty – really – and the great future she had ahead of her if only she could harness all that nervous energy. Like she didn't know that already. Jesus wept. Take that stupid bitch in Clapham, the sunny red-brick house. It existed all right. The couple wanted her all right. Sure, they were kind people, it had to be said – dickheads – whatever, but it was really Steve they wanted. It was a son they'd lost. Not a daughter. And butter wouldn't melt in his mouth in them days. He was always a good boy. Blonde hair slicked to the side. Just enough puppy fat to be cute. Big blue surprised eyes. And easy like runny butter. Yeah – he was just the kind of cherub the dickheads fell for every time. Nicola was always that much sharper. In her head and in her features. Shifty eyes, she heard one of the bints say about her one day. Stupid cow.

Still, shifty eyes or not, sharper-faced or not, Stevie boy wouldn't go nowhere without his Nicki. It was two for the price of one, the cherub and the magpie. When she wanted to move on again, he moved on with her. Even that time in Clapham when he wanted to stay put. But Nicola had big plans for the pair of them. She'd been trading penknives from the age of eight. It was only a matter of sweet time himself before she moved on to greater things. She had stars in her eyes and putting stars in other people's eyes was her business.

She understood the dangers same as Steve. But that was the difference between them. He started using. She never used.

232

He'd stopped using. Stopped dealing. Nicola never stopped. Never. When he wasn't her guinea pig anymore to sample the gear, there was always fresh blood to try stuff out on. The women in this place, for example. They kept up a constant stream to her door for the contents of her little black box. Got a make-up into the bargain. Nicola was into extras, value addeds. Which was how the punters with habits got to know of her. Two quick fixes for the price of four. Easy money. And a safe place to come home to after a hard day's work. Not some sleazy bedsit with a shadowy doorway and a blade waiting for her throat, someone not happy with her encroachment on his turf. Yeah, there were downsides to every business.

Take the profit margin on smack these days. Bloody market was flooded. Nicola knew when it was time to move on. In every way. She was going into LSD tabs, knew someone who could source and make them with her. It was a complicated process, getting the mix exactly right, diluting it so that each dropperful onto each square tab of paper would contain the correct microgram dosage for hallucinatory bliss. Trouble was, it took a while, a day dropping, a day off, because the constant fumes filled a room after a while and heads and hands grew a bit unsteady. Nicola didn't want any mistakes happening – not in a fresh market. Wouldn't do her reputation any good at all.

A knock on the door interrupted her machinations. She took the money, handed over the package, applied a brush of mascara and a dollop of gloss – another satisfied customer. Not too long now before she could hand over the dog's work, run a few of the whores here maybe, from a clean, safe eyrie up west. Do it all on a mobile then. She'd take driving lessons, buy a red car, one of those sports jobbies and live in an all-white apartment. Chunky suede furniture, clean lines, nothing fussy – like the rooms in the magazines she bought every month. All sorted.

If Steve wasn't doing her head in. She frowned at her own reflection in the mirror. Absently lathered another layer of lipgloss on top of the several coats there already. They'd a good tight team going till he lost his bottle and cleaned up. But his head was bollocksed anyway by the time of the last OD. He'd been going spazzie for years in any case. Useful enough with his fists when they started out. Could slice a brick wall with one butt of his head. She used her head another way though. Did all the figuring out, the making contacts, the clickety-clacking while he did the protecting. In the early days he was good at that. She could establish them just about anywhere. And did, just about everywhere. She'd be rich by now if they hadn't been done over by another team working the same patch. Still, she was lucky to be alive at all after that one. A close call. Steve wasn't so lucky that time though. Two broken arms, a fractured thighbone, collarbone and his head practically caved in on one side. Not much use as a protector after that, was he? So she dumped him. But the freak kept following.

She locked the box away in a trunk under her bed. Fixed her face one last time and headed downstairs. A quick look outside – yep – there he was, thinking he was hidden behind a bus shelter. Just another one of the dickheads now. She couldn't even run in these heels. Why wasn't that silly bint keeping an eye on him anyway? Nicola would have to track her down. Spin her another load of bollocks. Do her face, make her feel pretty maybe. It worked with the rest of the hookers, made them grateful, softened them up. Loosened the miserable bitches' fingers on their purses.

Meantime, there was her collection later today. She'd have to think of a ruse to shake him off. She began to strut in the opposite direction, expecting to lose him a few corners along. Out of the corner of her eye she caught him tracking her steps.

Why couldn't he get a fucking dog or something?

Robert waited outside Richmond Station for hours, rubbing his aching jaw. No sign of Angela. She wasn't turning up. He had to face it, take it like a man. Thought he'd take it like a man, with a pint, in the pub across the road where he might still look out – just in case. Three pints later, his eyes bleary with strain, he decided to cut his losses and go home. He'd overstepped the mark by kissing her. She didn't see him in that way and the shock had sent her fleeing back into the arms of her lover. Robert muttered a few words to the barman, nodded at a familiar face by the counter, stuck one hand deep within a pocket and left, whistling a little tuneless tune to himself. Probably for the best anyway. No harm done. His jaw throbbed mercilessly.

On the way home along the river it occurred to him that there was the slightest chance that he'd missed her. Maybe he'd looked away for an instant. In fact, several instants, when he'd left his post to buy that newspaper. That could be the answer. Maybe she was waiting, albeit growing impatient, by the houseboat this very minute. He broke into a run. It turned into a sprint over the footbridge. He was Icarus himself as he flew along the last section of towpath. To find – nothing.

Inside the houseboat he tinkered with the painting. But his heart wasn't in it. She simply was not coming and that was that. He decided to give her another couple of hours. Just in case. After all, there were the preliminary sketches of Anita to be getting on with. She'd turned up yesterday as usual with the girls and reminded him that she was next. He was going to start next Saturday. The portrait of Tammy and Nessie was nearly completed. He'd cheated a bit with Nessie's ticcy eye, making both eyes the same size, a fact that Tammy nearly blurted several times except that he'd managed to divert her attention on each occasion.

All things considered, he'd been feeling pretty good about himself throughout the week. He was painting again. The Victorian flower restoration had come up like a dream. Bonnie was off his back. What did it really matter if he never saw Angela again? He could easily finish the portrait now without her.

He slumped in a chair, sore chin in his hands, staring at the cleft on her cheek. What did it matter? That's not what he'd said to himself in the supermarket yesterday. Robert groaned and pulled his hands up over his face and hair.

He'd finished his session with the girls and Anita, and had headed out to get the ingredients for the meal he was going to cook for Angela this evening. He had a vision of them on the top deck, checked tablecloth, nice bottle of wine, rib of beef. Not enough time for lemon mascarpone but he could always get fresh strawberries. He was going to thank her profusely for giving him so much of her valuable free time. Was, in fact, going to toast her. Would not under any circumstances refer to anything more intimate than that so she might feel secure still more about the arrangement they had. And would continue to come with an easier mind. If the words didn't stick in his throat he might even bring himself to ask about her man. What was he like? Oh very nice. Lucky guy. Leave it at that.

He'd just chosen a punnet of strawberries and was heading for the checkout with a laden trolley when he came across them. A big hulk of a fellow with tattooed biceps like oak trunks was trundling down the aisle toward him, carrying a young boy on his back. At first the excited shrieks and hollers signalled a harmless bit of fun. Then the boy was wriggling, trying to get down. He was uncomfortable. A cry with an edge of pain caught Robert's attention. He looked at the man's face and saw the glazed, taunting eyes of a dozen Misters. Remembered how the games would spill over to the point of violence. The boy was whimpering now, the breath crushed out of him. Robert recalled arm wrestling matches, just a laugh to begin with. Then the shooting pain all the way up to his shoulder and the bunched crackle of his fingers within some Neanderthal vice. Bonnie was never there when the chumps asserted their masculinity. And Robert never told. He could see the same burning shame, the furious impotence emblazoned on the captive boy's face at that moment. The hulk, definitely a Mister and not a father, was taunting him. Telling him to try harder, see if he could break free. The young lad pummelled his captor's head, the man laughed cheesily, then with a vicious twist of his mouth, pressed the arms ever tighter around the boy's back. Making him sob in real agony this time. People scurried past. Too terrified of the huge hunk of meat that passed for human to try saying a word. Supermarkets were full of such incidents. Boy was probably some sort of psycho himself in any case. Or would be.

Robert told himself to leave it. The brute would stop in a minute anyway. They always did once they'd drawn the tears which made them feel so powerful. He made to move away with the boy's anguished gasps ringing in his ears.

'Hah? Hah?' the man was saying over and over as he cinched his arms tighter.

Angela would have mashed the punnet of strawberries into his ugly mug.

Before he had time to give it a second thought, Robert drew back the trolley and lunged it full force into the aggressor's stomach. He grunted, expelling air in a long whoosh. It had caught him right under the solar plexus. The boy slid to the ground, gasping at first, then a huge grin cracked on his cheeks. Robert just stood there. Well, he could hardly walk away right then. Even if his legs were begging to run. Neanderthal was holding his stomach, snorting like a shire horse. He staggered across to Robert, who had time for only one thought before the chunk of fist that was winging his way met his chin:

God yes. He was deeply and hopelessly in love with Angela.

That was all his mind would say. Over and over. Even as he sat there now, desperately trying to find a new mantra. Something more along the lines of – win some, lose some. C'est la vie. Would never have worked anyway. Oh well. Anything with a touch more self-protection than the bald naked fact of having fallen in love with a woman he would never see again. But the words imposed themselves and there was absolutely nothing he could do to stop them. He had trusted again to his bitter cost,

trusted that she would turn up every Sunday, that was his first
mistake, trusted himself not to let her get to him, his second
monumental mistake. Third? That he hadn't locked her in a room
when he had the chance, keeping her for ever just for himself.

The doorknob rattled and he nearly fell off the chair. He
turned with his mouth already open to tell her all this. If she
ran, he'd run after her and lock her in that room until he could
wear her down, make her love him back. Call in a hypnotist if
need be. An anaesthetist to knock her out if need be. Jesus,
Bonnie herself, if push really came to shove. His heart thunked
mercilessly.

It was Peter. Looking around in an owlish way.

'No Angela?'

'No.'

'Mind if I join you?'

'Yesss.'

'Who's stolen your bun then?'

'Get out, Peter.'

Peter's laugh tinkled. Thought that was a big joke.

'She's not coming back, I take it? Angela?'

Robert couldn't for the life of him figure out the gleeful fleas
jumping in his friend's eyes. The satisfied smile on his fat lips.
What had he ever seen in him all these years?

'No, she's not coming. Today,' he added pointedly.

Peter was eyeing him a little too shrewdly for his liking.

'What happened to your chin?'

'I hit myself shaving. Never mind my bloody chin. Look – I
want to get on with things here if you don't mind. Maybe I'll
drop by later. Before I go home.'

'No, you won't,' Peter said succinctly. 'You're always saying
that lately. And you never do. Are those of Anita?' He stepped
into Robert's space anyway, lifting the sketches in a pro-
prietorial fashion. 'Make sure you do both eyes the same size,
won't you? She's not in – em – the best of moods these days.
Hormones or something. Too many of them.'

'She seems happy enough to me.'

'Does she now?' Peter smiled but it didn't reach his eyes. 'Angela will be here next Sunday as usual?'

'What's it to you?'

'Well excuse me for breathing. Isn't a fellow allowed to ask a simple question without having his head bitten off? I want to ask her to dinner for heaven's sake. Seeing as you won't do it.'

'She doesn't have a lot of free time,' Robert snapped. 'Now if you'll excuse me, Peter, neither do I.'

Peter blinked rapidly for a number of seconds. Robert immediately regretted his curt tone, searched his brain for something to soften the situation which had grown increasingly hostile and brittle between them. Said: 'Look, I'll ask her next Sunday, okay?'

But Peter was still blinking. He turned sharply for the door.

'Well. Good to know she's coming back.' A metallic, hollow laugh. 'Shows she's more staying power than Mr Fielding at any rate.'

The door swung shut with a slam. Silence. Robert slumped miserably onto his chair once again. Angela's grey eyes twinkled at him from the portrait. A hint sadistically, he thought.

The priest was called off lookout and the doctor couldn't believe the rallying turn Auntie Bridie had taken in the course of just a week. Only nights ago he would have sworn she'd never see another morning. That's what he said to Bina and Angela on his way out. It wouldn't surprise him if she made the hundred, the way she was going. Angela thought Bina looked a bit forlorn at that but she didn't say anything and got back to work as usual. Evidently the prospect of purgatory had jolted Bridie into a rude recovery. She wasn't ready to commend her spirit into the hands of her Maker until she felt some kind of assurance that she was on the fast track to heaven.

There were subtle changes in the household though. Bina

239

had taken to shouting up at Bridie's persistent calls for things, that she'd have to hold tough for a while. Would have to wait until Bina found a free second to do or get whatever was required. Sometimes, she ignored the bleats entirely and Maisie was sent down to find out what was the cause of the delay, and Bina would send her back up with a flea in her ear and her hands empty. More to be in cahoots with her mother than anything – a delicious new feeling – Angela took to ignoring the plaintive wails as well. By the middle of the week she refused to take an extra tray up for Maisie who would have done any- thing for her elder sister, except starve. That was asking too much altogether. Though Bridie sort of asked.

By the weekend, Maisie was down, followed in cold pursuit by Bridie who was going to take up Regina's old cot in the corner of the kitchen just to spite Maisie. The endless bickering was in full swing with Bina lashing out at their asses with her dishcloth just as before. Bridie's gums were at her if her bunions weren't and now she could add the imminent onslaught of another stroke to the list of blackmail. But somehow no one was listening like they used to.

Angela decided it was safe to fly back by Friday evening. Bina walked her to the bus. Which was another subtle change in the scheme of things. Just before Angela boarded, Bina clasped her shoulder.

'Did you mean that? What you said to Bridie about making up your own mind when the time's right? You know, the vows?'

'Well, sure I did.'

'Good. 'bout time for you.'

Angela burst into a fit of laughing.

'Did you mean what you said about shoeing her hole?'

Bina's eyes twinkled mischievously.

'Night and day I'll be at it. Now I know the old buzzard's going to live. I've years of shoeing to catch up on.'

'Mam?' Angela hesitated, the bus driver was pointedly revving.

'Oh go on, let you. Sure of course I know there's a man. Didn't I see him in your eyes the minute you walked through the front door. Good luck to you now. And mind you make up your own mind and not let it be made up for you.'

Angela's mouth was agape as the door slid shut and Bina gave a backward wave as she strode back toward the bog. She was still wearing her navy flowery apron and wellingtons.

There were a million things to catch up on when Angela arrived back at the shelter. Mary Margaret hauled her into the office to give a list as long as a year's gin bill. Sr Carmel had been taken by some of the men to watch the hurling semi-final of Clare vs. Galway on Setanta in a local pub last Sunday. They'd decked her out – scarf, hat, banner – in Clare regalia and brought her along like their mascot. The feckers had slipped vodkas into her orange juice and Carmel had unwittingly imbibed the first drop of alcohol in her life. She'd taken the pledge at the age of twelve and never broken it. Until last Sunday, when she arrived back stotious, singing 'Four Green Fields' with a smile across her face to rival the Panama Canal. She hadn't been right all week. Pure useless for work. The giant of the Gorbals had taken his tallywhacker out that once too often and had been sent to Camden. The bleddy kettle was broken, sending the doctor into paroxysms of grief. And that fecker Steve was out all hours, swanning around the women's next door. What did Angela know about that anyway?

Angela shrugged her shoulders.

'I know I've a lot to catch up on, but could I have tomorrow afternoon off, d'you think?'

A silence like death ricocheted around the office.

'Would that be on top of Sunday or instead of?'

'On top of.'

'Jesus Christ Almighty.'

Angela felt her skin was on fire but she thought it best not to offer anything by way of explanation. With close on two

241

weeks off already behind her she might as well go for broke. Her intention was to call on Robert, to explain her non-appearance last Sunday. But she couldn't be sure that he'd be around next Sunday. Probably had a hectic social life like that friend she'd met, Peter. Saturdays, he painted his girls though. She remembered that and figured it was her best bet for catching him in. Mary Margaret was eyeing her with the face of a person who had just walked into a freshly steaming pat of dogshit.

'Holiday in the Caribbean next, is it?' She sucked on her Afton. 'So what's the attraction tomorrow? Let me see, we've art history on Sundays, I know, it'll be thermodynamics on Saturdays. Have I guessed it right now, Angela?'

'I've someone I've got to see,' Angela mumbled miserably.

The moustache bristled over the moue of lips the Superior made. The eyebrows were up up up. God, she might have extraneous hairs but she certainly didn't have any flies on her. The sceptical look said as much.

'Ah sure now.'

'Ah sure now – what?' Angela snapped. This was just so bloody typical. Five minutes ago she had been so contented to be back. Felt that she was in a home from home. *What?* No. What she meant was, felt that she was where she should be. Where she was destined to be. However. There was a measure of protocol to be observed. She wished to extend her polite apologies for her absence last week to a man who deserved no less than an apology. Even if he had been a bit forward in the course of their last meeting. She wouldn't like him to think that he'd rocked her foundations or some such. Because he most certainly hadn't. And it behoved her to tell him just that.

'You have a ferocious amount of catching up to do, young lady. Ferocious.'

'I'm perfectly aware of that, Mother. And I will. Catch up. Auntie Bridie sends you her regards by the way. Only yesterday she was telling us how you were her perfect student. Brighter than paint is what she said.'

The moue was so tight now, hairs were bunched up dark as an evening shadow on a wrestler. Mary Margaret poured herself a decent swig of Gordon's.

'Get out, Sister. And mind you don't trip over your nose as you go. There's a girl.'

'Tomorrow's all right then so?'

Mary Margaret clicked her tongue, swigged, nodded. Angela bounced out before she changed her mind. She immediately went looking for Steve. But there wasn't a sign of him anywhere. His cluster was neat and tidy, the bed made and the few clothes he had folded and stacked on a chair. An item under the bed caught her eye. It was a small photograph in a cheap plastic frame. A girl and a boy about eight and nine respectively. Nicola and Steve with their arms casually slung around one another's shoulders, their mouths wide with laughs, wind teasing hair back from their faces. She could make out a faint line of blue sea in the background. They looked so happy and innocent on the annual Residential Home outing. Margate no doubt, or Bournemouth. When she thought of Steve's face now, the mashed up, furrowed lines of it, the scabby hands, dead blue eyes, she had to swallow a rock in her throat. Nicola too, a thin, elfin little thing in the photo, such hardened emeralds her eyes had become. Moments of contentment by a seashore were few and far between for children like them. Jewels to be treasured evermore if the carefully polished glass within the frame was anything to go by. Angela smiled sadly to herself, replaced his treasure and launched herself into the dozens of tasks which awaited her.

Later that night, close to midnight, still no sign of Steve but he might have slipped up to his cluster without her noticing. She was up to her eyes in so many things. With her legs trembling from exhaustion, Angela made her way upstairs to her studio bedroom. She slumped into an armchair and lit a cigarette, eyeing her virginal bed through slitted eyes. It seemed to mock her. She began to undress where she sat, thumping shoes

243

onto the floor, wriggling as she hauled tights off, the fag butt held between her winched lips. Making her think of Mary Margaret. Maybe this was how it started, the doleful thought struck her. A few sneaky fags at bedtime, the empty bed, the spartan room, prayers and the long night ahead. All the other long nights ahead. A little snifter of gin to help those long nights pass more quickly. Followed by half a bottle. A short step then to most of the bottle. And still the sleeplessness. The restlessness.

She took off every stitch and stood before the mirror. A different person somehow to the young woman who had, and not so very long ago, pranced on the bed making faces at her reflection, mithering on about cappuccinos and the like. Her hands cupped her breasts, teasing and tweaking nipples. For a moment she imagined that Robert was standing behind her and it was his hands that were wrapped around her torso, stroking her, touching her. She wondered what his hands would feel like. What it would be like to wake up next to him in the morning. His lazy grin as he would reach for her. She felt a moistness like runny honey between her legs. The same wetness she had tried to ignore every time she sat naked under the silk shawl while Robert studied her, turning his head from side to side. The thought of his hands and not his eyes exploring her body, gently, intimately, made her eyes close. A tiny mewl escaped her lips.

Would these sensations ever fully subside? Or would they take her over entirely so that gin would no longer anaesthetize the longings? It was a fearsome thought, the rest of her life with only herself. Only her own hands to touch her body. No one ever to look and really see her. No one ever again to watch her as Robert did as though he could see her without her clothes on. Yes, she had enjoyed that heady power in his company, the overwhelming intoxication of being the subject of another's undivided attention. Had enjoyed, too, the frisson of exquisite torture in the knowledge it could go no further than mutual glances between them. Perhaps she had even enjoyed tormenting him.

And that thought was next to unendurable.

One of Angela's eyes prised open reluctantly. There was yet another reluctant concession to honesty she had to make. Her face screwed up into a tight wince. She wouldn't exactly mind seeing what Robert looked like either. Wouldn't mind taking a good long look at him. The other eye shot open. She stared into the dilating pupils of the reflection in the mirror. Herself, of course. But she did not know the eyes that stared helplessly back at her. Hardly knew the breasts she still cupped tightly in her sweating hands. The rest of her life with just herself – a self she knew not at all. Perhaps she had sought self-knowledge through an idea of helping others. The journey other women embarked upon through marriage and childbirth and the subsequent turmoils and upheavals they weathered until they reached a landing place from whence they could look back and know themselves through the past map of their lives – perhaps this was what Angela sought from her vocation. A way to look back at the map of her life. And make sense of it.

But the doubt was looming, a charcoal paw of cloud drifting upward, breaking through from her hidden self. Perhaps she had chosen this particular journey because it was easier to deal with other people's feelings than acknowledge her own. A tawdry little self-delusion which could ultimately leave her floundering in the future – childless, loveless, and utterly alone. Moreover, alone with a vocation which turned out to be no more than a screen. From herself. It had to be said, and her bloodthirsty mind was insisting on saying it: as long as she could perceive herself as the giver of care, the minder, the altruistic keeper of men's souls, she was also occupying the lofty, airy spaces of the higher ground. Take away that image and she knew she would have to walk the flat, muddy lowlands of ordinary mortals and the prospect was quite terrifying.

A spasm of bittersweet loneliness shot through her naked

body, causing her to tremble convulsively. She mentally chided her reflection for giving in to such a deluge of self-pity. But the tears were flowing now and she could not stop them. The newfound questions as to her own identity remained unanswerable. An identity apart from the Aunts, her mother and Uncle Mikey. Suddenly she saw the little girl she had spent her whole life running away from. The confused, fatherless child who had first surrendered her own mother to the Aunts and then surrendered herself. It was so shabby really. Nothing grand and noble and self-sacrificing like life in the Missions about it at all. Her hands fell limply away from her breasts. Doubt chased after doubt within the foggy labyrinths of her brain. But if she wasn't cut out to be a nun, what else could she be? She wasn't equipped for life on the outside. Least of all a life that encompassed mean, scabby, sordid impulses, base thoughts and ignoble deeds which would make short shrift of the shaky construct of herself she had always clung to, but clung limpet-like nevertheless.

If she did really begin to doubt her vocation and she had no notion of allowing that particular doubt space to roost – but if she did, she would have to consign the new construct of herself to the flux and flow of lay life. The stuff of ordinariness, the quotidian confusions, feelings of worthlessness and grandiosity, despair and elation, depression, joy and self-disgust, in short, the stuff of everybody's every day. And what of love? The risks people took! Look at all the unwanted feelings Robert had already managed to invoke – the hurt, the anger, the giddy hopeless joy – when she wasn't even in love with him. Not by half. No, it couldn't possibly be love if it made you feel this bad. How could it? Angela gazed around the arid room with a feeling akin to desperation. She felt trapped and breathless with panic.

'Ah who are you at all?' she asked the reflection who was busy squinting back more luxurious tears.

Her mind raced. If she stayed in the room another minute

the course of her life would alter unutterably. Of that much she could be certain. The vocation question mark was in, hooking its way with blithe abandon through the only parts of her she had considered ineradicable. It would take an enormous effort on her part to expunge it again. She needed a safe place. At least there was still the chapel, her final refuge. She quickly shunted into a thick tartan dressing gown and shot out of the room away from her own accusating eyes in the mirror.

Sr Carmel was just leaving when she got downstairs. The tiny nun gave Angela a shamed and guilty look.

'You heard I took drink, Sister?'

'Oh, Sister Carmel, what of it? Sure it wasn't as if you straight out asked for it or anything. You know what the men are like. Probably thought it was a huge joke. Don't you give it another thought now, d'you hear me?'

'I know you're right.' Carmel chewed a bonbon pensively. 'But I'd it in my head to go to my grave without breaking the pledge.'

'Well it isn't as if Our Lord has anything to forgive you for, when it was beyond your own control. It was taken out of your own two hands as surely as – '

Angela bit her lip. God alone knew what she was just about to say. To admit, more like. She chewed the lip mercilessly.

'You're pale out, Angela pet.'

'A small bit of a headache only. Sister Carmel, can I ask you something? And I want you to tell me what you think honestly.'

'Fire away, pet.'

'Well it's – what I'm trying to say is – d'you think I'd make a good nun, Sister? I mean, have I it in me?'

'Course you have.' Sr Carmel didn't hesitate. She patted Angela's upper arm. 'Sure wouldn't you be good at whatever you've a mind to be good at.'

'You really think so?'

'Faith then indeed I do. You could be a fine wife and mother too. If that's what you turned your mind to. Our Blessed Lord'd

247

let you go and be only thrilled for you if maybe you decided to go off in another direction, if you follow me.'

Angela clasped Carmel's tiny pincers.

'Are you saying . . . ?' Angela began but the tiny nun screwed up the lower half of her face. Little eyes danced mischievously in the dim light. She put a finger to Angela's mouth.

'Hush now,' Carmel urged. Then she winked, adding to Angela's confusion. Carmel stepped away, a pit pat of tiny steps along the tessellated tiles. Angela shook her head and called after her.

'Carmel? Sister Carmel?' The nun turned and waited. 'I love you,' Angela said. 'I really do.'

'Ah sure now.' Carmel beamed benignly and trotted off.

Angela made her way to the front of the chapel. A few candles cast spluttering, dying glows under the statue of the Virgin with her arms outstretched. She genuflected and knelt in the first pew, clasping her hands in a tight knot. Her head felt like the interior of a huge, rambling train station. All flux and flow, connections and misconnections. Bodies criss-crossing everywhere. And somewhere, floating aimlessly above it all, her own spirit hovered, looking down, at once a part of everything and part of nothing at all.

Chapter Thirteen

That afternoon, before Angela could head off for Robert's boat, she was waylaid by an urgent summons to Nicola's room. When she got there, Nicola was in a terrible state. She was crying and wringing her hands. Steve was haunting her, she said. Haunting her night and day. Every corner she turned, there he was, his two eyes burning holes into her skin. She reluctantly held up a wrist for Angela to inspect: there was a circle of red raw flesh as though someone had tried to restrain her against her will. Steve, she said. He was well out of control. Bang out of order. Angela sat with her knees pressed together, hands folded on her lap. She nodded her head sympathetically. Wondered what she might do about this dreadful situation at all. Nicola sat beside her. Idly began to run gel through Angela's hair, teasing it into stiff spikes.

'You've got to talk to him again, don'tcha,' Nicola said, applying a deeply orange-looking foundation to Angela's white face.

'What are you doing, Nicola?' Angela peered at her strangely tanned face in the mirror.

'Calms me nerves, innit.' Nicola applied black liner, making Cleopatra eyes. Then rusty blusher and a scarlet line making Cupid bows of Angela's lips which she filled in with geranium gloss. Angela was fascinated, in a peaceful daydream. It was so nice to have someone tinker with your face and hair. Even if the effect was a million miles away from anything she would do herself. Glassy-eyed, she held her fingernails out for matching scarlet lacquer. A sharp rap on the door made her jump.

Nicola prised it open just a touch, so that whoever it was could not be seen. She spoke in a terse, authoritative whisper. Told whoever to come back later. She was busy right now. Yeah yeah, so they was desperate, wasn't we all? Get out of my face, wouldya? Slammed the door tightly shut. Stopped Angela's curious enquiry with an airy wave of the glittering talons.

'Forget 'em, she'll be back. Now where was we?'

Angela shifted in her seat about to go. She reached out for a wad of tissues and a cleanser.

'You can't do that!' Nicola was horrorstruck. 'Look at you.' she swivelled the mirror. 'Bloody transformation, innit?'

'I can't exactly go out like this, Nicola,' Angela said hedgily, afraid to cause offence.

But offence had already been caused. Nicola's face was a glowering thunderstorm. Her lips curled derisively.

'All right for the tarts, huh? Nice girls like you don't look like that. I get it.'

'No,' Angela protested though it was the truth. 'It's just – well – I never wear make-up. Really. It's too much all in the one go. If you see what I mean. I don't want to hurt your feelings, Nicola, honest.'

'No, it ain't too much, I wear tons more than that.' Nicola softened a little. 'All what's wrong is the gear and the shoes.' She reached for a pair of patent heels, not quite stiletto but high and murderous. 'Here, try these for size.' She slipped Angela's feet in and they fitted. While Angela was trying to settle her balance, her ankles wobbling perilously, Nicola hitched up her plain navy skirt around the waist and doubled, then trebled over the band at the top. It took five inches off the hem, bringing the end to a couple of inches above her knee. She undid the top buttons of Angela's severe white blouse and pulled out the large crucifix around her neck to let it dangle on the outside. Finally Nicola backcombed Angela's hair and gave it some fixing spray so that it stood high like a mountain ridge. She turned a full-length mirror that had been faced to the wall.

'Whatcha think?'

Angela's jaw nearly dropped to her ankles. Her immediate reaction was one of abject horror. The person in the mirror wasn't her at all. She swivelled around, pulling her mouth down at the corners. It had to be said the legs weren't all that bad from the back. Not bad at all.

'Great pins,' Nicola confirmed. 'You should show 'em.'

'I don't know, Nicola,' Angela muttered doubtfully. She turned about again. Certainly it was over the top but she had to admit – yes – there was something, well, festive, for want of a better word, about her whole appearance. It was beginning to grow on her by the second. Perhaps it wouldn't be any harm to turn up at Robert's a bit more decked out than usual. Especially if that Anita one was there: she wore plenty of make-up and lots of jewellery too. And her clothes that time she'd met her, would have made Angela feel pretty drab indeed if she hadn't that lovely shawl wrapped around her shoulders. What was wrong with a bit of frippery anyway? Show them all she was a woman of the world herself. With her own hectic life.

'Hmm,' she considered.

'It's my gift, innit?' Nicola beamed. The emeralds were flashing in such a delightful way it would be such a shame to dampen her enthusiasm. 'I don't expect you to take care of Steve for me for nothing you know.'

For nuffink. Why, it would be downright churlish to throw Nicola's gift right back in her face now, Angela thought. And she could always pop in on her way back to take the warpaint off again and return the shoes.

'Thanks, Nicola,' she said shyly. 'I can't promise anything with Steve, you know that, don't you?'

'You can handle him. I know you can. Just get him off my case. I'll be sorted in two, three days tops, anyway.'

'Sorted?'

'Figure of speech.' Nicola placed a hand against Angela's back, propelling her toward the door. She yanked it open and then further bemused Angela by suddenly placing both hands on her shoulders. The green eyes danced and sparkled, almost childlike, and Angela remembered the little girl in Steve's photo. No matter how old, raddled or haggard people grew, everyone still had brief moments when they looked like the child they once were. She was touched.

'Put you on the streets here and we could all shut up shop.' Nicola offered her greatest compliment. Her smile was quite sincere.

'Thanks. I think.' Angela smiled back.

Later, when events had run their course, she would be glad that the last time she saw Nicola's pointy little face, it had been twinkling with a genuine smile.

The girls were done, oohing and aahing appreciatively as they admired their own considerably enhanced portraits. They nibbled at the plate of cookies Robert had set out for them and slurped from their glasses of milk.

'Why not Coke?' Nessie asked.

'Because I told him,' Anita remonstrated. She was seated on the sitter's chair, while Robert finished a few hasty sketches. He was doing his level best to put a brave face on the whole thing but his heart was seriously not in it.

'Whyd'you look so sad, Uncle Robert?' Tammy asked.

'Hush now,' Anita interjected. 'He doesn't look sad. He's concentrating. That's all.'

'Is it Angela?' Tammy asked. 'Did she break your heart or something?' She crunched blithely on her biscuit. Robert had to conceal a smile. If only she knew.

'He was only doing her portrait, Tammy. It wasn't what you think. Was it, Robert?'

'Umm.'

'He looks like his heart is broken to me,' Nessie offered.

252

'Well.' Anita tapped a foot. Then she tossed her head and Robert had to settle her into the pose again.

'I could come on Sundays instead,' she said.

'We'll see.' Robert smiled. 'Anita, d'you think you could wear just a little less jewellery – not that it isn't lovely of course but –'

'She wears too much,' Tammy obliged. 'Jingly like a Christmas tree when she walks.'

Oh they thought that was hilarious, clanking around emulating their mother who shot them a twisted smile with her eyes narrowed.

'And – maybe – just a little easier on the lipstick,' Robert faltered. 'And that stuff on your eyes. Perhaps.'

'I understand,' Anita said soberly. 'Is she coming tomorrow or isn't she?'

Robert shrugged. Felt his heart clunk down into his shoes. It had been clunking all week long.

'I really don't know.'

'Well you can ask her,' Nessie chirruped.

'I would. If I knew where she lived. Or had a number.'

'No. I mean now,' Nessie said from her spot glued to the window. 'She's coming here right now. That's her, isn't it? She looks all different. But I'm sure it's Angela.'

Robert dropped the charcoal. Craned his head out. It certainly was Angela, he'd know that walk anywhere, even if it was a touch lopsided and wobbly. What had she on her feet? As she got closer, his eyes widened into dinner plates. What had she on her face? And what was with the hair? It was Angela all right, and at the same time, it wasn't. She looked ridiculous. Like – he couldn't begin to think like what. She nearly brained herself several times on the ludicrous heels as she staggered down the towpath. He pulled the door open and shot out, followed in hot pursuit by the girls.

'Angela?'

He did his best to keep his face straight. Not show his

253

disappointment at her strange appearance. Not show his elation at her sudden appearance. At any rate, he failed miserably because she stopped stockstill a little distance from the boat and glared at him. Looking anything but the angel he'd taken her for.

'Something wrong?' she snapped.

'Angela, you're all painted up!' Nessie cried.

'What if I am?' Angela directed the question at Robert. 'Maybe this is the real me.'

'Very – very colourful I'm sure,' was all he could offer. He really couldn't find it in his heart to say he liked this new look. Angela would always be milky skinned and natural to him. 'What happened last Sunday?'

'That's what I was coming to tell you. I had to go home. Auntie Regina passed away, may she rest, and Auntie Bridie had a stroke.'

'Uncle Mikey's all right though, isn't he?' Tammy chimed.

'Yes. Thank God,' Angela responded. 'Though you can never tell which one of them'll be next.'

'Won't you come in?' Robert made way for her. But she cast a cool eye over his shoulder at Anita still sitting on her chair, discarded jewellery on her lap. Lipstick swiped off.

'I don't think so. Thank you very much,' Angela said primly, which almost made Robert laugh, the crispbread voice with the way she looked. 'You're very busy. I just wanted to explain why I didn't come round last Sunday – no other reason,' she added pointedly. 'And to offer my sincere apology forthwith.'

'*Forthwith?*'

'Precisely. Forthwith. Now I won't be keeping you from your business.' She swivelled on one heel and very nearly pitched into the river. Robert caught her arm.

'Angela – you will come tomorrow, won't you? Please say you will. Please?'

She hesitated, staring at his hand encircling her arm. He immediately released her.

'I'll have to consider my position,' she said in a tart voice.

'Your position?'

'Yes. See if my schedule will permit another visitation.'

'Jesus, Angela! Visitation?'

'Precisely.' She was tottering down the towpath again. Robert was about to run after her when Tammy tugged his sleeve.

'Don't run after her. She'll be here,' she said with a knowing smile well beyond her years.

'How can you be sure?' Robert asked, feeling quite desperate.

'Obvious,' Tammy said.

'Go on. Quickly. She's getting away, for heaven's sake.'

'She didn't ask to see her picture,' Tammy offered in her most reasonable voice. 'She hasn't seen it yet, has she? No. So she's not going to not come back. Without seeing it first, is she?'

'Tammy. Promise me you'll never settle for anything less than rocket science. Promise me,' Robert laughed, giddy with relief. She was right of course. No one would sit week after week for a portrait they never got to see.

'You know I'm going to be a hairdresser, Uncle Robert,' Tammy remonstrated, but gently.

'And I'm going to be a supermodel.' Nessie jumped up and down.

Robert smiled at her with his head cocked to the side. Not with that gammy eye, my little darling, he thought.

'Course you are,' he said.

When they went back inside, Anita had scrubbed her face clean. Her many pieces of jewellery were in a little shiny pile on her lap. Robert had never seen her face without adornment before and it took some getting used to. A lot of getting used to in fact. But he felt so incredibly happy at that moment, he felt that he could have painted anyone beautiful. He sighed with satisfaction and clapped his hands. All business.

'Right. No more sketches. I think we can make a start on the real thing.'

Anita flushed with pleasure.

255

'You prefer me like this, I see.' She beamed. 'That's – that's really wonderful.'

'What? Oh yeah.' Robert didn't see the aural glow radiating from her face. He was frenetically mixing pigments. His fingers itched to get started. His fingers itched to get finished. The girls were raiding the secret stash spots he kept out of sight from their mother in the kitchen. Deeply satisfied crunching could be heard.

'Oh, Robert,' Anita sighed contentedly.

'Yes?' He glanced up.

'Nothing. Just Oh, Robert.'

'D'you think you could tilt your head to the – yep – that's it, chin up a bit – perfect.'

'*This* is going to be perfect,' Anita said. 'I can feel it. The best thing you've ever done.'

'Anita, d'you think you could open that left eye just a – great.'

'Didn't Angela look strange?'

'Well, yes. A bit.'

'I'm so glad you prefer the natural look. Now that she's out of the picture so to speak. We can concentrate on me. Can't we?'

'Hmm?' Robert mixed fuschia and a creamy ivory. Really he was going to have a devil of a job getting her high flushed colour. Never realized she was so damn red before.

'Sorry, Anita. I'm afraid I go into a world of my own when I'm mixing.'

'Of course you do. Of course. You're an artist, darling. Not an orthodontist.'

The orthodontist had been doing a little creative mixing of his own earlier that afternoon. It was no easy task achieving the perfect mix for the perfect weekend away with a tearful, emotional and hormonal wife. But he thought he just might have it sussed. A four-poster with a jacuzzi in a little hotel in the

Chilterns. Michelin-starred restaurant. Bollinger and white lilies in the seventeenth-century bedroom. A little walking, a lot of eating, guzzling, talking perhaps, some serious shagging and Bob's your uncle. She'd be back to her former reasonably discontented self.

He was still smarting from the summary dismissal at Robert's last Sunday. Needed to put things back on an even keel again. That is to say, an even pedestal from whence to look down. Things would look immeasurably better once he'd handed over that travel wallet with the little satin ribbon, from his own perspective at least. The girls would ooh, Anita would read the details with her mouth slightly agape, perhaps a little nervous – apologetic even – tremble in her fingers. Robert would look on, as Robert always did. Voila! Contentment in East Twickenham once more.

It was all planned to the nth degree, the sally forth, the waving of wallet, the takeover of the boat or take back if the absolute truth be told, when he saw that funny walk again. No. It couldn't be, not done up like that. He had to squint furiously from his position at the back of the bush he'd jumped behind. Good Lord. She looked like – well, like those girls who had cackled so demeaningly at him when he'd last followed her. And lost her. Well he'd be damned if he lost her again.

Peter ran after her. She was running on those high heels. Running no less. Did his 007 behind the pillar at the station. Remembered to buy a newspaper to hide behind this time. Held it wide and ostentatiously before his face all the way to Whitechapel. This time he dogged her steps so closely there was no way she could disappear into thin air. He didn't care if he looked a mite suspicious, walking, or trotting along like that with a spread *Telegraph* in front of his nose. She was so fast for such a little thing.

She'd stopped outside what looked like an ancient, dilapidated warehouse. Tripped on a step, nearly pranging her nose in the subsequent fall. A couple of women were coming out of

257

the door. One of them bent down to help Angela up. She talked and laughed with them for a number of seconds, before disappearing inside. The women sashayed down along the street. Skirts up to their asses, heels like ice-picks. One of them stood on a corner with a hand on her hip. Good Lord! Trade! That's what they were. He would have laughed if it wasn't so terribly tragic. All his life Robert had been waiting for an angel. Oh someone far superior to anyone Peter could nab. Namely Anita. And what had Robert managed to nab in the end? A hooker. A dirty little prostitute with her eye on the main chance. Oh rapture!

He sang from *Carmen* all the way home. Didn't care if there might be clients looking at him. Bugger *them*. He had Salome's prize, the head of Robert the Baptist on a platter. He could hardly wait to spill his guts out when he finally inserted the key into the Mock Tudor in its tree-lined cul-de-sac in East Twickenham. Could barely get his shaking limbs up the wide-fronted staircase to the en-suite where Anita was taking-a-bath. Usually-a-no-go-area. Not tonight, Josephine!

'Get out,' she snarled.

He looked at her soapy breasts. Hesitated.

'I've put the rib of beef in the freezer,' she said. 'You can do chops or something for yourself and the girls tomorrow. I won't be doing Sunday lunch.'

'No?'

'No. Robert's doing me tomorrow instead. He doesn't know yet. But I'm going to surprise him.'

Little did Robert know just how surprised he was going to be. Peter cast a sprinkling of aromatic something or other into the sudsy water. Cast his wife a dazzling smile.

'Thank you.' She sounded a little suspicious.

'No. Thank *you*.'

The weekend wallet *and* his little nugget of information. That pedestal was just begging Peter, singing to him, up here, buddy, back where you belong.

'You look very cheerful for yourself,' Anita said with slitted eyes.

'I'm just a cheerful kinda bloke.'

'Aren't you just.'

Peter felt so goddam good in fact, he tweaked one of her nipples. She slapped him away with corrosive disdain. He had to run back out to the bedroom, couldn't remember when he last felt this excited. Except maybe that time when she was doing those pelvic floor exercises at her Callanetics classes. Vagina with a clutch like a vice back then. It would hold him again.

A fellow could grow far too lonely and much too vulnerable, on the outside.

'Angela Frances Xavier Teresa Doolin!'

Angela stopped in her tracks. Closed her eyes with terrible resignation. She was caught. All evening long she'd managed to avoid Mary Margaret. And now the final disaster after a thoroughly disastrous day. There hadn't been a sign of Nicola when she returned and the door was firmly locked. She had cursed herself loudly for not checking in advance. Her shoes were in there. She'd dithered about for a while trying to figure the best way to approach next door. Wiped some of the lipstick off with the back of her hand but there was tons of muck on her face still. Not to mention the upright hair. Finally, she had decided on a lightning streak, a dash to her own bedroom and maybe she could move so fast, no one would even catch a glimpse. She unrolled the waistband of her skirt and slipped out of the shoes, figuring they'd only slow her down.

But as usual, she had walked into two dozen calamities all occurring at the same time. A fracas in the television room between Paddy and some new arrival. The soup cauldron had been allowed to boil dry for the first time in years and Sr Oliver told her that there had been some serious trouble earlier with young Steve. He had been exceedingly hostile to Sr Carmel when she'd tried to take his penknife off him. Even threw a bonbon in her face. No one knew where he'd gone. Sr Oliver explained that Carmel hadn't said a word about the incident to the Superior on account of Angela's bond with Steve. Her lips were sealed unless Angela herself decided it was the proper thing to tell on him. Angela immediately told Oliver that Carmel had done the right thing. Keep her mouth shut and everything would be just grand. He'd had a little turn was all. Oliver didn't appear quite so convinced.

Then, just as Angela had been about to slink up to her quarters, Sr Aloysius took it upon herself to fall into a dead faint from the heat in the kitchen and had to be fanned back to life. There were a few queer glances in Angela's direction but no one had time to say a word about her new appearance. Running around like a lunatic in her bare feet, she'd forgotten all about it herself. Until a quick reminder of her reflection on the glass swing doors of the refectory just a couple of moments ago. The face of a gargoyle Barbie was what she saw. She was tiptoeing past the Superior's office, shoulders hunched, lip chewed, when the loud holler of her full monicker had resounded from within.

'Get in here this minute,' Mary Margaret bellowed.

'Yes, Mother?' Angela strolled in, making sure she kept the door ajar behind her.

'Close the fecking door!'

'Yes, Mother.'

Mary Margaret lit a fresh cigarette from the butt of her old one. She mashed the butt into wispy shreds. Stood up with the new fag clamped between a rigid line of lip. A hand slapped rhythmically at a thigh as she circled Angela, eyeing her up and down. Angela could only hop nervously from one bare foot to the other. Finally the Superior spoke on a belch of smoke.

'A beauty parlour. Is that where you took yourself?'

'No, Mother.'

'No?' One incredulous eyebrow. 'You mean you did that to your own self?'

'Well, not exactly. One of the girls next door. She was just trying out on me like.'

'I see. And what were you doing there at all?'

A little runnel of sweat dribbled down the side of Angela's left temple. If she told of her arrangement with Nicola, to keep Steve out of the way, he would be out on the street by nightfall. Simple as that. Mary Margaret wouldn't brook any complications with her charges here. Next door was off limits and if a woman was being hounded then the hounder would be sent to Camden and if there wasn't a cluster to be had in Camden, he could go to hell. Everyone knew there wasn't a whole lot of difference between them in any case.

'This young girl, Nicola's her name, well, I thought I could interest her in studying or something. You know, sort of get her off the street or what have you.'

'Next door is next door's business, I'd have you know, young woman. Just because they don't run a tight ship like what I do here, doesn't mean you've the right to go poking your nose in where it isn't wanted. Them girls aren't your responsibility.' She took a deep suck of the fag, folded one arm across the heft of bosom, which meant she wasn't finished with the bollocking by a long shot. Angela's shoulders slumped further.

'Now so.' Mary Margaret held the cigarette upright and studied the burning tip. 'I think it's about time we'd a proper talk, you and me. I've me eyes on you this long while. And them same two eyes are sending me messages.'

'They are?'

'Indeed they are. I don't know the full gist of it all yet, but what my eyes don't see my nose is smelling. It's smelling hoodwink and stunt-pulling of every kip. But whatever you're up to, you're out of your depth. I can tell you that much.'

'I'm not up to anything!' Angela was growing angry now. She was tired of the constant sarcasm, the constant deprecation. 'You're always on my back.'

'It's my job to be on your back,' Mary Margaret snapped.

261

The atmosphere between them was the most strained it had ever been. Usually the Superior delivered her punches with a measure of weary resignation, anger tempered with a degree of drollness. But this evening she was deadly serious and Angela felt that she was deliberately pushing her, goading her into a response whereupon she would have the ammunition she needed to get rid of her.

'The trouble is, Sister, you don't know *your* job well enough.'

'That is so unfair,' Angela shouted. 'Nothing I do pleases you. Nothing!'

'You mightn't see it this way but I actually have your best interests at heart, Angela. I see that you've the height of intentions. You're a great worker, I wouldn't take that from you. But you get involved, girl. That's the what all. You think it's your lookout to change things. Cure people. We're not doctors or nurses. Most of the men are incurables. That's why they're here. We don't judge them – we feed them. Put a roof over their heads for as long as they want it. They break the rules, out they go. Some other poor fecker gets the bed. On and on it goes. People have the right to go wrong. Sometimes it's their own fault, most times it isn't. Either way. We feed them. Put a roof over their heads. Let them walk away. You're only here yourself because a shower of Lulu aunts made you step out of one asylum and straight into another. Ah close your gob, you'll catch flies. Amn't I only trying to tell you what'll dawn on yourself in years to come in any case. And then you'll turn bitter but it'll be too late and then you'll just go on being a nun because it's all you know how to do. You'll never make a proper nun. Angela. Your head is too far up your own arse.'

'Oh,' Angela gasped. 'Oh.'

This diatribe on top of the look on Robert's face today when he saw her new persona, it was all too much. Everything was falling apart in front of her very eyes. The very skein of her life was unravelling. She felt terribly sorry for herself indeed and the way Mary Margaret's mouth was sloping to the side

262

like that, she wasn't going to get much by way of comfort or remorse there. The mouth had opened as if to verify that very thought.

'Don't mind looking at me like that. Right. I've had my say. Now get out. And take that slop off your face and put a pair of shoes on your feet.'

'You've had your say, well I'll have mine thank you very much,' Angela suddenly exploded. She couldn't take any more. She stabbed an accusing finger at Mary Margaret's heaving chest. '*You*. You have the cheek to tell me I'll never make a good nun. Take one look at yourself, would you? With your gin and your fags, the effing and blinding that goes on in here every day. What kind of a nun are you? Cruel and hurtful to everyone including poor Sister Carmel. Not even the men would stoop that low. You're a bitter twisted ould cow of a woman and it's no wonder that everyone round here hates your bloody guts.'

She had an all too fleeting moment of satisfaction at the slight blanching of the woman's face. But Mary Margaret remained perfectly composed as she inhaled a deep drag.

'I don't ask anyone to love me, Sister. I don't even ask them to need me. Unlike your good self. I only ask that they do what I say. And that's why I'm your Mother Superior. You'll oblige me by thinking on that while you're scrubbing your face. Oh and Angela?'

'Yes?' Angela's tone was considerably deflated.

'If you still want to take the vows in two weeks time – then we'll go ahead. In the meantime, pray long and humble, Sister, and look fierce hard to your guardian angel for guidance.'

'Yes, Mother.' Angela felt thoroughly miserable now.

She hesitated at the door.

'I'm sorry for what I said. Not everybody here hates you – what I mean is –'

But Mary Margaret stopped her with a raised hand. She stubbed out the cigarette with the other. If anything, she looked perfectly placid. Water off a duck's back.

'We've had our say,' she said. 'If the world and his dog hated me, Sister, it wouldn't cost me a lick. But I'd be here till I'd moss growing out of my ass before I could make you understand that. I'm all reconciled with the one person what I needed reconciling.'

'Our Blessed Father?' Angela tentatively asked.

Mary Margaret gave her a crooked smile.

'Him too,' she said.

Chapter Fourteen

Angela had the devil of a night. She had tossed and writhed and gritted her teeth so hard, her jaw ached in the morning. Ached right through early Mass, a plethora of chores and a prayer meeting in Gaeilge for the local Irish vintners association. Then she supervised the men waiting for their methadone fix in the television room as they watched *Power Rangers* with silent, numb expressions to a man. She made stock for a new cauldron of soup and smelt so strongly of chopped onions she had to rub salt on her hands which stung from the constant chafing. Then she made a half-hearted stab at a little studying, something else which had been slung very much to the side these days. All the while she kept up a constant check for Steve and Nicola but they'd disappeared off the face of the earth.

So much work, distraction and more work and still she couldn't get her head around the thing which was really bothering her. The meeting later with Robert. By the time she finally headed out she was feeling cranky as hell, disorientated, premenstrual, and not a little angry that he had managed to invade her life, her everyday thoughts, to such an intrusive degree. She tried telling herself that it was perfectly natural that frequent contact with any man who wasn't missing a limb or a brain, might have such an effect. When she wasn't used to whole men as it were. At least with broken men you knew where you stood, what needed to be fixed. How could you possibly tell what needed fixing with a complete person? For that matter, nothing at all might require fixing, in which case, she would be entirely redundant. Something Angela did not altogether wish to be. Once you got used to being needed, it was a bit of a come-down to being needy.

The whole way there, she told herself that this would be the final meeting. She would say goodbye, crisp and businesslike, a handshake maybe. She would ask to see the portrait, mutter some words of praise if they seemed appropriate, if she hated it, she wasn't going to lie. Angela was done with lying. Or at least the withholding of full and absolute truths. Or at least the putting herself in the way of obstacles to her vocation. Mary Margaret had been entirely wrong. She, Angela, would make an excellent nun in the fullness of time. Excellent. She would go to the Missions, and leave the Superior's negative attitude far behind her. Of course it was possible to make a difference, to change things or people, or their situations. What was the point of a vocation otherwise? And God alone knew, there were so very few of them at all nowadays. Why, Angela would be a rarity, so young by nun standards. Quite unique. It might happen that she would be interviewed in magazines and such like, and would do the Sisters no disservice at all by her accounts of such a satisfying and fulfilling life. Other young women might see fit to join. Not everyone wanted marriage and babies. In fact, when it came right down to it, Angela considered that she might very well be the epitome of a modern career woman.

Two weeks and everything she'd ever hoped for, planned for, would finally come to fruition. After so many years, so many stops and starts, a fortnight was no wait at all. She felt certain that the actual vocalizing of the vows would consign all doubts into oblivion. She felt certain that the vocalizing of said vows would do no such thing. She had to sit down. Her legs were shaking so hard.

'Me – I'm Marty,' the man with the can of lager on the bench said. His eyes took in her trembling state and his hand snaked out with the can. Maybe he figured she was in withdrawal. Angela shook her head and cast him a feeble smile.

'I'm Angela,' she said.

He nodded. Slurped from the can and stared with clamped lips across the river to the other bank. Angela thought that her heart's palpitations must be shaking the bench. She stood up. Sat down again. Groaned with her head resting in the spread palms of her hands.

'Oh for God's sake, what's the matter with me?' She uttered a muffled cry.

'Broken heart, eh?' Marty mumbled.

'Not that. No,' Angela snapped, pulling her head back sharply.

'Sorry.' He shrugged and sipped, mumbling something to himself with his shoulders going up and down in some internal conversation.

'I'm just a bit confused is all,' Angela offered in a softer tone. 'Here – I will have a slug of that.' She grabbed the can and swallowed half the contents. Marty's hands itched to grab it back but he had been brought up to put manners above all else. No little contributing factor as to why he was on a river bench.

'Better now?' he asked hopefully, mentally reckoning what was left in the tin.

'Grand. Thank you.' Angela returned it to him, wiping the back of her hand across her mouth. 'Actually it's my career that's bothering me. What I have to think about.' She swivelled on the bench to face him. 'Look it, if someone said to you that you could have everything you'd ever dreamed of – I mean everything – in just two weeks' time, wouldn't you be happy? Wouldn't you be just thrilled if someone said that to you? Well?'

'I s'pose so, yeah,' he responded, dubiously. Hand tightening instinctively around the lager.

'That's my position,' Angela cried. 'I should be ecstatic, shouldn't I? So what's wrong with me?'

267

Marty declined to answer that. It was his experience that usually when people didn't know what was wrong with them, they invariably wanted the contents of his can.

'You're right of course,' Angela continued, as though he'd spoken. 'It's all got complicated by a man.'

'Oh,' Marty offered.

'And even if I – well let's say, if I wanted this man before my career, how long before he'd be treating me just like the mother of his two children? Hmm? How long d'you think?'

'Dunno.'

'Precisely.' Angela warmed to her theme. 'I mean, say I didn't go ahead and take the thing I've wanted all my life, say I decided to go down another route altogether – how could I be sure that *that* would make me happy in time to come? How could I even consider throwing everything away for no security at all? What sort of a choice is that, I ask you?' Her eyes tightened, resting on the scaly, scabrous patch on the back of his neck. 'You've a small touch of scabies,' she said.

'I have?' He sounded surprised.

'You're probably not eating properly, are you?'

'Probably not.'

Angela quickly scribbled the address of the shelter on a scrap of paper and thrust it at him.

'If you call in there one day, they'll take a look at it for you. Sort it out once and for all.'

'Thanks.'

'Don't mention it.' Angela stood. 'Look, just forget we had this conversation, will you? I'm just mixed up today is all.'

'Oh.' Marty waved a hand expansively, tossed his head back. Forgotten already, his gesture implied. No sooner said.

'Thanks for the beer,' Angela said.

'Oh.' Another wave. Another toss.

'I'd better go.' She added reluctantly, 'I have to say goodbye to someone.'

'You can have what's left, if you like.' Marty proffered the can. 'But it won't help, that much I can tell you.'

'I'm sure you're right. Thanks anyway.'

Angela felt immeasurably touched by his kindness. She walked away with a slow, ponderous gait quite unlike her usual lively trot. It occurred to her that in all the time she'd been dealing with the men at the shelter, the broken, damaged outlanders, she had never before revealed anything of herself. Never sought an opinion or allowed a moment's confusion to show. Never once behaved as thought they might have something to offer her. Which of course they had – every day they offered her a good opinion of herself. The price of her then, to end up on a park bench sipping from a vagrant's can. Even Auntie Bridie returned to her head for a brief scalding moment, to hoot with laughter. Angela felt small and mean and entirely superficial as the houseboat loomed nearer. So she did what most people do when besieged by such feelings – she gathered all the various emotions into one multicoloured bouquet, knotted the stalks – directed the feelings outwards – and came up with anger.

As a heron on the far bank shifted weight from one foot to the other, it suddenly became quite lipsmackingly clear to Angela that this whole dilemma she found herself in was entirely due to Robert's interference in her life. The blame for her vacillations, these quite unspeakable waverings and self-doubts rested firmly by his feet. Once she had eliminated the problem of Robert, the map of her life would set itself firmly in her sights again but she would be a better person for having endured and indeed conquered this final Everest. She was, after all, a modern career woman and this sort of thing was just par for the course. The stuff of office politics to others. Angela pulled her mouth down and clicked her fingers at a group of ducks. Like *that* she would deal with him, expunge him from her life for ever.

The thoroughly modern career woman had a splitting

headache and a kind of buzzing noise in her ears as she picked up pace to stride purposefully along the remaining towpath toward the boat. She knocked quite peremptorily. Decided, no, she would just wrench it open. Wrenched it open. Stepped snappily over the threshold. Bounced down the five steps. A few more faltering footfalls.

Straight into Robert's waiting arms.

'Angela! Thank God. Oh sweetheart.'

'Don't call me that,' a muffled wail from somewhere between his chest and armpit. She didn't dare to lift her head. He was wearing a loose, baggy overshirt made of some sort of a jersey, fluid material. Smelt of sweat and beer and linseed oil. A lovely warm familiar odour. Her face nuzzled closer and closer. It felt so safe standing there with his arms locked tightly around her.

'What's the matter? Why are you crying, sweetheart?'

'My head is sore and I'm all mixed up.' She snuffled deeper.

Robert cupped her face and gently lifted it back so he could look at her. She meant to turn away but craned up and kissed him instead. After a very long time, she pulled away and rubbed her mouth with the back of her hand.

'That was for goodbye,' she said.

'Well I'll be looking forward to hello then.' He gave her a lopsided look. 'Will I be killed for saying you look much better without all that gunk on your face? Do you mind? It's just that you look like you again.'

She spun around, hands spiking her hair in a frenzy.

'But I was never me. That's the problem. Leastways not the real me. There's something fierce important I've to tell you, Robert. You're going to be shocked. Look it, maybe you should sit down for a sec.' She held a chair out but he ignored it. Instead, he placed his hands on her shoulders.

'Whatever it is, can wait,' he said. 'First we're going to finish the portrait today. Then I'm going to fix us a really nice meal. We'll go up on deck and eat in the sunshine. And then we'll talk and talk. For ever maybe. Or for as long as it takes to settle everything between us. You agree we do have to settle things?'

Angela nodded. Then she opened her mouth to add something but he put a finger to her lips and drew her to the passageway.

'Later. Put the shawl on and let's get this much out of the way. I understand you feel bad. It's difficult when there are other people involved. But we can't help the way we feel now, can we?'

'Robert –'

'Go on,' he laughed, his hands made shooing signals. Angela sniffed. Thought maybe he was right. It would be nice to just sit there like so many Sundays before, just letting her mind drift, letting the teeming train station in her head come to a halt for a while. Before she told him about the Missions and all the rest of it. Not a word of advice from Auntie Bridie. Where was that woman when you needed her anyway?

In the bedroom she slipped off her blouse and cotton camisole. Stretched up for the hat box on the top shelf of the wardrobe. Unaware that Robert had left the passageway and was now standing in the sunken living area with his jaw dropped somewhere down around his shoes.

'Anita?'

She was standing on the top steps, slipping a sheer muslin dress from her shoulders. She kicked the bunched material around her ankles to the side and moved toward him with her arms extended, wearing nothing but the huge beaming smile on her face.

'This is what you meant. How you really want me, Robert. Isn't it?' Her arms slid around his neck and before he could so much as breathe she yanked his head down and drove her tongue halfway down his gullet.

'Jesus Christ, Anita!' He just about managed to break free. 'What – Are you gone – What are you *doing?*'

'What I should have done a long long time ago.' Her eyes

271

were heavy lidded, tiny little gasps for air. He backed away but she caught his shirt in a clench of fist and hauled him to her again. Threshing her breasts and crotch against him.

'You know you want to, same as me,' she moaned softly. 'You've always wanted me. So here I am.' She grabbed his hand, dragging him toward the bedroom. 'Take me. Oh God. Take me!'

Angela dropped the hatbox, spilling the shawl on the floor. She caught a glimpse of quivering naked thigh, heard the last husky entreaty from an advancing Anita, before she jumped into the wardrobe, pulling the door shut as hard as she could without attracting attention. She stood in the darkness with her knees knocking and her arms crossed over her bare breasts. She could hear the loud creak of Anita's body as it flipped back onto the bed. One muffled moan from Robert. Her eyes shot this way and that in the gloom of what was now her bolthole. Her ears were red from straining to hear. It sounded as if Robert was trying to get rid of Anita. He was pleading with her to come to her senses. Angela's blood could have boiled eggs. How inconvenient for the two-timing, wife-stealing, back-stabbing *bastard!* She wanted to scream that word at him. But first she had to have her clothes on.

So this was the carry on as soon as she left every Sunday. Maybe Saturdays too for all she knew – while those poor little girls watched a video or something. He didn't even want them or their mother until another man took them over. Now he was cuckolding that very man who was willing to bear his, Robert's, responsibilities in the first place. Oh it didn't bear thinking about. She didn't get a whole lot of time for thinking about it at any rate because the next thing she knew she was blinking like a startled racoon in the light from the hastily opened door.

'Jesus – it *is* Peter,' she heard Robert exclaim.

Anita was standing beside her in the wardrobe now. The door slammed shut on the two of them. The women could just about make out one another's doleful face as Peter's booming

272

laugh permeated through from the living room. A stunned silence in the wardrobe.

Robert rushed out. Peter was standing there, laughing, calling his usual hell-ooo? Anybody ho-oome? His wife's discarded dress by his ankles. Robert dived across, rugby tackled the dress out of sight much to his friend's amusement. For heaven's sake, man, Robert hardly had to tidy up for him, after all these years. He was perfectly used to the mess on the boat. Why, it was charming in its way, if you liked that sort of thing. Where was Anita?

'Anita?' Robert panted. 'You've got your days mixed up. Anita comes on Saturdays.'

'Well she comes on Sundays now too, or so she said. I wanted to surprise her with something.'

There wasn't a lot Robert could say to that one, in truth. He was all surprised out himself. The main thing now was to get Peter out too.

'What's the matter with you anyway?' Peter was studying him. 'You're running a temperature, I'd swear. Go and lie down. I'll get the thermometer and a glass of iced –'

'I'm fine, Peter. It's just – it's just hot today. Don't you think? Very hot.' He blocked Peter's move toward the kitchen, running a finger around the collar of his shirt. 'Phew. Hot.'

'It dropped nearly five degrees overnight. You're not well. And your pupils are dilated.'

'Are they? That'll be the – beer.'

'You think?' Peter said doubtfully. 'I'd have a beer if it was going.'

He tried to step past Robert again, reeling back from the force of the nudge Robert sent his way. More like a wrestling throw than anything. Peter was a little winded.

'No beer,' Robert said. 'Sorry.'

Peter's chubby legs were being forced to backpedal. He did not take kindly to this treatment at all. Two curt dismissals from the boat in the space of a couple of weeks, well, it was

273

more than any man could be expected to endure. Even a gentleman with an innate equanimous disposition.

'Stop pushing me,' he squeaked, mustering an hauteur which sounded on the faint side even to his own ears.

'Sorry, Peter.' Robert pushed again. 'I'm up to my neck in it today. You'll never know how up to my neck in it,' he added forlornly. 'Tell you what though, I'll just finish up here. Be down to you with a six-pack in oh twenty, thirty minutes say.'

'Better still,' Peter rebounded cheerfully, 'I'll settle for a nice cold glass of – '

'Out! Now!' Robert could not mask that high treble of near hysteria.

'What is the matter with you these days?' Peter was horribly shocked.

'Just get out, Peter. Please. There are things I just can't explain. Trust me. You're better off not knowing.'

'Is that so? Well before I go – I think there's something you should know, buddy. Something only a real friend would tell another. But you wouldn't understand anything about that, would you? Oh no.'

He was gathering himself, muttering oh no over and over, flattening his ruffled collar, smoothing his ruffled feathers. Jamming a parchment-type wallet back into his pocket again.

'Before I leave, and leave I shall, probably never to return I might add – ' He waited for Robert's hasty interjection, continuing when it did not arrive. 'There's a little something you should know about your *new* friend Angela.' Good. That had caught Robert's attention. Peter climbed two of the steps toward the door. Just to be on the safe side of a speedy getaway should somesuch be required. 'She's not the little angel you take her for. Quite the opposite as a matter of fact. Quite, quite the opposite. It might interest you to know that your new little friend is nothing more than a – '

In the wardrobe Anita sneezed, the hand covering her crotch shot up to her mouth.

'Pardon me,' she whispered.

'Bless you,' Angela returned, sourly.

Their eyes rolled sideways, met once more in the dim gloom. Rolled away once more with apoplectic embarrassment. 36B at the very least, Angela thought miserably. Her arm tightened further across her own 34A. The sound of Peter's voice had grown increasingly muffled and now faded entirely until they heard the resounding slam of the boat door. Neither of them dared to make a move until Robert pulled the door open. He quickly averted his eyes.

'It's safe to, ah, come out now,' he offered.

Anita shot through to the living room, an electrical charge of quivering cellulite. The sound of thrown furniture everywhere as she rummaged for her dress. A number of expletives. Whipcrack of the door closed. And she was gone. Angela wasn't about to make a move until Robert stepped out of the way. When he left the bedroom she tumbled out. Something fell behind her. It was a framed picture which had been tucked into the wardrobe facing the wall. As she hurriedly dressed it caught her eye. There she was. Naked as the day she was born. A smickering little smile on her face. There were no depths left for this man to plumb. So that was what he was up to – pornographic drawings no less. She caught the picture and slammed it against the bedframe so that a wooden knob on the headboard stuck through. She hauled it off with difficulty and slammed again. Robert's voice called to know what she was doing. She stormed through to the living room, her eyes stinging with most grievous tears. The very least she might have expected was a contrite face, a hint of remorse – but no, there he was, slumped on a chair, sending *her* an accusing look. Before she could so much as open her mouth to let him know what an unspeakable, truly reptilian, slithery slimy creature he was, he said:

'You might have told me, Angela.'

'Told you? Told you what?' she shrieked.

'What you are.'

'What are you on about?'

'Peter followed you yesterday. He saw where you went. Told me what you do for a living.'

'Oh, I see.'

'Why didn't you tell me yourself?'

'It's my own business, isn't it? It's my vocation – nothing in the world wide to do with you.'

'*Vocation?* My God. Is that how you justify yourself? You're a class act, I'll give you that.' His mouth twisted bitterly. The way his eyes were travelling up and down her frame so derisively boiled eggs in her blood again.

'Don't you talk to me about justifying, Mister. Not with the way you've been carrying on. Oh the barefaced cheek of you. The gall.'

'I didn't ask Anita to – to whatever, if that's what you mean. I had no idea she was going to come here today and do what she did.'

'Bound to catch up on you, wasn't it? Your dirty little tangled web.'

He was trying to figure something, running his hands back and forth across his head. Eyes glazed as though he'd been stunned in a boxing ring.

'All those men, Angela. I mean – doesn't it ever bother you?'

'Why should it bother me? It's my bleddy job, isn't it?'

'A job? Are you so desperate for money? You could have asked me. I'd have given you anything. Anything at all.'

'Desperate for money, is it? Sure I don't even get paid half the time as it is. It's far from desperate I am I can assure you, Mister.'

'You don't – God – it's not for the love of it. Surely? Please don't tell me that.'

'Why else would I do it? D'you know, I can't figure you out at all at all. You sit there, pointing the finger at me. What I didn't tell you. And all the stuff you didn't tell me. Where do those poor misfortunate little girls sit in all of this? It's tantamount to child abuse what you're doing.'

'Tantamount to what? What are you on about for Christ's sake?'

'Oh yeah. Bring Him into it and all. I'm getting out of here. And I won't be back. You're a – a fakah of the highest order and so you are.'

'A what?' He stood up. 'Don't come back. That's fine by me.'

'I won't. Don't worry.'

'Why should I worry?'

'Why should you indeed.'

They were inches away from one another now, glaring furiously. Each waiting for the other to back down, even a little. She could see that he was wrestling with something. Turning it over and over in his head, trying to reconcile his newfound knowledge with his original construct of her. To prove to him that she really was leaving for the last time, she stomped over to her portrait on the easel. Whipped back the covering. Thought she saw his shoulders slump in defeat a little. Looked at her own reflection smiling back at her. Wondered how anyone could know her so well, and know her not at all. He'd even caught the Aunts in her eyes, she thought, gazing with her mouth slightly agape. The portrait was sadder than she'd expected. Even if her mouth was curved into a permanent smile. Fine. Let him remember her that way. She said as much. Firmly keeping her back to him so that he wouldn't see the hot tears coursing down her cheeks.

'I was going to tell you anyway, today,' she said with a hopeless shrug.

'Angela?'

'Oh well. You have your road to travel. I have mine. End of story.'

'I suppose you're shocked that I'm so shocked. In this day

and age. I mean – if that's the life you live every day, I suppose it seems normal to you.'

'Perfectly normal, thank you very much.'

'Angela.' He was approaching, hands making shapes in the air tentatively. 'Angela – could you even tell me that maybe, maybe you'd been considering giving it up. Considering even?'

'The thought wouldn't cross my mind,' she responded tartly.

'I see.' He looked crushed. 'I'll worry about you, you know. There are a lot of very dangerous men out there. Psychos. Maybe you've just been lucky so far.'

'I deal with psychos every day. Well able to handle them. So you won't need to worry.'

He was blinking back shock at that. She knew she was ladling on the bravado somewhat but it was nothing short of the truth. Half the men at the shelter were psychotic at the best of times. There wasn't even a word invented for what they were at the worst of times. But she thought he looked ineffably sad. Then she remembered Anita and his girls again and her face hardened.

'And I'll worry about your girls,' she said. 'Don't just stick them in front of a video while you carry on. It's not fair to them. Poor little things.'

'But they like to watch videos while I do Anita. It passes the time for them.'

'Oh dear God in heaven himself.' Angela made a strike for the door. She would suffocate if she stayed a moment longer. How could he own such tender eyes and be so terribly cold-hearted?

'Angela – if I said that I – if I said I could try and learn to live with, well, what it is you are. What you do. Would that –' He broke off, tortured. 'I don't want to lose you. Is what I'm trying to say.' A hand ran through his hair repeatedly. 'But I don't know if I can –' He stopped again, eyes suddenly blazing with a million unspoken accusations. 'I thought I'd fallen in love with an angel, for pity's sake. I need time to take this on board, any man would.'

Angela snorted. Tossed her head at the portrait.

'Well at least you kept my clothes on for that one.'

'What's the matter?' he bitterly returned. 'Feel you got duped? I suppose by your standards you did. Here –' He emptied his pocket of coins and notes. Threw them on the ground by her feet. 'Consider my time with you paid for. Just like the rest of them. I wouldn't want to cheat you.'

Angela looked at the rolling coins through a gauze of tears.

'Why not me, Robert?' She swung the door open. 'You're cheating just about everyone else.'

She ran out. Fled down the towpath so fast she couldn't hear the sound that rang in Robert's ears as the door slammed shut behind her. A pursing, compressive sound.

His heart contracting into the smallest, tightest butterbean once more.

Steve was well and truly out of it, seriously out to lunch, his mind AWOL. Whatever way you phrased it, the upshot was the same. Angela was long enough in the business now to know a try on, a sideshow to entertain the troops – happened every day one way or another. Someone would start bawling his head off, fisting walls, fisting anyone. Or threatening to kill himself, feebly slashing at wrists with a blunted razor. Most of the time, Sr Carmel could handle any one of them, all by herself. Several of them altogether, all by herself. They were just cries for attention, of abject hopelessness, of interminable boredom and nobody took much notice.

This was different. This was the real thing. Mary Margaret ran frequent lectures on the signs the nuns should look out for. Eye rolls to the point where only the white was on show. Muscle rigidity throughout every part of the body, in particular, fists that would not unclench. An appearance of something akin to lockjaw in the lower half of the face, flecks of spittle or foaming.

A singular, repetitive motion such as constant headbutting of one section of wall, or a flinging of the entire body back and forth, knocking it with sufficient force to make the nose erupt into a volcanic bleed.

Steve's nose was streaming, eyes were rolling and there was a scum of dried-in spittle at the corners of his mouth. He was thrashing about in the refectory, smashing chairs into splinters, firing huge tables across the length of the room with a single heave. There was a wall of energy surrounding him. Almost tangible. He fed from it and spewed it out again. A self-perpetuating cyclone. Mary Margaret had cleared the room and left him to it in the hope he would burn himself out, but she was heading back to her office to call the police when Angela arrived in the middle of the storm.

'What happened?' she asked Sr Carmel.

'We don't know, pet. He keeps on about some girl called Nicola. It's hard to make head or tail out of what he says. Something about not being able to find her. Do you know who she might be, pet?'

'His sister.' Angela chewed her lip.

Mary Margaret stepped back again.

'What else can you tell us?'

Angela hesitated and the Superior caught her shoulders and shook. Hard.

'Whatever you know – tell us. Right this minute. Something that'll give us an edge. How many times have I told ye before, ye've to use anything, anything at all that they might care about.'

So, accompanied by Steve's incoherent and tormented howls of frustration and fury, Angela told what she knew. Mary Margaret's eyes slitted as she confessed her own duplicity, how she had managed to keep Steve away from Nicola through persuasion and false promises. The eyes slitted further when she told them about Nicola's lifelong ambition to set up her own beauty clinic and how that simple little dream had touched her own heart. When she finished to the crescendo of a table being hurled through a window next door, Mary Margaret lit a cigarette, nodding to Sr Carmel as though the elderly nun would have come to the same immediate conclusion as she did.

'She's dealing,' Mary Margaret said succinctly. To Angela's surprise, Sr Carmel also nodded in agreement.

'What d'you mean?' Angela asked.

'Oh for feck's sake. That's the oldest screen. You should've known straight away. Doing the women's faces is the front for peddling her stuff.' She indicated Steve with a toss of her head. 'Didn't yer man give you any hint?'

Angela dropped her eyes.

'I see. He did. But you weren't listening, my girl, were you?' The Superior let out a heavy sigh on a stream of smoke. She winched the cigarette into the corner of her mouth, clapped her hands for attention all around and snapped out orders with military-style execution.

'Right. Let's be having you. Listen up now. You – Aloysius, trot next door, see if you can find one of the women called Nicola. If she's not there, tell whoever's on duty to send her here the minute she turns up.' Sr Aloysius trotted as best she could which was more of a hobble than anything. Mary Margaret turned to Oliver and several of the older nuns. 'Keep the men in the clusters. I don't care how you do it. Get them out of the way, next thing we know this'll start spreading. Lasso them if you have to. Go on! Go!'

They skittered in every direction, coralling wild beasts with their arms spread out like the days on the farm when they'd herd the sheep into compounds.

'Sr Carmel – mash up four or five Mogadon in a mug of strong coffee, stand by the kitchen entrance on the far side of the refectory.'

'What can I do, Mother?' Angela faltered.

Mary Margaret cast her a withering look but this wasn't the time or the place for censure. She caught up a chair, smashed it on the ground in a couple of deft swings. Slid a broken leg

281

through the double handles on the refectory swing doors.

'That should keep him in there. Carmel will hold the other door with the Mogadon. I'm calling the cops. You, Sister – just keep watch. Don't say one word to him. D'you hear me? Not a word. He's past all reasoning. Roar out to me if it looks like he's heading this way.'

Angela nodded. Within seconds everyone had dispersed and she was left to gaze forlornly through the glass at the top of the doors at the foaming hunk of raw human suffering which was all that remained of Steve. She had played this one so badly. So ineptly. He emitted one long bloodcurdling howl which almost put the heart crossways in her chest. She looked around: the corridor was entirely empty. There had to be some way of salvaging something out of this. Some small shred of hope. Her lower lip was so chewed she could taste iron. She took a deep breath, looked up and down one last time, slid the baton out from the doors and with one hold of a long inhalation she quietly crept inside. Knees knocking so loudly they could have been an African drumbeat.

He didn't notice her at first. She took a few tentative steps. Already starting under her breath the familiar animal sounds she used to make to Uncle Mikey. The nook-nnook-nyahh that had managed to calm Steve before. She was making the sounds as much for her own sake as his. He froze when he saw her. She stopped a couple of yards away. Nyaahh.

'You fucking cunt!' he bellowed, only the white of his eyes showing. And Angela realized she'd really made the mistake of her life this time. It was too late to run back, he could catch her in time. There was nothing for it now but to brazen it out. She held onto the one remaining upright chair in the room. Thinking she might use it as a shield if necessary.

'You told me she was safe, din'tya? How you was going to get her and me together. Now she's gone! I can't find her nowhere. Lying bitch!' He'd just about managed to cover the distance between them in a couple of strides. Angela felt lightheaded with fear. Quickly saw, from the corner of her eye, the penknife glinting in his hand. It had been sharpened to a fine line of glittering, honed edge.

'Steve.' Angela swallowed. Trying desperately to adopt that grown up voice which would mask her terror. The worst thing she could do now was reveal fear. 'Steve, pet. You've got yourself all upset over nothing. Why, they're finding Nicola right this minute. Even as we have this little chat.'

'They won't find her.'

'Now now. How can you say that for certain?'

''cause I just *know* don't I?' he bawled, suddenly slicing the knife back and forth across his thigh. Slashed denim mingled with zig-zags of dark blood. 'I lost her yesterday – after you was with her,' he added in a hiss. 'You knew what she was doing. You knew. And you didn't even try to stop her.'

'I swear I didn't, Steve.'

'Just another lying twat. Same as the rest of 'em. That's all what you are.'

He was covering the last few steps between them now, in a slow, menacing glide. Angela's hand tightened instinctively around the chair back. Rivulets of sweat dripped from her temple and swelled in a band over her eyebrows. Her throat had constricted so hard she could barely get his name out.

'Steve? Take it easy now. No, Steve! Don't –'

But he'd lunged the final yard. And caught her around the neck in a fierce clutch of elbow. The breath whooshed from her lungs. Tiny star points flashed in front of her eyes. She could smell the madness from him. He was muttering, almost cackling. The knife blade radiated spears of dazzling light around the room where a shaft of sun caught the acute blade. She was losing consciousness. Knees sagging limply. Fingers unfurling from the chair. A spray of spittle flecked her earlobe where he muttered over and over that she would never lie again. Never. How could she – with her tongue cut out?

*   *   *

283

Robert didn't move when Bonnie descended the steps, her eyebrows up, looking around for signs of Angela. He kept his slumped position in front of the portrait. Wondered briefly what story to spin her, didn't need to say a word in any case because she must have instantly clocked the situation from the hump of his back.

'Oh,' she said.

'Yes, well.' He circled a series of brushes in oil. 'Painting's done. That's an end to it.'

'She's not coming back?'

'Nope.'

'Mutual, I guess?' She cast him a look of deepest scorn. 'Just like always.'

'I don't want to go into it right now, Bonnie. Drop the subject, all right?'

'Oh sure.' The sarcasm was dripping like beads from her mouth. 'I get it. Let you down, did she? Didn't live up to Robbie boy's expectations, huh?'

'As a matter of fact – yes,' he responded, in a voice that sounded blase enough, though his teeth were gritted. He stood up. Yawned and stretched. To show how little he cared.

'Even you might be surprised by the truth of this one,' he added with his mouth still stretched open.

'Try me.'

'Never mind. Main thing is – it's over. Whatever "it" was in the first place. Nothing much really. Good portrait though, don't you think? I'll try the Royal Academy – so no time wasted after all.'

'Time to waste is what you got, I guess.'

'Yes. My time. My waste.'

'Your life. Sure, hon.'

There was a little brittle pause. This wasn't the way it played out usually. Robert felt a touch cheated by the lack of serious confrontation. Where was the scathing peroration? The general recount of his hapless love affairs? Hang it all – the back catalogue, the list that was at least long enough in the recounting to make him feel careless at worst, quite the chauvinistic pig at best? He waited.

'Did you eat, hon?' Bonnie asked.

'What?'

'Food. You know – it goes in your mouth, out your butt, that stuff?'

'I'm not hungry.'

'No? Sheez, I'm starved. You need to stock that fridge of yours a whole lot better than you do already.'

'I couldn't possibly eat. Couldn't possibly.'

'Pasta, I reckon. That's what I gotta taste for. A big bowl of steaming noodles. Chilli oil. Parmesan if I got any.' She was rooting about in the kitchen, clanging metal pots on the stove. She called out to him:

'Robbie – try to remember noodles for your place. Next time you get groceries. I'm talking about if maybe you're gonna do some more portraits. You know – like maybe other girls on Sundays.'

He was beginning to feel seriously aggrieved.

'There won't be other portraits. Other girls for that matter. On Sundays. Or any other days.'

'No?' She popped her head around. 'That's a shame. Look – am I doing pasta for one or pasta for two?'

'Pasta for one,' he grated.

He picked up the portrait and carried it under his arm to the door. A little pause once he'd opened it, just in case she decided to deliver a little censorious homily after all. But she was smiling from the kitchen, busy preparing food. Her fingers curled in a little dismissive wave.

'No point in being upset about it,' he said. 'She's gone and that's all there is to it.'

'Who's upset?' Bonnie blithely called.

Robert waited some more. But she was busy some more. Finally he stormed out, swinging the door so violently behind him, it yanked open again. The tap tap against the side of the boat accompanied his stride up the gangway.

Really. She could have shown just a little more concern. Just a little. Anyone would think she didn't give a tuppenny damn about him – the way she was behaving.

Vooompp!

Mary Margaret swung the club of table leg one more time over her head. This time she caught the other side of Steve's crown. He went down like a duck – quietly, with decorum – more of a fluttery swoon than anything. The stolid legs of the Mother Superior stood several feet apart, her mouth was twisted to the side while she swung the club over and over, batting air helicopter fashion, just in case he signalled a retaliative strike. But nothing. He was unconscious.

Angela held her throat, gasping for breath. Her tongue was still coiled tightly at the back of her throat where it had instinctively reflexed once Steve had plunged a hand into her mouth. He was so intent in ripping or severing it that he hadn't heard the soft pad pad of Mary Margaret's footfalls behind him, or seen the outrageous swing of her weapon as she circled the air above her head. The fervent, demonic gleam in the Superior's eyes subsided as she gave his inert body the once over. She quickly checked his breathing, his pulse, bruised temple, then, satisfied that he would live, she turned her attention to the breathless Angela.

'Cops are on the way. Tie his hands up while we've the chance.'

'What'll I use?' Angela looked around desperately.

'Use your bleddy tongue for all I care,' Mary Margaret barked. She was dusting herself off. Wiping her hands together. Another day, another casualty. Sr Carmel ran up with the mug of Mogadon and coffee. Both Angela and the Superior stretched out simultaneously for it. But Carmel was on her knees, gently cradling Steve's head, forcing the liquid down his throat.

Mary Margaret stormed off. Angela fell to her knees to help Carmel. She was shaking so hard she keeled over sideways. Carmel's little wren pincers helped her upright.

'Ah, pet.'

'I keep messing everything up,' Angela blubbered. 'What'll happen to him?'

'He's in the hands of our Blessed Lord now, pet,' Carmel said, gently stroking the bruised temple.

'But shouldn't I – I mean – the police, couldn't I –'

Carmel looked sadly at Angela. But there was the world of gravity behind her tired little blinking eyes also.

'Our Blessed Father, Angela. Let it be now. Put your trust.'

'But I can't!' Angela wailed. 'There must be something I can do.'

Carmel fished for a bonbon. Looked at her again. And in that instant Angela saw the gaping chasm between them. And it was not merely a matter of generations. Carmel understood that there were things she could not change. That she might wish for them to change was as natural an instinct as breathing air to her, that she understood that it was not within her personal remit, an equally natural understanding. Angela kept trying to second-guess her God. Would never be able to entirely trust that His eye was on the ball at all times, especially when there was always too much irrefutable evidence to the contrary. Certain lingering doubts, only every now and then, might well be prudent in lay life; utterly redundant as a salient proposition for a nun. Carmel popped the bonbon into Angela's open mouth.

'Think of your Mammy,' she said, with a soft tap to the lower jaw, to close it.

'Umm.' All Angela could respond.

For the next few hours, Angela spent her time in the chapel, praying herself into a transcendental state. She didn't want to watch them taking Steve away. She felt riven with remorse and a dark despair that told her she had made things worse for him if anything. The train station in her head, which had replaced the Aunts, shrieked and clattered with violent motion. And every departing train left her standing forlorn and lonesome on a deserted platform. There wasn't a suitable carriage with room for her. Though they trundled by, gaining momentum as they passed her feet, every coach turned up bereft of passengers and starkly empty, just as she lifted her head to look.

Even when she tried to conjure Robert's smiling face to soothe her teeming brain, it wasn't the usual crooked smile playing on his lips. More a sneer of disdain. Clearly he felt duped by what he would consider the childish infatuation of a would-be nun. The naivety of her silly schoolgirl crush. Wasting his time, not delivering the goods. Angela didn't believe there could be further depths of mortification left to plumb, quickly remembered Mother Superior's face earlier in the refectory and revised this opinion. The depths were as infinite as space itself.

Before bed, she put her head around Mary Margaret's door, wishing to get the crowing over and done with as soon as possible. The Superior glanced up, took a long swig of gin, returned her attentions to paperwork once more.

'I just wanted to say,' Angela stammered, 'just – I'm very – sorry.'

'And so you should be.'

'Night then.'

'Angela?'

Angela bounded in. Desperate for any word of comfort.

'Go home, Sister,' Mary Margaret urged in a devastatingly soft voice.

'Home?'

'For the couple of weeks you're making up your mind. Go back to what you know. And then make your decision. Now get out. Goodnight.'

Angela nodded. She slipped back into the corridor. The dim light from wall sconces lanterned her way to the stairwell. Her head hung down onto her chest. She thought of all the dreams and childish fantasies which had brought her to this place. The immeasurable joy she thought she would experience when Uncle Mikey took that first stair-tread down from the attic. Her own sense of achievement when that would happen. Bells tolling in a frenzy. Birds scattering in every direction. Life affirmed, renewed. Because of Angela. Her persistence. Her vocation. Just her – in reality. Whoever that was.

She remembered her mother's parched face, fingers squinched in a tiny huddle, threading needle after needle while somewhere in the background an aunt fizzed and fiddled with the futures of those around them. She thought of the hill of disappointment, heaven turning into bog before her very eyes. And she wondered if Robert was already painting somebody else in his mind. That she would never see him again, she might be forced to accept, if only he hadn't appeared so devastated by the revelation of her vocation. Maybe he really did care for her after all. Then the image of Anita's 36C quivering in the closet sprang into her mind. How long before he took her out of the closet? How long before he taunted Angela with the existence of his lover? He hadn't managed to give her up for his best friend, it was hardly likely that he would give her up for Angela.

No, she decided, she could never see Robert again, that was the only thing that was absolutely clear in her scrambled head. The certain knowledge brought with it a sense of piercing grief as though she were experiencing a bereavement. And the comprehension of her loss also brought with it the comprehension of her love. She could finally cut through the screening veil of her own intrigues and self-delusions to admit that irrefutable fact. Not that the admission helped in any respect. If anything, she wished she could stuff that acknowledgement behind some cobweb in her head. What use was it to her now when their paths would never cross again. Never. A long time. The longest time. The time a nun like Sister Carmel, right this very minute, scuttling into the chapel up ahead, had willingly consigned her soul.

Angela slumped on the first step of the stairs. The last step seemed inordinately high up. Beyond reach.

And her heart just wasn't in the climb.

Chapter Fifteen

Nicola was dead. The skinny little Cleopatra had tried to make that one deal too many, had tried to swell her business empire to incorporate the new ultra-desirable gear, on ultra-restricted turf. She was found on the Monday morning, slumped in a doorway with her throat cut from ear to ear. Her bag was long gone, even her stilettoes, but a small locket was found around her neck. It contained two miniature photographs, smiling children, herself and Steve. Long faded angels.

Angela had been packing to leave for the airport when the news was relayed from next door. She wanted to stay for the funeral or whatever meagre service the likes of Nicola merited from state funds. But Mary Margaret insisted that was not a good idea. She said she would represent Angela herself. Steve was in a local psychiatric ward and would not be told until a course of drugs sedated him sufficiently. He would remain drugged to the eyeballs until release, and Angela could pretty much tell the score from then. A few skips, dosshouses, couple of benches – his life emptied of the one thing he cared about. A creature of no importance, least of all to himself. The maniacal rages taking him over, stronger and more frequent with every passing day. Until the final bench. The rip of his chest wide open, retribution from a hand he'd broken on another bench, some night previously. On the streets, at Steve's level, the devil you knew was always the one who got you in the end.

All morning Sister Carmel had tried to reassure Angela over

and over again that this course of events was not her fault, but Angela could not exonerate herself. She had allowed herself to be duped by Nicola, in turn had herself duped Steve and her Superior and all in the wanton belief that she was ultimately doing the right thing. That she was really helping people. There were degrees of honesty and acceptance required of convent life that Angela had not acknowledged before. And she was doing so now to her bitter cost. The mantle of her vocation which she had blithely worn for so many years weighed heavy and cumbersome upon her shoulders.

Her knees were practically melded to wood when Mary Margaret happened upon her in the chapel. Angela did not see the glance of warm sympathy which suffused the Superior's face because Mary Margaret's swarthy features had settled into their usual businesslike expression by the time she slipped into the pew beside her riven postulant.

'Sister?' The Mother Superior cut across Angela's prayers. 'It's nearly time for you to be heading to Heathrow.'

'I know.' Angela anxiously checked her watch. She quickly made a sign of the cross. But her body slumped again as though she couldn't bear to be wrenched from her last refuge.

'I do love it in here.' She sighed heavily.

'I know that, girl.'

'I'll never make a world class theologian or some such.' Angela cast a self-deprecating smile. 'I wouldn't want to think it all out. But I do have a feeling of God, you know. In here – the peace, just the sound of the candles sizzling sometimes when they come to the end – I just know He's out there. On the lookout for us. I don't need to know any more. Really.'

'The chapel'll still be here, Angela,' Mary Margaret said softly. 'It'll always be here for you, you know that, don't you? Whatever you decide.'

Angela cast her an anguished look.

'I can't hardly breathe with the guilt,' she said hoarsely. 'I've made such a mess of things.'

'We all make plenty messes.' Mary Margaret shocked her to the core by squeezing her hand. 'And you know the grand thing about being a Catholic is we get to say sorry and move on to the next mess.'

Angela's jaw dropped but she saw that the Superior was winking mischievously.

'Seriously, Sister,' she was saying. 'All the Steves and Nicolas in the world, they're not your fault. For that matter Uncle Mikey isn't either. People live sad lives. We've to accept that fact and not live sad lives ourselves. That's the best thing we can do.'

'Don't you get sad sometimes?'

'I *am* human, even if you might find that a tough one to swallow.'

Angela flushed and opened her mouth to apologize for all the mean thoughts she had voiced internally about her Superior but the older woman was waving a hand to cut her off.

'Look – I might be sad same as the next person from time to time, but I don't live a sad life, Sister. Far from it. It took me a long long time to come to the decision yourself made so early in the day. You set your sights on being a nun from the age of what – ten maybe? Twelve? And I'll tell you something else for nothing, the world would be a better place if it was filled with the likes of yourself and our own Sister Carmel. Indeed then it would. But it isn't. And that's the way of it. And if the pair of ye were running this joint the lunatics would take over the asylum and there'd be a pile of ashes around yer darling little feet, because good intentions are one thing but they have to be kicked into results by a tough old boot like me.' She stopped to chuckle to herself for a moment. Continuing when Angela glanced in bemusement. 'D'you know sometimes I do laugh to myself when some fecker from a committee, or what have you, says to me how it must be *sooo naice* to be sheltered away from it all like a nun or a priest sometimes. Like we don't see and hear things every day what would put the hairs standing on their balls. And what do I say? "Oh it must be fierce hard being out there in the world we live in these days. Oh oh oh," says I, shaking my head, a look of pure torture on my face – and me hand out for the spondulicks what'll fix the hole in the roof, or cover the drain clearing or what you like. I swallow my words and keep my own counsel.'

Angela laughed at the image of the Superior doing the humble mendicant routine. How it must stick in her craw.

'You'll do the same. When it's your turn.'

'You think I'll get that chance?' Angela tentatively probed. Mary Margaret made a moue of her lips and stared penetratingly.

'There's something else in the what all of this, isn't there?'

Angela nodded but her mouth remained clamped.

'I see.' Mary Margaret considered for a while. 'Well, you're entitled to your privacy I s'pose.'

'It's just – just I don't think I'm ready to tell you. Yet.'

'Fair enough,' Mary Margaret sighed and slowly heaved her bulk upright. She reached back and massaged her lower back with spread fingers which made the egregious stomach stick out like a tyre tread of a two-ton lorry. 'Bloody back is giving me gip again, not to mention the fecking shingles,' she muttered. 'Anyways, time for yourself to be making tracks.'

Angela rose and genuflected as bidden. If she hurried she would still have time to bring a small bouquet of chapel flowers to Nicola's room next door. Part of her would always miss the spiny little creature who had lived by her wits for so long. Until the same wits killed her.

'And Angela,' Mary Margaret was saying in between winces, 'if you do decide to come back to us – no, don't say anything right this minute – if you do decide, then it'll be thought out the right way. Nothing'll have changed in this place, only yourself. You'll still be dealing with hopeless cases every day until a bolt from the blue comes when one of the men goes straight or sees the light or whatever way you want to put it. But you'll understand that it happened because of the law of averages. And not because it's your due.'

'I have a lot of changing to do,' Angela said glumly.

'You could look at it another way – maybe you're just grand the way you are.'

'But –'

'It all depends on what you want to do with the rest of your life. T'would be a very sorry world without idealists in it. The biggest joke of it all is – the last place they should be is in a convent.'

Angela had her head sunk low on her chest, digesting these words. When she looked up to say something, the Mother Superior was gone. Angela quickly lit a candle, for the first time in her life for her own intentions, and plucked a small cluster of carnations from an urn. Then slipped from the confines of the chapel, her elongated shadow casting a dark, fluid shape along the panelled walls.

'There it is – look!' Peter pointed out the blackened bricks of the women's shelter. A couple of women in minuscule skirts and *faux* fur jackets were making their way down the steps. Robert's heart sank as though weighted down with concrete and thrown into a river.

They were watching from a distance, Robert having insisted that Peter take him to the place where he'd seen Angela as good as ply her trade – his words. The women lit cigarettes and parted company, one of them was approaching now, her eyes keeping up a constant sideways vigil for any obviously decelerating cars.

'You're just torturing yourself, mate,' Peter offered, relaxing into the casual lingo of their childhood. All morning he'd refrained from curling that top lip over his teeth, which Robert took to be a sign of comradeship and he was touched. It took a lot for Peter to drop that awful nasal accent. To drop the affectations which had come to seriously annoy Robert in recent times. Not to mention taking a whole morning off to come here with Robert who had found himself pouring out his heart to his friend when Peter dropped by at a late hour the night before. He hadn't meant to, but suddenly found the words tumbling out of his mouth, revealing himself in a way he would never have deemed possible before.

'Oh, for God's sake, don't draw her on us.' Peter clapped his forehead dramatically as he watched Robert bolt forward to speak to the approaching woman. Too late – Robert was unpeeling bank notes from a furl like a man possessed. The woman was also clearly thrown by such overt behaviour also. She hastily looked right and left, sensing a trap of some description. Robert reached out to stop her retreat and she hollered.

'Look, I only want some information,' Robert panted as Peter reluctantly sidled over to join them.

'Leggo my arm!' she cried.

'Here – take all of it.' Robert thrust the roll of money into the pocket of her jacket.

'Please! I just – can you tell me anything about a woman called Angela? I mean – does she work with you? Hair like so – half runs instead of walks . . . D'you know her?'

Peter had to avert his eyes. Really, his friend sounded like a madman. The woman thought so too if the way she was frantically looking around was anything to go by. She was trying to wriggle her pinned arm from Robert's grip. Peter went to her assistance but Robert ignored his chubby friend's prising fingers.

'Robert – let her go,' Peter cried. 'For heaven's sake, man! What d'you want her to tell you anyway?'

'I just want to know if Angela is safe.' Robert trained hypnotic, trance-like eyes on the woman. As if he could mentally compel her to speak. 'Just tell me she's not taking any crazy chances. That's all. Please can you tell me that?'

'Who the fuck are you?' the woman shouted. But the hard edge of her fear had subsided. 'Look, mate, I don't know no

Angela. Ask someone else, right? I'm new to here. What's she up for anyway?' Her eyes narrowed comprehendingly. 'Oh I get it. You're the father, yeah?'

Robert could only glance helplessly at Peter. She would think that, of course, they both realized at the same time that this young girl was barely over the age of consent herself. A simultaneous thought struck Robert and he let go of her arm. He ignored the wad she was reluctantly thrusting back at him. When he turned to Peter, his eyes were ablaze, glittering with some kind of demented hope.

'What? What?' Peter asked as the young prostitute slipped sideways, holding the money tight as anyone not wishing to look a gift horse in the mouth would.

'Look, she doesn't know her,' Robert, the gift horse clutching at straws, said. 'I don't know. Maybe we jumped to the wrong conclusion. Maybe we've got our wires crossed somehow. Oh I don't know. Anything!'

'But she told you herself, didn't she?' Peter tried to gently nudge Robert back toward the tube entrance.

'It was the look of disgust on my face. I was judging her, Peter.' Robert shunted free. His eyes moved from side to side to keep time with the thoughts darting through his mind. He was restructuring, reconstructing, trying to salvage any morsel of hope from the last conversation with her. 'I mean – maybe she was actually coming round to thinking about giving up. And I blew it!' He gripped Peter's shoulders in a frenzy. 'That's it, don't you see? She just needs time.'

'It's possible.' Peter nodded dubiously. He scratched an eyebrow. 'But what if she really does want to go on being a –' He stopped and winced apologetically. 'Well, you know. What she does. Anita says she always thought there was something, emm, off colour about Angela. A bit different.'

'You told Anita?'

'Well. Yes. Shouldn't I have?'

'What else did Anita say?'

'About what? Angela?'

For the life of him, Peter couldn't understand why Robert seemed so agitated about what Anita might have said or not said. Suddenly the clouds parted before his eyes.

'Oh I get it!' he exclaimed.

'You do?' Robert's eyes were glued to his shoes.

'You're planning on keeping it a secret, aren't you?'

'I am?'

'My God!' Peter slapped a palm to his pink forehead. 'You've really got it bad, old mate, old chum. That's why we're here. You'll take her on any terms, won't you? I see. But what if she never gives up? What then? You can't keep a secret like that for ever, you know. People are bound to find out. And what if there are kids involved? How're you going to explain to them where Mummy's off to every night in her fishnets and spikes?'

'I've thought about that,' Robert said dolefully.

'Look here, Robert.' Peter's chest swelled expansively, his tongue poked around within an ample cheek. 'Take it from one who knows about these things – women can be very, make that *extremely*, obstinate about certain things.'

'Is that so?'

'No need to look at me like that.' Peter felt the soothing balm of condescension suffuse his blood. It felt so good to have that lofty pedestal in his sights once more. He tried to stop, but couldn't help himself. 'Learning how to handle them only comes with experience.'

'Really?'

'You're annoyed.' Peter sighed wearily with the air of a gentleman casting pearls at swine. 'But you said yourself that you didn't handle the situation all that well. Hmm?'

'That's true.'

'You were outraged. Disgusted. Hmm?'

Robert nodded miserably.

'In point of fact,' Peter enunciated pithily, warming to an image of himself as Queen's Counsel, 'you were highly critical, would it not be fair to say? Ah-hah, precisely. And being critical of what she does is tantamount to criticizing her. And if there is one thing a woman simply will not stand for, it is being criticized. How could you know this, old chap? You're not married. Never have been.'

'Unlike your good self,' Robert muttered through gritted teeth.

'Quite so.' Peter smiled with a hint of sadness for his bachelor friend. 'Take Anita for instance, when she asks if the blue dress makes her look fatter than the black dress, it's a trap of course. Now *you* might be inclined to ponder the question, wishing to give a considered and honest opinion. Whereas *I* would immediately say that both dresses make her look exceedingly thin.'

'She is thin.'

'That's not the point. The point is – I know what she wants to hear. How to keep her sweet so to speak. D'you follow? Robert – why are you rolling your eyes like that?'

Robert opened his mouth. Caught the twin glints of shivering terror in his plump chum's eyes. Sealed his lips once more.

'Good Lord!' Peter exclaimed suddenly. 'That's her. Angela!'

Robert spun around to see the slight figure trotting up the steps of the building the two prostitutes had come down moments earlier. She was dressed in a sombre black suit, perfectly respectable he thought, with a huge measure of relief. She was clutching a small bouquet of flowers. He dashed across the street causing drivers to beep in fury but she had gone inside by the time he reached the bottom step. Peter panted behind him.

'You can't go in there!' he cried, grabbing Robert's arm.

'Why not?' Robert tried to shrug him off.

'It might upset her even more. Think about it, Robert. How mortifying it would be for her if you turned up at her door out of the blue. Her place of work, don't forget. Why, you'd be like a red rag to a bull. She could be working right this very minute. Could even be in the middle of –'

'All right. Enough,' Robert cut across with a pained wince. 'So what do I do?'

'Leave it to me.' Peter smoothed his lapels. 'Let me do the talking. You go and stand around that corner there. I'll wait for her to come out again and I'll find the right words.'

'The right words?'

'Yes. Well, if you mean to go on with her by hook or by crook, the right words will have to be found, won't they? I mean, you're hardly the expert in these matters.'

'And you are?'

'Well, considerably more so than you it would appear,' Peter said, his lip curling vehemently over top teeth. 'I mean, correct me if I'm wrong, but was it me or you who blew it with her yesterday?'

'Me,' Robert said forlornly.

'And why? Because you said the wrong things. You were hasty, my boy. Precipitous. Precipitous never won fair maiden. Think on.'

'Oh shut up, Peter.' But Robert was thinking on. He stepped back a little. 'Look, maybe you're right. She might listen to you.'

'I never met a woman yet who –'

'I'm going to deck you in a minute.' Robert feverishly clutched Peter's lapels. 'Listen – just tell her I'm sorry I reacted so badly. Tell her I just want a chance to talk. To put things right. Tell her I'm –'

'Crazy about her?' Peter interjected.

'Well, yes. And –'

'– You really don't care if she's a hooker or not?'

'Well, yes,' Robert agreed, a touch more reluctantly.

'And you really don't care if she goes on being a hooker or not?'

'Well . . . umm.' Robert chewed his lip. That was the toughest call. 'Look, you can let that bit for me. Just get me to that point, okay?'

'Essentially –' Peter smoothed his fingers over the ruffled lapels, '– what you wish me to do is to sweeten her up. Sweetening up is something we're agreed I do well, is it not? Considerably better than your good self. Hmm?'

'Jesus, Peter, some day I'm going to kick that fat ass of yours clear into the River Thames,' Robert hissed, but he was desperate and desperate measures called for desperate toadying. 'But yesss. I agree. I agree to anything. Just – sweeten – her – up.'

'Fine. No problem. You could have said that in the first place,' Peter said, slightly abashed, then his eyes widened. He was staring over Robert's shoulder. 'I think that's her coming out,' he added in a rush. 'Quick! Run around the corner. I'll do the needful.'

Robert's feet steamed with speed just as Angela stepped through the door. She blinked several times when she saw Peter standing there, leaning against the step railings with the nonchalance of a true gentleman.

'Angela!' He smiled.

One of her feet poised hesitantly in mid-step. Peter couldn't be certain if she intended bolting back inside or stepping down.

'Peter, isn't it?' she said with her eyes squinting. Then a quick scan to see if he was accompanied or not.

'No. Only me.' Peter's grin broadened for reassurance purposes. 'Not working today then?' He indicated her black suit.

'I often wear this suit for work.' She frowned, puzzled. 'But as it happens, today I'm wearing it because we've lost one of the girls here. She – she had her throat cut. It's horrible. Horrible.' She gazed away hardly seeing him there any longer.

'No wonder Robert's worried about you,' Peter said. There had to be a way of using this information to further his aims. She was clearly distressed. Maybe she was waking up to the dangers to her own safety.

In fact, as he arched his back along the metal railings, spreading both arms on either side, he was beginning to feel that his finest hour might very well be upon him. He savoured the delicious words just resting on his tongue, just waiting to roll off and with the rolling, there, crystallized for all to see, for Robert to see, would lie the incontrovertible, irrefutable and exquisitely ineluctable truth, that compared to his boyhood buddy, Peter was indeed a superior beast.

'What are you doing here anyway? What d'you want?' Angela asked. A tad too snappily he thought.

'I'm a man on a mission.' The smile was beginning to make his cheeks ache.

'What're you on about?'

'Our mutual friend Robert of course,' hastily adding as her face darkened, 'I believe you're aware that I'm guilty, yes guilty, of appraising him of certain informations concerning your good self?'

'Ye-es.' Her eyes were narrow slits.

'And I further believe that his reaction was somewhat, shall we say, dismaying?'

'Well, he did get a bit of a shock.'

'Quite so.' Peter twiddled with his chin in a manner appropriated from a particular actor he admired. Now he was ready to drop those liquid gems, watch them crystallize. 'Well, Angela, I'm here to tell you at his behest, that he entirely forgives you –'

'Forgives *me?*' she cut across. Making him frown, he wanted a good clear run at things.

'Why, yes. Moreover, he's made up his mind that he will accept your past entirely, may even go so far as to accept your present, in fact anything that is required in order to pursue your relationship.'

Angela's mouth opened and closed. Her face was so fiery red, Peter felt that Robert's magnanimity might prove a touch too much for her to take. It was the last thing she was used to, he supposed.

'Are you telling me,' she finally managed to spit, 'that no matter what I may be now or in the future, he wants a *relationship?* Dear God above in heaven. The man's a pervert.'

Her ears were stinging. She could hardly believe it possible that she could have misjudged Robert so entirely. Then again, in the light of her recent misjudgements perhaps it wasn't so terribly surprising after all. But so gobsmackingly hugely? Yet, here was the evidence. Delivered by a man who was himself being duped and, to top it all, was now being used by Robert to acquire a nun for his harem. An acquisition that had clearly grown more and more appealing to him throughout the course of the night.

'Come, come,' Peter interrupted her outraged thoughts, 'pervert is a bit strong, don't you think?' Though he had to concede, with a dollop of satisfying relish, that indeed there was a touch of perversion to this whole sordid affair. Still, if Robert wanted a hooker, then Peter would always maintain the morally superior position, possessing himself, after all, a normal, proper wife.

'I'm – well I don't know what to say at all at all.' Angela shook her head. Peter eyed the constant nervous wringing of her hands and felt a pang of pity for the wretched creature. Cast so low in the flowing stream of life's misfortunes. A noble spasm clutched his heart. To be a part of this unfurling earthly drama. Oh it was gratifying in the extreme. Still there were serious considerations to be, well, considered.

'If it were to develop – this relationship – he would have concerns as to the children, of course. If you couldn't bring yourself to give up.'

'The children?' Angela shrieked.

'They would be the unforeseeable dilemma in all this. How they might react.'

'Good God Almighty!'

'Well you can't sweep the issue of kids entirely under the carpet, you know. Dear me, no.' He added with a chuckle and what he thought was an endearing roll of the eyes. Hard-pressed father of two. 'Much as one would like to sometimes. But you know – see no evil, hear no evil and all that stuff. Ha ha. Angela, are you seeing a ghost or something? You're awfully pale.'

'I'm not sure I'm understanding this right,' she faltered, afraid to confirm the terrible thought. 'Are you telling me that you're worried about how your kids would react if Robert and me –' She broke off, eyes gleaming the thrust of the unfinished sentence. He was pooh-poohing, waving a hand.

'Don't be silly. *Your* kids. Yours and Robert's of course.'

'So you want to get rid of them?'

'I beg your pardon? I don't see what the word "rid" has to do with anything. I don't even know them yet, do I? For that matter, neither do you.' Peter puffed out his chest. 'Look here, Angela, this is just idle semantics. I'm only talking hypo-thetically.'

'Don't you want to take the time to get to know them?' Angela was sundered by a shaft of pity for poor little Tammy and Nessie. Not only was their father a wastrel, but their adop-tive father cared so scantily for them, he hadn't even bothered to take the time to get to know them.

'Well, I will. In due course,' Peter replied, scratching his head in some bemusement. 'Just as you will, if that's the course of nature.' It suddenly occurred to him that this whole children issue had something to do with Angela's pathology and subequ-ently the prostitution. Ah-hah, his churning thoughts exploded. She was afraid. He levelled his most earnest gaze. The one he used at university throughout the psychology course. To cover the fact it was all going over his head yet somehow into some unfathomable recess of him which throbbed with a terrifying redolence. Which was why he went into teeth.

'I understand your fear,' he said.

'You do?'

'Well, you won't be left all alone. With kids to mind. I can assure you. Robert and I share everything. *Everything*. We always have. That's what best friends are for. His affairs are my affairs and vice versa. That's why I'm here after all. Ask Anita, if I tell a lie.'

'A – Anita?'

'She knows Robert and I go way oh way back. She is fully complicit in all our dealings.'

'I don't believe I'm hearing right.' Angela exhaled in a gasp. 'I mean – you know? He's actually spoken to you about the children? And you're willing to go along with this affair of his? What kind of man are you? My God, there's a pair of you in it.'

Peter didn't like her censorious tone one little bit. Thought it a tad rich coming from one so lowly. Much preferred the hand-wringing repentant harlot.

'I don't think you're in much of a position to be casting judgements if I might so say, my dear. After all, you are the one who initiated this deception in the first place. For my own part, I have deceived no one at all. My conscience is quite clear, thank you very much. Robert is my good friend, whomsoever he chooses to have a relationship with is his own business. I am simply acting as the facilitator, if you will. Now, I think he's being jolly reasonable about this whole issue of your – emm – chosen ah career. Is that an acceptable way to put it? Anyway, let's get to the point and no more shenanigans – what message would you have me relay to him? Come come, what shall I tell him?'

At that moment, Robert shot out from around the corner. He had spent the last few minutes in a frenzy, trying to snatch glimpses of their exchange so that his neck ached from bobbing back and forth. But he hadn't been able to hear a thing, much less ascertain from Angela's dazed expression the way things were progressing. It had suddenly and gut-strikingly hit him that Angela might make mention of Anita's performance on the boat yesterday. He was blanching, his face in a rictus of guilt as he sped toward them, in time to hear Angela's gelid tone as her gaze seared through him.

'Tell him to fry in hell,' she said.

She glided down the steps, brushing past a somewhat sheepish looking Peter and was about to stomp clear of the licentious pair until Robert caught her wrist.

'Please, Angela! Just let me talk to you,' he began, almost recoiling at the glittering contempt in her gaze.

'There's been quite enough talk,' she hissed.

Robert glowered at Peter who was busy doing just about everything he could possibly do not to acknowledge that glower. Humming fatly under his breath, no less.

'Look – I don't know what this *moron* –' another evaded glower '– has said to you, but I came here with the best of intentions, Angela.'

A tiny inarticulate squeak issued from her lips at that. Robert tightened his grip on her wrist.

'Please – just listen to me. I know I'll find the right words, if you'll just give me a chance.' He was distracted by Peter's urgent mumbling, encouraging him on. 'Could you excuse us for a moment, Peter?'

'What? Oh right. I'll just be . . .' He followed the sideways swerve of his own head to a safe distance.

'Okay.' Robert tried a watery smile but she was Antarctica. 'Look, we seem to have our wires crossed here somewhere along the line.' He lowered his voice so that Peter wouldn't hear. 'I'm not having an affair with Anita. I know, yesterday, the wardrobe – well, it was just one of those crazy things that, well, now that I think of it, *never* happen to people. But it happened to me, she's going through some sort of a breakdown or something. I think.'

'One of the few things I've managed to learn from my dealings with my men, Robert, is that they lie all the time. I thought you were different. I thought you were, I don't know, a whole person. Not like the broken people I deal with all the time. But you know, I think you're more damaged than the most of them. You just scrub up better.' She raised her free hand to stop his interjection. 'Don't say any more. Peter seems to be okay with your little arrangement, what's it to me? He's even taken the time to consider the long-term effects on the kids, for heaven's sake.'

'What? Oh my God! What has that buffoon said to you?'

'The laughs the pair of ye must have.' Two ebony slats where her eyes should be. 'Have you no shame at all?'

'*Shame?*' he cried. 'What about you? I came here willing to take all *that* on board. The thoughts of all those men touching you, seeing you first thing in the morning, last thing at night – and you speak to me of shame? Who are you, Angela? I only know a painting of you.'

'Ah, Robert,' Angela said, her shoulders slumped, the resisting wrist stopped wriggling. She looked as if she had collapsed into herself. He had struck home. When she turned her head to look at him, the dilating pupils were further magnified by two huge glass beads of tears. 'Ah, Robert.'

In the ensuing silence, Robert was reduced to contemplation of that 'ah'. What did it actually mean? What could it imply – such a tiny, useless, redundant word? If a word at all for that matter. Yet it was a peculiarly Irish thing the way they wielded the sound. Conferring just about any meaning at all, from approval, gratitude, pleasure, indulgence, to the strictest of rebukes. Such was Angela's 'ah'. Disappointment, disillusion, disgust, just about dis-anything. A hundred voiced reprovals wouldn't have had the same effect. He had covered all this distance, he felt, not physically, rather emotionally, to be scuppered at the post by a ridiculous exclamation. All his contempt for himself had thrummed instantaneously there on Angela's vocal chords and he suddenly felt a coruscating spear of anger toward her. She wouldn't so much as give him the benefit of the doubt. He was having an affair with Anita and that was that so far as she was concerned. No ifs, buts or maybes.

'Yet it's all right for you to give yourself to anyone at all,' he said bitterly, finishing aloud his own train of thought.

'Not just "anyone",' Angela replied. Robert let go of her wrist and it fell limply by her side. 'I don't know how you can say that. My work means everything to me.'

They continued to lock eyes in stalemate. Peter could contain his agitation not a moment longer. He'd crept back and caught the end of the exchange. Drops of sweat pricked his furrowed brow.

'Go on! Push it! Find the words,' he urged Robert in a terse whisper.

But Robert was already walking away, shaking his head sadly, heedless to the squealing brakes and furious hollers extracted from approaching traffic. Peter hesitated for a moment, torn between both of them until his quivering thighs elected chase after one true friend, one true buddy, and when he cast a quick glance over his shoulder, Angela, it appeared, had vaporized. She was gone.

'Robert! Robert, wait!' he called. And continued to call the whole way to the tube station where Robert finally turned around to stab a finger into Peter's chest.

'If you know what's good for you, you'll keep well away from me.' he spat.

'But Robert –'

'Did you hear me?' Robert stabbed with each word.

'But Robert,' Peter cried. 'Didn't you get the feeling some-how that we were all talking at cross-purposes?'

'And whose fault is that? What in Christ's name did you say to her anyway? To put that look in her eyes. That bloody "ah" in her throat? I should've known better. What made me think for just one second that I could trust you – trust anyone?' He took a deep quavering breath. 'Right. Well, that won't happen again. Never ever again. So long as I live.'

'I was only trying to help,' Peter wailed after the rapidly receding figure.

'Help yourself,' Robert called back. 'You puffed up, opinion-ated, pompous, fat fuckerrrr!'

Peter stood transfixed, only his eyelids moved to blink with enough velocity to fan an inferno. A small child kept gawping at him and he couldn't think of a more appropriate, dignified way to retreat, so he pulled out his tongue. The little girl ran crying to her mother.

Just as Peter ran, almost crying, for the subway train.

Chapter Sixteen

The Aunts couldn't do a thing with Angela. Though they fizzed and fussed with every ounce of their not inconsiderable powers, they were reduced to watching and sucking their teeth as she went through the motions of eating, living, sleeping – since her arrival three days ago. Alone with Angela in a rare, quiet moment Bina tentatively inquired about the man she'd seen in her daughter's eyes and received the merest shake of a head by way of response. Nothing going to happen there? Nothing. Bina backed off, she knew a broken heart when she saw one. Even Auntie Bridie retreated with her hands raised when Angela sent her an excoriating look at the very mention of vows and purgatory.

The only place that felt any way comfortable was up in the attic with Uncle Mikey. It was as though he sensed her heartache and enveloped her in hugs and tight squeezes as she huddled up with her head placed against his chest. He allowed her to clean the last of the skylight window and stood beside her as they gazed out over the bog in silence. Flock by flock the various birds were leaving, filling the grey, leaden sky with flickering shadows. Soon they would be entirely alone again, with just the odd funereal crow for company.

'I've less than two weeks now, to make my decision,' she said to him, early evening of the fourth day. 'I wish I could magic up the future, Uncle Mikey. See if I'll do the right thing.'

He nodded. His head made a sweeping arc following the swoosh of migrating geese above the rooftop.

'It's all got so complicated,' she continued. 'But maybe that was meant to happen. Maybe it's a way of making me know for sure ... Well –' Her voice trailed off and she shrugged. Gazed out the skylight window again with her eyes trained on the hill of disappointment in the distance. 'I mean, d'you think things happen for a reason, Uncle Mikey? Some things?' She turned and he was nodding rapidly.

'That's what I think too. But – but, if I tell you the thing that's really bothering me, you promise you won't be shocked?' The nodding increased in fervour. Then he trained the dark eyes on her face and waited.

'Oh I can hardly say it!' Angela's hands flew to her eyes but she peeped through a gap in the fingers. 'You see – I'm fairly certain I'd be taking that first set of vows in just over a week, if only I hadn't met that ould Robert fella I was telling you about before. But nothing's going to come of that,' she added hastily. 'Still, the problem is the feelings I've grown for him. Like they just won't go away. No matter how much I tell myself to cop on. And, if they never go away, the feelings, I mean, well – love – I suppose you'd call it, though why anyone would want it never mind survive it, is beyond me, but if this love business does stay – then I won't be taking up my vocation for the right reasons, will I?'

He was nodding so hard she thought his head would come off. 'I mean it'll be because I don't want anybody else. So I might as well be a nun. D'you follow? And if I'm not a nun and he's all I want – then how could I possibly look those poor girls of his in the eye? Knowing his carryings on. Dear God in heaven maybe he'd even be looking for foursomes or the like with that creepy ould friend of his. Ughh!' She shuddered. 'If you saw him. Pink and porky just like a pig.' She made snorting, porcine grunts and Uncle Mikey nearly keeled over laughing. She had to smile herself. 'T'wouldn't be one bit funny,' she

311

added, her own grin broadening. 'And that's the least of it, I tell you. You're not going to believe this bit, the porky pal tells me that I could go on being a nun if that's what I wanted. Robert would be okay with that. Can you imagine? He'd take anyone at all. Probably go after Mother Mary Margaret if I introduced them. Sister Carmel even! Now that would be some foursome!' Angela added in a shriek. She couldn't tell if she was laughing or crying with the tears streaming down her cheeks. 'Ah Uncle Mikey – stop laughing will you?'

To oblige her, he stuffed a bunched fist into his mouth but he couldn't prevent the up and down roll of his shoulders. Angela tried to glare at him but she was overtaken with a convulsion of mirth herself and they bellowed and hooted together until she came to a gasping halt and wiped her eyes.

'Sure the joke's on myself,' she said. 'I thought I was like, kind of fond of this good, decent man. And now I find myself in love with a shit.'

They brayed for another few minutes, honking until Angela had to hold her sides.

'Here I am, supposed to be considering my vocation – and all I can do is think about him.' She stopped wheezing suddenly and cast him a penetrating look. 'But you do think I'd make a good nun, don't you, Uncle Mikey?'

He didn't like the question. Screwed up his face when she repeated it sharply. Then he looked her straight in the eye and slowly shook his head. His own eyes apologized but he shook his head again just in case she didn't get the message.

'Oh!' Angela exclaimed. 'God Almighty – not you as well. There isn't a sinner left to believe in me. No one at all. Not even my own self.'

She grabbed the supper tray, ignoring his pleading hand gestures and flung open the trap door. The tray was balanced in one upraised palm as she stomped heavily down. Her foot crashed through a rotten stair tread causing her to trip and catapult forward head over heels until her head met quarry tiles below with a resounding crack. She remained conscious for a few brief headsplitting moments before a huge rolling thundercloud of darkness descended. In that velvet darkness, very faintly, at some great supernatural distance, she thought she could hear a sweet tremulous voice sing to her. And she knew beyond any shadow of doubt – that she was listening to the voice of an angel.

The sky over a full, brimming Thames was a richly opulent blue. A brocade evening blue. Uniform in intensity all the way up to Twickenham Bridge. Peter sat next to Marty on the bench. He was in despair. No one would speak to him. Neither Anita nor Robert. She just gave him a look of derision every time their paths crossed, which she made sure was not often. As if she could hardly bear to breathe the same air as him. And Robert refused to take his phone calls and wouldn't return the answering machine messages. It was one thing to lose Anita. Quite another to lose Robert. Peter felt like a man in mourning.

'Me, I'm Marty,' Marty said.

'Me, I'm Peter,' Peter responded hopelessly.

Silence reigned for another ten minutes.

'I think I've lost my wife and my best friend,' Peter said, just as Marty was gathering his belongings to go.

'Oh.' Marty stopped gathering.

'Not together you understand,' Peter hastily added. 'But separately.'

'That's hard,' Marty said.

'I've been thinking for the last hour here,' Peter continued. 'About having one last try with one of them. Right this minute. I think I've just about got the energy for one the way I feel. There's only so much shit you can eat at a time.'

'That's true,' Marty said, staring across the river with his jaw clamped.

'Which one though? What do you think?'

313

Marty considered for some moments.

'Which one is closest?' he asked.

Peter stared up and down the towpath, the bench was precisely equidistant from his own house and Robert's.

'Robert is closest,' he said, standing up. 'Thanks, mate. Wish me luck.'

'G'dluck.'

They separated, each walking along the concrete track in the opposite direction. Peter broke into a run at the top of Robert's street. The perennial sight of Mrs Leitch trying to get her buggy into her pathway caught his eye. He figured a good deed might bode him well.

'Fuck off!' she cried as he tried to manoeuvre the steering wheel.

'I'm only trying to help, you old bat,' he muttered. She yanked the stick into reverse and rolled over his toes. Peter hollered at the top of his lungs.

'That'll teach ya,' she sniffed.

Robert was one of the neighbours summoned to his door by the sudden yowl outside. Peter stopped hopping when he saw him.

'She rolled over my bloody foot!' he cried.

'Pity she didn't roll over your fat head.' Robert grinned and beckoned him inside.

Once they were seated in the front living room with two large tumblers of whiskey by their sides, Peter examined his squashed toes. He wiggled them.

'Nothing broken. I think.'

'That's all right then. You'll live to interfere another day.'

'No word from Angela, I take it?' Peter asked.

'No. Nothing.'

'Sorry, mate. Look, I don't know what I said to make her go off half-cocked like that. I swear I don't.'

'It's all right,' Robert interjected. 'Doesn't matter now anyway.'

'You're not going to try again?'

'Nope.'

There was a long silence.

'I have tickets for the Rugby Saturday week. If you're interested?' Peter offered with one eye closed.

'Sure.'

Peter exhaled, drained his glass and stood up.

'Look, I might as well tell you,' he said in a hot rush. 'I don't think we're going to make it. Anita and I.'

'I'm sorry, Peter. Really I am.'

'Ah well.' Peter rubbed a speck from his eye. 'What about the painting?' He directed his attention at the portrait of Angela propped up in the corner.

'Who cares?' Robert said bitterly. 'I've done with all that.'

'Maybe I should never have told you about her – what she turned out to be. I suppose the best thing would have been to let you find out for yourself.'

'You were just doing what any friend would do under the circumstances.'

'Think so? That's all right then.' Peter paused, shook his head. 'No. I must be honest. I don't think my motivations were all that honourable if the truth be told.'

'What do you mean?'

'Oh, I don't know what I mean.' Peter sighed. 'I'm not sure I know anything any more. Ah well – friends, right?' He manfully extended a chubby hand. Robert felt a little bemused but he stood up and reached out to shake it.

Peter wouldn't let go, he kept right on pumping. Robert smiled, tried to extract his hand, said:

'Friends.'

And to his horror, Peter erupted into a burble of tears. He clung to Robert, rocking them both back and forth while huge quivering sobs overcame his portly frame. Robert could only stare into the distance past his friend's heaving shoulder with his own eyes rounded, unblinking, his back frozen rigid with unspeakable mortification. Truly, if the ground could have opened up, he would have jumped right in.

'There there,' he murmured after a while. Because it was the thing you said, when there was nothing to say.

'Sorry sorry.' Peter eventually pulled free. He drew a sleeve of sweater under his runny nose, as he used when they were boys. Robert awkwardly patted his shoulder.

'You'll get through this.' He tried for a hopeful note.

'Is there somebody else, d'you think?' Peter pinned his deepest fear onto the wall. 'Please tell me, Robert, is there something I should know? Something you know, that I don't?'

'Absolutely not.'

'You're certain?'

'Absolutely. Absolutely certain.'

'One absolutely would do.'

'Absolutely then.'

'Okay.'

Peter cast him a feeble smile, found a rag to blow his nose. Straightened up, flattened down. Garbed himself in his gentleman's armour once more. Much to Robert's relief.

'Right,' Peter said in his clipped businesslike tone, upper lip stiff as a board. 'I'll just have to try harder then. Yep. That's all I can do. Try harder. Thanks for the emm – you know – ear, as it were.'

'Any time.' Robert patted his shoulder then quickly retrieved his hand just in case there was any more unspeakable burbling. There was just so far a man could go for a friend. And that distance could only withstand so many naked tears.

'Am I really a puffed up, opinionated, pompous, fat fucker?' Peter asked over his shoulder.

'Course not.'

When Peter had gone, Robert covered the squally seas he had been working on with an oilcloth and took Angela's portrait out from the corner. He poured another stiff whiskey and sat morosely staring and sipping, unaware that Bonnie had crept in and was staring at him staring at Angela, with her arms folded and her head cocked to the side. He jumped when she spoke.

'So this is how you pass the time.'

'I'm actually quite busy, Bonnie. Come back when I'm free.'

'Busy,' she sneered. For whatever reason she had managed to stay away since the last day on the boat and Robert had steered well clear of her. She lifted the portrait up, examining it in the fading evening light from the window.

'You got her just perfect,' she had to concede. 'Now you can stay in love with her picture. Whoopeedoo!'

'Who says I'm in love?'

'You just did, hon.'

'Bonnie –'

But his words choked in his throat. She had raised the canvas over her head and smashed it on the back of a chair. Robert jumped up, tried to grab it from her clutches but she smashed again. Angela's face was slashed into mosaic pieces. Robert howled and finally managed to prise it free.

'What – how dare you? Jesus! Are you crazy?'

'Sure I am.' Bonnie just stood there, her voice flat, emotionless.

'Get out of here!' He was pushing her toward the door, afraid that he might do serious harm if she stayed another second. But she clung to the doorframe like a beast sensing the slaughteryard beyond.

'Now you listen here to me.' She was gasping with the effort. 'That girl is perfect for you. The real thing. Not some pretty picture you pulled outta your head. I hoped you'd come to your own senses, without me prodding – but I see I gotta prod after all.'

'If you don't get out of here, Bonnie, I'll be the one doing the prodding. With my shoe. Get out!'

'No!'

He had his arms around her formidable girth now, hauling toward the front door, but she appeared to be possessed of superhuman strength and clung to either side of the door with screwed-in fingernails. Robert took a deep breath. Tried to exercise some calm.

'Bonnie, if I have to physically throw you out, out of my house, out of my goddamn life, then so be it. I'm only going to ask you one more time. Now please get out.'

'I only want for you to be happy!'

'I'm sure the majority of mothers would say they want the same thing for their sons. However, it is the manner of their execution of that want that invariably – results in the exact opposite.' He added the last in a snarl.

'Oh fuck you and your shmancy talk!' Bonnie shrieked. 'The point you're missing is I do want you to be happy even if right this very minute I don't think you deserve squat, you little shit. That girl would make you happy. I seen it in her face. And you just threw a lovely thing like that away. Just threw her away. Like all the rest of them.'

'The rest of them weren't prostitutes, Bonnie!'

'What?'

'You heard me.' His voice had flattened. Hands fell limply by his sides. Now that he'd said it, tossed it into the open, the fight ebbed away in him. His mouth twisted bitterly. Bonnie was still reeling with shock. 'There,' he said. 'So now you know.'

'Well.' All she could muster.

'Yes. Well.'

'You spoke to her about it?'

'Oh yeah. She has no intention of giving up. In fact, she loves her work. Deals with psychotic men every day and says she's well able for them. To coin her phrase. It was Peter who found out. He followed her to the – well – knocking shop, I suppose you could only call it. I even went there. But she wouldn't listen to me. Just "ahhhed" me.'

'Ahhhed you?'

318

'Never mind.'

Bonnie moved to the sofa and slumped back.

'Well.' She shook her head.

He'd never seen her lost for words before. It was a most peculiar sensation having the last word with Bonnie. And now that the moment had finally arrived in his life, he wasn't able to enjoy it in the least. He took a slug of whiskey. She indicated with her eyes that he might get one for her too and he did. She polished it off in one deep draught. Wiped her top lip dry. She looked so forlorn he decided not to say another thing. None of the words he might have felt compelled to use if she'd kept up the attack. How it was clear to him now that no one was worth trusting after all. How avoiding that very thing all his life had been time well spent in fact. How it had been confirmed to him with rapier succinctness that behind every facade was a tissue of lies hiding another false veneer masking yet another layer of untruths. How sincere paintings were, with however many flaws and strata of varnish and botched restorative pigments, in contrast to human beings.

How the sound of the men's throaty laughs would haunt his dreams at night.

'Sheez.' She was trying to mull over his revelation. 'Hot diggety dog.'

'Oh drop the phony Americanese for a second, would you,' Robert disparaged. Sick to the back teeth with the constant aural assault.

She went rigid momentarily. Then issued a loud exhalation; it sounded like air hissing from a burst tyre. Her head swivelled and the cobalt eyes pierced the distance between them.

'Fine then.' She shrugged. 'I will. It was getting dated anyway, even to my own ears.'

'W-What?' Robert's jaw dropped. Not at what she'd just said but the way she said it. In perfect London Estuary. Not a trace of American twang.

'You heard me,' she said.

319

'Bonnie – what are you telling me?' Robert was totally confused now. It couldn't be true. Could it? 'You're not from New York? Upstate New York?'

'Farthest west I've ever been is Hanwell, darling. Farthest South – Peckham. Where I was born.'

'I think I'm going mad,' Robert was reduced to shaking his head. 'I *am* going mad.' There was no way to make the least bit of sense of this. 'Why, Bonnie? For Christ's sake what possessed you to – all these years? All my life?'

'Don't pretend it didn't make things easier for you in some ways. All alone with the crazy Nooo Yawrk mother. Instead of all alone with the fat slapper from Peckham Rye.'

Robert felt a sharp spasm of guilt. Before he could say anything in denial she waved a hand airily.

'Oh, don't bother denying. It's not your fault.' Bonnie exhaled a weary sigh. 'Look – a day before my sixteenth birthday I just upped and left home. If that's what you could call it. You don't want to know the nitty gritty details, the hows and whys, believe me. Let's just say, no one came rushing after me. And that was okay by me. Then I woke up one morning, I'm not about to say where – and decided to go the whole hog. I'd make a new past. A new me. And that's what I done.'

'I can't –' Robert paused. 'Is your name even Bonnie?'

'Sure it is, hon,' she chuckled in familiar twang, adding in a more sober note, 'At least now it is. Oh close your mouth, Robert, you'll catch flies. Listen, the reason I'm telling you all this is I want you to understand that Bonnie's my cloak. I made her. Invented her. And she protected me. Now she *is* me. I wouldn't know how to be anybody else. She's not such a bad old bat, is she?' She added the tentative probe.

'No. Quite nice actually. In small doses.' Robert smiled in a daze. He still couldn't get his head around the normal-sounding voice.

'Find Angela, Robert. Talk to her again. Try harder,' she suddenly urged, grabbing his arms.

'Don't be ridiculous.'

'If you love her, you can get past even this. Get her to see – I dunno – a counsellor or something.'

'Oh, for God's sake.'

'Don't you care about what danger she might be in? Aren't you in the least bit worried about her?'

Robert drew his hands down his face. She was hitting his most vulnerable spot. No, not hitting – hammering. He'd hardly slept a wink for the past few nights. And when he did manage to drop off, his dreams were the stuff of cheap and nasty horror movies. Skin flicks. Slash films – and centre scene – Angela, but a grey-skinned, ripped Angela. The grey eyes hooded in pain. The men in her life, shuffling like shadowy zombies all around, surrounding her, until she was out of sight. In the dream, Robert would hear his own frantic breaths as he ran toward her slight frame. Faster, faster, his hands in a frenzy, tearing at the surrounding bodies, peeling them back until he could reach the centre. And there, he would find, nothing. Angela would have evaporated.

'Listen to me,' Bonnie was saying. 'Maybe it's some trauma in her past. That uncle in the attic – there's something real fishy going on there. She needs your help!'

'What? Be her pimp?'

'You know full well what I mean.' She feverishly rubbed her hands along his upper arms, cobalt eyes gleaming with her fresh reconstruction of the situation. 'Go to her. Tell her you couldn't give a goddam what she does. You're so crazy about her – you'll accept anything. Jesus, anything! No woman could resist that. Then – when you got her – change her. That's how it works!'

'I tried that, Bonnie.' He paused, reconsidering, then shook his head. 'No. It could never work.'

'You are crazy about her, right?'

He nodded miserably. She pressed his hands tightly. 'Then find out what she's cloaking,' she persisted. 'We all do it, Robert.

Every last one of us. It's our shield. You'll never really know love until you force yourself to see past that. Push your way past it.'

'Bonnie –' He wrenched his hands free. 'There is no *cloak*. She's a hooker. Got that? End of story. Who knows, maybe I could live with that –'

'Sure you could.'

'But she likes being a prostitute. That's the real problem. She likes it.'

'No one *likes* being a prostitute,' she bawled. Face pressed up to his. 'You think I did?'

Angela was sure she was dead. If she opened her eyes and saw bog, then she could be certain of it. Her head felt like a kicked-in melon. There was the high-pitched keening sound again. Such a melancholy lament. One eye prised open, no bog, hall ceiling, thank God. The other slitted enough to let in an anxious peering face. Both eyes shot wide open. Uncle Mikey. He was wringing his hands, stroking her head, in a terrible state. In spite of the shooting pain when she lifted herself onto her elbows, she cast him a huge smile. He had finally come down from the attic. For her. Mary Margaret had been right after all, you did have to use the thing they cared about. And clearly, she was the thing Uncle Mikey cared about. She hugged him in a tight embrace, wincing a little as her skull throbbed hellishly, but she was all right, still in one piece. There weren't any bits of her spread out along the floor. At least not that she could see.

'Oh, Uncle Mikey. You came down. Look, I'm fine. Nothing broken at all.'

But he did not share her elation. He was squinting in the dim light of the hall which was stronger by far than the shadowy, filtered beams which streamed through the skylight window. After his initial grin on seeing that she was all right, his body grew tense and agitated. His eyes looked up longingly, seeking shelter in his familiar cocoon. And when he looked at her again, it was with such a burning sadness, Angela could hardly speak.

'You want to go back up?' she whispered finally.

He nodded.

'All right then.' She got to her feet, taking him by the elbow. 'Let's go.'

They climbed the stairs together, skirting the gaping holes in the treads. Once inside, he scrabbled happily to his usual corner, watching her face to see if she was cross with him. But she shook her head. This was his place. Where he belonged. And she could see what Mary Margaret had been trying to tell her over and over again. There were people who were simply born without the right equipment. Or they lost the necessary equipment for survival along the way in what was deemed the normal world. They had too little skin for protection. Or too much skin so that it trailed around in their wake, causing them to trip and wound themselves with every step. All her life, she had wanted Uncle Mikey to come down from the attic. And all his life he had wished to remain there.

'At least let me open the window – just a little,' she asked.

He smiled his assent. A breeze of pure clean air filtered through the attic, licking into corners deprived of air for so long. Bringing with it the heady, peaty odour of marshy bog, oak leaves and piebald heathers. He sniffed, filled his lungs, and nodded. This was as much as he wanted. As much as he needed. They stood by the open window for hours, watching the sky darken to true night. A pale golden moon suspended low in the horizon, just above the crest of the solitary distant hill. From far away the sound of dogs howling carried to them. And Angela watched in silent entrancement as one stray moonbeam danced across her beloved uncle's face. He threw back his head and laughed with delight. Angela laughed with him. There were no more questions. Her decision was made.

The young prostitute chewed gum in his face, sizing him up, checking him out. He described Angela again, about so high, spiky dark hair – a flicker of recognition in the girl's eyes. She jerked a thumb in the direction of the next doorway along. He was about to thank her but she turned her back on him and stomped up the steps in platform heels high as shoeboxes. All pretence at interest in him dissipated as soon as she understood he wasn't punting for her. He couldn't help but wonder if Angela was ever so stony-faced about business. It was a hard concept to swallow. But swallowing was what he was here for. Pride, squeamishness, the meagre set of precepts he'd managed to live by thus far. Nothing much really. Just the stuff of a lifetime.

He knocked on the heavy oak door. A tiny woman in a nun's habit opened up, squinting as if unused to normal daylight. She looked like a little wren. One cheek swelled out in a peculiar bulge, a sweet or something. Her smile was incredibly gentle though and he felt slightly heartened.

'I'm looking for Angela,' he said. 'I tried next door but they sent me here. Is this where she – lives?'

'Did she promise a bed to you, pet? Is that it?' She was eyeing him up and down, in some confusion it appeared. 'You don't look enough desperate,' she added with a little curl of frown creasing her brow.

'I only want to speak with her, if I may.' His voice Arctic now. Gelid. But not a blink from the wren.

She stepped aside to let him enter. The hall was dark, wood-panelled walls, a smell of must and decay. Male body odours. A few decrepit men shuffled past wafting that malodour in his face. It tore at his heart to think of Angela in this place. Whatever had reduced her to this? He was grateful at least that there weren't any more of the women like next door to be seen, at least not yet.

'I'll take you to the Superior,' the little nun was saying, leading him down a long dank corridor.

'You actually run this place, do you?' Robert called after her.

'Ah sure we do our best.'

324

'I see.' He was bristling now. 'I imagine you have to keep your eyes shut to lots of things.'

'The half of it you wouldn't figure,' she smiled gaily, giving a dark cumbersome door a timid little knock.

'What?' a voice barked peremptorily from within.

'It's a man, looking for Angela,' the elderly nun explained. She patted him inside and tiptapped away with a speed that belied her years.

'Close it,' the chunky woman with a distinct moustache ordered. Robert closed it. Stood there feeling as if he'd been brought up to see the headteacher. Albeit a very strange captain indeed, with rolled-up shirt sleeves and arms like beech trees, a burning fag set in the corner of her mouth, making her eyes squint even as they studied him, a touch too salaciously he thought.

'And who are you?' she asked.

'I'm Robert –' He didn't get any further before she interjected.

'And you're looking for Angela.' She settled back in her chair, took a long drag and through the screen of smoke he could clearly make out twin gleams dance in amusement.

'Ah, sure now. The picture's coming clear. You'll be art history Sundays, or is it thermodynamics Saturdays?'

'Beg your pardon? Look – if you could just call her for me, or tell her I'm here. I'll wait outside if you prefer?'

'She's not here. Gone home.'

'You mean to Ireland?'

'No, to Beirut. Where d'you think I mean? What d'you want with her anyway?'

She hadn't asked him to sit down. Robert shifted uneasily on his feet.

'If you don't mind I'd rather talk to her first. It's – it's personal. Can you give me an address?'

She eyed him in silence for a while. Squinched out her cigarette. Looked at him once more, as if making up her mind, then with a shrug, tore off a sheet of paper from a pad and wrote something. Her tongue stuck out of the corner of her mouth as she drew a map.

'It's not the simplest place in the world to find.' She thrust the sheet out, withdrew it slightly again when he reached for it. 'But you look fierce determined, I'll give you that.'

'I am determined.' He tried to snatch the paper but it was on her lap now as she folded it over and over. Eyes pinning him to the ground. He was starting to feel a touch angry, at the lubricious, knowing glances of this whoremonger, for what else was she – for all her dictatorial tone. 'Can I have the address please and I won't trouble you any longer,' he added frostily.

'And what d'you want with her anyway?'

'That's my business.'

'Angela's future is my business,' she snapped.

'No. I think her past was your business. Not any more,' he blurted, anger rising with every passing moment. He smelled sour gin for the first time. No wonder Angela went off the rails a bit when this was the creature she had to look to for guidance. Probably made a fortune from the cut she made from the poor unfortunate women. All housed under the perfect foil. It made his blood boil. He felt compelled to let her know exactly what he thought of her. 'You could have helped her,' he said. 'Instead of letting her go on the way she was. Has she been hurt?' It suddenly occurred to him.

'I s'pose you could say that. But I'll have you know, young man, I've me back broke with the height of trying to help her. She's a stubborn piece of work, don't make any mistake about that.'

'How hurt? Will she be all right?'

'Her pride'll heal in time.'

'Pride? I hardly think it's a matter of that. Didn't you care? Don't you even try to stop them? Out there night and day, dealing with psychos and God knows what else? Who was she

326

doing it for? Not the money, she told me that. Was she doing it for you? To please you?'

She frowned. Lit another cigarette.

'Nah,' she scoffed, inhaling deeply. 'For the Aunts of course. That was the fecking problem from the very beginning.'

'The – the Aunts? I see.' Though he didn't see at all. 'Well anyway, just show me where to find her and I'll take it from here.'

'You'll have your work cut out for you, I'll tell you that for nothing. Talking her out of it.'

'I'll manage.'

'She'll always be looking to give too much of herself –'

'The address. Now!'

'And even if she's done with here, and I hope for her sake she is, no doubt she'll still be forever banging on about serving the community –'

'– Oh for – What kind of a woman are you? Don't you have any morals? Any scruples whatsoever?'

She gave him a curious look. Sucked hard again.

'Shingles,' she said, 'is what I have.'

'Well, good. That's all I can say.' He lunged across the desk and snatched the paper from her grip.

'Oh, now.' Her eyes widened and her teeth had to grip the cigarette butt, her grin was so broad. 'Off with you then. And be sure to tell her thanks from me for all the hard work and –'

'I'll tell her nothing from you. Nothing!' Robert steamed to the door. Wrenched it open. Couldn't wait to get away from the ghastly creature.

'Sure you're probably right. Doubtless she's it in her own head at long last that she's no business in the world wide being a –'

'Thank you. Goodbye.' Robert slammed the door.

'– nun.'

He stalked down the corridor. The little old lady was dispensing bonbons and cast him a huge beam. He stopped in mid-track. Turned, stared back at the office door in a state of petrified shock. A what? A what? Said it aloud:

'*A nun?*'

Angela pulled off the ear protection pads for a moment to call up to Uncle Mikey. She was strimming all around the house, in an effort to improve his view. For the past couple of days since, he'd allowed her to open the window in the roof. She had hacked back the brambles which threatened to choke the lower half of the house and pulled at snaking skeins of ivy with her bare hands so that they were raw and bloodied now. She had patched the rotten staircase with a hammer and enough nails to seal a battleship. Scrubbed, scoured and disinfected the attic from corner to corner. She'd pasted photographs and cutouts from magazines along the walls so that internally he might have something to look at too. The scratched fingers and throbbing head were small exchange for the reward of seeing his face light up every time it appeared at the window above. Yesterday, he'd even extended his hand, just a little, to wave to her. As she'd waved madly in response, a lump the size of a small television had formed in her throat.

At least there was this. If nothing else. If not Robert. Probably painting someone right now, even as she strimmed. She had to pinch her nose to stem the tears. All that fuss and now she wouldn't even make a nun after all. The evening she walked her uncle back up to the attic, settled that. But it was too late for Robert. She couldn't shake the memory of his face that last time from her head. The patent horror – that anyone sane in this day and age, should elect to join a religious order. She was some kind of freak, his confused eyes had said. Unnatural. No, Robert would insist on a perfectly natural type of woman. Like that Anita person, she sniffed to herself. To act as foil for his own perversions. Well. Good luck to him anyway. Wherever Angela ended up now, whatever she ended up doing – and she had absolutely no idea whatsoever – which was extremely scarifying, but no matter, she snuffled, she would put him behind her. All those lovely long talks, the smiles, the way his hands worked across stretched canvas. All gone. To be forgotten. As soon as possible. Sooner. Well, soon enough at any rate. She sniffed again. Never ever ever. Her mind wailed. It was uncanny how honest it insisted on being now that her vocation was a thing of the past. If he walked up the track this very minute you'd – the newly frank mind began. 'Shut up!' Angela shouted, clamping the earmuffs tighter to her ears.

To take her mind off him, she forced a gay wave up again to Uncle Mikey. But this time he didn't see her. His eyes were squinting, fixed on the distance of bog ahead. Angela shrugged and got back to work.

Up at the other house, Auntie Maisie also had her gimlet gaze fixed on a stretch of heathery turf.

'There's someone coming,' she said.

'Who is it?' Bridie asked from the cot in the corner where she had spent the morning in a silent sulk because Bina had again given her a white egg instead of a brown one. Bina had been up to all sorts of skulduggery these recent days. Telling her, Bridie, to get things herself and what have you. And stop her going on. As if you couldn't go on when you managed to reach Bridie's age. How else could you pass the time of day? And not alone that, there was the impatient handwaving of the niece. Telling her not now, Auntie Bridie. Later when I've time, Auntie Bridie. Ah shut up and leave me alone. And all that only a precursor to the very worst kind of bombshell yesterday. No more vows, no more nun, no more salvation from the flames of purgatory for Auntie Bridie.

When Angela had told them over the breakfast table in a flat almost disinterested way, Auntie Bridie had clutched her heart.

'Ah I'm fecked!' she'd shrieked. Cursing for the first time in their memory.

'That's my decision. It's final,' Angela reiterated, keeping her eyes well lowered from the frenzied antics of both surviving

329

aunts. They were wrapped around one another in a miasma of suffering. Such terrible bloodcurdling cries issued from their quavering lips. Maisie's keen rising not to be outdone by her elder sister. The whole room shook in the ensuing cacophony.

Until Bina banged a fist on the table. Causing half the crockery to hurtle to the floor, the sound of smashed cups and saucers adding to the feverish noise level.

'Shut yer gobs! The pair of ye! Or I'll walk out that door, never to be seen again . . . Hush up! Not another word. Not a squeak now – or I'm walking . . .' As if to hammer home the seriousness of her intentions, Bina wrenched off her pinny and took a few steps toward the door, and turned with her head cocked to the side, challenging them.

There followed a stunned silence. Auntie Bridie's mouth opened and closed rapidly. Maisie momentarily looked to her for guidance, then sensing the final and unalterable shift of power within the dynamic of all three sisters, and being the cute whore that she was, she stepped slightly to the side of Bridie. Creaking down to pluck the broken shards of a cup. Impervious to Bridie's accusing glare.

'Well? Will I walk?' Bina persisted.

Angela held her breath as the silence also held. The sisters knew they could no more fend for themselves without Bina's help than gold chalices were going to drop down from the sky above. With an outrageously aggrieved air and waves of silent recrimination emanating from her scrawny body, Bridie kept her jaw clamped shut. She pulled out a chair and sat in a rigid, upright position. Hands folded tightly on her lap. Maisie plumped down on a chair beside her. Their eyes darted nervously toward their sister who was still poised with one foot pointed away from them.

'Good,' Bina said. Oblivious to their gasps of relief as she retraced her steps to the table. 'Now so. You'll be getting a white egg this morning, Bridie. Seeing as there's only the one brown left. And I've a taste for it myself.'

Bridie pursed her lips.

'Fine sure,' she said meekly.

No more vocation, her younger sister's mutiny, white eggs two days on the trot and now a stranger coming over the bog, little wonder Bridie suspected more skulduggery in the offing.

'Who is it?' she now rasped again.

Maisie scratched her heifer rump, turned her head this way and that.

'I don't know,' she said. 'A man.'

Bridie was over to the window in a shot, howling bunions notwithstanding. She put her forehead to the glass but cataracts blocked her view.

'There's no man. You've Alzheimer's.'

'Show me.' Bina pushed them both out of the way. She gazed intently where Maisie pointed, then a huge smile broke out on her face. The sisters were baffled.

'Who might he be?' Maisie asked.

'There's no he, I tell you.' Bridie stamped her foot with frustration. 'I can't see no one. No he.'

'A stranger,' Bina said with satisfaction.

'How d'you know that?' Maisie enquired.

'Cause he don't know the road. Look – that's the third trip he's taken since I'm looking out. Oh – there he goes again. He've no eye for the potholes.' Suddenly she made a hurried sign of the cross, confusing the sisters further.

'A priest, is it?' Bridie asked hopefully. 'I was never told there was a new one.' A thought struck her with horror and she scuttled back to the cot. 'Did ye put him on lookout for me?' She buried down beneath the quilt. 'Well ye'll have to interview him at the door. Tell him as I'm not ready.'

'He's not here for you, Bridie, shut your ould gob.' Bina slung her dishcloth at the cot. She went back to kneading brown cake, pummelling, punching with her knuckles, flying the floppy disc of dough through the air, powdering with flour, then kneading again. The fixed grin on her face gave the sisters a bad dose of the heebie-jeebies. Only the top of Bridie's head peeped above the coverlet. She eyed Maisie with deep consternation. Maisie returned the gaze with a frown, then looked out the window again, the frown faded as her mouth fell open. Her eyes were round as the pennies that had dropped in her head.

'Oh,' she said.

Far down below, the object of Maisie's 'oh' stumbled for what seemed the tenth time. Really, this road wasn't even a proper track. More a curving leeway through marsh, flattened by footsteps over the course of years. An idea of road. The fact that his hands insisted on remaining plunged deep within his pockets didn't exactly help with the balancing act but it was as if they were intent on disclaiming all responsibility for the present trajectory of his wayward feet.

And in truth, Robert could hardly blame them. The patterns of his life had never been all that clear. Certain comforts in that, it had to be said. What you couldn't see you didn't have to run after. But somewhere in the distant future, he had seen a wife, babies, a reasonably executed painting at the Royal Academy perhaps. Lunch at Peter and Anita's every month. Dinner occasionally perhaps. Long evening walks by the river. Not much to some people. But enough. For him at any rate.

The last thing on earth he would ever have seen was a vision of himself stumbling through a bog, hands thrust deep in his pockets, to confront a woman he'd considered an angel, then a prostititute, now as close to a nun as made no difference. A woman who would most probably send him away with various fleas in his ears and a hollow thrum in his heart that would last for ever now. As he staggered along he began to feel more and more angry with her. After all it wasn't as if he'd put himself in the way of a spiny-haired creature who unrolled ten-pence pieces on the subway like other people phooted gum from their mouths. He could have ended up reasonably happy with a Jennifer or a Marjorie, why just like that – one cowardly hand crept out to click its fingers. The drubbing of the other hand reminded

332

him that it was unlikely anyone was actually called Marjorie these days. Just an example, a figure of speech, he wanted to shout to it.

Apropos speech, what was he to say to her anyway? God, the very idea of making a naked declaration was enough to make him break into prickly sweat. How did it go in books? Angela – I love you. I'm deeply in love with you, Angela. Darling, I can't live without you. Oh Christ! It took years of practice to be any good at that sort of thing. Years. Millenniums. But he had sworn to himself, boarding the plane at Heathrow, that he would wear her down with words. But what words to use? He'd never been very good at those. Peter thought he was and look where they'd landed him? As close to losing his wife as made no difference.

Another stumble and this time he landed on his knees. Of course the callow hands were too busy elsewhere to break the fall. Oh God, he muttered over and over. Got up. Went on. There was a house up there somewhere on the left. Maybe they'd give him a glass of water. Maybe his senses would return and likewise he would also return. To his three-up two-down. To a normal everyday life, thank you very much. To the loneliness of life without Angela spewing out of Richmond Station, her grey eyes scanning for catastrophes. He might just have got by if she hadn't inhabited his dreams at night. She had a lot to answer for, in truth.

On the subject of truth, Bonnie had landed another shock on him that evening in his living room. Mr Fielding was not his father, not even close, she'd said. Remember old fat, baldy from Staines? Yeah, the human cigarette. Mr Gibson himself. And he hadn't run out on her either. She wouldn't have him way back then. Oh no. Figured she was due something far far better. He was married since, with two girls of his own. Quite happily as it turned out. Always kept up contact though. Remembered her birthdays, bought her that lovely shawl. Might even have made her happy, well leastways not too unhappy, if she'd settled

333

for him. It got lonely when you reached a certain age, thinking of all the people you hadn't settled for. Remembering all the people who didn't settle for you. There comes a time, she'd said, when you didn't keep an eye out for all the things you wanted in a person any longer, you added up, made a few deductions, found an equation somewhere between what you thought you wanted or needed or just plain felt you deserved, and what was actually on offer.

He'd considered that very harsh at the time. A bit too deflatingly blunt. But then she'd gone on to say, in a quiet voice, that somewhere in the middle of the totting up and paring down, you got to look at all the things that weren't there in a person. The things that would drive you crazy in time. The things that were mercifully missing. He'd had to think long and hard about that all through the night. In one way it sounded so negative, in another he saw that there was a certain perverse logic to her way of thinking.

As he'd lain there, tossing and turning, he'd come to the realization that first you fell in love with the parts of a person you didn't know. The shadowy pockets full of possibilities. What they might turn out to be. And as they turned out to be whatever it was they really were, you had to fall in love all over again, and yes, there might be some disappointment with the real thing. But the point was, you'd have looked, sucked your teeth, said yes or no, and gone on either way. Not much different from picture restoring in fact. Stripping back, further and further until only the bare bones remained. The truth. Covering up again. Adding new colour, fresh texture, a protective veneer of clear varnish. Because wasn't that what couples offered one another in the end? Mutual protective coatings. And if they didn't, nothing could ever cover up the cracks. And they had to separate, yolk from white.

It wasn't what people turned out to be that bound people together in the finish, it was all the things they turned out not to be. The gaps. The raw product. The tears at night. Fears, vulnerabilities, unspoken dreams. Things no one else ever got to see. This was the stuff of love. Or something like it. Or nothing like it. Depending on the day the hour the minute. In a minute you could love or hate. You could go on on. Or stop altogether. These thoughts had never troubled Robert before. He had just assumed you fell in love and that would be it. He hadn't realized that commitment was only the beginning. Never an end. The end was two shrivelled people on a bench in Bournemouth staring out to sea, dazed, wondering if they'd made it. Knowing that they had, as they passed across egg mayonnaise sandwiches. No need for smiles, that would be smug. There was nothing smug about making it through the rest, the last of your life with someone else. But there was something vaguely triumphant. Something true. Something entirely incandescent. It might be familiarity, fear of the unknown. God alone knew, it just might be love.

He was up to that house now. More the remaining crust of a house in reality. There was some sort of movement up by the roof line. He looked up. It had to be – could only be – the hermit uncle. The grinning face flitted back out of view. Robert's eyes carried down to a huge clump of hewn brambles to the left of the building. And there she was.

He watched her for what seemed like minutes. She was busily strimming, her back to him, earmuffs on either side of the spiky hair. He cleared his throat. Oh those damn words. What should he say? He didn't want to say anything at all if he were being totally honest. Just wanted to wrap his arms around that slender frame and never let go again. It wasn't often a man got a woman to cling the way she did, these days. Clematis, he thought. The shy vine moved away a little, strimming in a fury, doing that funny half walk half run, darting at stray bushes as if she could rip them out with her teeth. He thought of how his life used to be, before Angela. How it had been since her arrival. Thought of that tiny bead of sweat dripping from her scalp to the nape of her neck. Nothing would ever be the same again. There was

335

no choice. He had to think of something. The right words. Absolutely.

He walked directly behind her. Tapped her shoulder. She started. Quickly swivelled around pulling the earmuffs away. She didn't say anything for a second. Just stared at him with her mouth open. Her pupils dilated like twin black balloons, and he could clearly see two miniature Roberts gazing back at him. Could hardly believe how happy he looked. Still, to use her word, it *behoved* him to say something. Didn't it?

'Ah, Angela,' he said.

Her mouth twisted. He couldn't be sure if she was going to laugh or cry.

'Ah, Robert,' she said.

It was the right 'ah'. The one he'd been waiting to hear all his life. Without another word he lifted her into the air, swinging her around and around. She laughed. When it came right down to it, there wasn't any need for another single, solitary syllable.

From high up in the roof, a simultaneous joyous laugh drifted down to them. Maybe it was his imagination, but Robert thought it sounded like the distant peal of church bells.

He had heard that sound once, a very long time ago. The tinkle of laughter and raised, hopeful voices coming down the track from the house above, the day Bina got married. And he had been so glad that one of them had managed to escape. It had always been his deepest wish that the small thing would escape too. But for years she seemed so intent on burying herself within his eldest sister's dream.

Listening to her now, looking down at the happy smile on her tiny heart of a face, the way the tall fellow held on and would not let go, the way their hushed voices tripped over the thousand things they needed to explain, he thought his heart would burst. She had fallen after all. The fall he had wished for her throughout every thought and dream. Through all the years. Not a silent, acquiescent meltdown into the grave of Bridie's sophistry.

For his own part, he had fallen too. Fallen in with Bridie's hushed and oft-repeated exhortations that he should stay up here – where she had consigned him so very long ago. Out of harm's way. Out of her consecrated sect. It had never bothered him. Others maybe. The small thing certainly. But never him. For he knew that here was something they could not understand.

One great concentrated lunge and he performed a perfect cartwheel. And another. He clapped his hands with sheer delight and laughed so loud the world outside might hear him. For didn't they know? Couldn't they tell?

Here was a man – content with himself.

Acknowledgements

I would like to express thanks to Sister Maire Nally for her advice on religious life, also to Hilary Pinder, for sharing her expertise on picture restoring, and heartfelt thanks to my brother Michael for the stories and experiences he shared with me, perhaps never realizing how intently I was listening.